Treasure

1. Rear View Mirror
2. Silk Road to Atlantis
3. Subterfuge

a trilogy by Vanessa Leigh Hoffman

For more information or to order additional books, please contact:
vanessaleighhoffman@gmail.com or visit
www.vanessaleighhoffman.com

*To all our heroes who have
fought and given their lives for
our freedom
in the fight against crime
and terrorism.*

Rear View Mirror

PART ONE

Prologue

"*I love you!*" She wanted to scream that phrase over and over again throughout her neighborhood that night, but she didn't. She knew that she had to free up her mind, so she could start writing in her journal about a heart-wrenching nine month drama, involving two semi-sweet love affairs that should have taken off to new heights. As she looked out her bedroom window at the star-filled sky, she wondered why they weren't allowed to. She had to come to grips with the *strange turn of events* in this final chapter of her life. Sitting in her candlelit room, dressing, while watching her new husband pace up and down the front yard walkway, she suddenly knew that her future wouldn't be allowed to evolve into anything due to *fate...greed... and...deception.*

Introduction

It started one warmish March day at the St. Petersburg Pier at an open-air bar named Captain Al's Waterfront Grill & Bar. Camille had been laid off her "so called" permanent teaching position at a rather snobbish naval academy for elementary and middle school students. Her young students were surprisingly down to earth, however. She didn't know how that was possible. She decided that when the clock struck two fifty-five, she was out of there. Why stick around? She had given the best she had during the past two years, and they had snubbed her, took her for granted. She was ready for a drink, some sun and fun and relaxation, so she headed straight to Captain Al's.

Camille slipped into a lawn chair, as soon as she arrived, and started gazing at the boats, and at the skyline of her new found city on Tampa Bay. She had moved here from Canada one year and a half ago, and it was still heaven to her. She felt exuberant sitting there, until she got a taste for a cold beer, so she walked up to the bar. Nonchalantly, she sat down on a stool that was next to an empty one and noticed that there were cigarettes lying there. Next thing she knew, an older man was sitting next to her. They started talking. Vibes were there. This man was older, still attractive, so much so that anyone could tell that he used to be a looker, a real looker and cooker.

He was a distinguished gray-haired gentleman of medium height, very well-groomed, with a hint of expensive cologne on his well-manicured and postured frame. He walked eloquently to his stool.

He asked her name, and she of his, and they immediately broke into a conversation of their lives. He said, "Call me Kenneth."

She said, "Call me Camille."

He was magic to her. It turns out, there was a twenty-six year age difference between them. She was forty-two. He was sixty-eight. Something attracted them to each other. It was like a need that each of them had, in which both of them satisfied the other. The course was now set. They were destined to meet the next day at the same bar, same time.

Along with the other daily bay cronies that frequented the bar, there were a few "new-timers" to the scene, like Johnnie, who lived downtown and worked at the Veteran's Hospital as an electrician, and Kat, or Spider, either name applied. The latter rode a ten foot tall tricycle which he used for transportation, as well as for a sales model. He was selling his invention for *only* eight hundred dollars. That was a pretty steep price in her estimation for a novelty item like this contraption.

There was one intellectually-looking, dark-haired young lady, who wore black horn-rimmed glasses and tucked her silky hair behind her multiply pierced ears. She always sat at the table right beside her, reading some avant-garde book, whenever Kenneth was late. On one of these occasions, Natalie, as she introduced herself, asked to join her. The intellectual dramatically expounded on her addiction to crystal meth, her obsession with the Green Peace Movement, and her insatiable desire to make out with the long haired blonde tricycle inventor. Camille was so glad when she saw Kenneth's face coming toward her. She never sat near the intellectual's table again.

There were tons of tourists who flocked this bar daily. Some were clean and good, others were cunning and bad. The other thirty-three and a third percent were comprised of weird ones and lunatics. These were the types Kenneth told her he encountered every day, as he sat and stared, while casting a line out into the Bay. This was his recreation. Kenneth never killed a fish. He only did this as a sport. Once he snagged a line, he removed the catch, and sent it back to live in the calm waters. You see, he was just too kindhearted to kill anything, even an insect. It seemed he possessed everything needed for happiness in life---sportsman, socialite, rancher.... What? Rancher? Yes! She was definitely impressed on that first day of introduction.

He proclaimed that he had a ranch near Sarasota, in a small livestock and citrus town called Parrish. It was a big ranch, five thousand acres of prime orange-growing and cattle producing land, stretching from near Ellenton to the Skyway Bridge. Kenny had a white picket fence circling around his massive property and told her to come on out, if she got a chance.

He said, "It's easy to spot. Call me, and I'll come out to the gate."

Kenneth continually expounded on his enormous house, with its wrap-around porch and balcony, and its lush amenities. He noted that his house was dressed up all in white, with green shutters. Kenneth equated it to a Georgian plantation house, back in the day. He was supposed to have many workers living on the land in their own houses, as well as his wife's niece, Jude.

Jude was the veterinarian on site, as well as his stability, he said. Gimpie was the manager of the ranch, who came in every morning promptly at seven, and who was the only one who did not live on the ranch. She happily lived in Ellenton with her newlywed husband, where they rented an apartment. Now Jude, on the other hand, was single, flirtatious, spontaneous, and when mixing with her best friend, Kimmie, who was an outstanding jockey on the West Coast, they became every man's worst nightmare. Jude lived on the ranch and had an office and bungalow in Pinellas Park. She had a veterinarian clinic on the busy corner of 66th Street and Park Boulevard. Jude, his niece, was the only thing remaining from his marriage. She loved Ken and moved to Florida, where he helped set up her veterinarian practice.

Jude was in California about every weekend visiting her mother, Ann, Jane's sister. She had her uncle's pilot fly her on Ken's Learjet. Yes, Kenneth said he also had a sharp, cool Boeing sitting in the backyard of the ranch house, waiting to take off with her in it at any moment.

As she began to leave the bar, after her third draft, Kenneth asked Camille to sit for a few more minutes, because he had to tell her… something very important…something she might not believe. He told her of his military duties in Korea, Vietnam, Kuwait, Afghanistan, and Iraq.

"Being a two-star general leaves one with no time to ever be at home," he said. That was why he said he retired to Florida when he reached the early age of fifty-five, sacking a net worth of five hundred and twenty-five million dollars, four hundred and seventy-five of this net being liquid.

She didn't even flinch. It was at that point that she realized money and status was not what was keeping her hooked on the man, but instead, it was the time, place, and circumstance.

She met Kenneth by the Bay every day, promptly at three-thirty, and they drank beer until six. He would then walk her to her car and take off himself, oh, not in a fancy auto, but rather on foot, with fishing pole and tackle box in hands. He was definitely an eclectic spirit, and she treasured him from the start. He said that he owned an apartment building downtown, near the Pier. He kept the front living space for himself, when drinking at Captain Al's.

They began to call each other several times a day, just to chat and laugh. They were really beginning to enjoy each other's company. To her, he was fun, smart and witty, and had a really cool Boston accent. Some of his words sent tingles down her spine, and the fact that he was a two-star general who now owned a ranch located thirty minutes away from her house, didn't hurt matters at all.

Chapter One

The Pier

As I sat on the edge of my bed, looking out the window and feeling uneasy with all that I was looking at, I wondered if I had truly erred. I thought about that life changing early march afternoon, and I scribbled some words on a page, with quivering penmanship. I was lucky enough to have a few empty moments, and so I let my mind drift back to the beginning, to the start of the amazing cycle of events that took place over these past nine months.

As I wrote, I remembered the sounds of the swirling winds blowing through the rough waves, causing crashes on the sea wall of the St. Petersburg Pier. My small red convertible was racing down the lane, ready for a valet parking attendant to ask for its keys. It was a warm day, plenty of sun for all of the fishermen who were straddled out on their Florida Gator lawn chairs, just waiting for a short, taut pull on their long, sagging lines. *These memories have never faded...I Continued writing.*

I strolled past these sportsmen who couldn't keep their eyes on the water. I looked at my watch, and noticed it was three sharp.

"Yes," I thought. "Time for a cold one."

I sat at a sunny bar table, ordered a beer, then I soon noticed an empty stool in the cool shade. And so I sat solo, next to the sunglasses and cigs sitting by themselves on the bar. After five minutes, an older gentleman returned to occupy his empty seat, not knowing that our lives were about to change, and I mean forever. We chatted and laughed, sometimes even hysterically. *Kenneth didn't even dream of what they had in store for him at this point. He found out a little too late.*

The next day, Kenneth returned at three sharp, as he said he would. I stayed at the bar for only an hour. Kenneth bought beers for the patrons and told war stories. He had fought in the Korean, Vietnam and Gulf Wars. In the Gulf War, he sliced Khomeini's cheek. In Vietnam, he had been a Prisoner of War and had his teeth knocked out by a shovel, at the hands of his Hanoian captors. At the beginning of his US Air Force career, Kenneth was transported to Korea to act as an Air Traffic Controller at the US Base at Seoul. He was shot with shrapnel pieces throughout his body during his first week out. He was immediately flown to Boston, his hometown, for treatment, then discharged with a Purple Heart. This was sounding more and more like a B-rated movie to me, but I let it go.

Kenneth was a staunch Democrat, which I thought to be a little odd due to his strict military beliefs. His wife, Jane, had been a strident Republican Party member until her rather early death at fifty. Jane and Kenneth had only been married for two and a half years when Kenneth told Jane to pack up and move back with her parents. There was a fifteen year age difference between them. He constantly referred to Jane as his child, of which he never had.

One day, after returning from Colorado Springs, where he had been speaking at a war memorial event, he walked into his house and down the hall into his brown leather wall study and found Jane's parents mulling around his personal paperwork, which was piled up on his desk. They were nosing through bills, pay stubs, and banking receipts. He immediately ordered everyone out of his house, called his lawyer, and a divorce was set in motion. He never stopped loving Jane, however, only her family. He thought he was just too much of a free spirit for her.

One night, when Kenneth was in his twenties, he and his Air Force buddy stumbled into a local sushi bar. Very drunk already, they ordered two more each. The establishment agreed not to serve them any more alcohol at that point, so Kenneth proceeded to kick the huge fish aquarium, spilling water and goldfish throughout, ruining the restaurant's newly installed plush carpeting. The police were called, but Kenneth and his buddy "Rock" were gone, gone to the next bar where they were apprehended by authorities and taken to the city lock-up. Luckily, Rock's uncle was a state prosecutor and got both boys released with no bail, no pending court appearance.

Ten years later, when Kenneth took Jane out to a dinner on their two-year anniversary, he took her to the same "Nagasaki Kitchen" in Boston. There was no more fish tank, however, and it appeared more elegant and expensive.

As the couple strolled through the entrance, the proprietor shot one glance at Kenneth, then escorted him through the exit door. He pushed Kenneth out the doors and said, "You're not welcome here, and don't come back." Jane was furious with Kenneth and very embarrassed. She asked him what he had one to cause this. He told her the truth, with the usual "I'm sorry" puppy dog look on his face.

Coupled with this episode and others like it, when Kenneth would leave her alone in movie theaters, shopping malls and churches, so that he could go drinking at the nearest bar, she became very disgruntled with her marriage. This inspired Jane's parents to look through his papers to see how much money he really had. To everyone, it seemed like Francis spent *so* much money on his own extracurricular entertainment. Everyone thought that Jane deserved more respect, as she was the backbone of their marriage. Up to this point, Jane had threatened to leave him three times, so when Kenneth walked out on *her*, she and everyone else was devastated.

Chapter Two

Quebec City

We had been meeting at Captain Al's Waterfront Grill & Bar every day for six months at the same time, except for on weekends, when we met at noon. We made more and more friends--patrons, bartenders and managers of the establishment.

One day, however, Captain Al's was closed due to flooding from a near miss hurricane, and so we went upstairs to the top floor. We found an open-air place called "Xanadu". There, Ken told me of his massive wealth, and that he had acquired this solely through raising Angus beef and Florida oranges. He did have a little stock on the side.

My expression never changed, even as he raved on and on about his Learjet, and of all Kimmie's escapades. Kimmie was Kenneth's god-daughter. She had been the actual daughter of one of his servicemen friends who lived in Salem, Massachusetts. His friend and his friend's wife had been flying to Bali for a long-awaited twenty-fifth wedding anniversary celebration trip when their jet voyage took a turn for the worse. The airplane went through an incredible amount of turbulence from a massive rainstorm, then plummeted downward, on its side. It was lost on the radar screen, found the next morning by a fisherman who had strayed off course from the shore of his native homeland of Borneo. He reported seeing an incredible amount of different sized shiny metallic shapes, floating on top of the water. Crews searched the wreckage of what was found to be Kimmie's parents' doomed flight, but found no survivors.

Being Kimmie's godfather, Francis had been given the responsibility of raising her, if anything ever happened to her parents. She moved in with him at the ranch, went to a brand new private academy and proceeded to become a narcotic-filled recluse.

At the age of seventeen, right before her high school graduation, she was given a horse which she rode daily, for hours at a time, at an incredibly fast speed. She had taken plenty of jumping lessons as a child, but enjoyed the sensation of racing more. She fell in love with her thoroughbred stallion named "Marty" and gave up everything bad in her life.

Marty became faster than lightening, as they galloped through the ranch fields in back every morning and evening, partly due to Kimmie's expertise with horse obedience and health issues, but mostly because of his golden genes. At nineteen, she signed up for her first derby. It was a small town race in Georgia, where she placed a reputable third. Kimmie knew what she now wanted from life---to become a famous female jockey, and she was off to a good start with her talent, her horse, and most of all, her godfather's money.

Kenneth invited me to fly out to Los Angeles to see Kimmie's race at the Hollywood Downs. He said I could stay in my own room at the Beverly Hills Hotel, sip on champagne by the pool and eat dinner nightly at the Brown Derby.

I took him up on his invite for some time in the near future. I advised him that I was scheduled to take a trip up to my birthplace of Quebec City next week for a two week stay. There, I was to help in a massive carport sale that my mother was scheduled to have. She was seriously thinking of moving down to my area of St. Pete.

Kenneth asked me how I was able to keep up car and house payments with no job. I said that it was very tough at present. I had a little bit of savings, and only the hope of getting a phone call from a stern-sounding principal, offering me more money than I had in my contract before.

It never happened. Well, it hadn't happened yet, but I told him I wasn't giving up hope.

Kenneth told me he had a plan of getting my former position back…if I wanted it. He served with the one-star general who was offered the position of getting the slacker teenage boys disciplined, or thrown out, at my former academy. This general supposedly would do anything Kenneth asked of him, so if I wanted my job, I could get it back.

✳ ✳ ✳

Boarding the plane for Quebec City, I got a strange feeling of urgency to get the job done, so that I could hear more of Kenneth's life. After three hours, I landed in Quebec City. With baggage in hand, I hailed a cab for my mother's home. She lived in one of the more exclusive areas of the city, close to fancy shops and elite churches and schools. She wanted less of a strain in her life, however, as her bills and property taxes were soaring. We started the selling of some of her more prized possessions, along with some of her lesser ones. After three days, the huge sale was over. There had been cars and people lined up and down the driveway and street, waiting for the doors to open, as if in a much publicized estate sale.

The next evening is when I got the call from Kenneth. He said that he was flying his jet to Fort Bragg, North Carolina the day after tomorrow to commemorate a war hero, who died in action during the last days of the Gulf War. He was asked to come, at his widow's request. He told me he could swing by the airport in Montreal to pick me up, and maybe go out to dinner, then continue southward.

He wanted me to be his dressed-up lady to the hilt at this military funeral. He informed me this would take place in four days, and he told me to bring something cool to change into after the ceremony, as it was extremely hot and muggy in North Carolina in June. I agreed and went to sleep, dreaming of castles, maidens, and knights in shining armor sitting at my doorway, waiting for me---for whatever fate has in store for me.

Camille Bisset's fairy tale dream-state was about to be ruined by an incessant loud ring of what seemed to be an alarm clock, or a telephone. It was the latter, as there was no clock in her room. She got out from underneath her smooth, clean sheets, quickly put on her long, flannel robe, which she wore on many nights in Quebec, and groggily answered it, with the receiver stationed at her ear. When she heard Kenneth's gloomy voice, she woke up right away. She stood at attention. What was wrong? Was there some problem? Why was he calling at five-thirty in the morning? She wondered this, as the phone continued to ring incessantly.

When she finally got enough courage to answer it, Kenneth told her that he was feeling lousy and had been up all night. He had seen the doctor earlier that day. He said that his intern ordered him not to fly any type of aircraft, feeling like he did. The malady seemed to be, perhaps, a type of walking pneumonia. The doctor wasn't sure, without further tests. Obviously, they weren't going anywhere....not to North Carolina, and not to the Hollywood Downs....not anytime soon, at least. *Ohhhh.....how fate wheelz and dealz.*

Chapter Three

The Garage Apartment

I came home to St Petersburg two days later with a little bit of spunk and enthusiasm--couldn't wait to call Kenneth to see if he was alright. Nobody answered his phone number but a machine on which I left a short message of "Hello, just checking on you. Call me later." *I felt like something was in the air.* I got a return call not more than four hours later at two o'clock in the afternoon. The voice, however, sounded different, a bit more anxious and nervous, not as subdued as I was used to from his character. When I finally talked to him in person, he quickly asked me to meet him at Frezzios, a local bistro at the Marina, where "*The prices are right and the martinis are sizzlin'*". When I had entered the restaurant in the past, he walked up to escort me to the table, and he always said that phrase to me, not today, however.

I saw Kenneth from afar, waiting for me, sipping a Heineken, contemplating life. He arose from the table as soon as he saw me and greeted me with, "Hey Zahz." Kenneth loved using nicknames for people, instead of their "boring given names," as he always said. When he found out that I used to call myself "Zahz" when I was young, he started calling me, "Zahz". He loved the name, and it stuck. He extended his arms to embrace me, but not in his usual fashion of hugging me, while rubbing my back.

I thought to myself, "Oh well." Then, he pulled out my chair, sat back down, and ordered another brew.

He sternly told me, "I have news to tell you. I am really a four-star general who is still over command of troops in Iraq." He said that he just feels too boastful to brag anymore of his accomplishments, so he just leaves it with everybody as, "Yes, I'm a two-star general, but I only supervise in this capacity from time to time." But yes, oh yes, he was so much more than that to me. He was strong and tough.

My hero said he wanted to live with me at my house, until the ranch was ready for another tenant, the other tenant being me. He said that it would probably be for only a month. I quickly said, "Sure…just help me with the mortgage, and you're golden." He quickly added, "Soon, I'll have my two boys come to your house to do some light remodeling and finish out the garage apartment, then we'll sell the place."

Right now, it had on itself an array of code violations from its previous owner and of which I had to carry the burden. "Never worry. All things work out. Good always comes to those who wait patiently and faithfully," my grandmother used to always say, when my brother and I stayed with her in Nova Scotia and looked in the huge toy shop windows at Christmas time.

We loved our Grammy. She basically raised us. We spent all summers and most winters with her. Our mother and father divorced when I was three and Bradley was one. It was hard for mother to make ends meet when we were little, until she got a pretty good job in management at a top clothing store in Quebec City. We didn't know much about our father, other than he died five years later from a heart attack, while digging out land to lay some railroad tracks. He only gave my mother money from time to time, and when we weren't around.

Coming home early from grade school one day, I looked in the front window and saw my father holding cash in his hand. He was cornering my broke and almost desperate mother in the kitchen. She cried. He then picked her up and carried her to the couch in the den, where he raped her. I heard *"ma mere"* screaming. My mother never knew that I had seen and heard this, and I never told her I did. This had been the only time I ever saw my dad. I didn't know who was actually at fault in their marriage. It seemed obvious to me, though. My mother never spoke of the divorce, or my father, for that matter.

✳ ✳ ✳

Struggling to get out of the heavy, pensive mood I laid upon myself, I added apprehensively, "You know, I would love to have some company on **my** ranch." I had a fairly big front yard for a St. Petersburg home, very shady, with gardens on either side....MY paradise....*for now.*

The next day I picked up Kenneth in the front yard of his city apartment. He was holding three tool boxes, an electric saw, and a fishing pole. He proceeded to climb into my small red convertible, and we journeyed to my tiny home in the center of the city. My house was three miles from the bay and three miles from the Gulf in both eastward and westward directions. The breeze felt at the location where I inhabited was so invigorating, especially during a potential hurricane. Hurricanes in Florida seemed to be fortune-filled for builders and building supply manufacturers, but only an out of control paranoid joke to the seasoned, veteran inhabitants of life on this flirtatious *Mid-Floridian Gulf Coast.*

We went to my house, unloaded everything, and Kenneth proceeded to organize the work on the completion of my garage apartment. He was like a work horse to me. He had so many years on him, but so much spirit and strength left. I loved him even more for helping me with this project...and was even more looking forward to moving into his kingdom on the hill in Parrish, on Tampa Bay, where fairy tales were to turn into reality tales......*hopefully.*

Chapter Four

The Ranch

A few days after moving in with me, Kenneth was called back to the ranch for a week's worth of duties that consisted of breaking in wild horses that were just bought by his hand, Emilio, and for a very cheap price.

I called him and asked, "Kenneth, when do you think I'll be moving into the big house?" He replied, "Whenever you think you're ready."

"What did that mean?" I wondered, and so I continued to wait. He told me he was to schedule his two ranch "fixer-uppers" to come to my garage apartment to redo its violations.

They had never showed up, not for three days.

Finally, one afternoon, after talking to a very serious Kenneth about this issue, and who was filled with excuses, my obnoxious, yet harmless, next door neighbor and I journeyed to the heavens and back, by way of the Skyway Bridge. It connects Pinellas to Manatee Counties, stretching across where Tampa Bay meets the Gulf. After ten more minutes of interstate, I saw the exit Kenneth always told patrons was the route to get to his place. Every day at the bar he asked its drinkers to come visit him at the ranch, never thinking that any one of them ever would. I just *had* to go there. I had to finally get a glimpse of the estate grounds for myself.

Bobby and I continued a short while on Kenneth's route, until we came upon the massive white cross-barred fence of which was constantly being mentioned by Kenneth. He was very proud of this feat. He referred to this as his greatest accomplishment to date, as he had fenced the entire five thousand acre ranch himself, with the occasional help of the two laborers. I sped up to the ornate gates on which spelled out *The Ranch* in cursive type. Here, I found a nonchalant, evasive Kenneth that never even invited me through the gates and onto his grounds. He just waved, turned and walked away. I was dumbfounded.

Bobby said, "See, I told you he would turn out to be a jerk, and bipolar besides. You know, you've only dated him for seven months." I put my used, but dependable, Cabriolet in reverse and got the hell out of there. We drove back to our respective residences in silence.

I waited all evening and night for a phone call from the man whom I thought I loved, and who loved me, but no go. I waited two more days, and still, nothing.

Almost one week before, Francis had been surveying the grounds of the ranch, watching Kenneth when he was on property. He knew he must drug Kenneth over a period of time, so he plotted. He sneaked into the manor home late one night and replaced the codeine pills, which were given to Kenneth on a regular basis from the Veteran's Administration Hospital, with mild, slow-acting arsenic. Now, Francis prioritized confiscating Kenneth's infamous clientele book, duplicate keys to the black, ranch Escalade, and silver Learjet, but most importantly, all of his checking account withdrawal and deposit information. It was now the time to set out on his life-long planned mission.

❋ ❋ ❋

It was a cool Halloween night, the vampires and gargoyles were cheering, as Francis silently strolled inside the massive manor home. He knew exactly where to go, as he had done this once before, when he had replaced Kenneth's baby aspirin with low-dosed arsenic tablets. He had ordered architectural home layout renderings from the county code compliance department in downtown Bradenton, immediately after his first meeting with Camille at Frezzios two weeks prior. Both times he had entered the mansion, he wore black leather boots with gripping rubber soles, and he went up the stairs and down the hallway. The floor never creaked. These boots he thought to be the perfect device for a smooth entrance and speedy exit, and they evidently were.

He nudged the door, which was already ajar, until it was fully open. He entered into the cozy, professionally decorated, maroon-walled bedroom and sitting lounge. This was where he found an Escalade key chain on the nightstand in front of the sofa, with a Learjet starter attached, a thick clientele book, and a check book. He gathered all these crucial items and glanced across the room. He was aghast, looking at a man with an uncanny resemblance to himself stretched out on the mattress. It was at that point that Francis felt like he was looking into a mirror. He couldn't believe his eyes. In his almost seventy years of living, he had never seen two people who looked more alike than Kenneth and himself. Francis' birthmark had been the only trait that distinguished them from each other.

Francis knelt with head in hands, weeping, not for the deed he was about to commit, but for a life in which he had never even been given a mere chance to acquire. As he was in this sullen state of emotion, he abruptly fell into unconsciousness.

Chapter Five

The Pregnancy

When Emily walked into the unwed mother's shelter looking for a hot meal and warmth, she was greeted by an array of peddlers trying to sell their wares to adoptive families. She had never even entertained the thought of selling her baby. As Emily appeared to be a young, pretty, healthy girl in her middle teens, she was approached by all kinds of *wheelerz and dealerz*. They each had photos of their perspective families and homes, along with income verifications. Amounts of money were offered by each dealer. Her head was spinning, and she felt like she was sinning even talking with these people, who resembled players in one of her father's many late night poker games. Emily took a long, deep sigh and stated to each party, "I'm much too sleepy to make a huge decision like this tonight." They offered to come back to the shelter in the morning. She said, "Fine, just don't have me waked up if I'm still sleepin'."

Uprooted from a dairy farm in southern Maine, five-year old Emily and her brother of four moved to a tenement structure in Boston, because of lack of funds. "Artie", her father, had a gambling addiction. Artie had put up their home, farm and dairy cows as a bet in a poker game. He lost. The new owners now lived in luxury, due to the prosperous business they had inherited. Artie and his family now lived below poverty level standards. Artie kept saying to his family, as he always did, "Don't worry. This will soon pass. The Gods are just testing our strength."

Well, it never passed, and the family lived in Boston until Artie's death six years later, which was soon followed by his wife's dying of a broken heart. Artie had been sick with emphysema, as he smoked two to three packs of cigarettes per day. It finally got the best of him. His immunities simply wore out.

Emily and her brother were tossed from one family to another, like jugglers throwing colored balls from hand to hand in a side show, staying two months here, half a year there. One day, however, Emily was tossed alone, to a rather opulent couple from upstate New York. Emily never heard from her brother again. She adored her new family and felt like Mr. and Mrs. Jehl were her real parents. She went to a high society private school, made good grades, and went to dances, followed by dates, with eligible young men.

On one of these dates, however, she found herself in an uncompromising position in the back of a pickup truck, as she and her suitor were parked in a hay field close to the girl's academy that she attended. Emily knew only the young man's name and that he was enrolled in a preparatory school nearby---nothing more.

At sixteen, when even one day late for a period, intense fear and doom hover over any girl. Needless to say that in the nineteen thirties when a young girl of sixteen was seen with a protruding belly, it raised many an eyebrow. Emily couldn't bear telling her foster parents the sordid truth, so she left her fancy home. She skipped town, hitching rides along the way, until she arrived back in Boston. This was the only place she truly felt comfortable.

Emily stayed in homeless shelters for the first three nights and days, until she was told to check out an unwed mother's shelter. "In Holsbrook," Emily heard, "they take care of everything." So, Emily went to the shelter one evening, only trying to seek refuge, and she never left alive.

A rich Manhattan couple, the Redmans, who had recently moved to Holsbrook, offered her "dealer" a very good sum for her baby, which she took. She felt there was no other way out. She had no home and no money to raise a baby. The baby's father never claimed responsibility, as doing so would have ruined all of his chances for getting a law scholarship at Harvard.

When she finally went into labor at the shelter, she gave birth to twins. From the start, she had had such a high fever, which never cooled down, not even for one second. She simply went numb and gave up on life. Emily died, leaving her twins' lives in two powerful, feuding grips, one in the hands of God, the other in the clutch of Satan.

Her dealer felt very fortuitous upon hearing about the twins. He thought that perhaps he might make another few thousand from the second baby. After the babies were cleaned, checked for health issues, then left to sleep for hours, they were given to Emily's "dealer". Of course, now that Emily had died, there was no monetary distribution. It all went to the broker.

The first baby was a boy, with blonde fuzz and freckles. The second was a boy baby as well, with blonde fuzz and freckles. He was identical to the first, except for a massive red birthmark found under his left eye. The broker did not want anything to do with this "mistake baby", as he referred to it, as did no other broker. The shelter was forced to release this "mistake baby" to the area orphanage. In the black market world of baby buying in the nineteen thirties, everything had to be perfect, otherwise there was no deal.

The "perfect" baby boy was carefully placed in the hands of his new found inheritance. The three of them stumbled to their coach, carrying bags of jewels and feathers. They proceeded to gallop onward, toward the pulley drive that acted as a bridge over the moat to their castle.

It was the perfect life for any toddler to have, with numerous friends, parties, games, pets, and most importantly, toys. The "mistake baby", or Francis, as the orphanage decided to name him, grew up not having the perfect life. He never saw an animal, only during a one hour long visit to the Boston zoo. He never experienced a toy, a game, or a party in his first years of childhood. Fate had really dealt Francis a bad blow from the start. In primary school, he made failing grades. In junior high, he made passing grades, and in secondary school, he made the honor roll. Francis had begun to feel a glimmer of hope, but he was still fighting one major obstacle.......*no money.*

At eighteen, Francis left the orphanage and went to work for a small landscaping company outside of Boston proper. This lead had been given to him by one of the administrators at the orphanage, along with a recommendation. He made a fair living, not enough, however, to pay rent for his own apartment. He answered an ad in the Boston Globe under "Roommate Wanted".

When the advertiser answered his phone, "How much money per week?" was asked by Francis, and "only ten dollars" was the short response given.

Francis thought this to be a fair price, so he agreed to meet with the occupant to complete the deal.

The next morning Francis took the train from the shed where he was bunking on the landscaping company grounds, and which the owners were nice enough to let him stay, until he found shelter somewhere else.

A local train took Francis into Boston, near Beacon Hill. This was where he found the apartment's address. He stumbled up to the door and knocked.

He heard a loud, brisk, voice say, "Who's there?"

Francis answered the voice.

The screaming reply was, "Well, get the hell up here." Francis carefully walked up the rotted planks of wood on a staircase that had no railing.

When he reached the top, there was only one apartment door, and the tenant stuck his filthy head outside of it. He gazed at Francis blankly and yelled, "Well, don't just stand there staring at me. Put your body through this opening and entre," trying to speak his last sarcastic utterance using a bad French accent. He came off sounding like an East Coast redneck. Then, the man bowed, showing Francis the make shift path of entry. Francis had to squeeze between dusty objects and dirty clothing rags to get to a closet-sized back room where the tenant pointed to a large card table with a stack of messy papers on it.

The landlord said assuredly, with arms folded, "This is the place."

The small room smelled like mildew and had a wet, clammy feeling. However, Francis had no choice but to rent the room. He had nowhere else to go. This was the fork in the road that finally made him realize, he must work in some other line, so that he might be able to live a decent, normal sort of life.

He had acquired a small savings that could get him through almost one month, and with this in mind, he turned in his notice at the landscaping firm. They wished him luck, and he hit the pavement in search of money. This quest proved more difficult than he had ever imagined.

"We're not hiring." "You have no qualifications." "Don't think so, young man." "No experience?" were a few of the remarks made to Francis on a daily basis. He soon went from being a jovial, hopeful and somewhat irresponsible young man to a cynical, calloused, and serious worn soul from this entire experience.

One evening, at the end of his month long job search deadline, craving trivial conversation and lots of libation, he moseyed into an Irish pub near Faneuil Hall and ordered three Guinness' and one corned beef and cabbage. The smell made him remember those Friday nights at the orphanage, when corned beef and cabbage with new potatoes was served religiously. It was one of the few treats that the orphanage provided its "inmates". They looked forward to this meal all week long.

The cook was from Ireland and only worked two days and two nights per week, as that was all the orphanage could afford. During the other five days and nights, leftovers from these four meals and canned and jarred foods were served.

Francis had become great friends with this cook they called "Mr. O'Sullivan". Mr. O'Sullivan even let Francis cook the meals with him from time to time. Francis never forgot Mr. O'Sullivan's recipes and his knack for knowing the correct measurements of spices and other ingredients needed for flavor, without ever using any measuring device, just gut feelings.

Since Francis Cranford, the surname which was posted on his birth certificate, was supposedly from Irish decent, he was very interested in learning more about his culture. He really loved picking up a British Isles geography book, or an Irish cook book.

Francis used to tell Mr. O'Sullivan the made up story which was given to him by the orphanage. He would drone on and on about how his parents came over on a ship from Ireland to Boston where they both acquired malaria during a horridly hot summer. They soon perished, leaving his twin brother and him to be placed in separate city orphanages. Again and again, he thought about his lifelong desire of meeting his twin, and he always asked himself the questions, "I wonder if he's getting through life alright? I wonder where he is right now?"

As the meal was placed in front of Francis, he thought the aroma to be scintillating. He eyed the first piece of cut meat, savoring the thought of that scrumptious bite of juicy corned beef, and he placed it in his mouth.

"This is no good," he shouted, as he began to chew, "Not real, not the way it's supposed to be, ya hear?"

The cook came over and asked him, "What's the matter with it, son?"

Francis knocked the plate off the table and demanded that he go to the kitchen and prepare the dish "the way it's supposed to be".

After serving up several Irish dishes later that night to more than satisfied clientele, Francis was immediately offered the cooking job at the pub. He grabbed it. He was now to make more money. Soon, he would be able to move into a small one-room apartment by himself, which he treasured the thought of. Everything was going great now, both personally and professionally.

✳ ✳ ✳

Getting everything he asked for "at a moment's notice", Kenneth Redman became a crashing bore, filled with temper tantrums which seethed out at any given moment. He became very hard to live with in elementary school and junior high. He was simply a smart, conniving young man who wanted everything for himself. He decided that he liked the act of "taking" much better than the act of "giving". He felt destined for the thriving, successful business of "pulling the wool over one's eyes". As a teen, he began to make a lot of money, becoming a master con artist. It came easy for him. He had watched his intelligent, but extremely *clever* father do it for years.

In his senior year of high school, Kenneth held every heart in the class. He had girls waiting in line for a chance to go out with him, or just be seen with him.

Kenneth had a huge ego and did not even want to waste time with "mere mortal activities, like sports," he would always tell his cohorts. He chuckled to his classmates during one lunch period. "I'm going straight to the top just on my charm and wit." He was soon offered two scholarships, a partial one at Yale and a full one at Florida Southern College in Lakeland. He chose the second offer, as he had always enjoyed vacationing in Sarasota, at his family's Gulf-front bungalow as a youngster. He absolutely adored the horse industry there, so much so that Kenneth went out of his way to become an expert horseman through and through. Being an equestrian was unbelievably his number one interest, *for a while.*

After a two year stint at Florida Southern, he decided that college was not for him, and *neither were horses.* He felt like living the entrepreneur life of his father. He had become a clone of his foster father, Thomas Redman. Ken left school and got a job at a Miami bank. There, he moved to selling stocks, bonds and mutual funds. He learned how to double, even triple an allotted sum of money, and what investments most generally provide for this type of yield.

After a few years however, he felt he had hit a brick wall. There was no more room for his intense desire of growth, both in ego and wealth. There was nothing more to learn about making scads of money that the financial news wouldn't provide. He felt at the end of his rope, and he became very bored. Hating to leave Florida, he felt he must return to Holsbrook where he was raised and move in with his parents for a little while. They finally convinced him what to do next. Kenneth did whatever his hero dad advised him to do, without any questions asked. Listening to his brilliant father's teachings always ended in success for Kenneth, so he took Thomas at his word.

Thomas said, "Enlist in the military. It will toughen you up, bring you down to earth, and you'll realize your vulnerability. It's hard, but you'll grow to love it." He was right. Kenneth became a United States Air Force War Hero in both genres, fighting and commanding.

Chapter Six

The Date

Kenneth's visit to Holsbrook, Massachusetts turned into fourteen years of tumult. He enlisted in the Air Force when he first arrived in Holsbrook and was quickly flown to Seoul, Korea to act as an Air Traffic Controller. This happened to coincide with a crucial air strike in this war of the nineteen fifties. Kenneth originally dreamed of becoming a fighter pilot, but instead, the Air Force thought his highly strategic mind to be an important tool in getting US jets safely on and off the ground.

Late at night during his first week of duty, he was trafficking solo. Suddenly, a Korean plane flew straight over the tower, almost hitting its roof and blowing shrapnel pieces around an exciting, bright, star-filled sky, almost like confetti being thrown at a party. Kenneth collapsed on the board. The next thing he knew he was looking out a window at a dreary snow-filled sky. He asked a lady who was dressed in a white smock standing before him, "Where am I? What happened?"

She smiled and answered, "Why, you're in a Veteran Administration Hospital in Boston. The Air Force flew you back home after you were hit with shrapnel in Seoul. You seem to be doing swell now."

Kenneth asked, "When can I leave?"

The nurse replied, "Give it a few days anyway. Do you have to be somewhere?"

Kenneth chuckled and answered, "Always!"

Kenneth was discharged thirteen days later. He had bumps all over his body from the pieces that were locked in his skin. However, the doctors said the lodged shrapnel would pose no threat in later life. Kenneth received a Purple Heart for his heroism and begged to be sent over once again to complete his mission. The Air Force agreed after more recuperation. This time, Kenneth served for one year as a fighter pilot. Then, he was elevated to the rank of US Air Force Lieutenant.

When the next Asian war broke out in the sixties, the one in which we joined later, Kenneth was sent. After two years of intense fighting in the sky, he was promoted to United States Air Force Captain.

One afternoon while on assignment near Hanoi, his helicopter was hit by fire. It spiraled downward, one hundred feet to the ground.

Luckily, the copter had just taken off, so there was no fire upon impact. The Vietcongs took over the helicopter and its soldiers. Kenneth and his boys were taken to a small, dirty thatched hut, with no furniture to speak of, just a sturdy palm leaf that was glued with sticky tree sap onto three small pieces of wood. This was where the enemy commanding officer sat while assessing situations.

This hut contained six American Prisoners of War. They each slept in their own space of slightly dug out dirt. Kenneth told his soldiers to do this with their hands, remembering what his two German Shepherds, Belmont and Mattie would do in the heat of summer by the Gulf to keep cool. They would dig down deep, and once they got low enough, close to the water that ran beneath the sand, they felt comfortable. This was the only remedy for surviving the "jungle hot mug" in Vietnam, as the soldiers put it.

The captors only fed the prisoners one small meal per day. Most often, it consisted of one tiny piece of fish from the pond out back, some unusually textured, strange tasting peas, bought cheap, from the vendors that strolled by, and a piece of unripe fruit picked from a tree alongside the hut. Sometimes, it was simply a bowl of tasteless sticky rice. The six months the emaciated prisoners lived there seemed like an eternity.

One night Private Wilson asked Private McRee, "Hey, do you want to flee this joint? Today, I found an opening in the wire fence about five hundred yards away. We could squeak through, then go back to get the others out. Maybe, we could get some kind of recognition, or medal, or somethin'."

Private McRee said, "Count me in, and maybe we could find some weed along the way," he laughingly added. "I really need some…I mean…WITH All THIS STRESS… It's been way too long."

Private McRee enlisted in the Air Force as a way to escape jail for bringing three joints from Mexico back into Texas. He would have done anything not to have to go to jail.

At eleven thirty pm, the two boys left their hut, trudging through swampy fields until they arrived at the opening in the fence. They were weak from not eating or drinking much. When the two Privates ripped the fence open, a succession of bullets sounded through the night. They were killed instantly. It seems that the rip in the fence had been placed there on purpose, in order to tempt the prisoners. It worked, and now all that were left were four.

Another three weeks passed. Finally, one rainy afternoon, the Hanoians made four nooses and hung them four feet apart from each other. The four Americans knew what the enemy intended for them at that point. Two of the remaining soldiers pleaded on their hands and knees to be let go. The Vietcongs strung those fellows up first. The two remaining captives knew there was no other way out. They had to chance escape, while the enemy was performing the two executions.

Forgetting where he was positioned, the nervous Sergeant ran in the opposite direction of the hole. Kenneth instinctively ran towards the hole, jumping over creeks and marshy areas. Now, he was really wishing that he had participated in that Olympic qualification track meet his father suggested he enter and train for.

"My father was always right," he said to himself, as he jumped and straddled deep ravines, which held muddy rainwater, fearing for his life the entire time. "This sure enough brought me vulnerability, made me more down to earth, but I don't know about the toughness part."

Kenneth made it to the fence in record time, crawling through the sharp, broken ended barbed wire pieces that surrounded the wide hole. As he dragged his final body part through the jagged opening, he heard a shot ringing through the fields.

"Dammit, those bastards got the Sergeant," Kenneth yelled, hearing his echo resounding in the distance.

Francis worked as the cook in the Irish pub for three and a half years, before beginning a decade of moving from town to town, always near Boston, however. He stayed in a one room apartment in Beverly for three years, but after this, he rented one month at a time in each small town, never getting bored in stagnation. Francis loved living life as a gypsy. One night while at a local dive near Revere Beach where he was living at the time, he met two girls. One of them was named Tina. She sheepishly told him, "Hi, my name is Tina, and I'm from Holsbrook. Where are you from?"

Francis nonchalantly answered, glancing around the room, then at this woman whom he thought had pleasant, but rather ordinary looks.

"I'm from everywhere," he said.

Tina said, "You know, you look and sound just like a former boyfriend of mine from high school."

Francis said in a snappy way, "Okay. What's his name?"

She replied, "Kenneth Redman, a doll and very rich." She drunkenly slurred, "He was so lucky he got adopted into that life. He had everything and every girl you could ever imagine, just made of gold. Kenny was pretty cold hearted though...had too much going for him...just too much ego....but I liked him still."

This perked up Francis' ears. He wondered, "Had he hit the jack-pot?" He excitedly told the girls he had to go. He had business to take care of in the morning.

The provocatively dressed Tina slipped her phone number into Francis' rugged hand and whispered softly into his ear, "Call me some-time." He nodded and walked out of the bar to his apartment, where he was to plan his quiet attack.

The next afternoon Francis drove to Holsbrook, went to the county records office, and told the officials there of his relentless desire to meet his twin. He informed the workers that the two were supposedly separated at birth. He found out that "Kenneth Redman" was born on his own birthday, in the same year, and in the same shel-ter. This was the break he had been waiting for. There was no current address for Kenneth however, only the address of Kenneth's parents, at the time of his birth.

Smiling Francis walked out of the office chanting, "Well, at least I'm getting somewhere."

He revved up his small, but powerful engine. He left the county municipality and headed over the creek and up the street, until he arrived at 508 Arbor Lane Drive, as the address read. He turned onto the cracked driveway of the overgrown plot of land, which displayed what looked like a large ginger bread house, in great need of repair. It was situated smack dab in the middle of overgrown foliage. Francis got out of his vehicle, hesitantly, and proceeded to begin the investiga-tion into his twin's life.

Kenneth got through the Vietnam War with honors. He was promoted to major and sent to Germany. He stayed in Munich for close to five years, conducting routine practice missions throughout Western Europe, until he had enough. He requested one week off to simply go back to his home in Massachusetts and visit his father who was very ill. This request was denied by his commanding general, General Bryant. When he got this news, Kenneth went straight to the nearest bar and had several *biers* with several *frauleins* who took him upstairs. He dozed-off, then awoke, with a pounding headache. He said *auf wiedersehen* to the *damen* and hailed a taxi to take him home, where he began to plan his getaway to the states.

As soon as he opened the door to his apartment, he ran to the kitchen to phone several of his officers and tell them each what he wanted. Most importantly, Kenneth requested a military jet, orders, and clearance papers. He found these could be arranged through General Smythe, whom he had flown with in Vietnam.

When General Bryant found out about Smythe's overriding of his own denial, he tried to get Smythe court-martialed. Bryant couldn't accomplish this however. Both Smythe and Redman had impeccable military records.

Two days later, Kenneth's appeal for temporary leave was granted, and he flew to Boston. He bunked with his father in his private hospital room. Kenneth had been there for only one week, when Thomas turned cold and blue, and died. He had contracted pneumonia. Kenneth would have given up his entire military career just to be with his hero at his end. Kenneth had become a very heroic and respected man, a far cry from what he had been as a teen.

Kenneth requested an extended leave, in order to get his estate affairs in order, as he was the executor. He was granted this request. At the reading of the will, Kenneth was to receive five million dollars. His mother was to receive the other five million, and the home. Kenneth's mother, Kate, who was in her sixties then, put Kenneth in her will as the sole beneficiary. It was during this leave that he met his wife, Jane.

Francis got a call late one evening, while fixing a pot of homemade chili with plenty of diced onions and shredded sharp cheddar. He had the six o'clock news cranked up, while he sizzled sirloin on the stove. This was his usual "day off" meal, and he looked forward to it with passion, enjoying every moment of its preparation. Chili, chips, and light beer was his favorite anecdote to a busy week.

Standing his large spoon in the large pot of thick chili, he picked up the ringing wall phone. He immediately stood at attention when he heard a deep voiced man loudly say, "Hello, this is Anthony Farres, Maitre d', and I'm with Countess Cruises." He inquiringly asked, "Is this Francis Cranford?"

Francis replied, "At your service."

Anthony bluntly told Francis that the cruise line was interviewing for the position of head chef on their Mediterranean runs. They needed a highly qualified master chef for the two ships that have a two week run. He said the cruise line received several commendations on Francis' gourmet cuisines.

Sounding direct, Anthony stated, "Both are hard runs, very demanding, but they will make your pockets stretch out."

Next, he gave Francis the bi-weekly schedule. He stated, "The first ship leaves Barcelona on Saturday and continues to Palma de Mallorca, Marseilles, Monaco, and Florence, disembarking in Rome the next Saturday. From there, the second ship leaves Rome for Sicily, Athens, Santorini, and Istanbul, from Saturday to Saturday as well." He clarified that the run is scheduled from October through May, and that the base pay is seventy five thousand dollars a year. Anthony quickly added, without a breath, "And of course, the head chef gets tipped in a major way, if the job is done well. You know, only wealthy guests board our elegant ships. And by the way," he added, "our chef is given lavish room and board. It's a run with nice, cool weather besides."

Smiling from cheek to cheek, Francis agreed to an interview the very next morning at ten at the cruise line headquarters in Providence.

"This is the break I've been waiting for," he screamed throughout his apartment, as he reached into the fridge, took out the cheap bottle of bubbly, which he had saved for a special occasion like this one, or a cheap date, and he popped the cork. Pink champagne spewed everywhere. Francis laughed hysterically and drank the whole bottle while cooking his chili.

The next morning he awoke with a start, looked at the clock and saw it was only four, not five, which Francis had originally set the alarm for. He got up anyway, made himself a single cup of java and sleepily cooked up some hot oatmeal from scratch. He thought this to be the perfect breakfast, one that was small and light enough to keep him energized all morning, while not weighing him down for the drive, or the interview ahead. He poured whole milk over the steamy oats and mixed in two teaspoons, one of brown sugar and one of butter. Francis quickly ate.

Then, he finished his *Caffe` Americano*, which had just a touch of espresso mixed in, only to get him going in the mornings.

Finally, he got ready in the bathroom and decided on what apparel would be appropriate for a "Master Chef" interview.

He had never been on an interview like this, as he had mostly worked in dives up and down the coast of Massachusetts, where it didn't matter how he dressed. Francis quickly decided on a tan and green, long-sleeved striped polo shirt with khaki pants and deck shoes.

He thought to himself, "This makes me look rock solid and confident, but not too arrogant, *the perfect combination to get what I want in life.*"

He made it to Providence in what seemed to be record time, probably because he was thinking about his twin the entire ride and how he might meet up with him, and his money. After finding the three story, old brick building in the center of town, Francis carefully climbed out of his used, two-door jalopy, but which displayed a new coat of slate gray sparkles. It did have a good working engine. The car had never let him down. He reached into his back pants pocket to get the information that Anthony had recited to him the day before, and that's when he found it…Tina's phone number. He thought that he must have worn his khakis that evening he met her at the bar. Francis felt this to be an omen and promised to himself, saying to the air, "If I get this job, I'm gonna take this female to the Ritz for drinks, food, and sex. That way, I can find out more about my brother."

He had not been able to find out anything about his brother's whereabouts, except that he was a high ranking officer, stationed somewhere in Europe. He had found out this information by talking to the Redmans' former neighbors who lived next to this "ginger bread" house. The "baby boomer" neighbors saw Francis through their window and darted over that day, asking how they could help him. The couple informed him that the Redmans had moved from there about ten years ago. Francis asked if they knew to where the two had moved. The man and woman shook their heads and told him that the Redmans were said to have moved to a very large house located on a few acres outside of town in the countryside. They had also heard that Mr. Redman had been in and out of hospitals over the past year. He evidently was in a perpetual state of illness. Francis was not able to receive any more information about his twin from that chance encounter. He knew what he should be concentrating on now...the large house, near the edge of town, and when he was going to talk to Mr. and Mrs. Redman.

✳ ✳ ✳

Francis told the elderly, yet seemingly competent receptionist in the lobby that he had an appointment with Anthony Farres at ten. She buzzed the Maitre d' upstairs, and in what seemed like two minutes, a rather large, jovial, dark brown haired and skinned Italian with a rosy round face and menacing gray eyes sauntered out from behind the elevator doors.

He said, "Follow me," in a take charge manner, as he led the way down the black marbled hallway, until it dead-ended into a dreary, boxy conference room. It did provide some comfort that nervous Francis craved, as the stale room looked out onto an elaborate Japanese garden with small wooden bridges. Here, Francis showed Anthony photos of some of his most flamboyant concoctions, along with several dessert samples that he carried in a Tupperware dish.

Anthony was impressed by everything, especially Francis' "take charge" demeanor. The Maitre d' thought to himself, as Francis raved on and on about his dishes, and how much the patrons loved them that "this might be the guy we need."

He had not been able to find a permanent replacement for the former head chef who had left three years before, due to illness. The others had been too "thin-skinned" for all of the criticism and pompousness that a chef had to endure on a daily basis. In general, the snooty clientele seemed to be getting harder and harder to please.

"Francis might be the guy to pass my complaints and requests onto. Why not? He'd be the new kid on the block, and he needs to be broken in," Anthony rationalized to himself, contemplating all of his moves, while wrinkling his forehead.

Francis had never felt like such a big shot than before the night that he got Anthony's all important call. Now he felt special....like some former angel was now looking up at him, showing him where he should go and what he should become. He was feeling powerful and manipulative, deceitful, and dirty.

Anthony called Francis the following morning at nine sharp and told him Countess Cruise lines was prepared to offer him the head chef position.

Elated, but not wanting to appear too excited, Francis calmly told him "Sure, I'll take it. Why not?"

Paperwork was sent back and forth, between the two parties.

Francis was scheduled to depart for Greece in one month, and with only three days left, he made sure he had gotten all of his affairs in order, and he had, except for one. That was when he again saw her name and phone number, this time lying on top of his dresser, and he decided to give it a chance and ring her. "I have nothing to lose and lots to gain," he whispered to himself.

"What's up?" tall, auburn Tina asked in her sultry voice, as she picked up the receiver, seeing Francis' name on caller ID. "It took you a long time to give me a shout. How's come? You don't like me or sumpin'?"

"No, I like you fine...JUST Fine," Francis murmured almost inaudibly.

"What? Can't hear nuttin!" she interrupted, speaking loudly.

Francis restated, "Of course I like ya. Otherwise, I wouldn't have called you to ask you on a date tonight."

Tina asked, perking up, "When? And where?"

"Eight o'clock at the Ritz Carlton," he replied.

"Wow, did you strike it rich or somethin', babe?" Tina asked.

"Well, sort of. I'll tell you about it later. How's 'bout we meet at the bar in front, then go to dinner from there? You never know what might happen after that, toots," Francis indiscreetly added.

He knew she was a loose broad, so he didn't have to worry about play acting with her. He also surmised that she was lying about knowing Kenneth in high school. She had probably been a "Pro" and he a "John" when they met, maybe even on numerous occasions.

"What you see, my fiery, slutty Tina, is what you get, and you for sure want me! It's obvious," he sang in a made-up, mundane, two-note melody.

After three very strong, salty Martinis from the bar, the two decided to get a room and order room service. Francis ordered them both beef tips and rice cooked in a mushroom wine sauce and asparagus with hollandaise sauce. For dessert, they had Cherries Jubilee with strong black coffee, which was waiting on the huge round tray on the coffee table.

Tina didn't have dining etiquette, or really any etiquette at all, for that matter. She complained about heartburn from the mushroom sauce with every bite. She didn't even try the asparagus, said it looked awful and that she hated vegetables. She only ate the vanilla ice cream, scraping off the fancy liqueur and sweet cherries from the Cherries Jubilee. She couldn't stand the taste or smell of coffee, either. She said she drank iced tea with saccharin in the mornings. Since gourmet dining experiences were so important to Frances and a major part of his being, Tina proved very boring to him from the start.

After this disastrous candlelit celebration, Francis decided to load some Sinatra into his portable compact disc player, hoping it might lift his spirits, so that he might find the information he wanted so desperately. He seemed to get sidetracked however, about why he had even asked her out in the first place, whenever Tina unexpectedly took off her busty, transparent, long-sleeved spandex shirt. He had stared a hole through it the entire evening. She then pulled off Francis' sweater and started licking his hairy, muscular chest. Moaning, he lifted her skirt and massaged her private parts. Then, he took her from the chair and carried her into the bedroom alcove. It was apparent, she was merely a sexual toy to him. The love of sex was the only thing he had in common with her, and the only thing that Francis even liked about the girl. She reached many orgasmic heights throughout their session. He did too, but only through oral sex, which was his favorite by far. She seemed a bitch to him, and a serious nymphomaniac, but in his horny state, he didn't care.

At midnight, Tina silently got out of bed. She dressed and left the room, without even a note. When he awoke at eight fifteen, Francis was panic-stricken. He did not even know where she lived or worked. He called her number, which was still lying on top of his dresser and heard only a three note melody on the other end, followed by a computerized recording of a female voice saying, "The number you've dialed has been disconnected". The only leads he had on where to find her were the Revere Beach bars where she supposedly hung out. He banged his head on the wall, thinking about what a stupid fool he had been the night before. He had not even had the chance to ask her if she knew Kenneth's parents and their address. No, nothing had been accomplished. She had gotten the best of him, and he had gotten "nada", except for an expensive evening with a cheap dame.

"The dame would have cost less at a bordello and probably been more sophisticated," Francis said out loud to himself.

The following afternoon he went up and down the beach asking establishment workers whether or not any knew the girl, giving her name and description. They all said that they'd never known, nor seen anyone like that. Except for one old time proprietor at "Greensleeves", an English club across from the beach, who told Francis, "Yeah, I have known her since she was a young stripper in Springfield. She was never any good. She lived in ill repute houses, since she was about seventeen. She never really went to school, never had much of a family, just an alcoholic mother and a dead beat father who left them both to marry a waitress from Hoboken. She would always come around and try to sell her 'product' for money, whenever the rent came due. I'm warning ya bud, stay away from her."

Francis asked, excitedly, "But did she ever go to Holsbrook High?"

"Are you kiddin'?" was all the old man uttered, as he glared in disbelief. "She never even made it to high school," he continued, as he made his way to the entrance to open up shop.

Francis knew then he had been had for sure, and he left the establishment, angrily taunting himself. He repeated, "You should have been smarter and abstained. You're better than that. If you ever see her again, it's definitely lights out for the skanky dame."

✳ ✳ ✳

Kenneth again saw the pretty, young, hazel-eyed girl with ash brown hair at the shop where he always picked up postcards to send to his officer buddies. Not thinking he stood a chance, he approached her nervously at the counter.

Surprisingly, she told him, "Hi, I'm Jane, if you need any help."

"Thanks," he shyly replied back.

Slightly batting her natural eyelashes at him, she aggressively said, "You know, I've seen you here many times before and always wished you'd talk to me. You haven't until now, but we still have time."

Kenneth flirtatiously responded, "Time for what, dear?"

Jane cunningly answered, "For whatever life has in store for us."

She looked into Kenneth's dark gray eyes and asked rather shyly, "Would you like to go out for a coffee?"

That evening when she got off work, he met her at the shop, and they went to an open air cafe on the fishing pier in Camden, where they both had Maine lobster and coffee and brandy. They instantly fell in love with each other, as they laughed together in the early September foggy moonlight.

Jane and Kenneth dated for two years before getting married. She had just turned twenty-three, he was thirty-eight, when they took their vows. They lived in a large four bedroom, two and a half bath home in the outskirts of Holsbrook, near his mother, and located on three wooded acres. It was a nice retreat for Kenneth, when he returned from England on a bi-weekly basis to spend four days in his "kingdom", with his faithful young wife. They had many acquaintances, parties and possessions, but only a fair marriage from the start.

Kenneth's mother died when Kenneth had just turned forty-one. She had had a short bout with brain cancer. Kenneth and Jane moved into the inherited estate right before he served Jane with divorce papers.

Not knowing how to behave in a committed relationship, as he had never really been in one, not in his entire life, not even in a true friendship. He had not given his fair share to the marriage. He had only used people for his own wants and desires. This was why Ken thought that he, himself, had ruined the marriage. Ken had never been there for Jane, not even when he had physically been beside her. Never had his mind been on his wife, only on himself, in his pursuance of victory. He earned and accomplished more and more, but never once included Jane in any of his pursuits, never really included her in anything, for that matter. After reaching his final ranking of two star general, he became very aloof and cynical whenever Jane came near him. He had been given such huge tasks and challenges in Europe during their marriage, that he became a mastermind in air strategies. He was given "US General" status at a huge soiree, where Jane wasn't even in attendance. The celebration was in England. She was in Holsbrook. Ken didn't even inform her of the occasion, or ask her to be his escort.

Thinking of this past event, he drunkenly told her, while guzzling brandy late one night, "You are far too good for me and deserve better. I've always thought that."

They divorced two and a half years later, and he knew that he had done Jane wrong. He told her so in a long letter. He was slowly being lifted by the hand of God, up from the heat.

✳ ✳ ✳

Francis didn't have time to delve into his brother's existence. He was now ready to depart for his job of a lifetime, ready to make some cash and have some fun. He didn't care now. He put his sibling on the back burner. "I don't care if I ever meet the rat bastard. I don't need him, never needed him in the first place. He's probably bogus anyway, ya know? Doesn't even have a dime to his name. Yeah, I'm the cool one *now*," Francis whispered this soliloquy to the flight magazine he was reading while crossing the Atlantic.

Chapter Seven

The Napkin

Francis jumped up the next morning with a start, thinking that his twin was standing before him, staring at him. All night long, he had had a very restless sleep, in which he tossed and turned, dreaming about twenty year old cruise ship scenarios. Right before he awoke, he had one of his ongoing Mafia nightmares. He began to have these nightmares when he started work at the beach pub. Many of the clientele there belonged to the Irish Mafia. Francis heard about all of their escapades over brews and became very good chums with all of them. They would sometimes close up the bar together, all becoming inebriated.

A few days earlier, Hugo Henry, one of the most respected of the Irish mobsters, made an entrance at the pub. Hugo was born in Belfast, but raised as a teenager in Boston. He was the son of the most infamous criminal mind in the British Isles, Patrick Z. Henry. Hugo and his mother, Maddie, moved to Boston to begin a new existence, when Patrick Z. was placed in the confines of a Northern Ireland penitentiary.

Maddie was tired of the constant ups and downs, living life with her good-looking, but unstable Patrick. He was a perpetual playboy and renegade.

Hugo had also been a renegade all of his life too, from birth in Belfast until now. He "coolly" and suavely glided through life, wherever and whenever. All heads turned to look whenever he entered an establishment.

Hugo had a tremendous ego, as everyone could tell. He felt he could do anything to anyone, without any repercussions. His four ex-wives had testified to that trait of his personality at each of their divorce hearings. They each said that Hugo would bedazzle them with his kindness at first, winning their trust and affection, then "bam", he would change overnight and become an egocentric mad man, just like powerful Tyrone, his selfish, *thug* older brother. His *sane* older brother, Theo, was a clean Irish farmer.

Hugo walked over to Francis, smiled mischievously and placed his finger on Francis' upper cheek, tracing a squared-off circle over his blemished area. Francis uncomfortably backed away. With his mouth open in bewilderment, he wanted to say something but could not.

Taking one last swig of his pint, Hugo smirked, "When are you gonna take care of that, boy? You've been wearing that since your cruise days."

Francis laughed, "Well, how can I, bloke? It's permanent...from birth. Hey, don't I know you or something?"

Hugo said, "Nah," and scribbled something on one of the bar room napkins, pushing it down the bar to Francis.

Francis asked, "What's this shit?"

"Call the number and see for yourself....but it will make your life change," Hugo said wild-eyed, as he flung his jacket over his shoulder and waltzed out of the pub.

For an instant, he thought about his eldest brother, Theodore, and what a boring life he must have, with a farm in Ireland. Hugo felt so glad he had moved to Boston as a boy with Maddie, *so glad*.

When the alarm clock which laid on a pile of much read recipe books began to belt out tunes from the "fifties", Francis got himself up to make his morning one cup of sanity. He learned a unique way of fixing a mug of piping hot java from Mr. O'Sullivan, without a percolator.

He cupped one industrial-strength paper towel, which was filled with ground coffee beans, and placed it over his mug. He then boiled water in a tea pot and poured this water through the paper towel, over the ground coffee and into the mug. The strong aroma of steaming, fresh, robust brown liquid filled the room. This was the easiest, most efficient, and least costly way to start the day for him. Only when he had a date or a dinner party with friends was this method not functional.

He saw the number that the Irish dude wrote on the napkin, which Francis had placed on the kitchen counter by the stove. He dialed the number on the napkin and waited for over ten rings, until a perky voice answered the call, "Facial Surgery with Dr. Martin." Francis hung up the phone.

"What the hell?" he thought.

Five minutes later, there was a forceful, what sounded like the palm of a hand, banging at the saloon door. Francis dressed in his apartment upstairs, then, he walked downstairs into the bar to see what was wanted this early in the morning.

Francis looked down the sidewalk, squinting through the latched chain. He saw Hugo standing there, wearing a sly smile on the left side of his fair-skinned face. Hugo's salt and pepper hair looked as if it needed a trimming badly, and Francis thought the bald spot on the back of his head to be getting bigger by the moment. Francis annoyingly unlatched the door and asked Hugo what he wanted with him this early. Hugo handed him a white box with a red ribbon on it. Francis just stood there, looking at him harshly.

Hugo stared at Francis and exclaimed, "Well, what are you waiting for? Open it!"

As Francis did this, his expression changed from annoyance to astonishment. In the box was more money than Francis had ever seen before, along with a card underneath the pile that read:

"This is to remove your birthmark with Dr. Martin, along with a stash of recoup dough. Call Martin to make an appointment, and listen to me Fran. I'm the one you answer to now."

Back upstairs, Francis found the crumpled-up napkin on the floor by the garbage can and unraveled it. He dialed the number once again, but this time he spoke with the perky-voiced girl on the other end. He asked her how she was, and she answered, "I'm very hot, thank you."

He smiled to himself and asked if she could squeeze him in sometime soon to see Dr. Martin about a birthmark scar removal.

She asked, "How's about tomorrow afternoon, honey?"

Unsure about how he got an appointment that quickly, Francis answered robotic-like, "Perfect."

After waiting the following afternoon for nearly an hour, flirting with the blonde, bubble gum-chewing receptionist who wore red spiked heels on her high-arched stripper feet, a clingy white tank top and black low-riders, a redheaded pudgy middle-aged man wearing a long white jacket and green scrubs entered the room. Francis sat at the long conference table. The man introduced himself as Doc Martin, facial surgery specialist. The Doc immediately took sight of the abnormality, and assuredly nodded and said, "This should be no problem. I'll have you looking like a million bucks by tomorrow."

"Tomorrow?" Francis asked.

The Doc replied, "The boys want it done the sooner the better, so I'll make it my first priority of the day. Be here tomorrow morning at nine," and he abruptly left the room.

"Wow," Francis murmured to himself. "What is going on here?" At that moment, he again thought about the twin he wanted so desperately to meet and about his chance encounter with Tina at the dump on the beach. He had been thinking a lot about his brother lately, so he had decided that the first thing he was going to do after he healed was to find his twin.

＊ ＊ ＊

And did that ever happen. Francis didn't know what was in store for himself, or what he was about to turn into.

＊ ＊ ＊

When he got up at six the following morning, so he could get to the doc's clinic at nine, he walked into the cozy kitchen and remembered he wasn't supposed to drink or nibble on anything. He couldn't even the tasty banana bread he had made the day earlier. He phoned the restaurant and told them the Doc said it might be a few days 'til he could return to the hot kitchen. The restaurant asked that Francis just drop off some of his new lobster sandwich recipes that he had concocted and which everyone seemed to adore. The "Stuffed Lobster Roll" became the favorite at the beach bar.

Francis had served Countess Cruises well over a twenty-five year period. Many thought he had been the best *Master Chef* the line had ever had. Francis had all the females and even a few of the males wanting to go up to his balcony suite for the night. He had become such a con artist because of this entire experience. He was by no means rich, even though he did bring home a healthy pay check. He had acquired no assets, as well as no liabilities during his employment. He had lived his life up 'til now like there was no tomorrow.

At the ripe age of sixty-five, he felt he needed a rest. He was becoming less energetic and more tired of his monotonous routine. Plus, his fan base was dwindling. He looked and felt like a worn out rag. He told his best friend, Anthony about his decision to retire from the cruise line. Tony understood and thought it best, too.

It was on his last two week run that he met a striking dark Irishman about forty years old. His name was Hugh. They became acquaintances on board ship for the week, as they talked about Boston, about

Ireland and their Irish backgrounds, and of course, their Bostonian hangouts. They exchanged email addresses but never kept in touch.

On that last bittersweet morning when docking in the port of Piraeus, Francis packed his bags, picked up his last pay check, cashed it on board, and disembarked from the ship....FOREVER.

He flew from Athens to Boston, went straight to his old Revere Beach hangout, where he was greeted royally. He was offered a full time cooking job there his first day back, which he accepted. He was to work there for the next three years. He felt like himself again.... down and dirty, lean and mean.

He felt good, wearing his old faded jeans and muscle shirt, and cooking his favorite...Lobster Rolls. He was still toned for a man of his age. He ran the beach and lifted weights daily. The cruise ship had provided him lots of opportunities to meet fancy, sophisticated people, but that scene wasn't really him. Long term commitments with prestigious men and women never interested Francis. They pushed him away, far, far away. He had to have his space, freedom, and smut.

He strolled into the clinic a little after nine, after hurriedly giving the recipe copies to the part time cooks. The nurses rushed him into a laboratory to test him for any allergies and check his pulse before they put him under anesthesia. He was in good physical condition, tests showed, except for an occasional heart murmur, which could be a problem, if left unguarded. He did have an unknown allergy to penicillin, which they took special priority to note in their filed records. Having this crucial information, the anesthesiologists began to place tubes and needles in his arm.

"One hundred, ninety-nine, ninety-eight, ninety-seven, ninety-six, ninety-five...," he muttered to himself before falling asleep.

When his eyes opened three hours later, there were five of Francis' fair *friends* from the mob surrounding his bed. They were supposed to take him back to his apartment and make sure he was comfortable.

The boys were really catering to him. He wondered why. He struggled to get up out of the bed with the help of the boys and one mousy brown bouffant headed petite nurse. They walked with him over to the bathroom where he dressed, so that he was able to leave the clinic as soon as possible. He splashed cold water on his face, and he felt ready to go and see what was in store for him. The Doc came into the room and said that everything went well and said that Francis should be able to take the bandage off of his face in seven days. The mob boys then escorted him to a waiting limo and drove him instead to one of the boys' estates, near the harbor.

"This must be where they're gonna talk to me," Francis surmised.

Francis now started getting tense and worried, as he saw the emotionless, sullen looks on each of the mob boy's faces.

As they started walking down the flower laced brick pathway leading up to the massive mahogany front doors, Hugo emerged.

He said, "I'm glad you could join us all in one piece after your surgery. It's now time you listened to what *we* have to say. Come inside, and please, please make yourself comfortable, and we'll tell you what we expect from you." Francis walked inside with the others.

The boys got extra pillows and propped up Francis on the elegant mauve velvet sofa, and Francis comfortably heard the details of their elaborate scheme. Hugo revealed the entire plot. He told Francis that he was to double as his twin brother, Kenneth Redman, in order to get vital information and take Kenneth's place in society.

Francis freaked, looking down at the ground and said, "You mean, this is how I'll finally get to meet him?"

"I suppose you're wondering why? Ain't ya, Fran?" asked Hugo.

"Just tell me what you're trying to get from me killing my twin brother," Francis barked in amazement, "Tell me. What's the real deal?"

Hugo answered, "The real deal is that you got half a million dollars in a box to kill your brother. Over the next few months, you are to trace each of his steps and moves, get to know his friends and acquaintances and all about his businesses, clients, and bank accounts. When the time is right, a ten million dollar life insurance policy on Francis

Cranford will be taken out by his twin brother Kenneth Redman, with Doc Martin's written A+ evaluation of Francis' health."

"I still don't understand," Francis blurted out.

"Oh, you will," Hugo grinned, and he began the drama. He pointed his finger at Francis and lectured, "You, Francis Cranford, alias Kenneth Redman, will receive a red hot check for ten million dollars, and you will in turn, give us all proceeds. You see, Francis Cranford has mysteriously died from a misdiagnosis, with wrong drugs being administered and prescribed to him. You will be the one who gets into Kenneth's manor home to switch pills in two bottles and begin pumping poison into his veins.

We'll arm you with a stun gun to knock him out so you can give him that first dose. After that, it's all downhill, except you have to bring him to us. You think you can do it?" Hugo asked, and he quickly added, "For a job well done, there's also a hefty bonus. It's fuckin' easy....You don't even know the old geezer."

Francis immediately said, "You know I'll do it." His soul had definitely now been transferred into one of the devil's clutches.

Francis counted down the next seven days, almost in desperation. He called Doc Martin's girl on the third day and told her of his intense pain. Even with the black market pain killers given to him, they weren't killing the agony, just making him woozy and lightheaded. He wanted the Doc to know this and call him back. The Doc did this right after his scheduled surgical procedure. The doctor told him to take these pills with a glass of brandy, if they weren't working.

He added, "You need to acquire a taste for brandy anyway, if you're going to portray Kenneth. You know, he really loved the stuff, became dependent on it. I've never seen anyone who had such important responsibilities become so addicted." Doc stressed, "Pills and brandy are a dangerous mix, so please be careful."

On the fifth day, Francis felt much better. With the codeine and brandy combination, he slept like a baby for two long nights.

On the sixth day, the pain had gone completely. On the day of unveiling, Francis was ready to see if Doc's magical reputation and skill rang true.

Before Francis started, he downed a shot of brandy, so that he would feel no pain as he ripped off the surgical tape. The cotton gauze that covered his left cheek was attached to the skin by what seemed to be a type of gluey ointment. Now was the time of reckoning. Would it be a miracle, or a disaster? He ripped off the bandage.

Chapter Eight

His New Face

Francis pulled off the sturdy bandage, lifting it up at its edges. Keeping his eyes shut, he painfully took the covering off. Francis took another swig of his new found pain remedy, brandy, before opening his eyes. He let the brandy trickle down his trachea pipes, then popped his eyes wide open, as if in a horror flick. He gawked at what he saw. He traced where the blemished lines were in the mirror from memory, because they were there no more. No, not a trace. Some pinkness and swelling protruded slightly from the upper part of the cheek, but looked as if he simply bumped into something.

He called the Doc to report-in and tell him about the protrusion, but he was in surgery, and again, Francis left a message for the Doc with Kathy, the "hot" receptionist.

Doc Martin called him back three and a half hours later. He told Francis that he knew the procedure would turn out perfect.

"I'm good," he stated. "Some even say I'm great. All I do is my job, the best way I know how. And about the pinkness and the swelling, well…that's normal. It's just irritated from the surgical shock on that very fragile, sensitive area. I had to be particularly careful with the eye being so close to where I was working. I'm glad it looks perfect, but I knew it would…and with that, I'll dismiss you from my care, unless you run into a problem, which you shouldn't. I have other matters to tend to now."

Francis knew to what he was referring, and he left the conversation alone. He assumed that Doc Martin had a thriving business, judging from his expertise and that he did this kind of funny stuff on the side for a lot of extra dough. It's not like he didn't already have millions, but he wanted more.

"What a greedy son-of-a-bitch," he thought to himself, before bidding him, "Adieu".

Francis called Hugo after he hung up and gave him the news. Hugo sent a limo for Francis to come to the estate where pictures and films of Kenneth's dealings were to be displayed in the basement. When Francis arrived, the mob boys had champagne flowing, plenty of pretty girls in tight mini-skirts, and a blue's band wailing in the back yard. Everyone was amazed at the sight of Francis' face.

The scent of *Ben Franklins* filled the air.

Francis looked at an array of photos and film clips. These included Kenneth's meetings with dignitaries in the United States Air Force and Marines Corps, along with officials from other lands. He seemed very smooth and gracious in all of these social affairs. As far as business meetings were concerned, Ken appeared very stern and astute, patient, *yet hurried.*

There was a client of his in one sharply defined photograph with whom he seemed jovial, almost flirtatious. This client was the rich cosmetic queen herself, Cassie Cay. The picture was taken at her ranch, near Ocala, Florida.

Francis was then played a tape which was dubbed into a sequence of film clips of one of their conversations taken from the chips placed on Kenneth's watch link and motor vehicle. Kenneth spoke quick and direct to her, but in a playful manner. He obviously enjoyed doing business with Cassie, but who wouldn't? Cassie was a distinguished looking multimillionaire who owned a prestigious estate located off the interstate, heading south to Tampa. Cassie appeared to be a trifle older than Kenneth. She was tall and slim, and still in good muscular shape. She had long, shiny, black hair which she twirled on top of her almond-shaped head. She placed only two long bobby pins in her hair to keep it secure. She constantly bragged about this. She had very defined facial features and naturally red lips. She wasn't stunning, but had a unique look which attracted men. She had a dramatic way about her, and although she was elegant and refined in social life, she was rough and tough in business. Kenneth liked this.

Kenneth sold her his two mares, shoved the cash in the pocket of his tight, cowboy jeans, and he began to walk down the hill toward the gate of the estate where his Escalade was parked. Cassie walked briskly beside him, her shivering arms folded, looking to the East for the sun to fully rise and provide some warmth on this chilly early February morning.

She pointed to the right of where they were standing and said, "This is where the famous country singer, Becca McClain, is going to build her second home. She bought five acres from me last week. She's supposed to put in a recording studio out back. It'll be a pretty busy place around here until she gets her palace built and moves in."

Kenneth said dryly, as he climbed into his ride, "Until next time, Cas. See ya," and he gave her a wink, followed by a salute.

Cassie was obviously saddened by his departure, but revived herself, when she heard the phone ringing from afar. She galloped up the front walkway, like one of her race horses, desperate to get to the house before the ringing ceased. She had been waiting for an important call regarding a special ingredient that supposedly keeps lipstick on the mouth, never smearing. This was how she kept in such good shape for her age, by walking, running, and horseback riding throughout her massive property.

She wished that Kenneth would get off his ass and ask her out on a date. Cassie knew they'd be great together, as they were both attractive, both thought alike, and both lived life in grand style.

Cassie also gave a tremendous amount of her earnings to an assortment of charities, mostly for children, as did Kenneth. Kenneth and Cassie especially loved children, but religiously helped anyone in need.

✳ ✳ ✳

Francis ordered a tall brandy from the gorgeous, orange-haired busty playmate who was taking bar orders with a hoarse voice. As he was contemplating the entire situation, Hugo nudged him in his funny bone. Hugo showed him more photos of Kenneth's boys who manage the apartment complex for him, and who of course drink with him nightly at several of the small, seedy taverns on Central Avenue. They looked like a goofy, intoxicated bunch. He saw clips of his twin and his buddies mooning female bar patrons, while these heavily made-up customers were displaying their boobs back at them. Francis wondered how Kenneth could have gotten so far in life behaving like this.

"There's no audio or film on this set of characters," Hugo interjected, "just photos, bios and applications, with personal information that should be helpful in getting to know the cast and where they come from."

Hugo gave Francis illegally-retrieved financial statements from the general's LLC and all the cast's personal affairs. Judging from these records, Chase McCarty was the most professional and definitely had the most money. He was the general manager of several "in need of refurbishment" small apartment buildings in the downtown area of St. Pete. These were all owned by Kenneth and bought at very low prices, which made him hundreds of thousands of dollars yearly from rental revenue. He hired two other cast members named Peter Sciara and Blaine Hampton.

Hugo recited his spiel, "Peter is said to 'wash clothing for the accounting department'. Even though he is a supposed jerk and a know it all, Peter knows how to hide money well. He came from an upper middle class family in Queens, where his dad was a pediatrician. They sent Peter to Yale, where he majored in International Finance. Peter lived on the Spanish Mediterranean for seven years, where he worked in a major bank with American customers. He never felt comfortable there, because he couldn't get a handle on the language, and so he returned to the states when he was thirty. He then got a job as a broker with a mortgage company, as merely a consultant. Peter was next offered a job in an *up and coming* brokerage firm, as a vice-president in the mortgage department. He took this position in a heartbeat and stayed there until he took early retirement. Kenneth had accumulated a couple of million dollars, and he thought this plenty to start the quiet life he had always wanted to lead. Kenneth was Peter's bar buddy at one of the places in downtown St. Pete. Kenneth asked him, when he first acquired the place, if he'd be interested in working at the complex part-time. Peter said 'yes', and part-time soon turned into full-time. The Internal Revenue Service audited Kenneth's books three times in the last ten years, but found no wrong-doings," Hugo rambled on.

"Kenneth had so many investments, properties, cars used for business, and a multitude of other deductions, that he and his LLC appeared to be in the red, two out of the three years. For the third audited year, Kenneth only showed a slight profit and had to pay a minimal amount to the government. He was clean and always has been. He enjoys drinking and being loud and rowdy, but that is as far as it goes with Ken. He likes living life on the up and up, never having to look over his shoulder," Hugo continued in a matter of fact manner.

"As far as Blaine is concerned, he's a nice chap, birthed from British parents who immigrated over the Atlantic to Philadelphia on a freighter in the mid-sixties, immediately after their wedding at a church in the Cotswolds. His father worked at all types of jobs, until he found his calling in ship building. He became a ship builder for the coast guard in Philly. Blaine was born several years later. His father was then transferred to the Coast Guard station on St. Pete Bay five years later, where he worked until his retirement. Blaine calls St. Petersburg, Florida his home. He attended ten years of school there, until he got a wild hair at the age of sixteen to join a rock band and go on the road. The band never made it, never even paid its bills. The members had to work two and three jobs to even exist in the industry.

One day," Hugo reported, "the lead singer was found shot to death in a gas station restroom. Supposedly, it was suicide, and that was the end of Blaine's music career."

Hugo said that Blaine learned the construction trade after that. "He lives a simple life downtown and always has steady work. He works on Ken's apartment complex, and any other venture, whenever they need him," Hugo stated.

Chapter Nine

Camille Bissett

Hugo had gotten more intense and more animated with the expounding of each new character in the scenario. He was now at edge of his fold-out lawn chair that he kept in his cabana permanently, alongside a long, rectangular white painted table with chipped paint on its edges, and adjacent to that, another lawn chair where Francis sat, awaiting an explanation.

Hugo had never looked more serious than whenever he stared at Francis and raved, "It has been over three days, and now I feel is the time we've been waiting for, time to tell you why we have to acquaint you so much with your brother's past....*it's Camille......Camille Bisset....uh....his girl.*

Camille is a forty-two year old chick, born and bred in Quebec City, Canada," he began the story. "She was a figure skater, winning many awards, but never made it onto the Olympic Team. We heard that her brother had been a second string quarterback for Saskatchewan's Canadian football team. At eighteen, she was offered a scholarship to Rutgers. She moved to the United States two months later and got citizenship. Half of her family lives in Northern California, and her second cousin is the former Mayor of Eureka, which made her attempt easy. She didn't know her father, nor ever spoke of him. She and her mother, Genevieve, are still very close, however. Her mother has been retired from Smith's Department Store for six years now. She lives alone in Nova Scotia, in the same house her mother lived in, and where Camille and her brother Bradley stayed most of each year," he explained.

"Camille graduated with honors four years later. She worked in sales and marketing for a large media firm in Philadelphia for years. She loved Philly with a passion, until her rent got too high, and her salary too low. She noticed an ad in a local rag for a teaching job down South. Well, she got it," Hugo informed Francis. "It was teaching French at a private academy close to the beach in Florida. She flew to Tampa, stayed on the campus, and had lots of students. She loved the position, but two years later, she was let go."

Francis, who had been listening attentively up to this point, butted in and asked, "She's no good at teaching, huh Hugh?"

Hugo clarified, "No, she's very good. She speaks and knows French very well and loved the kids, you know, but there were massive budget cuts and lots of the teachers were let go."

"So what happens next in the drama?" Francis asked Hugo.

Hugo followed with, "That's where you come in. It's all up to you. You see bud, Kenneth dated her for about seven months up 'til now, and they know each other pretty well, inside and out. Twenty-six years separates them," Hugo said. "Kenneth is a mentor to her, since he's so smart. Camille loves intelligence, always has," Hugo said smiling slyly, getting up out of the chair to get two Heinekens from the fridge.

"Camille has a striking look about her," he went on. "She has long, straight silver blond hair, with streaks of dark brown running throughout, which she parts down the center. She's tall, slender...has a boyish figure with no curves to speak of, except for her 'J Lo' butt," he chuckled.

"She's classy as shit. I'm just telling you this so you know how to act around her," Hugo finished. He told Francis to come and walk outside by the pool with him.

When Hugo caught sight of the sexy orange-haired playmate wearing a pink skin tight, V-neck t-shirt, with low-rider shiny black hot pants and tall white boots, he impatiently snapped his fingers at her. She ran over to him. He placed two drink orders with her, while stroking her neck and back. She giggled. He smiled.

"I guess you want me to impersonate Kenneth with Camille, right?" Francis asked in disbelief. "There's no way, Hugo…no way.… can't do," Francis replied with his eyes wide open.

"Francis, I have photos, tapes…bits of footage of their meetings at restaurants and bars, and even at her home and her school," Hugo confirmed. "Everything's mint. It'll be an academy award winning performance, but you have to be confident, otherwise, you're right." Hugo stressed, "There's no way it'll work. It's totally up to you…the ball is in your court…and don't forget…"

Francis nervously broke in and asked, "Don't forget what?"

Hugo questioned him, "Remember, I said there was a bonus for a job well done?" Francis asked, "What cut of meat are you throwing to me?"

Hugo answered, "A prime cut, for a job well done. You will have more money than you've ever dreamed of. Again, you'll be Kenneth in mind and money, with more broads than you've ever seen. Kenneth could get any woman on this planet, you know that money buys the world, man. To be straight, you'll be taking in all his money, except for the split.…but we'll talk about that later when everything's said and done.

Are you with us?" Hugo asked him.

Francis shrugged his shoulders, mouthed some words, and shook his head in disbelief.

Seeing this reaction, Hugo flipped out and went into a tirade, punching his fist on the cabana wall. He screamed out, *"Fran, don't fuck with us."* Hearing all the commotion, the boys gathered quickly and mulled around the cabana, scoping out the situation. Francis was now angry, as he felt disgraced and disrespected by Hugo.

Francis was given a brandy to settle his nerves and escorted to a huge bedroom that had an elegant four poster bed and French doors which led to a Jacuzzi bathroom with black marble tile throughout. The orange-haired playmate was waiting there for him, wearing only a chain around her hips. She led him over to the bed, stroking his private parts while tearing off his clothing. She laid her long orange hair over his entire genitalia. He tried to abstain, but couldn't. He rolled her over, inserted his manhood in her, and then squealed in ecstasy to his demons. A few seconds later, Francis was asleep, passed-out, and his playmate had absconded, along with Francis' five one hundred dollar bills in her hand.

When Francis awoke the next morning, he was dazed and confused. He didn't remember what had happened the night before. Then, he put on his trousers and noticed that his money was gone from his pocket. Suddenly, he remembered everything. He realized that he had to play this game with the mob, in order to stay alive and to acquire his deserved fortune and to not lose everything he already had.

He went downstairs, found Hugo at the breakfast table, and committed himself, "I'll do it Hugh."

Hugo laughed and said, "I knew you would. Now about Camille... you'll love her, probably end up marrying her, if I don't first. If you can, try to settle her down and stop her gibbering about her obsessive political beliefs."

Hugo added, with a sly smile, "She talks a lot, probably too much for most men. She has strong beliefs about her party, which she acquired through her Political Science Professor at Rutgers. You know she's a closet Socialist. Camille can have a bad attitude. She's true to her cause. I know you told me you lean toward the right, and she leans toward the left, but if you both lean more inward, toward each other, you'll both meet in the middle. You can't be stubborn, because Camille already has a very stubborn side to her. You must play this out for us," Hugo stressed.

"Thanks, but no thanks," Francis rebutted.

"Oh, and there's more. Camille was married once, ten years ago, to a super sharp-looking, Irish-Italian guy named Jamie McIntyre,"

Hugo revealed through police reports the boys got from a cop buddy on the take. "She kept her maiden name, Bisset, during their marriage. Jamie was tall and dark, with a good physique and chiseled facial features. He had wavy hair that swept over the right hand side of his forehead, like he put it that way on purpose. Jamie was suave and smooth, always saying the right thing at the right moment…a real con artist. He had one fetish, however, and that was hitting Camille, followed by plenty of rough sex. At first, Jamie did this only once in a while. Camille would leave, come back, and the cycle would begin again. He beat her on a regular basis, for the last three years of their marriage, smiling after each episode, and going out to meet the world with wit and charm. Sometimes there was a period of weeks where Jamie showed no signs of misbehaving, being the perfect husband, but when restless Jamie got tired of playing this role, he started fighting with her again, calling her names. The slapping started next, followed by the hitting of her head on the bathroom walls," he stated.

"One night, around midnight," Hugo painfully informed him, "when Camille came home from a girl's night out, Jamie met her at the door with a smile and a hug. Once fully inside the door, however, he slammed it shut and carried her into their bedroom, where he beat her up, almost killed her. Jamie beat her in the dark for three hours, raped her, and then held her in his arms all night long. He evidently slammed her face into the bedroom walls so many times that the walls had permanent streaks of burgundy. They all had to be repainted with a darker colored purple paint to hide any remnants of that insane night.

Also, hospital reports state that Camille has permanent damage in the muscle of her left arm. She can't bend it past a certain point anymore, because he slammed her chest and arms into the wood floor so many times. She was a mess."

Next, Hugo pulled out a photo of a pretty young lady with a page-boy haircut and said, "Are you ready for this?"

Unsure about what Hugo was talking about, Francis nodded, shifting his eyes, looking around the kitchen.

"There is one main character left in the story and that is his only wife, Jane," Hugo went on to say, pointing to the photo, as he rambled.

"They have a fifteen year age difference, no kids…didn't have any ties. Kenneth met her near Portland, Maine when he was in Boston on leave before his father died." Hugo said that Jane worked in a souvenir shop by the water and when Ken walked in, Jane's heart seemed to stop beating, as he showed her a photo of their initial encounter. He went on to say that they were inseparable after this first date, until Ken could take no more of the straight life and began to carouse around town.

"She overlooked this in the beginning," Hugo added.

"Well, he asked her to marry him," he continued with the story. "However, it lasted less than three years. It seems he cared more about his career and his provocative social life…drinking…and yes…. women, than he did about his wife."

He whispered slightly, "She told her parents about this, and they ransacked Kenneth's and Jane's mansion one night, trying to find evidence for a divorce settlement. Can you believe it, Fran?" Hugo asked. "They committed a crime in the law's eyes…breaking and entering. The police were called, attorneys were on the scene, and they were divorced one month later." Hugo added, "Kenneth was the one who started the proceedings. He knew everyone and could get anything done.

After his marriage, Kenneth invested in real estate ventures in the Tampa Bay area, where he liked living so much. He even bought a house on the Gulf in Sarasota, which he quickly sold, as property taxes that year skyrocketed. He moved northward to Saint Petersburg, where he found the small city to be dignified and classy, yet laid back, just like him. He quickly made an offer on a hotel downtown, which the owners accepted. He turned it into a money making enterprise. He bought and sold a few properties, and he stayed there for years, until the urge to buy a ranch hit him. He never saw or talked to Jane again," Hugo finished the scenario.

Chapter Ten

Red and Yellow

Hugo took out the keys from one of his Italian slack's front pockets. He asked Francis to take a spin with him in his Lamborghini. They drove through the countryside to the coastline parallel to Nantucket Island.

Hugo was silent, as they motored at close to two hundred miles per hour on narrow, winding lanes. Hugo had been on the circuit as an Indy driver once upon a time, so he handled the road extremely well, especially at top speeds.

At first, Francis was very nervous, clutching his seat belt tightly, but when he saw that Hugo was more than in control, he felt safe… *pretty* safe.

Even when a pro is driving at top speeds, he never knows what fate may have in store. When they drove into the next small town, located about five minutes north of Hugo's house, Hugo slowed way down around the first curve and started conversing with Francis. He said that he had one more important piece, probably the most difficult piece of the puzzle, and of which he must expose.

Francis said, "Okay, shoot it to me."

Hugo interjected, "Hey, are you hungry?"

Francis hesitantly shrugged and said, "A little."

"The best patty melts and fries with mayo are served up right over there," Hugo told him, pointing toward the water.

They pulled into a diner named "The Onion Grille" and ordered two patty melts, fries, and coffee. Hugo started his spiel. He said that Kenneth has been subpoenaed and said that he must testify at the Tampa Federal Courthouse against an accused murderer who supposedly had a law degree and had passed the bar. This trial was to begin in eleven days. Hugo lethargically went on, as he sipped his hot, steamy coffee, which had just been poured into his cup, and onto his saucer by a short, medium-built, gray haired waitress.

"Kenneth sometimes works the front desk of his city apartment complex when he's stayin' there." He then told Francis that the boys had a lot of sound and video recordings.

"One day," he went on, "a gentleman dressed as a construction worker, carrying a hard hat entered through the open doors of the apartment complex, came up to the desk and asked, 'Are there any rooms for rent? The sign out front says there are.' Kenneth told him, 'We've got whatever you need, one or two bedrooms, even a studio available for weekly or monthly rates.' The man answered, 'A studio is all I need, for a week at a time.' Kenneth stressed that the rent was due on Monday of every week. 'A one hundred dollar deposit is due, along with the first of one hundred fifty dollars,' he specified. 'No problem,' the renter affirmed, as he laid out three one hundred dollar bills on the counter. He then stated, 'You can put the change on my account.'" Hugo mimicked the renter, and added that the man was given his key after Kenneth photocopied a copy of his driver's license.

"The man's name was David Crabtree," Hugo said. He was careful to point out that Kenneth had told the authorities that he did not know much about the accused, if anything, and he definitely did not know about any crimes he may have committed in the past, or even what he was doing for work at present. Kenneth stressed to the police that David was merely a tenant. Hugo stared at Francis, as a teacher angrily stares at a pupil.

He slowly stated, "At the meeting with the state prosecutor, Francis, you must know the day and the time that their agreement was consummated and the amount of cash that was taken in. These answers must glide off your tongue. The hotel is not providing us with bookkeeping records for every tenant. So Francis, you're to retrieve these records before the questioning," Hugo sternly added. He emphasized that copies need to be made in case the prosecutor wants to view them.

Francis finally got a word in edgewise. He broke in with, "What did this guy do, anyway?"

"A lot," answered Hugo. He continued, "He would call up numbers in the want ads. You know, people who were selling their cars. He'd arrange a time to meet 'em and drive the car. He would tell them that he needed to test drive it in an open lot or field to see how the car handled on rougher terrain. The individuals, or the couples would accompany him, and once away from view, David would shoot the person, or persons in the head and leave the scene with the vehicle."

"By the way, the cars in the ads had to be imports. That was how he made his living. He would sell each car in the black market, pocket the money and do it all over again. He's a sick mother fucker." Hugo grimaced, "I don't know why he had to kill people just for stealing cars. I think David enjoyed shooting people dead, with one shot in the mouth, or between the eyes. He got some fuckin' thrill from it. Anyway, the defense is trying to blame the murders on a black man named Henry.

He's out on parole. He lived in the same building as David. The black man's Identification card was found next to the most current set of bodies in Tampa. The card probably fell out of the man's pocket, or was stolen by David, then placed by the bodies to pin it on Henry. David has left a trail of these 'want ad' killings from Texas to Florida and hasn't been convicted yet. However, with the prosecution team and state attorney having so much evidence and so many witnesses, David should now be able to find his place in society, either in solitary confinement, or on death row.

You will be a key player in this trial, so don't blow it. Just listen to the tapes and watch the video clips 'til you get bored from repetition. You'll do fine. And remember, you only have eleven days, and Fran, you've got to trace his signature and learn how to scribble it fast. You never know when you'll have to sign somethin', especially the back of a check. You know what I mean?" Hugo chuckled and gave Francis a wink.

After fifteen minutes, the sandwiches arrived at the restaurant's wobbly table. Hugo asked for more coffee and "red and yellow." Gray head came bobbing out of the kitchen, holding a big coffee pot in one hand, and two small jugs of mustard and ketchup in the other. A glob of homemade mayo had already been placed inside each basket next to the fries for dipping, as was their signature. They both gobbled every morsel on their plates.

After about fifteen more minutes, the sun had set completely, and that meant the party at Hugo's home would soon fizzle out. Hugo and Francis sauntered out to Hugo's Lamborghini, where they found a gathering of people who were stationed around the car, admiring it. Hugo unlocked the doors with his key pad. "This is what you have to look forward to, Fran," Hugo slurred under his breath, his head high.

"This ain't too hard a life for ya boy...IS It?" he smugly asked, as he climbed inside his toy. The race car peeled off in the direction of Logan Airport. It was now time to begin the drama.

Francis flew first class down to Tampa late that night with Hugo by his side. They drank stiff gin and tonics that the pretty little Korean flight attendant continually presented to them. When one was half gone she brought another, and another, then another. Finally, she asked if they needed anything further, as the jet descended.

Hugo screeched loudly in an obnoxiously drunken way, "Of course, sweetie! Where will you be after I get my bags?"

"I will find you," the sweet one replied sheepishly.

"Okay," Hugo smiled. He knew he had scored.

At baggage claim, the Korean girl was waiting for Hugo who had stopped in an airport bar to get a beer with a more sober Francis. When Hugo finally arrived downstairs, drunk, the carousel had stopped spewing out baggage, but the patient, submissive Korean was still waiting there for him.

Francis took control at that point and went into the baggage claim office where the female working behind the counter pointed to two bags and officially said, "Are these two yours? They were just brought in. If they are, you need to show me some identification before you can leave with them." He showed his ID, picked up his sport's bag, then went back to get Hugo's identification.

Walking back slowly, he looked around the claim area curiously. It was empty of people. There was no one in sight. Hugo was gone.

Francis signed for a nondescript utility sports vehicle at the heavily occupied lot on the fourth level, and he sped off to the ranch, not knowing when or where he was to meet up with Hugo again. On the interstate, he called Hugo for instructions.

Hugo answered, then asked, "Are you there yet?"

"Just about," Francis dryly answered him, hearing giggles in the back.

"Get him," Hugo ordered, as Francis sped to the hotel in Bradenton.

Chapter Eleven

Penicillin with Arsenic

The cool Halloween wind was howling, with frightening yells. The unlatched windows were banging. Francis regained consciousness a few hours later. He felt the back of his knotted bloody skull. His hand felt wet, when he rubbed his head and neck that were both soaked in blood. He wondered to himself, trying to remember what had happened, "What could have caused this?"

He would soon find out, as he looked around the now littered sitting room. One open window was coming off its hinges with the strong, blustery wind gusts that barged their way inside the bedroom and swirled the foliage lying on the carpet around the room. Francis strategically raised his body off the floor, as he stretched out a hand and grabbed a nearby chair for support.

When he finally got up to a vertical position, Francis saw the huge pieces of branch which evidently were the cause of his head injury. They were lying throughout the sitting area, splaying the couch and chairs with dirt and holes. He looked over and saw Kenneth, still sound asleep, unbelievably, having had such a sudden, violent storm in his room. Francis breathed a huge sigh of relief, when he saw the almost emptied crystal brandy snifter sitting beside the bed. He then knew why Kenneth was sleeping so soundly. Francis also knew he had to execute this plan before the break of day, and it seemed about to enter the room and say "Hello" at any moment.

Francis replaced the pink baby aspirin that were in the aspirin bottle, and that Francis took once a day, with the mild-dosed arsenic pills. He then pulled out the stun gun the boys gave him and shot it into Kenneth's lean thigh. He forced the first set of sedatives through his twin's wind pipes, then pushed the needle that was one quarter filled with a very mild dose of arsenic into Kenneth's flat derriere. Next, he pulled Kenneth off the bed. He dragged him into the large walk-in closet which was filled with all types of military garb. Francis gagged Kenneth with one of the many bandanas found on the shelf. He stuffed this cloth inside his mouth and tied another around his head, over Kenneth's eyes. Then, Francis sloppily dragged Kenneth down the hallway and down each one of the tall specially-crafted steps.

At the bottom of the staircase was the large mahogany floored entry. Francis had to be particularly careful not to slip on the highly polished real wood floor while holding Kenneth. He knew he had to place Kenneth in the Escalade before the girls started their daily duties. He put a black tarp over Kenneth's body and dragged him to the utility vehicle. In this way, it appeared that Kenneth was perhaps a piece of machinery that needed some attention at a nearby repair shop. Francis shoved Kenneth inside, leaving his legs bent and arms dangling under the tarp that was placed on top of the back seat.

His first acting scene of the drama seemed about to begin, as he glanced up, while climbing into the driver's seat, and noticed Gimp's sparkling midnight blue Dodge Caravan coming down the estate's gravel roadway. It appeared to be several years old but still in mint condition. Francis revved up its engine, locked the doors, and let down his window, and his guard, and began his spontaneous script.

"Hey Gimp. Glad you could join us today," Francis yelled out to the driver of the Dodge Caravan, who had a slight limp due to a fall in her youth. Gimpie boldly pointed out that she was fifteen minutes *early*. Those two had had a running feud for years, which

Francis played to the hilt. With two and a half weeks of watching his twin socialize, in photos, and from afar, through binoculars, he knew all of the correct moves to fit each mood of Kenneth's personality. With the microscopic bugging chip placed between one of the links on Kenneth's watch, which Kenneth wore religiously, Francis perpetually knew the right words to say in any given situation, along with the exact sounds of speech to make, which mimicked Ken.

As Francis pulled out of the ranch and headed up the interstate toward Hugo's estate in Mass., Gimpie screamed to him, "Hey, what's with the new Chevy?"

Francis shouted back, "It's a rental. I've got a long sales trip ahead of me. Didn't want to put the mileage on my Cadillac, Gimp."

She nodded, smiling in approval, as good business managers do when their boss has made a practical decision on his or her own.

He knew driving to Massachusetts would be a long, hard ride, so he decided to take the more direct route and go up ninety five the whole way, after taking interstate four to Orlando. Hugo's basement was the decisive location for keeping Kenneth until they completed poisoning him, because it had such spacious living quarters. It was a very comfortable spot for the procedure to take place. Here, Dr. Martin's injections for Kenneth's demise could be administered, without any interference.

Francis got a call on the car phone before he reached the interstate. He felt hesitant to answer it when he saw the name flashing, "Cassie Cay". Remembering all of the race horses he recently sold to her over the phone, and what she was going to pay for each, he took the call.

Sounding short on time, just as his brother would have, he agreed to meet Cassie at her home in Ocala that afternoon to discuss the sale of one of his favorite and most promising colts. He promised to bring her race horses with him in the trailer as well. Francis turned around on the two lane highway several minutes from his property, which led to the interstate, and forged back to the ranch to hook up his trailer and load it with *"pieces of gold"*.

*** *** ***

Two days later, Hugo was at the end of the drive waiting on Francis. When the Chevy turned into the pebbled driveway, Hugo told Francis to park near the basement entrance in back. There was no one on the property, except for Doc Martin, who was standing at the back door, holding a big, black medical supply bag.

As Francis wearily parked, Hugo came running up from behind, and Martin gently maneuvered Kenneth out of the vehicle and into the house. The Doc dragged Kenneth down the basement stairs with the help of Francis. Hugo was on the phone with one of the boys, as he scoped the situation outside.

When Kenneth was laid out on the bed downstairs, Doc Martin told Francis he was going to inject his twin with penicillin and a "bit of arsenic" every day for several weeks. "A little at a time, until he "pops off", Martin explained to Francis and Hugo, who had just come downstairs. Over a period of time like this, it seemed plausible to die from simply an allergic reaction to penicillin. The autopsy would not show the miniscule amounts of arsenic administered to Kenneth on a daily basis, causing a slow, undetectable poison-filled death.

"Francis, you really are allergic to penicillin, so Kenneth, who has become Francis, unknowingly, must be allergic to penicillin too. Francis Cranford will die from injections given by a young, incompetent candy striper who by the way, is scheduled to arrive here at any minute. She will be his live-in caretaker."

Breaking in and taking over the story, Hugo continued, "Doc will put penicillin in the bottles marked codeine, and you can guess what happens after that." Hugo ended up by saying, "Start being Kenneth right now, in your body and in your soul, 'cause you've got lots of things to do and places to be as Kenneth, and you know, he'll be dead in a few short weeks."

Francis asked Hugo, "Why does he supposedly need pain pills anyway, Hugh?"

Martin dryly answered, "Because he has just had his birthmark under his left eye removed by me. Remember, he's you, and you're him."

Francis continued the questioning, "What's going to happen to the nurse who ends up killing him?"

Hugo shrugged his right shoulder, lifting it high, saying nothing.

Francis felt another tinge of sensitivity, but quickly dismissed it when Hugo placed a five hundred dollar bill in his black Polo shirt pocket, one of the many Polos that now made up the bulk of his new wardrobe. He looked at Hugo and asked, "What the fuck is......?"

Then, a heavy door slammed above the staircase and a young wall-eyed freckled face redhead came trotting down the stairs, singing, "Soory m late.... Gut cuot n trafk".

Francis looked at Hugo in disbelief.

"Yes, she is kind of retarded," Hugo murmured pitifully..."Oh well."

✳ ✳ ✳

Francis went ahead and brought the colt with the other two race horses over to Cassie's home the afternoon that he began the drive to Hugo's. He ate a late breakfast at a run-down diner in the area, where he was served burnt bacon and toast. The coffee was okay, but nothing like his own. He greeted the cosmetic queen with a hug, as he had seen the two embracing in Kenneth's photos, and he very animatedly spoke to the woman, not sounding short on time now. No, now he was patiently awaiting a big, fat check in exchange for the thoroughbred horses he was about to unveil, and the promising colt. Of course, she had to have the colt when she laid her eyes on it. She reached in her designer hand bag and pulled out a wad of cash, handing it to him, and she gave him a peck on the cheek.

"This should be more than enough," she stated. "Count it now."

He turned away from her, as he had seen Kenneth do on many occasions, and shook his head, "No".

After about an hour of nonsensical chit chat about the weather, the economy, and what not, Francis left Cassie Cay's property with cash in hand.

He drove to one of Kenneth's banks in Ocala, deposited half and kept half. All of Kenneth's horse sales were done on strictly a cash basis. He provided he client with a better price, not having a paper trail. Of course, he reaped the benefits this way. He could stash these benefits right in his jean pockets.

Francis traveled across Florida selling horses and colts to wealthy names and addresses. His Black Angus cattle was sold to popular grocery store chains. Francis now felt he was going to accrue tens of thousands for himself, just from his brother's ranch business, and in just a matter of weeks. There was to be a split, however. The mob would more than likely receive tens of thousands in profits from the citrus growing business, in a short period of time. Each entity agreed to run one of the two enterprises completely and solely by themselves, so as to avoid disagreements and stalemates.

The mob had a horrible grudge against Kenneth. Kenneth was supposed to give the boys half of all profits from the ranch and estate for the first five years, and one third from then on. Kenneth didn't hold his part of the bargain, hence slow, painful pay back. He had paid principal and interest on the property for only a couple of years. Then he stopped, hording all of the money.

After thirteen years, the Irish boys decided to finally get back all the principal and interest loaned for start-up costs on the multimillion dollar enterprise, plus a lot more.

When their scheme was to fully unravel, the boys were to make millions, through the life insurance policy, but more importantly, through the five thousand acres of citrus groves, producing citrus products for shipment throughout the country, all year long, with costly prices attached to them.

Francis was given sole rights to the horse and cattle business. He was the only one who knew anything about these "animals". The boys knew nothing about these business ventures and didn't want to be bothered with "pets", as they referred to the horse trade. With his newly-acquired evil attitude, Francis did extremely well in both of his businesses, even better than his brother did. Now, he was finally able to live the life he had always dreamed of.

Chapter Twelve

Execution and Manslaughter

Dreaming of his favorite submarine sandwich, consisting of crab meat stacked high, and thinly-sliced Swiss and provolone cheeses, placed on a crisp, seasoned Italian roll and topped off with Francis' secret, spicy butter and mayo sauce, a char-grilled onion, and three tomato slices, Francis slept soundly, unaware of his radio alarm clock playing "fifties" music for close to half an hour. He was finally awakened by the ringing of the telephone on the nightstand next to his bed.

"Yeah," he muttered, as he coughed.

The voice on the other end yelled, "Asshole, wake up, or you're going to blow everything."

Francis jumped out of bed, recognizing Hugo's voice, looked at the clock, then hung up the phone, saying nothing to Hugo. Francis was in a panic, as he realized that he only had an hour to get dressed, eat something and drive all the way to downtown Tampa.

"Shshshit!" he stuttered, as he squeezed into his faded Wranglers and cowboy boots. He grabbed one of his tight black muscle shirts, hanging in his closet and slung it over his rugged shoulders. He splashed cold water on his face, brushed his teeth and hair, grabbed a stale bagel from the bag on the dusty motel dresser, and flew out the door.

Francis had flown in with Hugo the night before. Francis didn't realize the air-conditioning in his Escalade needed coolant, since he hadn't driven it for a while. He turned off its unit completely. He was miserable and began to sweat profusely, and he thought that he should take the rental back as soon as he got back to Boston. He sped along the city interstate, until he reached the tall, massive Tampa Federal Court House building. He parked in one of the few lots that still had space, got out and sprinted into the building. He was soaked in sweat. At this point, he was fifteen minutes late.

When he ran from the elevator into the lobby, outside of the trial room, he was greeted by a displeased Hugo. Hugo said something that Francis did not understand, and he pushed Francis inside. It seems that they had just called Francis to testify, and Hugo told the bailiff that "Mr. Redman" would be arriving momentarily, which thankfully he did…for Francis' sake.

Francis held his own in the trial. He did a superb job of reciting the facts of his several short conversations with the accused, and of course, he had paperwork, and dates and times of contract signings and payments received from David. He managed to confiscate all needed files and receipt books from the locked back office at the apartment building. He had picked the lock. Hugo brilliantly had showed him how. The prosecutor had Francis on the stand for only about twenty minutes, as his testimony hurt the defense, due to contradicting statements made by Francis.

When the defense attorney who was tough as nails and able to bring any one down in the witness box, let Francis step down after only two of his questions, Hugo felt relieved. "Sorry, bud…," Hugo humbly told him, as he wrinkled his forehead, "but you did magnificent." Hugo patted him hard on the back, saying that there should be no more hassle with the authorities with this situation. Hugo felt that the jury would find David guilty and give him life in prison, or death, for sure.

The next morning the verdict was in. It proved to be the latter.

✳ ✳ ✳

Before Francis was to drive back to Boston, Francis had to go over the previous month's accounting records with Sciara and McCarty. This was done like clockwork on the first Monday of each month. He drove over to the apartment complex and entered in the same back door that he used to confiscate the needed records for the trial.

Francis strolled into the lobby wearing a white Izod shirt, shorts, and sandals, with socks. This was Kenneth's daily attire. He got used to wearing socks with sandals from his days in Germany. He enjoyed not having his feet perspire this way. Francis walked down the hall to the building's hidden office and opened the large frame of the big black door by its shiny brass knob, which was hung a little too low. He cheerfully acknowledged the two men with, "Hey guys, you's ready to do it?"

Pete frowned and said, "We've got to."

In two hours, they completed their project and went to the bar up the street, like they always did. Blaine came shufflin' through the entrance, laughing, "Hey, studs, what's up?" He told the fat bar maid to pour him a draft and a schnapps, which he always drank together. After a few more rounds and conversations with scantily-clad women, Blaine was sufficiently hammered and couldn't walk back to his apartment. Francis offered to take him home. Blaine accepted, and fell down, head first. The bouncer came to his rescue, picked Blaine off the floor and placed him vertical, on solid ground.

The drive up the road to Blaine's proved disastrous. Francis did not know exactly where his place was and couldn't ask him for help, as he was passed out in the back seat. He had to call Hugo. Hugo gave him the address. It was only two minutes up the road, and Francis stayed in the Cadillac with him until the booze wore off. After fifteen minutes, Blaine awoke and walked upstairs, by himself, into his abode.

✳ ✳ ✳

"It's now time," Hugo told Francis. "Kenneth should be out of his misery in about one more week."

Martin said that Kenneth was like a vegetable, unable to speak or move. "He is in a virtual coma anyway." He assured the two, "It won't be much longer."

In the basement, Kenneth was completely incapacitated, just lying there, staring at the ceiling. Francis got one last twinge of guilt, as he looked into Kenneth's lifeless eyes. He was sure they once gleamed and glowed with delight and passion. Hugo moved his own hands up and down, as if to break Francis out of the trance he was in, and it worked.

Still in a state of thought, Francis watered up the syringe and had the candy striper place the needle in Kenneth's left hand where the veins were strong and sturdy.

Francis, Hugo, and the retarded girl continued with this procedure on a daily basis for six days. Every day Kenneth became more and more like a vegetable, having very little ability to move any part of his body.

On the seventh day, Kenneth awoke with a startle, his eyes wide open, but didn't have any feeling, anywhere, then he simply closed his eyes with a snorting moan. The retarded girl came into Kenneth's room with a tray of injections. While trotting down the narrow staircase to administer a new dose to Kenneth, Hugo and Francis heard a blood-curdling scream. They were apprehended by a hysterical young waif in a candy striper's uniform. She grabbed the two, each by one arm, and pulled them over to the bed. She screamed, "Uh, m gud, whut di'i du?" Then she burst into tears and screeched, "N' pulz! He deaad!"

The retarded candy striper hadn't understood why Kenneth wasn't improving, only getting worse, and she could not defend herself against accusations made by Hugo. The detectives were called, hand-cuffs placed on the girl, and a determination was made by the courts that the curly redhead was to be held with no bail on charges of manslaughter.

Chapter Thirteen

The Swiss Bank

There was no funeral. The mob boys simply dug out ground in the back of Hugo's grandiose estate and plopped the body down deep inside. They covered the now filled hole with dirt and wedged a wood branch in the top so that they would remember its location.

Not many people really knew him, so the supposed death of Francis did not really affect anyone. In his personal and business life, Francis kept very close to himself, letting few inside his realm.

Getting greedier and greedier with time and events, the real Francis now wanted to sell Kenneth's estate and pocket all earnings. He was getting so clever and so bold that he didn't even care about cheating the almighty Irish mobsters. He felt a little nervous at this prospect, but said to himself, "Oh, what the hell. This life's no good without it, without lots of the green shit, so I'll take the risk and even consider it fun."

Five days after Kenneth's death, Viola Hopkins was formally charged with manslaughter and sentenced to life in an insane asylum. Her retardation was the key factor in this determination. The jury thought her to be schizophrenic, needing to be monitored twenty-four seven.

On the news later that night, Francis saw the nurse sobbing hysterically, but he didn't get any twinge of sorrow or guilt. The twinges were all gone. He had no more sympathy left in him. Now, he was completely in the hands of Satan, administering the devil's wishes to whomever and whatever.

✳ ✳ ✳

Francis contacted two developers who had left their cards in the "R" of "Ranch" on the electronic gate several days before. The first one offered five million, the second one offered six. He met the second developing firm to complete the deal that evening. It was now done. Francis had scammed the mob. He had become very brazen, but knew he still had to be weary and careful of everybody and everything.

Francis called Doc Martin and requested his help. He told him he would pay him one million dollars to fake his, or Mr. Redman's death. Since Kenneth was a closet chain smoker, Francis thought it fitting that he die of lung cancer, which was diagnosed too late. Worshiping money, the Doc smiled from ear to ear and jumped at his proposal. He also wasn't worried about going against the mob.

The next morning Martin got "Mr. Redman" admitted to the Veteran's Hospital near Clearwater. Having a pet scan done, Martin determined that it was inoperable cancer, too far gone, and he proceeded to transfer him to the hospice unit. The news crews were all over this story. Hugo called the Doc in hysteria. The Doc told him it was true.

"Francis has lung cancer. He sure didn't seem sick when we all first met him up in Boston. He seemed just fit and trim, but now it's almost over for him. When he's dead, I'll arrange to have him placed in a fancy casket and flown to Arlington. I'll call the State Department to notify them of these plans," Doc Martin advised Hugo.

"Well, that's good news for us. Now we don't have to whack him, and we already have the insurance money and citrus contracts. We just need to either sell the estate for a massive profit or learn the *pet* business," Hugo belted out in a smirking tone.

When Camille found out that Kenneth was dying of lung cancer, after reading a blurb in the Tampa Bay Times, she drove to the Veteran's Hospital to see him at once.

When she arrived, however, she was told that no one was permitted to see him.

Camille raised her deep voice one octave and said, "But, I'm his girlfriend…Doesn't that matter?"

The nurse who was escorted down the hallway by Doc Martin said, "You must leave."

Camille stormed out, shaking her long streaked hair. She had no idea what she had done wrong.

"Why is he so damn mad at me? What did I do? *J'aime Kenny beau coup, mere. C`est que ce?"* she called her mother in Quebec to ask.

The following day, Camille drove to the hospital where she marched straight upstairs to Kenneth's private room. Getting ready for a major battle with the nursing staff, she breathed deeply several times, in and out.

As she approached the nurse's station she heard, "Oh my God!" proceeded by quick, heavy footsteps trudging down the hall.

"In here…there's no heartbeat. Let's pump it out."

Camille burst into the Kenneth's closed room, panic stricken.

Doc Martin put his arm around her, looked at the ground and said, "Kenneth's dead." Camille was devastated.

She ran over to a tranquilized Francis and kissed him on the lips, whispering "*Mon Ami*" into his ear.

Then she said to Martin, in a demeaning way, as she opened Kenneth's mouth to pull out his dentures, "Don't you and your crew know how to do your job?"

"These," putting her hands on his teeth, "should have been taken out immediately," Camille ranted, raved, and harped.

"You inadequate, incompetent retards, his teeth were knocked out years ago in the war. You should have known that."

Reaching her boiling point, she grabbed his teeth and tried to pull his dentures out. She tried and tried, but was unable.

Perplexed, she stared at his stained, but sturdy teeth, and looked up wild-eyed at Doc Martin and said, "That's not him, not Kenny."

Then, Doc Martin shot her with a heavy dosed of morphine. It took thirty seconds until she went to sleep. Doc then left the hospital by taxi, never to return, with a one million dollar check dated a week earlier on his person. His destination was Mexico, by way of Boston. Doc had to retrieve his belongings from his high-rise apartment. He was scheduled to fly to Cabo San Lucas the next evening, where he was to purchase a beachfront mansion, equipped with a staff of servants.

At a convenience store pay phone along the way, Doc left Hugo a belittling message on his cell.

"I outsmarted you, you dimwit."

After this episode, Francis knew he must also leave the country, leave the continent, for that matter, and quick. So he disguised himself, sneaked out of the hospital and flew the Learjet to Atlanta Municipal. From there he took a taxi to Hartsfield and caught a DC-10, non-stop to Bern, then onto Athens. Using his twin's credentials, he was able to get into Switzerland and Greece without waiting in each country's airport's tremendously long custom's line.

Once out of the airport in Athens, Francis was whisked off to the seaport in a long black sedan, to where the island ferries were docked. Francis had to wait in the blinding sun for close to an hour until the ship was ready for boarding. He carried his one bag with him on board. He only brought with him three pairs of jeans, one pair of shorts, and five shirts. His clothes horse days appeared to be over, even though he had over five hundred million dollars in his Swiss bank account and could buy anything he ever wanted. Francis had had this money transferred from Tampa to "Die Welt", a reputable Swiss bank in Bern. During his long layover in Bern, he went to this bank to add another authorized user to this new account, "Irwin Stuart", his new alias.

Upon walking out of the revolving doors of the tall, impressive bank, "Die Welt", and onto the sidewalk filled with fast paced, business-attired pedestrians, Francis accidentally bumped into a non-yielding, fair-skinned, rosy-haired man who spoke with an Irish accent.

"Sorry, chap," the young freckled face man quietly said.

"Oh, no. It's all *my* fault," Francis sarcastically mocked, as he flagged down a taxi to return to the airport.

Chapter Fourteen

The Funeral

Upon Francis', alias Kenneth's death, the "Irish clan" was to receive his property. Francis knew this and that they were playing him. This clause between the two parties had already been drawn up by the mob lawyers. It was at the bottom of the contract, in small print. Francis had read this with a magnifying glass the night after the signing.

"You guys will never see any of it," was the indistinguishable, strange sounding message left on Hugo's machine.

This message was left for Hugo the morning Francis departed for Greece. Hugo heard it, but didn't bother with it. He thought it to be simply a prank.

Feeling angry, confused, emotional, and dumbfounded, yet delighted at this twist of fate, Hugo contacted the mob's law firm. He spoke to the big, burly Chicago attorney about these unforeseen circumstances. Attorney Gambino said he would handle everything.

"I will tie everything up in a pretty package for you guys. I'll get back with you, after I make some calls."

Then, Gambino quietly said, "And for all the presents you sent my sick girl, this one's on the house."

Gambino's eleven-year old had been diagnosed with acute lymphocytic leukemia two months prior and was going through intense treatments. Her chances for survival were fifty percent. The boys sent her elaborate doll houses, toy stoves and ovens, along with rare, antique dolls. Alison received these presents every week, after each treatment. He said they made her so happy, forgetting everything she had just gone through. Gambino was very appreciative, to say the least.

Hugo fell asleep on his recliner while waiting for the call from Gambino. When he opened his eyes, he saw on his cell, which had mistakenly been on silent the entire time, that he had two missed calls and two urgent messages. He saw that one call had been from Gambino and the other from an unknown caller, so he hurriedly put in his secret code on the land line to retrieve the messages. He placed them on speaker and first heard, "Got real bad news, Hugh. Are you sitting down?"

Hugo said to himself, "No, but I will be." He called him back.

Gambino started the scenario. "Well Hugh, it seems that Francis sold the entire estate, horses, cattle, oranges, grapefruits…everything. He pocketed all of the change before he died. We don't know where it is stashed. It'll take some time, but we'll find out. But Hugh, now we're going to have to bill you."

Hugo solemnly told the phone, "I understand." He continued, "Why would he hide the money in a different account than Kenneth's anyway? He has been using that vault for over a month. They all know him there and think he's Kenneth. It was peachy, so why did he do this?" "Don't know, but we'll find out real soon," Gambino assured Kenneth. "I have to go, I'll talk to you." Then, there was a dial tone.

The second urgent message was from an unknown number that had a very recognizable voice from the immediate past. It was Doc Martin.

The Doc boldly raved, "I snowed you, bro. You are never gonna see any of it. You're history, so you better start packing, 'cause you're going down. Too bad that you can never find me now." Then, there was a click, followed by another dial tone.

Mad as a bull, Hugo raced his rented silver Porsche down the interstate from the five-star hotel in Sarasota to the Parrish exit ramp near Bradenton. He slowed down when he got on the two lane road that fronted the evil thousands of acres. He came to a halt, when he found Jude and Gimpie in the road, flagging down traffic. It seemed that one of the ranch hands had had a heart attack when he heard that Kenneth had died. The girls had called 911. It had already been ten minutes, and they were worried about permanent brain damage, if he did not get medical attention fast.

Sirens blasted throughout the air, along with screeching brakes, as the ambulance encountered Hugo's Porsche parked in the middle of the road. The paramedics brought out the stretcher and ran over to where Emilio was, on the other side of the rod-iron gate with his own pony staring down at him. They announced that Emilio was semi-conscious. They evidently had gotten to him just in time. The paramedics loaded Emilio onto the ambulance and sped off. The two girls asked Hugo to come inside for a drink, as an offering of "thanks", and which he gladly accepted. Hugo then told the girls how sorry he was to hear of their previous tragedy, as he had heard about it on the news.

Gimpie said, "He's sold the ranch, and I don't know where I'm goin' now." She cried, "I liked it so much here."

Jude added, "Well, I know where I'm scheduled to be in one hour…at my clinic in Pinellas Park. Wish I could have met you under better circumstances, but life must go on," Jude sighed in a carefree manner and waved good-bye.

Leaving the residence herself, Gimpie told Hugo that Jude would be fine, because she had such a thriving veterinarian practice in Pinellas County. "She's always been so independent. She can survive anything, keeping a smile on her spirited face," Gimpie described Jude.

At that moment, Kimmie hysterically came barging through the door.

"I can't believe he's dead. I was just talking to him last week, and he seemed fine, a little out of it. He didn't remember my most favorite birthday when he gave me a miniature pony, but I just chalked that up to age. I'm so sorry this happened. I hate that stupid doctor. How could he not have known about the cancer before?" Kimmie demanded to know.

"It was apparently a too late diagnosis, the news said. By the way, my name is Hugo," Hugo replied to her demand.

"How did that doctor ever get his medical license?" Kimmie blurted out, not caring about the rude introduction. "Kenneth always got an annual physical. How could this quack have not seen any signs, *then?*"

Hugo replied, "Maybe it happened that fast. They say *you never know.*"

At that moment, Kimmie fainted. "Let me go to the Ranch Infirmary and get some smelling salts for her. I'll be right back," Gimp said, running out. Hugo went to his car, reached in his carryall and opened the chloroform, drenching the white cloth napkin he also had pulled out of the bag.

Hugo met Gimpie at the back door, when she returned with the salts. He grabbed her from behind, pushing the drenched napkin onto her face, until she passed out and fell onto the tiled floor. Then, he gave her a boatload of sleeping pills to make sure she was knocked out for a good while.

Hugo picked her up and placed her on the couch he had been sitting on earlier and proceeded to look around the property. He ransacked all of the drawers, file cabinets, and entertainment centers but found nothing...no information. He began to walk to the tool shed, located way in the back of the rectangular shaped estate, when he noticed the Learjet was gone. He thought this to be very odd and called Gambino immediately. Hugo found out the jet was not reported as stolen.

"There's more to this story," Hugo blurted out to the cattle standing beside him.

Hugo stayed the night in the barn, behind the house, thinking about what must happen next in the scheme.

At seven in the morning, he was awakened by a long-axle cattle truck whose driver was herding the last of the cows into his "barn on wheels". Hugo went outside.

Acting like a ranch hand, he asked him who he was picking up for. The driver said, "My bills say, *Cannon Meat Processors*."

The cattle was all gone now, probably sold to processing plants and grocery store chains. There were no thoroughbreds in sight, either.

Hugo thought, "Francis must have sold all fifteen to Cassie, and the rest of his millionaire clientele before he died, or skipped town," as he now was beginning to believe.

✳ ✳ ✳

Hugo had no other choice but to call Camille. He looked up Ken's cell records to get her number.

She answered in her usual deep, but perky, slight French-accented voice, "Hallo."

Hugo stated, "You don't know me, you've never seen me, but I've seen you, a lot."

She didn't say a thing.

Hugo continued, "Please don't hang-up. This is not a crank. I've got to talk to you about Kenneth, uh...."

She immediately came to attention, and quickly interrupted and said, "Well, I was supposed to catch a cheap flight late tonight to Washington for the funeral tomorrow, so...."

"How 'bout this evening?" he asked, interrupting her, "at the Gulfport Marina. I'll rent a boat and bring some wine, okay? Oh... How's about six?"

By seven, they were both officially intoxicated. The boat was bobbing up and down, as it was tied alongside the walkway of the pier. There, Camille listened to an hour long confession of Hugo's. It was not one hundred percent accurate, however, not even fifty percent. Hugo was a master bull shitter and always had been. He just reported that Francis and Kenneth each took over the others persona for some money scheme. Francis died, and now Kenneth was dead too. She was astonished. She didn't even know he had a twin brother. That's why she drank more and more…not believing what she was listening to. Camille was in a state of shock.

It was unusually mild for an early December morning in DC. Arlington National Cemetery was overflowing with people, all friends of Kenneth. The mob boys did not attend, so as not to bring attention to themselves. Camille was there, dressed to the hilt, in black leather from Calgary. She and Hugo caught a red-eye after their encounter at the marina. Hugo rested at the hotel, and a limo was waiting to carry her back there after the ceremony.

When the long time US Senator from Massachusetts got on the podium to make his eulogy to Kenneth, before the burial was set to take place, the crowd went silent. Kenneth and Senator Kenard went back a long way. They agreed with each other's political views, agreed with each other's values, but put each other down in record time, on every occasion. This happened perpetually, especially when they met for drinks at the American Legion building near Beacon Hill.

The Senator started and ended his elegant tribute with applause. He stepped down and hugged Camille who was standing beneath the podium. Half of the time, Camille shed crocodile tears, and the other half, real tears. She still wanted to know where the real Kenneth was. She thought that maybe he was still alive.

Camille climbed into the black limousine, lifting her long black leather skirt slightly, so that she didn't trip on it with her high heels. They motored to Hugo's hotel on Interstate ninety-five. The limo arrived at the hotel an hour later. Hugo greeted her with a hug and showed her to his bedroom. Camille's mind was in a state of disarray, as she told him she knew it wasn't really Kenneth who died at the VA.

Chapter Fifteen

The Wedding

Camille wasn't ready for what was to happen next. Hugo ripped off her lacy blouse and said, "This is what you've been waiting for, isn't it?"

Camille struggled and finally managed to pull away from him. He tried to apologize, realizing how this impulsive flirtation could have ruined his whole plan. Camille caught her breath, looked disgustingly at Hugo and said, "I trusted you for some reason."

Hugo defended his actions by sheepishly muttering, while on his knees, "You're just so pretty. I couldn't help myself. Please forgive me."

Upon hearing this, Camille felt a motherly instinct to nurture Hugo. She almost felt sorry for her words, but still wanted to mend his ways. "It's alright," Camille said to him meekly, as she sat on the fluffy ottoman. "Let's forget this ever happened and try to find Kenneth, okay?" she asked.

Hugo nodded and stood up. He got a Heineken from the mini-refrigerator, popped the top and planted a sweet one on her naturally pink lips.

"Tomorrow, we start our plan of attack, so we can complete this jigsaw," he boldly stated, pointing to the table across the room, where he had started his own puzzle of a Monet.

Hugo slept on the recliner, Camille in his bed. They were both exhausted from the horrendous flight the night before, where the jet was bombarded with golf ball sized hail, as it put down its landing gear, and said simultaneously, "Too much traveling!"

Camille advised a thought provoked Hugo, "It takes the fun out of it when everything's on such a time schedule."

As their morning started, they each took turns getting ready in the huge bathroom. Next, they ordered room service. After eating corned beef hash and poached eggs, one of Hugo's favorite breakfasts, they took their strong black coffees with them. They climbed into Hugo's rental, which he signed for and picked up at the stand downstairs. This time the only foreign car that was available for rental was a convertible Jag. He thought that Camille would probably like it, so he took it. Hugo didn't know what was happening to him. All he could do was look at and think about this perfect girl, with her straight, yard long, silver and mocha streaked hair, wearing her tight jeans and worn out Rutgers rugby shirt with the sweet smell of baby powder all over it. Her thong sandals which showed off French manicured toenails really turned him on. This was his type of woman.

The sun was shining, but the wind was gusting as they made their way over to Arlington. The boys met the couple there, with shovels in hands. They had paid off cemetery guards to look the other way, as they exhumed the body. Digging for what seemed to be over an hour, the boys finally reached the ornate casket. Pulling it up slowly with four shovels underneath, the boys sweated and cursed. Taking off their jackets that showed four muscular, young physiques, through skin-tight, long-sleeved black shirts and "painted on" black jeans, they pried open the "box". They hesitantly did this, not knowing what they might, *or might not find.*

A puff of dust escaped from the empty coffin, which acted as a vacuum. Camille and the boys, simply stared at one another in disbelief. Hugo, frothing at the mouth, screamed, "Ohhhh…you are really gonna pay Fran!" He slammed shut the coffin and ran to the Jag, got inside, and peeled off. Camille sat on the resealed the coffin and cried.

A little while later, the boys put the hollow coffin back in the ground, leaving the mounds of dug up dirt on all sides. They carried Camille back to Hugo's hotel. She stayed there alone, all night, as a recluse. She put on footie pajamas and drank hot cocoa all night. She cried and watched classic movies, and still, no Hugo.

As the early morning sun glared at Camille through the balcony window, she awakened from her restless sleep. The irritating melody of her cell phone began to ring. "Hallo," she answered, with her eyes still shut.

"Camille? This is Doc Martin. Remember me? I was the one who pronounced Kenneth dead at the VA."

"Yes, I remember you," she spoke softly. "How can I help you?"

"I've got secrets to tell…big ones," he revealed. "I was supposed to get a big, fat sum for my services. Instead, I got a big, fat check from a closed bank account in Tampa. So, I'm ready to spill the beans, but I want to tell you in person, not over the phone. I'll have tickets waiting for you at Dulles at five.

When you arrive in Tampa, a brown hummer will pick you up at the arrival terminal. Come to a small table in the back corner of the cafe on the first floor of the Memorial Hospital. I'll be there with bells on." After catching his breath, Doc warned, "And remember, it's in your best interest to come alone."

Thirty minutes later, Camille heard Hugo outside the room, "Honey, are you still there?" He unlocked the door and stepped inside.

With a blank stare, Camille grabbed his toned arm and pulled him close to her. She hugged him tightly and took off her faded rugby shirt and his musky smelling gray turtleneck, rubbing her small firm breasts on his erect nipples. He laid her down on the leather recliner and had his way with her. The two fell asleep soon after their ecstasy, primarily due to exhaustion. It had been a harrowing few days for everyone involved with lies and schemes and set-ups which were all designed in the end to set Francis free, Francis and his millions.

Over lunch, in a cozy Italian bistro on *K Street*, near the air ticket shops, Camille couldn't wait to tell Hugo about the call she just received from Doc Martin, and he seemed more than interested to hear about it.

She told him, "The Doc said he was supposed to get money from Kenneth, if he said Kenneth died. Kenneth never paid him. It doesn't make sense to me, but he said he'll tell me the rest tomorrow at the hospital."

"What hospital?" Hugo asked. She shrugged her shoulders, not wanting to say anything, because of what the Doc had said to her.

"I have to meet him in Tampa tonight. He has tickets waiting for me at Dulles," she said.

"I'm going with you," Hugo insisted.

"No, no you must not," Camille vehemently stated, getting up from the table, pulling down on her knee length skirt. She hugged Hugo, walked out, and flagged down a taxi for the airport.

* * *

Camille briskly walked to the terminal exit alongside what appeared to be just another "snowbird", swooping in on the great state of Florida. He was a gray-bearded, feeble man, who seemed barely able to walk. He wore navy blue pants that went down to his ankles, and a jacket with sleeves that went halfway up his forearms. He carried a purple duffel bag that was much too stuffed to zip, with scarves and hair pieces drooping over its sides. She paid no attention to this old man, however.

Once outside, Camille immediately saw the brown Hummer one lane over and climbed inside. The old man followed right behind her in a red taxi.

Camille found the table where the Doc was supposed to be. She waited thirty minutes....no Doc. These thirty minutes turned into two hours, and still....no Doc. Finally, Camille called Hugo's cell. He answered with, "Haven't you figured it out yet?"

Camille replied, "Wait a second. Are you crazy, or am I? What the hell is....?"

Before she could finish her question, she glanced up and saw Hugo standing at the entrance to the cafe, with a wrinkled blue pair of pants draped over his right forearm and a khaki jacket resting over his sturdy shoulders. He smiled and motioned to Camille to leave with him. She jumped up and ran over to him. She grabbed his arm, this time not in a passionate way, but in a stern motherly fashion, and she sounded off, using plenty of gestures. She naturally used her hands in conversation, having grown up in a French-Canadian province.

"Let me talk. Don't interrupt me. I want to know everything.... and I mean *everything*....so....talk, talk to me, now....NOW I said," Camille yelled in his face.

Hugo agreed to on the ride back to her home.

When they got to his rental car, Hugo opened its trunk, took the jacket off his back and placed it inside the purple carryall that was lying on top of a gray wig and black dress shoes, with socks stuffed inside.

She questioned him, "What's all that shit for, Hugh?"

He slammed the trunk and opened her door, saying nothing. In silence, they motored past Camille's home, only doing about seventy, as he heard on the CB that the cops were out in droves. He quickly swerved off the two lane Gulf Coast road and into a public beach parking lot. He parked. They both got out and held hands. He took her behind the pavilion, adjacent to the parking lot, where a muddy beach area was. He confessed to her that he had the boys "hit" Doc Martin.

"The Doc had too much to say for your pretty ears, and he scammed us, too. No one does that to us. I don't want anything to happen to you, my precious. You see, I've fallen madly in love with you. I followed you from *K Street* to Florida, disguised as a geeky old man. The stuff you saw in my trunk was my costume. This case contains my bag of tricks. It's there when I need it, even when I don't. It's good for my survival...it provides for **my** wealth and security. Now, I want it to provide for **our** wealth and security."

Getting more and more scared with each syllable spoken by Hugo, she nervously broke into French without even thinking and asked, *"C'est que ce? Je ne comprends pa. Je sais que je t'aime seulmont."*

Hugo wanted her more with each foreign word that she uttered. He grabbed her and hugged her, hysterically broadcasting to Camille, and the seagulls, and the crabs on the beach, "What I want is for you to be my wife. My one wife, forever and ever. I've been waiting all my life for you." *He never mentioned to her that he had had four previous marriages.*

Shocked at hearing this proposal, Camille squatted down on the hard, compacted sand, her head in her hands, and after a silence, which seemed to last a good ten minutes, she looked up into his steel violet blue eyes that a street light was highlighting and whispered, "Okay".

Hugo thought it now the time and place for her to know the truth about him. He pulled Camille up from her squatting position and held her for a short time. Then, he pushed her from his chest, holding her at a distance. He looked deep into her green eyes and said, "I'm in the mob...the Mafia, the Irish version of it."

Camille's green eyes slowly closed, and her knees buckled underneath her.

Hugo caught her before she fell and revived her by slapping her cheek.

When she was totally alert, he clarified, "As a mob wife, you'll be part of this world too, so just keep your mouth shut, and we'll be great. You'll have whatever you've ever dreamed of...ya hear?"

"Tre's bien," Camille replied in an obligatory manner, as she held his hand and kissed it. They drove back to her house, this time continually talking. She changed into a sweatshirt, jeans, and sneakers. Then, she made a pot of dark, rich, French coffee, and the two of them began to plan their wedding.

Camille and Hugo married on Christmas Day at a massive Episcopal church in Cambridge. The church overflowed with guests. The elaborate reception took place across the street in two large banquet rooms, one housing gourmet foods and drinks, the other shared itself with both music and dancing and showed off high ceilings and three elegant chandeliers. Rice was thrown at the newlyweds, who were now dressed in appropriate attire for making their cool "NASCAR jump-off".

Snowflakes filled the sky and covered the ground, making it hard for Hugo's Lamborghini to execute a speedy take off. With Hugo's driving skill and experience, however, he quickly came to a respectable speed on the interstate, as they excitedly headed to Logan Airport.

After parking in the long-term lot, the bride and groom each carried a small duffel inside. They were headed to Florida. All that was needed there in December were a couple of shirts, and pairs of pants, shorts, tennis shoes, sandals, and the jackets they were wearing. They ran to the terminal which was a fair distance from their parked car and gave both bags to the luggage attendant standing outside, behind a podium. The couple took out their last minute E-tickets, received their boarding passes from the check-in machine, made a quick sprint through security, and arrived at the gate as the jet began to board. Their four-day honeymoon on St. Pete Beach was about to begin.

After their celebration, they were to list Camille's house with a reputable real estate agency in the area, and pack all of her important belongings and memorabilia and load them onto a very small rental trailer, which was to be hitched to her Volkswagen Cabriolet convertible. Boston was to be Camille's final destination, where a fairy tale life with Hugo was to become her new reality....*or was it?* Feisty Camille would soon find out. For now, however, she radiated peace and contentment from ear to ear.

Chapter Sixteen

The Taxi Driver

The fifth night in St. Pete, Camille found the missing piece to the puzzle in her mail box. The wind gusts were blowing and the rain was pouring, as she ran towards the house, carrying the mail, and her large, sturdy black and red-striped umbrella. She had owned this umbrella for over twenty years and had purchased it in an up-scale store in Montreal. It had been relatively expensive, but evidently worth it. She and her umbrella had survived numerous rain and snow storms, some quite severe.

She opened the front door, griping three pieces of mail between her lips and found Hugo sitting on the couch, Heineken in hand, asking, "What you got there, hon?"

Looking at two return addresses and one postmark, Camille answered in bewilderment with her nose crinkled. "Looks like two bills and a letter from someone in Santorini, Greece."

Wild-eyed Hugo jumped off the couch and barked, "Give that damn letter to me." She jokingly said, "Okay," and put it on top of his head.

He gruffly took it off his head and ripped open the envelope's back, pulling out a note that looked as if it had been written by a child, using crayons for the first time, or a foreigner who didn't know English. The hard to read message, written in purple and green read:

Keneth is buri d behnd

Orphanag ner fenway park.

Ma tyin nevr snubd ya.

It ws me. The mob maad me do it.

You wer so prety and sweete.

Pleese forgve me.

Camille cried hysterically, "Get out of my sight, Hugh. All you ever wanted was to play me, and my emotions."

Hugo grabbed her and shook her hard, until she calmed down and said, "No I didn't. I fell in love with you…MAD Love. Francis is playing games with everyone involved. He's like that. I never trusted him. From the minute I laid eyes on him, I knew it. You've got to believe me. He's gotten real good at it, too." With a pouty look on his face, Hugo sweetly told her, "We'll get him, though."

After an intense moment of silence, Hugo asked her, "Now, whatta say about being my date tonight?"

Camille nodded in approval.

"Now, go clean up and slip into your sexiest outfit, and we'll have the midnight buffet at that quiet, fancy restaurant downtown. You know, the Italian one you like so much. How's about it?" He asked in a smug fashion.

"I'm sorry I talked mean to you, Hugh. You know, I'd love to be your date tonight," Camille lovingly replied.

"Well then, get off your pretty ass, and I'll wait for you outside," Hugo said, his voice trailing off, as he walked towards the front door. He reached for the cell he had put on the entry table and walked into the front yard. He shouted that he was going to call the real estate agency to find out about leads on the house.

Staring out her bedroom window in dark silence, Camille watched Hugo ranting animatedly, talking to some other party on his cell. She knew he wasn't calling for the reason he said. No, it was for some other purpose, but she didn't care anymore. She didn't care about the secrets. She loved life with Hugo, and that was that. She didn't want to cause anymore waves. She quickly bathed, then put on a low-cut, tight mini-dress with high-heeled clear sandals, after painting her toenails and putting on her mascara, blush, and pink lipstick.

When she had finished getting ready, she encountered a quiet, more reserved Hugo out by the front gate. She asked him what the agents had said. Hugo remained silent. He grabbed her hand walked her to the Volkswagen, opened its door, and put her inside.

He handed her a fifty dollar bill and sternly said, "Go get a good meal tonight. I have a problem to straighten out." He shut her door, waved goodbye, and ran inside the house.

Irwin Stuart sat at his newly acquired beach bar, feeling the cool Mediterranean dawn breeze. The waitress poured him more strong coffee and served him some powdered sugar cookies. He was sitting in the direction of the infant sunrise, talking loudly to someone on his cell. He waited for three real estate agents to meet him for Bloody Marys, before checking out a hot new property that was only visible from his bar this property was located off the coast of Santorini and was its own private island, white cement cottage included. It intrigued Irwin when he heard about it, so he asked his boat hand to call the agency handling the listing to schedule an appointment.

Fifteen minutes later

The three real estate agents were shown to the bar by Nicholas, the boat hand, and introduced to a gracious Irwin. The waitress poured the already mixed strong, spicy tomato juice, with the bitter gin that was flown in from Athens. All four men looked at pictures of the island, while finishing their morning libations.

After thirty minutes, Nicholas yelled, with flailing arms, "Let's go guys." He loaded the motor boat with what appeared to be two rather large first aid cases.

After the cases were loaded, he motioned for the four passengers to board and put on life jackets with safety gear, because the current was so rough.

Once on the small boat, Nicholas hooked the jackets of the four guests onto their respective seats with aluminum straps and metal spring clamps. Next, he strapped heavy duty nylon seat belts around their waists, for "added protection"

After a very choppy ten minute boat ride, the five reached the uninhabited isle. Nicholas unlocked Irwin's life jacket and extended his hand out to Irwin, pulling him off the boat and onto dry land. Two of the remaining three were in obvious pain, displaying bloody cuts all over their feminine looking arms, presumably from the sharp, jagged inner aluminum corners of the boat. The two said they must tend to their ailments, using the contents from one of the first aid boxes. Nicholas asked them if they could wait for one second, until he got over to the chest. He said that he'd be back momentarily to unstrap and unhook them, but he had to first drop off the heavy medicine chest he was carrying at the base of the hill.

Nicholas impatiently said to Irwin, "Come on. We've got to hurry…Got to be back at the bar for the afternoon sunbather crowd."

"Are you sure you've got the right one?" the unblemished passenger nervously asked, without even thinking.

"Yep," Nicholas grinned, assuring him. Irwin eyed Nikko wickedly, as Nikko pulled out two saturated swabs from the chest and placed one in each of the two agents' hands. The agents just stared at each other, insecurely. Nikko then waved goodbye and started to walk up the sand dune with Irwin.

Suddenly, Nicholas swung completely around and threw the key in the direction of the motorboat. Laughing hysterically, he shouted to the helpless men, "Let's meet up at the bungalow soon…Okay?" he sarcastically asked, pointing up to the small cottage.

The panic-stricken redheaded and freckled face young agent shouted desperately, "This wasn't our plan, Nikko!"

Nicholas answered clearly, smiling from ear to ear, "I know," and he continued walking. Irwin smiled at Nikko and nodded.

A couple of seconds later, the three heard a ticking noise coming from the first aid box left on board. The petrified agents screamed and frantically stretched, trying to lift the box and toss it overboard. None could raise it, hardly even grip it, because of its distance from where they were strapped in. It seemed to be weighted down with lead.

The redhead screamed in a now detectable Irish accent, "I knew we should have hit you while you were still in the states…"

"And I knew," Irwin interrupted passionately, "that you realty boys were owned by the Irish mob and were paid to whack me. Nicholas told me you even paid him to do it," Irwin snickered, as the ticking continued.

Staring a hole through the redhead's fair face, a cocky Irwin stressed with "squinched" eyes, "One lesson for you boys to learn is that an Irish mobster can never come between me and my right hand man. Nik is as faithful as a puppy to me. He does everything I say and is highly compensated for it."

"I could have got you with one shot at that bank in Bern, but they said, 'No, wait…,'" the young man screamed out.

"Another lesson for you boys to learn is to *never, ever look in the rear view mirror*," Irwin sarcastically broke-in, knowing he possessed the winning hand. *"It could provide for your demise."*

"You asshole…"

Before the young Irishman could finish his comments of angst, a fiery explosion sounded and engulfed the motorboat with flames, sending body and boat parts flying throughout the mid-morning sky.

"Irwin" and Nicholas trudged to the other side of the isle, arm-in-arm and embarked on their yacht. Their planned deed was now done and over.

One Week Later at a Beach Bar in Sardinia

"Hey girls. Come on over here let me buy you a drink and tell you a story. Sit down. Daiquiris are on the way. My name is 'Tex', and I'm from Texas," Francis chuckled, stroking his new mustache.

He continued the charade, using his new found southern accent, "I come from generations of oil in West Texas. I'm rich, and I'm very successful," he boasted, as he flung his long, dark wavy locks of hair over his shoulder.

Nikko stood by and watched "Irwin" break into his new persona, laughing under his breath all the while, as he listened to the rehearsed script, thinking of the necessities he had learned from Irwin over the past few months, especially regarding role-playing. He also become aware of, quite frequently, how Francis liked both genders, and all ages. He moaned and groaned in disgust, as he turned his head away from the crowd, *"Onli won moore nite."*

When the bar emptied at midnight, he and Francis walked back to their bungalow. Nikko had seen and heard hundreds of Irwin's characters, "But this portrayal was by far the best," he told Francis, laughing all the while. He was sure that "Tex" would have become Francis' new identity......but NOW it was too late.......NOW the gig was up...... and NOW the time was right.

Francis walked into their room through the sliding glass door and said, "I'm gonna hit the sack. Join me when you can." Nikko nodded and opened up his suitcase on the patio and took out a bottle of codeine and a bottle of brandy. He shook out seven six hundred milligram pills and poured a large amount of brandy into a snifter.

Thirty minutes later, Nicholas nudged and awakened Francis by saying, "Cume on. Waak up. I jus wanna to have a nite cap wit ya," and which Francis readily agreed to, having many.

When Francis was sufficiently hammered and passed out, Nikko put him on the couch and stuffed the seven codeine's down his numb throat. Nikko walked from the room onto the beach and found a strong, thick rope, which he wrapped around a heavy piece of driftwood that he also found lying on top of the sand. He artistically wrote in the sand with his new found writing utensil, "Nicholas Sporkas, bote hand, alias Nathan Starkey..." He stopped and maniacally belted out a deep chuckle from his belly.

When he did this, he glanced in and saw Francis snoring through the open door. He loved knowing that Francis was so alive and so peaceful now, and in only a few minutes, he would be dead and gone from civilization, all because of him. Nicholas felt powerful now, for the first time in his life. Everything was going well for him, both personally and professionally. He had become a clone of Francis. No longer was he a struggling, non-entity on this planet. He knew he would become a billionaire in less than ten years, with all the right moves and strategies. He had learned from an expert.

"Nicholas Sporkas, bote hand, alias Nathan Starkey...." he continued with his dribble in the sand, "unemployd California beech bum, wil inhearit evrythin.... in won splt secnd. Th' five hundrid tuenti-five fukin' millon, now licuid, that th' mob, an Francis, haad schemd so longe and haard to get, now belons ta mi.........ALL TA MI........an ugli graade schewl drawpout frum Mykonos. I outsmartd the werld. An th' wird parte is......... *It was eezy!*"

Camille's old Florida cell phone rang, three consecutive times, almost off the hook. It would ring, then stop, then ring again. Alone in the house, because Hugo had gone to Boston for a supposed business negotiation trip, she hesitantly answered her cell. She didn't know who would be calling her at this number after eight at night. Her husband and mother only called on the home phone, or Camille's new Boston-based cellular phone number. She looked at the displayed number lit up in the middle of the receiver. Before saying anything, she screamed. The number on caller identification was Kenneth's ranch in Bradenton.

Frightened, she answered, "What?"

Then, a voice merrily sounded out, "Wanna meet me at Frezzio's, where the prices are right, and the martinis are sizzlin', Zahz? Can't wait, 'cause I love you so.

Her mistreated heart finally gave out on her. She sank down onto the carpet and withered away, not breathing at all. Since she had met Kenneth at the Pier that day, life had become much too rough for her. She had become frail and thin.

It was at that moment that her newlywed husband walked through the front door, went into their bedroom, and saw his bride lying face down on the wood floor.

"GOOD, dead as a doornail." He screamed in a now detectable Irish accent, "Now, I don't have to do it!" he haughtily chuckled, knowing he would soon collect the five million dollar life insurance policy he had just taken out on Camille, and he would be the one to collect all of her house proceeds, since she had put him on the quick claim deed a few days earlier.

Hugo boarded the jet for Athens, with his "bag of disguises". When he arrived in Greece, he was met in a vacant back corner of the arrival terminal by a timid Nicholas. He handed Hugo a large, heavy duffel bag. Hugo then forced the concealed silencer into Nikko's stomach and fired it. Nikko hit the tiled floor. Nikko's gun fell out of his limp hand. Hugo opened Nikko's duffel, saw the money stuffed inside, zipped it back up, and kept on walking, with bag in hand....toward the taxi.....toward freedom....smiling and laughing all the way.

"OH, how fate wheelz and dealz," he sang to himself, holding his brand new Maserati keys in hand, along with keys to his new ten thousand square foot villa.

He had bought both while living in St. Pete and were both waiting for him up the road.

"Will I ever know true happiness?" he thought, while becoming "Nikko", in the back seat for close to an hour.

His eyes watered, as a vision of Camille briefly passed through his mind. When the taxi came to an abrupt halt, however, his tears quickly dried up. The master of disguises had transformed his frowning face into a face with a lengthy smile stretched across it. He couldn't believe his eyes, as he stared at his elaborate estate, equipped with his favorite orange-haired playmate, sexy Sophie, sitting inside the Maserati. She was awaiting his arrival, having just flown in from Boston. Hugo paid the taxi driver who opened the back door for him to get out.

"Here, thanks."

The driver just stared at him, then he threw Hugo's money on the ground and pulled out a short revolver, staring at the Irishman's face in disgust.

He screamed to Hugo, "This one's for my boy, Nikko. You're not him, never will be. This party's going to end now." The driver then spit on Hugo, dislodged the bullet from his chamber, and drove through the electric gates, using his sensor pad, and onto the estate property, which was bought by Hugo, alias Nikko.

An Irish real estate agent whom Francis had known and worked with in the past called Nikko three days before and informed him that the keys to his estate were left underneath the gigantic front door mat at the mansion. Nikko and his father were more than surprised, and decided to play the scenario out to see what happens next in the plot. Well, they did, and they both found Hugo to be the evil force in the story. Nikko had first talked to Hugo on the telephone when Hugo called Francis from St. Petersburg late one night, shouting at him wildly and threatening him. Then, on only one other occasion did they speak. This was when Nicholas and Hugo agreed to be partners in another big money "characterization" crime after Francis' death.

To start off their partnership on the right foot, Hugo requested that Nicholas meet him that morning in the Athens airport to give him a portion of this last take. Nikko was carrying only a small amount of Francis', alias Irwin's stashed cash in a duffel, supposed to be Hugo's share of the take. Nicholas' father, who was waiting in his taxi outside of the departure exit, had planned to shoot Hugo with the short revolver, as soon as he plopped down in the back seat. Hugo, however, was too experienced to ever let this happen. He knew not to trust anyone, and besides, he wanted all of the take, not just a small portion. He knew *he* had to kill......*AND FIRST.*

✳ ✳ ✳

The taxi driver lived at the estate now. Nikko's father was sole heir, being Nikko's only living relative. One bullet sounded in the night. This high stakes masquerade was over, *in his mind.*

"This is all mine now," he announced to the world, stretching his arms way out, looking at the property, car, and Sophie...*in amazement.*

Hugo was bloodily lying face down on the driveway, *silencer by his side.*

✳ ✳ ✳

*"What a pity....but It **was** self-defense...," the current rich mogul boldly smirked, as he stopped in front of the garage, waving to his new found playmate.*

He handed her a tissue and quickly phoned for the Athens Police.

Then, he pulled out a chilled bottle and two flutes from his trunk and poured sparkling glasses of Prosecco, so they could toast, then savor.

Silk Road to Atlantis

PART TWO

Introduction

This is the story of a very old and important trading route dating back to B.C. Eras. This route was not exclusively for trading silk; many other items were traded as well, from gold, bronze, and other stones, to animals, spices, and plants. Silk was primarily for trade to buyers in the western part of this route.

The expression "Silk Route" did not originate from anyone in the Silk Road trading zone before the A.D. period, but rather it was coined by a nineteenth century German scholar named Von Richthofen. In these early centuries, all types of caravans and poorly built trading wagons climbed up the rugged mountain ranges through Central Asia and up towards and into China, carrying gold, precious stones and glass, which were not found in the country until centuries later.

Being transported from China was jade, bronze, lacquer and iron. These merchants were not savvy to the evils of the world and were not prepared to defend themselves against what and who lurked in the terrain, waiting to plunder, rob and kill. Forts and defensive walls were built, and this partially solved the problem, but nothing was full-proof.

Caravans simply began to work only in the areas which they were familiar with and then traded off goods with the next region's caravan. This was how the route developed and stayed for several centuries.

The most significant evolution of trading on the route was the switch from silk to religion. Caravans introduced new religions to Silk Road countries via transport of religious sculptures and paintings, such as the new Hindu art, never seen before by the Chinese and which came from India. In the grottoes which displayed the current art, the route showed the mixing of cultures which was taking place on a daily basis because of these traveling caravans and their goods from different lands.

Dress was developing and progressing and more classical facial and body features were coming into play. Countries were becoming more cultured, as they were losing their solidarity and traditions.

Trade throughout the following centuries definitely was heavily influenced by different religions and beliefs in each different region of trade. It remained fairly stable, however, until the middle of the thirteenth century, when the short-lived Mongol Empire disintegrated and trouble once again arose between the East and the West. The new Ming Dynasty did not care about trade with the progressive West. Soon, traffic along the road had all but stopped and everything that embellished the Silk Road was now simply underneath the sand.

The trade route has today reopened between the Russian people and several Asian Republics and the same between the Middle Eastern countries of Iraq, Pakistan and Saudi Arabia. In each of these countries, illegal and immoral trading are now common place. Clearly stated, money and power have always talked on the Silk Route, and they laid the ground work for what was to come. We see their current and constant addictions today.

Chapter One

At the Athens' Airport

He could hear the sound of distant feet pattering on the newly shined and waxed tile floor, evidently polished only hours before. Nikko could tell due to the intense shine that blinded him, as he tardily raised himself off the slick floor. The blood that had gushed from his torso at first, had now but subsided completely. When he stood up entirely, he noticed a 45-caliber shell on the ground beside him. He screamed to the heavens with thanks, as he realized that Hugo was not as great a shot as he professed to be. The bullet merely skimmed his abdominal area, no organs were hit whatsoever.

"I gotta be smartr next time. Whoever did this for me, thaanks for giving me this lesson in life. I cannt trust nothing, no person… no situation…..*never*."

Nikko did not know how to speak without using this double negative, as what was used in the romance language of Spanish that he was introduced to as a young boy, growing up in Mallorca. Palma de Mallorca was where he learned to swim, dive and socialize with the greatest of ease. It was here that he dropped out of grammar school. He had the life taken from his maternal side, so he absconded to

Piraeus, Greece with his father, who was intent on a career as a charter fishing boat captain. His father planned this, in order to escape his own grief. This did not work, and both never got over their loss. Nikko's father did not investigate the enterprise as he should have. Piraeus seemed to be more of a commercial port, rather than a fishing destination. He thought about taking his boy with him to one of the Greek Islands, which he had heard was the place to start a business like this one.

Right at their moment of departure, Nikko's father, "Pop," had another brainstorm. He converted his rather used and beat-up vehicle into a fancy taxi. He thought that he would use it to transport folks from the pier to the airport and back, and this did prove to be a fairly profitable business, at least for a little while.

Nikko's mother had had a severe case of rheumatoid arthritis which left her almost paralyzed. She was forced to use a wheel chair to go anywhere. One day, when pushing her wheels in a clock-wise motion down the small backyard hill, she lost control of her vehicle. The high speed had sent the cart tumbling down the cliff that overlooked the sea.

On the deserted spot of the island where they lived, there was no one around to help her, as she bled, displaying Christmas colors on the sea grass. It was not until much later, when Nikko returned home from school that she was found. He looked down and saw his mother, Maricela, lying on the grass and sand mixture, displaying black and blue marks all over her pale face, arms and long, once bronzed legs. She was lying in a pool of her own blood. She was dead. He screamed. No one heard him. He waited for his father to return from work. Nikko was devastated. His mother had been his world. She had taught him all about Spain and Greece at a very early age, since he was comprised of each ethnicity. Spanish and Greek were from his mother's side, and Greek only, from his paternal side.

His father left Greece where he had been doing hotel maintenance work to be with Maricela in her Spanish homeland. They had originally met at a hotel in Athens where she and her parents were visiting as guests. It was the same hotel in which he worked. He was thirty-two. She was twenty-four. They married and soon arrived Nicholas.

When his father arrived, he screamed "Maricela...Maricela... Maricela". He knew something had happened. He ran to the window and screamed for his boy, only to see him way down below standing over his non-moving and silent dead mother. His father screamed, "Oh my God, Nikki...Nikki...Nikki," the name he called his son in emotional or sentimental times, and he went running downhill in stallion fashion. He grabbed Nikko and started sobbing.

"I came home and found her dead," Nikko whispered, almost as if in a trance.

The authorities were called. An investigation was made as to what transpired, and the conclusion was such that she went spiraling down the sea cliff towards the Baltic Sea, perhaps in search of shells and sea urchins, perhaps as a means of escaping her rather new arthritic prison existence. "Pop" and son never contemplated this. They favored living life each in their own solitary confinement.

Withdrawing from society, not being able to concentrate on anything, and becoming a manic-depressive, Nikko dropped out of fifth grade. Nikko and "Pop" then moved to Greece.

At that moment of consciousness, upon waking up on the baggage claim floor, he was greeted with a barrage of medical staff, and behind it, news crews, who held microphones so far up into his face that they scratched the skin on his nose, making it tickle. He raised his arm up to scratch the itch and screamed. He was not ready for the immense pain that came from lifting his right forearm. Two paramedics wedged their way in front of the media and bandaged the arm, placing medication first underneath the glistening white sterile pad, then lifting the appendage into what appeared to be an old cloth sling that had been used many times, but smelled and looked immaculately clean. Nikko was lifted off the floor by the two male paramedics and taken to a stretcher, which was then placed in an ambulance. With sirens blaring, the ambulatory crew headed Nikko off to "health."

Nikko nudged the hefty one of the two fellows who was right beside him, preparing an injection for pain to be placed into Nikko's own sculpted and highly veined artistic looking hand, which was once used to play the piano at Greek weddings on the small island of Mykonos, where he and "Pop" had ended up. Nikko asked the fair-haired, green-eyed, thug-looking paramedic if he could tell him what was in the needle, and the fair boy answered dramatically, "What does it matter? It's good for you lad."

Nikko thought....Hmm...*lad*....that's odd.....we don't use that term anywhere in the Mediterranean, only in the British Isles. *Oh my God. It can't be.*

At that moment, the green-eyed monster stuck the terrifyingly long, sharp needle into Nikko's shaking hand.

"Where is my father?" Nikko made an effort to blurt a phrase out before the dizziness took over.

The other fellow who was very handsome, definitely of Greek heritage came out from the front, hearing that question, and answered compassionately, "I don't know, but we'll find him for you."

The other just smiled slyly, as he put away his tools.

Nikko began to shake, shake himself into a violent seizure, causing him to pass out.

The handsome Greek paramedic yelled to the other, *"Idiot, what have you done to him?* Let me see what you used in your injection base."

Looking at the bottles used which were out in plain view and not yet placed back inside the medicine cabinet by the incompetent Irish mobster, the real Greek nurse took the other by the collar, slammed him against the door of the ambulance. He knew the other had commented that he just moved here from Ireland, so he lectured him in English, quietly, but seriously, about administering the wrong mixture of drugs.

"I know you are novice, recently hired and still learning, but THIS CONCOCTION OF DISAGREEABLE ANTIBIOTICS AND MEDICINES THAT YOU PUMPED INTO HIS VEINS COULD PUT THE BOY INTO A COMA, AND YOU ARE RESPONSIBLE. YOUR LICENSE MAY BE REVOKED. I WILL SEE TO IT. I CAN ASSURE YOU OF THAT," the Greek nurse screamed, releasing his firm grip from his shirt and letting the Irishman fall against the door.

The only response given was, "And you think I care? I was sent here to make sure he was indeed dead and never talks…which now he shouldn't."

The Irishman then grabbed the long door handle latch and lifted it, flinging the door open into the busy traffic of Athens morning rush hour.

The real paramedic shouted to the driver, "Stop the vehicle!" When he finally had the ambulance in a stationary position, it was too late. The Irishman had bolted out, running for dear life into the traffic of downtown Athens.

The Greek got out of the van into the honking, now-stopped cars and pedestrians who all took out their anger in unpleasant words and gestures. The Greek saw no one who resembled the Irishman, who was obviously taught to meld into any crowd with the greatest of ease.

The paramedic climbed back in the wagon and shouted to the driver, "Okay, straight to emergency, not the doctor's office. It's crucial….I want this boy saved and want to hang that idiot….and I will….or someone will…you wait and see." He was almost foaming at the mouth, he was that upset.

The ambulance was weaving in and out of traffic trying to make it to the hospital in what seemed to be record time. Not trained in investigation, only medical procedures, neither the driver, nor the sole paramedic noticed a small black Audi which had been following them fast and furiously, making all the same turns and for more than three miles.

When the ambulance pulled into its emergency hangar, the Audi pulled into a visitor parking space directly across the street. Two strawberry blondes, one female and the other male, both dressed in suits, carrying briefcases, exited the Audi. They crossed the narrow street, as Nikko was being taken out of the ambulance by the Greek paramedic and the driver. Once the couple saw that the stretcher was fully outside of the van, they increased their movement speed to a run. They had to catch up with the three. Once they did, they each simultaneously grabbed a side of the stretcher, so as not to let it fall on the ground, and they each fired a silent shot into the fragile bodies of the two naive, but salvation-filled victims of fate. The thin bodies were then placed in the deep trunk of their Audi, after white jackets were taken off of victims. The two blondes quickly took off their suit jackets which were replaced with white medical jackets. They placed an already made name plate on each, covering the names which were already sewn on the jackets. The woman took out a thin tube of dark hair gel and got out a comb to produce a darker appearance. The man did the same thing in record time. The woman picked up all paper work which had been left inside the ambulance, and the file that was attached to the Greek's clipboard. They were now good to go, to transport Nikko up to his "death chamber".

It was unusually busy that morning, swarming with tourists that had sun poisoning, or food poisoning, or any other ailment used as an attention device. The couple got through without any questions or surprises because of this, as well as all of the noise everywhere. A person could not be heard over all the commotion that was ever present. The two, along with stretcher, proceeded to locate an empty cubicle downstairs before bringing Nikko upstairs. They got all the necessary paperwork and Mafia-made clearance cards out, in case they were asked to show something.

Nikko was awakening in spirit. The spirit of Camille was present everywhere where her ex, Hugo, had made his presence known. Camille was out for revenge, for herself and for anyone who had been burned by Hugo's evil, selfish and uncaring ways. Even though she wasn't present on Earth as a mortal anymore, she felt she would be able to defeat evil better as a spirit, swooping down on mortal Earth, then rising back up to where she now belongs. She now knew what her purpose for any existence was, not to live luxuriously, charmed and snobbishly.......oh no....to do so much more for mankind....to rectify it from the devil's influence.....so good always prevails. She had been given angel status.

Nikko knew that he couldn't let his conscious state show.....not now. He had to breathe very small breathes through the nose, keeping his eyes closed tightly and his muscles relaxed....very relaxed.

The two Irish received clearance to head upstairs. Their plan was well into effect. Tomorrow at noon, Nikko would be in a permanent comatose state, unable to ever divulge any impertinent information to anyone. He would be mentally dead and the next day his father dead, too. All monies would belong to the Irish mob again, where they belonged in the first place, and justice would be served in their minds. The strawberry blond twins had plane tickets in pocket for tomorrow's flight to Belfast for a huge celebration in their honor, for a job well done. They were both quite skilled and trained for any unexpected happening that might arise out of nowhere. They had always had easy targets....*that is before today*.

On the stretcher, going upstairs by elevator, the twins talked and laughed nonchalantly with several doctors who were headed upstairs for a patient meeting. It seemed an inescapable situation to be placed in, Nikko estimated. Camille's spirit was now blowing through the drafty hallways, enabling Nikko to remember all that had just happened to him in the airport, by his "trusted" cohort, Hugo. He had made a promise to himself, while lying in his own pool of blood, never to trust any situation, or any being, ever again. He had to remain strong, stronger than he ever has been before, in order to survive...to escape this insanity.

Once wheeled into a very large, and of course, very private room, Nikko continued the charade, scared as to what they were planning to do with him. The woman lifted his eye lids. Nikko played the whole scenario as perfect as ever.

"Let's look for more bottles of the two drugs, just in case, okay Jon?"

Jon answered, "Brilliant idea. One never knows and must be prepared." They left the room, talking to wheel-chair ridden patients who were lining the corridor.

"You ARE right, Jon. One never knows," Nikki chuckled to himself, as he grabbed onto a nearby window ledge to pry himself up from the stretcher. Once vertical, he went into his sleeping neighbor's room and struggled to yank a t-shirt out from one of the cabinet drawers at the foot of his bed.

Now Weak, but always strong-willed, Nikko took off his hospital robe, pulled up his jeans, which had never been removed, and simply slipped the stolen t-shirt over his nicely shaped, smooth chest, displaying world-wide soccer tournament dates. He quietly slipped out of his neighbor's room and into the dark, dank corridor. Nikko fluffed up his jet black hair, slapped his face to retrieve some color, grabbed some flowers from a perplexed patient's room, and proceeded to the crowded elevator for downward passage. The elevator door opened, and to Nikko's surprise, it was the blond couple. They angrily stared at Nikko and each other, unable to speak. He wedged himself in between its occupants.

Once on the lobby level, Nikko quickly squeezed out first and began walking through the crowds on the sidewalk, until he reached the first bus stop he saw. It must have been Camille's spirit that had a bus stop there to pick him up at that specific moment. The doors shut. Nikko saw the two running towards the bus, then pounding on the locked doors. It was too late for them. He thought he would never see the two again. Nikko was now off to find his father, but he didn't know where to begin.

He ended up at one of his favorite coffee hangouts where he used to go just to sit and to contemplate existence, and to study English, of which he was performing better and better every day. He ordered his favorite, a *mocha latte* with extra cream. He never had to worry about his weight. He read the daily news, which was free of charge, and just lying on the small, round cypress table where he sat. He read a long article about the Euro's benefits, and of it disadvantages, and of its value over the dollar. After this article, he turned to the local section. There was a slight mention about someone getting shot at the airport's baggage claim area. There was no word as to who the victim was or why it happened, but it said they would give a report after hospital records were released. "There will never be any records released you fools," he mouthed, as he sipped his steaming porcelain cup of latte.

Always taught to be generous, he left a sizable tip for the shop on the counter. He smiled and departed, to where exactly, he did not know. He knew Francis' purchased house, which had become

Nikko's upon his Francis' death, and then Pop's, upon Nikko's death, was located at the most scenic and prestigious inlet of Athenian waterfront homes. He couldn't remember the exact address told to him by Francis, but knew the approximate location.

Feeling better after relaxing over his scalding brew, he rented a scooter from a nearby family motor sport store and ventured slowly, out of the downtown commotion and into serenity and freedom. He searched up and down lanes, avenues, coves and passage ways, but to no avail. Just when he thought he should blow off the day and regroup for tomorrow's ventures, he saw the house that he remembered from Francis' pictures. Then, he saw the taxi.

"This is the place, and won't my father be amazed that I'm alive," Nikko screamed.

Nikko walked along the side of the house and up to the front which fronted the sea, and that is where he found him, hunched over an urn in the middle of a rose garden, crying his eyes out. Nikko had never seen his father in such pain. The pain he displayed made Nikko feel brutally special. Nikko had felt like a non-entity for so long, but for no longer.

Seeing the intense pain in his father's red-veined eyes was more than he needed to make up for his former lack of recognition and pride. Not seeing his boy at all, his father went back inside to pull a kerchief from the kitchen drawer. Nikko limped over the stones that were placed in strategic spots in the garden to get to his "Pop". They both met at the French door unexpectedly. Pop cried hysterically for almost fifteen minutes upon seeing Nikko alive and said that he had killed Hugo last night. He was then startled by the sound of a small boat pulling up alongside their dock which was located on the other side of the property. Two seemingly familiar faces jumped out, both carrying briefcases and both wearing wet suits, flippers, and bathing caps.

"What a strange duo," Pop proclaimed.

Drying his eyes again, his father got up from his chair and slowly walked over to see what was up with these two. As Nikko saw them

both unlatching their cases together, he recognized the body movements. He knew something was wrong, terribly wrong. Nikko flew
in mid-air to shield his father from what he thought was destined to
come, and before he could say, "Pop, watch out," his father was dead
beside him, with Nikko lying on the concrete alongside blood and
guts, and two murderers running towards him.

Nikko was now good and pissed. He grabbed a gun from the inside
pocket of his father's old jacket, where he knew he always had a gun,
and began firing, wanting to blow their heads off. The two blondes ran
speedily back to their boat and revved up the engine, firing defensive
shots at Nikko. Nikko was too fast, however, and in too good condition,
and too agile to take any bullet which was not marked for him.

"What do they want with me, and my family, and this property. I
must find out. I will use every waking moment of every day, every
piece of money that I own and every ounce of energy that my body
gives me in order to get justice and revenge. I will...I will...I," he
muttered totally correctly, as now very weak Nikko sank into oblivion.

The peaceful surge of waves, beating on the sandy Athenian shores
provided an aura of bygone days, thousands of years prior at the beginning of time as we know it, with huge coliseums for sporting events
and palatial ornamented ruins which overlooked the city.

"Oh, it must have been wonderful...and it will be again," Camille
whispered, as she gently stroked Nikko's head and hair.

She kissed him and promised to take care of everything. "I will lead
you on two routes. One path is to where diamonds and fine cloths and
spices are found, the other is a route of sin, greed, and death. They
each stem from one another, and may be the same in the end. You will
see. This has to be done. You are the chosen one, and you must choose
your destiny." His eyelids fluttered, then opened, full of attentiveness
and ambitiousness, kindness... and blindness.

Chapter Two

The Ballerina

Nikko did not know what power had happened over him, but he enjoyed the feeling. Even though the man whom he had always admired and treasured had just died, he felt as though he now had his own battles to conquer. He was ready, like never before. He kept getting strange images of a streaked blond heroin who commanded over him, as well as images of Francis resting peacefully in his bed, breathing, then not. He didn't even feel the smallest tinge of guilt. He felt like someone made him do the deed. Of course, it seemed to him that it was simply for the lust of money and power, and at first it was. Nikko had never felt this alive and important before, but the feeling was changing for him. It was as though he were on a mission, that he was placed on Earth solely for the task that he was about to take on.

He looked at his father, cried for the last time, then decided upon a burial spot that was between the lush gardens and the Mediterranean.

"You said that you would like to be by the sea forever, so here you will be. You have taught me strength, courage, and faith, which I will always carry with me, sir," Nikko proclaimed to his dead father, as he picked up a shovel and began digging up sand. "I will save the world for you and for everyone who has ever died unjustly. Never again will I be egocentric. That part of me is gone, vanished in the wind, and all that is left is a humble, sentimental, and goal-driven dude. That is for sure."

After a burial at sunset, Nikko began to plan his route, which he referred to as *his "Silk Road"*. One that will make him prosper, while bringing all degenerates down on their knees... "Where they belong", he announced to himself, while sketching countries and mapping the road.

Wanting to continue further with his renderings, he drew until his eyes shut. He fell asleep, on top of the map, lying on the thick glass table outside. It was pitch black, with only the illuminated light from the many stars, most of that which was coming from the North Star, Venus, and Orion's Belt. It was a glorious night, full of intrigue, desire, and hope. All of the qualities that Nikko now possessed. He slept outside that night, his head comfortable on the glass, snoring, with not a care in the world. Everything now felt normal.

His eyes squinted with the first glimmering ray of the risen sun. "Where am I? Did I sleep here all night?"

He began to collect his thoughts about what happened the day before. He glanced over at the slight mound of dirt under which his father was buried. There was a flower bush on top. Getting up from his table and chair, he went inside the house for the first time. He scoped the fridge and cabinets for strong coffee and something, anything, to eat. There was nothing in the place. Nikko started to leave to hop into the taxi to find coffee and eats, when to his surprise, he found a photo wedged on the marble counter top between the coffee maker and microwave. It displayed a very happy couple, alongside a shiny new black Maserati in front of this house. The woman was a beautiful light orange-haired, brown-eyed babe, the man was a nicely dressed older man, with gray hair and a heavy mustache who looked a lot like "Pop".

"It is Pop," his voice echoed in the empty house. There was no furniture provided in the sale of the house, so it was virtually empty, only some built in cabinets and counters. There was a wall-bed in one of

the smaller bedrooms. This must have been where his father slept the night before.

"Who was this woman?" he wondered, and where is the car?"

Nikko journeyed upstairs to the spacious, empty bedroom one step at a time. He noticed in this master bedroom that there was a note, full of cinders and ashes, holes and burns. Nikko managed to decipher the writing. It read:

"This is not for me. You're not for me, no matter the money. I loved Hugo and have always loved him. I am leaving with Hugo's stash of money that you put it in the safe last night. I have the combo. I watched you last night at the safe. I am also taking the Maserati. It is not yours. It belonged to Hugo. It was like his toy. He was a really great fella. I don't know why you hated Hugo. Why did you kill him? Why? He did nothing bad...ever...really...never."

"You dumb, slutty human being, you are first," he belted out.

Up near Shannon, on the West Coast of Ireland, was where the boss of the most moneyed and prolific Irish Mafia family existed, and quite well. He was one of Hugo's older brothers. He lived in a 15,000 square foot petite castle built in medieval times. The boys called him "Ty" for short. His full name was Tyrone Riley.

Ty was big and tall, with a very pronounced Irish accent. He had generations of Irish blood in him. He loved to eat, and especially loved to drink. One could find him in any one of the five Shannon pubs every afternoon between the hours of one and five, either guzzling a smooth, hearty Guinness beer or sweet, honey-based scotch Drambuie. Ty was a character. He could engage a bar in one topic of conversation for hours, never boring anyone. He simply had a commanding presence about him. People stood to the side, just to let him walk by. He had noticed this behavior ever since he was a kid. He often thought that this was how he got to where he was, by just being himself. He was meant for this life, and he adored it. Living in his castle, he felt like a King, or at least an Emperor.

Ty had a beautiful naturally blond-haired wife, in her early thirties and with the perfect figure, round and firm bosoms, sculpted arms, a long, slim torso, ending with muscular legs and slim, well-sculpted feet. Ty had first seen her at a ballet performance five years earlier in which she was one of the featured dancers. He thought she looked and danced marvelously then, and still does. He delved back into his memory, thinking of that special show and how he knew that he had to meet her, and perhaps take her out on the town that night. Ty sent a note downstairs to the stage manager, asking him to please give it to the blonde dancer, wearing the faded blue tutu and tights and who appeared to have very long hair, tied up into a large bun the top of her scalp. He handed the stage manager a fifty dollar bill and from the look on the worker's face, Ty knew he was going to get to meet her.

Ty waited for what seemed like an hour and a half, with performers going upstairs to meet family member, friends, or dates. He started to get a bit upset, displaying his arrogant and irritable persona, when suddenly his vision came out from nowhere, with note in hand. She smiled, offering him her hand, then her name, Cynthia, and he, his name only, Tyrone, and they were on their way.

Tyrone escorted Cynthia out the front of the century-old theater to an awaiting black limousine. Ty asked Cynthia if she were hungry, and she said that she was starved as per usual after performing.

The limo carried the couple to an expensive and well-known, long established seafood and lamb restaurant near his house, which was perched on the side of a cliff, overlooking the Atlantic Ocean. They talked very little on the ride, which he enjoyed. He appreciated a woman who was quiet, beautiful and non-confrontational, but still very sure of herself. This was exactly how Cynthia was.

The two had hearty meals, followed by Drambuie shots. They conversed about their private lives. Both seemed to be comprised of loneliness. After the two hour introductory meal, Ty escorted her to her apartment in Shannon proper, where he hugged her and kissed her on the cheek. He asked if she would like to go to the park in town for a picnic tomorrow morning. She agreed, and he said that he would pick her up at eleven.

The next morning Cynthia awoke abruptly and in a panic. She knew she had overslept, which she had. It was near ten o'clock. She quickly bathed and washed her hair. After drying off, she slipped on a pair of tight, faded jeans and a long-sleeved ribbed collar-less form-fitting brown shirt. She slipped into a pair of brown-leather boots, combed out her extra-long straight hair, touched up her face with a little make-up, grabbed her purse and waited... and waited.

Tyrone had had some unexpected "business" that he had to take care of in his castle's office, so he was close to an hour late. When he finally arrived at Cynthia's very small flat, he apologized profusely.... not once....but over and over again. When Cynthia began to smile, Ty knew that he was off the hook. They both piled into his Saab sports car and took off for the park, by way of one of Ty's favorite local pubs, where he ordered two corned beef sandwiches and two beers to go.

Heads turned in the pub, as the patrons recognized both Tyrone and Cynthia. They had another quiet, but enjoyable day, which soon turned into many of the same. The couple became quite well-known in South Ireland. They had celebrity status.

Six months later, Ty knew it was time to make this lady his wife, and so he proposed on their next date. She was flabbergasted, never really expecting this proposal was going to be verbalized. She loved Ty, sure, but she wasn't about to give up her career...not now anyway.

When she told him how she felt, he declared that she had freedom to do what she wanted with her ballet career, just so long as she didn't leave the country on a tour, and until they had children. She thought this to be a fair compromise, with a promising future for her besides. She took him up on his proposal, and they married the next month, after having spectacular arrangements made. They had a huge wedding on the cliff overlooking the Atlantic, on his property.

Once vows were taken, the party continued in the castle, with a symphony orchestra playing as guests danced and ate from the lavish buffet and cocktail area, attended by numerous handsome and elegantly garbed waiters.

The next afternoon he served his new bride breakfast in bed and surprised her with airline tickets and luxury hotel accommodations for the gorgeous British island of Bermuda. She cried, never knowing how happy she could be with her beloved Tyrone. They left for a week the next day.

Being as naive and vulnerable as she was, she never asked questions about his so-called pharmaceutical business and how he was able to have so much time off. She never really cared, not as long as he let her dance and live so happily. There was no need to know, until it happened, and it was bound to at some point. *She couldn't get pregnant.* All began to unravel and drastically change.

Tyrone started demanding expectations of her, which he never had before. He became obsessed with having a "son". He said that he *had* to have a son.

When Cynthia asked him why, he snapped back at her, for the first time ever, and said, "I just have to."

She again asked, "Why?"

He yelled at the top of his lungs, "A son has to take over my place in the business when I am gone."

Cynthia blurted out, "But you sell pharmaceuticals on a free-lance basis to various companies and individuals. What business do you mean?"

Now flushed, he went silent, nodded to his driver, and stormed out of their home. He sped off in the one of his three cars, parked in one of the three garages. His limo driver just watched.

"How could I have been so stupid....never asking anything?" she cried out the window. The limo driver heard her and went upstairs to the sitting room, only to find the door locked. He knocked, and she opened it, inviting him into her quarters.

Watching a perplexed and distraught Cynthia, crying her eyes out of her skull, he quickly went over to her and put a compassionate arm around her quivering, slender shoulders.

"Don't worry, lass," Ty's driver, named Robert, reassured her. "He'll come back. He always does. In the meantime, how would you like it if I took you to a little pub, on the 'wrong side of town', but where you can get a steaming bowl of cabbage and bacon soup and a nice, giant, hot cup of 'java' and Baileys? You know that a Bailey's is almost all cream and won't hurt you, only help you. It's getting mighty blustery and cool outside tonight. I think some warmth and libation will do you good."

She agreed and went to her dressing room to change into jeans and a sweatshirt and sneakers. She looked stunning, Robert thought, as she always did, no matter what she wore, even if he got her *pregnant with Ty's son. "This may be a feat that would pay me LOTS of money."*

Robert had never gotten to know Cynthia at all, up until this evening. He had been Ty's loyal assistant and "partner" for over seven years, never fraternizing with anyone else, and of course, demure Cynthia didn't ever engage in conversation, without it being engaged upon first. Robert *acted* more than ever disturbed as to the way that Ty had begun to treat *his dear, sweet, taken for granted damsel wife*, who now was in real distress. He really did feel something for her. She asked him over and over about the "business" that Ty had mentioned earlier. She thought that Ty had developed such a harsh manner about himself. Being loyal to his boss, however, Robert remained closed-mouth.

Ty had become like an enemy to her in the past month, right after she had sadly announced, "Your ballerina is having a hard time making a baby. My doctor suggests no dancing for the moment."

Surprisingly, Ty rebutted, "But ballerinas must never stop. If they do, they get old and fat. That better not happen to you, 'cause if it does, you can't stay with me. I have an image to keep up. Look at me. I have the perfect physique, and all the women adore it. So, I'll never be without," he chuckled.

The event of that summer afternoon, upon arriving from her doctor's office, was just too hard to get out of her mind. When they were first married, Ty couldn't wait for Cynthia to get pregnant with any gender, and then end her career, but now he wanted her to continue with it, and possibly forever. She wasn't happy like she once was.

Getting into her early thirties, Cynthia was feeling more maternal daily and really wanted a large family with her adoring spouse who she saw less and less of every week, except when he wanted her to do him a favor. Then, he would smother her with affections, words of praise, and plenty of lavish presents. These generosities increased with regularity, usually given on Tuesdays and Fridays every other week, when Ty presented her with what appeared to be a beautifully wrapped and packaged gift box. She was to leave it bi-weekly at the house of a Persian official who worked for the Irish and US Embassies in both Terrorist divisions.

"He's a real nice fellow who buys lots pharmaceuticals from me," her unscrupulous husband professed on one of these "gift" days. He said this without batting an eye, having no conscious whatsoever. "I have to be good to him, 'cause he's so good to me....and in turn... so good to you, my dear. He's providing for your life," Ty solemnly looked her in the eyes, with not a trace of a smile.

Cynthia noticed the first true glimpse of his own evil showing, then protruding from his being, as she suddenly smelled a new body odor that he now seemed to possess. The rotten stench of decay, acting as steam, escaped from his now fully-expanded facial and appendage pores in this slow-burning, pit rage that he was trying to keep all to himself. To his wife, this was the first sign that something was wrong...*something was definitely wrong.*

Back at the pub after a light, but very satisfying, non-talkative dinner, she finally ordered coffee with Bailey's. Robert excused himself from the table, then returned as the waitress was setting down the piping hot mug right in front of her.

After displaying the greatest of talents by carrying in her manly-sized hands and setting down two large mugs with saucers underneath and two medium-sized cordials of Bailey's without spilling a drop, she smiled and winked at Robert, flirtatiously waving "bye-bye" to the table. Bailey's had always made Cynthia feel so relaxed and at ease. She was feeling quite happy now, as the band returned performing traditional Irish medleys, and customers drank down pints of ales.

"This is great," she slurred to everyone in the joint. as she drank her gigantic mug of Bailey's with a splash of coffee, until the now two-headed, and what appeared to be slanted form of a full-figured bar maid in her vision, displaying medieval ornamentation, with low-cut patchwork robing her torso said, "No more for the lady."

"But I have had only one coffee drink, miss," she uttered, her eyes half shut.

Then, her dangling head fell on her neighbor's bar stool, who had just gotten up from his stool to visit a friend's table. She was discreetly taken to a back room in the pub where Robert, two dark-Irish bad boys and one Arabian injected her with a potion, causing her to go spastic. The Arabian reached into his long pocket and pulled out a wool scarf with the initials "TSR" embroidered on it. He carefully wrapped it around both of Cynthia's wrists, tighter, then tighter, the blood almost popping out of the beautiful dancer's arteries. He loosened his grip when he saw the chalkiness of his victim's skin almost blinding him. He knew she now was his captive. The Arab stuffed the scarf back inside his pocket and quietly went upstairs from the musty basement which was once only used for product storage by the previous owners. He then exited the building, as the other two Irishmen walked the victim to the steel shaft area of the basement.

These shafts were once used by generations of Celtic pub entrepreneurs for their loved ones' burials. Now, this spot was used as a world-wide terrorist headquarters and prison. Ty had thought this to be the most ingenious place to hide Cynthia, right in the middle of a working-class, protestant neighborhood on the Southwest Coast of Ireland.

"Who would ever think?" he asked himself. When he saw Robert coming upstairs, he testified, "I am a genius, and one day, Ty "Silky" Riley will own and command everything on this planet." His middle name of "Silky" was coined by the mob for the way he wore his hair, back from his face, swimming in hair gel, so that his curly locks would not show. *"Robert will for sure provide Cynthia with a boy," he whispered to the patrons. "Wow, money and a boy."*

Ty could not bring himself to be near the place of his wife's impregnation that night. He left the pub after his beer and traveled to the small town of Cobh, near where he was raised. His brother's farm was on the River Lee near Cork, where he was to put his plan in motion.

Once Ty arrived at the quaint, well-manicured farm house, he was pleasantly greeted at the big, red double doors by his brother, Theodore, and his wife, Susanna, who were the proprietors of this small hay farm. Theodore and Susanna, and their Labradors, excitedly showed the worried looking Ty inside. Ty was now showing signs of age and fatigue, not beauty.

"Prop yourself up on those two pillows from the couch, and here, take my chair. It's so damn comfortable, boy. It'll soothe you, taking all your cares away. Anyway, tell me how is the pharmaceutical business these days? It must be ripping popular, with all the cars you own. You know you've never invited me to your mansion on the coast. I do want to see it, and Susanna, wouldn't you like to also?"

"Oh, Theodore, where are your manners? You forgot to ask him about Cynthia. How is your talented wife, Ty? Is she pregnant yet? I know how you all want a child. You seem to have everything, just need a youngster." Susanna proclaimed, as she poured herself another cup of tea from the pitcher placed in the center of the main room's coffee table, which was used for high tea with the "right" guests. It was now long past four in the afternoon, so it was very still.

"Theodore….Sus…Susanna," Ty stuttered, "I have something to tell you, something shocking. I'm very worried, and I need your help."

"Well, what is it?" Susanna and Theodore both uttered at the same time.

"Cynthia has been kidnapped."

"Did gangs from Northern Ireland do this?" Theodore nervously questioned.

"No, I'm afraid it's worse than that…worse than I could have ever dreamed. How could this have happened to us, a simple couple. Sure, we have some money, but we work so shittin' hard.

I go over my quotas every month, and Cynthia is a damn good dancer, really popular, making a decent check too. Why did this happen? No sir….we aren't rich…well off, *maybe,* but definitely not rich," Ty added, lying like a lamb.

"Are you going to tell us, or just keep us guessing all night?" Theodore butted in.

"I'm sorry," Ty apologized, "but Cynthia's truly gone."

"Why? "When?" the couple both asked together in disbelief.

"I received a ransom note this morning." Ty added, "This organization wants you two to fly to a small Asian village in Northeast Asia, in the Gobi Desert."

"The Gobi Desert? What on earth for? Why us?" Susan asked astoundingly.

"Cynthia has been kidnapped by radical terrorists that hate women and think of Cynthia as the enemy, since her father is the United States Ambassador to Iraq and has been since the beginning of the Gulf War times in the nineties, when Saddam Hussein ruled the country. Well, the terrorists have questions they need answered.... and quickly.....before they harm Cynthia. All that they want is to harm Cynthia. All they want from you two is to deliver a bag to them at a designated location in the Gobi, then continue to another mapped-out location in Persia. They've left a note, and the route that you blokes must take. Here, I have it in my pocket."

He pulled it out with some dried blood stain chips which melded to the linen from another massacre which he instigated a few days ago involving a Macedonian couple, up at headquarters in Belfast. The two had betrayed the organization. Ty did not like betrayal. He would just as soon cut off a person's finger than have him or her say one non-positive remark against him. He had never truly loved or trusted anybody...not in his whole life. He was very much like his younger brother, Hugo. Ty knew that Hugo could not and would not be defeated. He was confident of that, with all of Hugo's brilliance.

"You're doing a great job for us in the States and in Greece. Keep it up bro," he had praised Hugo the week prior, when Hugo informed Ty of the "boating accident" that was to take place in the isles with "Red" in charge.

"Red", as he was nicknamed, was rising up the ranks of this new Mafia-based terrorist organization, as its members called it. Ty named "Red", the sharpest tack of all the boys he owns.

"I know you'll never let me down, now will you chap?" Ty questioned Hugo, laughing on his cell phone earlier that week, when Hugo had been in the front yard, before Camille went out to dinner alone, and before Hugo left for Athens to hit Nikko.

Ty unraveled the letter and read it from top to bottom to the couple. He read it out loud:

> We have your beloved Cynthia. You will get her back, providing you do one thing. Have your brother and his wife deliver a package to us in different destinations, in designated spots in the Gobi Desert, and possibly in a not yet disclosed dirt area in a lifeless part of Turkey. We will be in touch one more time via letter. Act soon and do everything we say. It's for your best interest, and the best interest of your wife.

The mapping of the route to be traveled was traced below the writing, with designated stopping points circled in blue. Down below the map was written, *Have them carry plenty of water. There will be none in the Gobi....more later.*

Chapter Three

The Route

The area which separated Europe from Asia did not produce the most sympathetic persons on the planet. First of all, this area was one of the most horrendous climate environments in the world, producing very little vegetation, a drop of rainfall, with countless deadly sandstorms. This place was and still is fondly referred to as *"The Land of Death"*. Death Valley in the western United States is tame compared to this region. Few travelers in bygone days, carrying their goods by caravans ever made it through alive. There were few roads and even fewer number of isolated oasis'. Temperatures in the summer months soared to almost 120 degrees Fahrenheit and dropped drastically as the sun set.

The Gobi Desert, in the vicinity of Northeast Asia, is just as bad. Some of the mountain passes in this region prove to be the most difficult to cross in the world. They are over 17,000 feet in altitude and dangerously narrow, with suicide drops at each ravine. Being so hot, intrepid and dangerous, the Gobi Desert was and still is the perfect destination to conduct "mischief" to set the world aflame, without anyone knowing about plans, and or fatalities. It has always en capsuled a virtually isolated existence. There are no sparser resources and no humanity anywhere. It is a dead place. Even animals cannot live in this environment for long periods in the brutal heat.

This was where the beginning of the Silk Road stood still in time. It always remembered its beginnings, embroidered with time in anti-quated university history books so boring, so factual, and so forgetful. No student ever remembered much about this part of the world. That was how Ty and his Middle-Eastern cronies preferred it, being as quiet as possible, until the shit hit the fan, and the world was destroyed, almost all of it anyhow, but of course, not Ty's egocentric world.

Since he had been a tot in diapers, Ty felt like he should rule the world, as many do at this psychological stage of life. The problem was, he was never provided a scaffold by his parents, nor shown the right way to behave. The three boys' father, Patrick, had been a product of two radicals who initiated this Irish mob clan, so Patrick had not been a particularly good parent himself, and his wife who was too scared to intervene in the raising of their children. She built walls so high that she couldn't look over them, so as not to see who the current forget-table broad was with whom Pat was spending plenty of time with and fortunes on.

Theodore couldn't stand his family's line of work. He was and had always been a fine, hard-working, honest male. He didn't know from where he got these qualities, since his father, grandfather and uncle had all tried their darnedest to get him into the dark, seedy world of lurid money and "legal" crime, as seen in the faces of hundreds of Irish cops on the beat who were paid off weekly to keep their traps shuts. Theodore attended church and Sunday school regularly and with con-stant desire. He always hoped that his brother would repent and start living the clean, pure, happy life, but as of yet, it had not happened.

Ty, he sensed, was always stressed and miserable. He thought this to be because of his lack of morals and his non-acceptance of God. Theodore always thought that without God, he himself would be an unhappy vagrant failure. He felt that God persevered with him through the most trying of times, when he almost lost his property, as well as his life, as doctors diagnosed him with an inoperable brain tumor which was sure to spread quickly. They gave him a month to live. So far, it had been two years of remission, "all due to God," Theodore would constantly tell people. There is work to be done.

"I have to rid the world of evil, slowly, but surely...one step at a time." He was the exact opposite of Ty, almost like Francis was of Kenneth. However, the latter two changed courses and became each other's moral beings.

"Susan, I'll do the deed. Are you game as well, my dear?" Theodore questioned his wife.

"I would never let you go without me. Yes, in your words, I'm game. When do we leave? What do I pack? How long are we going for?" Susan persisted with a long stream of questions.

"I don't know," Ty advised. "We'll play it by ear once you get there. I know you'll be superb."

"I know that *we* will be too," she replied. "We will play the role brilliantly and bring her home."

"You know that was my major at Oxford...theater. I wanted to be an actress in the worst way, and then I met Theodore. I can't say that I'm sorry about that. I have been very happy, very happy...regardless," Susanna professed.

"Regardless of *what*, if I may ask?" Theodore responded to the backhanded compliment.

"Oh, I just simply loved all the attention, applause and gorgeous *men*...It was loads of fun, but I am so happy to have a dear, sweet, thoughtful hubby like you. Love, we will play one hell of a theatrical performance to get sweet Cynthia back," Susanna interjected nervously.

"Alright, alright, enough with the personal drip," Ty expressed.

"I'll get our small gold ten seat Learjet to pick you up right here on property, tomorrow at eight sharp. Be ready and waiting. Fuel's ultra-expensive now, and we can't wait on *nobody*. You'll fly on a virtual straight course over Russia, then taking a southeast turn. You will be arriving in Kyrgyzstan, a small terrorist post north of Nepal and just to the northeast of Afghanistan. Bring a duffel. That's all. I have to get my Cynthia back. She's all that I have," Ty lied.

Susanna comforted him in her arms, stroking his back, as he forced water from his eye ducts. It was now easy for Ty to master this, as he had had much practice throughout all of his bogus, ultra-moneyed existence.

After several minutes, with Ty seemingly trying to regain his composure, he left their estate, climbed into his ride and sped off to the sleazy part of Belfast. He had to see his princess who had just flown in from her home in Kabul. He had nicknamed her Sunny, because she was always seemed so happy with her gleaming smile. Sunny was blessed with straight, silky jet black thick hair, a small tan face with round, glistening, opaque, brown eyes and a long slim nose with long, thin naturally red lips that displayed a "beauty mark" on their upper right side. Her body looked like that of a beautiful, mythical Egyptian. It was dark, thin, smooth and jeweled. It simply carried an overabundance of life, obedience, even death, as what was taught to her by her Culture.

Sunny's outfits were always loose fitting, sparse white garments, which showed off her physique, through the transparent material. She usually wore gold, medium-heeled strapped sandals. This turned Ty on....a lot.

Her aggressive, sinister and greedy behavior turned him on even more. He pulled in the stone drive and anxiously got out of his ride. He primped up his hair with his fingers, as he swiftly made his way to the narrow brick one-story IRA Headquarters, which he also used for her Sunny. It exhibited much need of much repair. He didn't feel the need to help Sunny with money much, because she never asked, so Ty never offered. He didn't feel it necessary. She was always there for him, no matter what, sometimes too much. He never had to give her one present, or even take her out to dinner. Sunny was always there waiting at that building, and she did whatever Ty told her to do, like clockwork. It must have come from growing up as a teenager in Afghanistan. Her brother, Med-hi, had been one of Bin Laden's best friends and followers. Her brother knew all of the illegals in the Mid-East and Asia Minor and all of their illegal dealings. He was quite well-known, trusted and respected by the underworld.

Ty tapped on the chipped door of his "office". Sunny, in desperate need of breath, because she had run from the back room as soon as she heard his car pull in, opened the door and let him in, crazily kissing him all the while. She was obsessed with Ty and would do anything he said. Ty knew this and took advantage of the situation.

He used her as a sexual ornament for Asian and North African men along the route, in order to make his power deals. Ty became obsessed with ruling his planet. He was the anti-Christ. Somebody had to stop him, but everyone was too afraid, so they let him continue to build more and more ammunition, concoct more and more elaborate plots, and simply destroy life as we know it. Bits and pieces of his shenanigans were now being aired on national news networks daily. He was building a following. He loved himself and felt invincible, as he strutted through his make-shift abode.

"Sit down Sunny, so I can talk to you," he whined, "You know you're the love of my life, my wife to be...only a few months longer... when all this is wrapped up. Will you help me with a problem that I have?"

She stared at him wide-eyed and nodded her head, "Why, yes."

"Arrange several meetings with high-powered fanatics throughout Asia, India and the Mid-East through your brother. I will have shipments of explosives and drugs delivered to each of their organizations. These shipments will be used as a means for my alienation from the rest of civilization, so that I may become the super power that I was intended to be in the first place. I will beg, barter, lie, and steal to become the world's financier."

"Oh, I want you so much! You are a genius! This is so exciting! I will handle it all by tomorrow evening, have the dates, places and times set. I can assure you, they will all pay handsomely."

"Good, large, large money can only help in my plan to rock the world with tragedy and detriment....and hopefully, I'll get a son. I will hold Cynthia down there for nine months, even with a ransom paid.

Got to leave now, but I'll call you tomorrow evening about six to retrieve all of the details. I'm closer to my goal, and that means we are closer to a wedding," he slyly grinned, walking quickly backwards to the door. He never touched her upon leaving, so Sunny ran up to him and planted a wet one on his "almost" virgin thin white lips.

"I love you, and you can count on me," she declared. "Come back tomorrow to hold me."

After climbing in and shutting the car door, he waved and wiped the kiss off his sterile lips. He had never liked kissing, even as a young enamored boy in school. Everything in life was merely a game to him---friendship, love, sex, work, and all money matters. Thinking of life in this way, Ty decided to play the game, not just for pennies on the dollar, but for high stakes...very high stakes. He was at the crossroads of his career. He was now positioning himself for more money and status than he had ever dreamed of, through high-tech bombing devices, high-priced drugs, and one billion dollars in ransom money for his beloved wife, Cynthia. He knew he would *never get caught* and *live forever.*

Ty drove recklessly over the short hills overlooking the northwest coast that continued from his native home of Belfast. Glancing in his mirror, he noticed a black car which was following him, keeping up the same speed. When he arrived in Shannon, he noticed the car had turned to the right and left his path. He motored ahead, straight to his castle. He felt he needed some shut-eye before he began his plan of attack the next morning. As he turned onto Water Cliff Road, he spotted the black car which had been following him. It had spun off onto the side of the road. Ty proceeded home.

After Ty's car was almost out of sight, the black car started-up and sped to Ty's castle. Two goons got out of the unmarked vehicle and walked briskly over to Ty's car which was now parked in the driveway.

Ty let down the driver's side of the electric window and asked, "How can I help you boys?"

"Step out. We want to see some identification. We heard from sources that you are running drugs and guns through this property. Is this true?" the more sinister of the two questioned.

"I sell pharmaceuticals to private enterprises and individuals and… lots of them. I had a family inheritance I used through the years, so I am able to live here and drive these cars. I don't have the morals to do anything as corrupt as that. I feel humiliated. I am an upstanding, decent human being. Now, I do have to hurry inside and attend to my wife. I believe dinner is waiting," Ty asserted.

"We'll be back," was all the two at the gate said, and they zoomed away.

Not even caring about what had just occurred, Ty sat down on his custom designed large sofa and drank a double scotch, before drifting off into a sound sleep, listening to the huge waves beating their way onto the cliffs, then plummeting down onto the coarse sand. The open windows in his sitting room provided him with a quiet solitude that he needed on occasions like this. Ty was a recluse and had always been. He preferred living like one, due to the many people that he had to come in contact with each and every day. Night had always been his favorite time of the day, when he could slip into unconsciousness and dream, dream about fairy tales with kings and queens and unlimited power, which he always wanted to have.

His dream was getting more and more surreal and enjoyable until a melodic sound disturbed his dormant state and made him enter into consciousness once again. Ty stumbled to the living room and looked for his cell. It was Sunny calling. He answered it in disbelief.

"Did I wake you, love?"

"Yes….what's on your mind?" Ty unhappily asked.

"My brother wants you to go to the Silk Road. He wants you to be a part of the action, too."

"Why me?"

"He just wants it that way, otherwise he won't help. He said he would call you tomorrow morning on your cell. He wants to meet you in one of the countries. I hope you're not upset."

"Fine," he yelled, as he slammed the phone down.

"This is going to be a lot harder than I thought," he whispered to himself. "How am *I* going to pull off a huge ransom, claiming that these Asian and Mid-Eastern gangs of terrorists have kidnapped my

Cynthia, if I am with them on the Silk Road too? I will have to think of something. I guess there is no trust anymore among friends," he sarcastically recited. "I will go, but I will reign and never be defeated. Nothing can stop Tyrone...nothing." He suddenly felt very tired, and he felt like he couldn't even climb the staircase, so he climbed into a large bed which was in a small bedroom downstairs. He barely made it there as it was. He pulled the quilt over his head and fell asleep, this time not waking until morning.

At seven, the help arrived at the castle to tidy up, and make strong coffee, poached eggs and toast. This was Ty's favorite breakfast. It energized him for the entire day.

Chapter Four

The Redhead

Nikko took the next day off to plan his strategy of revenge and righteousness at the Parthenon.

He could always think better being around a circus of antiquities. Nikko recalled every tidbit of information that Francis spoke to him about Parrish, Florida. He knew that he had to go to Parrish first, before venturing to points unknown that were filled with figures of terror, ammunition, plots and schemes.

Nikko had really always wanted to be anything but a grade school drop-out, but now, all he really wanted to be was back at that bar in Santorini tending to tourists' drink needs and scrubbing floors. It was an easier, safer and simpler life. He became aware that in order to become a czar in any of life's enterprises, one had to be corrupt, possessing no conscious. He was becoming more and more on the same page with Camille, his angel and goddess.

A flash of light appeared before Nikko, as he strolled downhill, away from the monument he was viewing. He heard a sweet voice whisper, almost inaudibly, "Go to Parrish." He knew where Francis' famed property was located, as he had heard about its whereabouts perpetually and seen the map tracing its location. It was off of Highway 301, about three miles from I-75. He had seen photos of the massive gates that displayed "The Ranch" in fancy cursive type. Nikko also knew of Jude and Kimmie, and all about their backgrounds. Francis rambled on and on about his properties, his brother Kenneth and Kenneth's wife's niece, the veterinarian, and his goddaughter, the horse racer. Nikko knew he had to talk to the girls to discuss the world-wide dilemma which would soon occur, if officials were not alerted. Something had to be done to stop these maniacs.

Nikko jumped into the Maserati and drove back to the neighborhood where his father had set up residence for one day before he got gunned down. He knew it had been done by the Irish mob, of which Francis knew too much about its dealings.

Once Nikko got to the mansion, he found it in disarray. It appeared that an intruder had done this, as everything in the place was on the floor. He grabbed the phone receiver in the sitting room, sat down on the love seat that now had a terrible slash through its beautiful tapestry cover, with stuffing scattered on top of the cushions, floor and end tables. He dialed operator assistance for the numbers of several airlines. He wanted the one that would have the best schedule and would get him out the soonest. He found that by flying on KLM and changing planes in Amsterdam, then direct to Tampa, he would have the best schedule offered. Nikko gave the phone agent the debit card used by both Nikko and the very wealthy Francis when he was alive. It was a Florida bank account.

Needing to depart from the doomed estate quickly, he phoned for a taxi to carry him to and drop him off at the Athens airport. It came in record time and got there in record time, as well. Nikko gave the driver a hefty tip, then exited. Nikko was and always had been a very good and moral person, up until the time he met the turned-evil dude, Francis. Francis' devilishness had left a mark on naive Nikko that Nikko was trying to dispose of, for good. He hoped that he would accomplish this, with his angel's help. Nikko had heard all about Camille, Kenneth, and Hugo, and surmised that Camille was a victim, just as he had been.

At the airport, Nikko printed his boarding pass and walked to the terminal. He was then escorted by an Irishman coming up the rolling walkway toward the gate. He stuck a piece of paper in Nikko's palm and called out to him, "Safe flight Nikko."

He knew he would never be Nathan. "I am Nikko forever," he muttered to himself convincingly.

Once on the aircraft, Nik settled into his first-class seat and ordered his first brandy. It was served to him by a cute male flight attendant. He unwrapped his note which read: "Don't ever come back to Europe. Stay in Florida. It's for your own good." Nikko was aghast. He knew he had a mission to complete with the Irish Mafia and mostly likely the scum-bags in between. He couldn't believe the note given to him by, of course, an Irishman. He desperately had to get to Parrish to meet the girls. Nikko needed comrades and prayed that everything would turn out as he had planned.

The cute flight attendant asked him if he wanted another brandy before they took off. Nikko answered, "Why not?" He needed an escape from the day's ordeals and devastation. He was going to be the victor, good over evil, and he knew it, especially with his angel's help. He fell asleep as the plane skyrocketed and headed close to the atmosphere's entrance.

He slept soundly and dreamed solidly, until an announcement came over the intercom, "Please take your seat. We are experiencing turbulence and an unexpected functionality problem with the aircraft's main engine. Please, remain calm."

Nikko knew that this was just too coincidental to be taking place with him on board. He knew that this whole flight had been a planned disaster, with 150 passengers going down, only because of him. He knew that he could not ever let this happen. He prayed to the heavens and to his angel, Camille, for assistance. His prayers were soon answered. The pilot announced to the passengers that all problems appeared resolved, with the help of an expert air mechanic that happened to be a passenger on this what was to be "ill-fated" flight. He was a master mechanic instructor who trained all who ventured into this field. His ingeniousness rectified the moment. Nikko looked up at the ceiling to give thanks. He knew that it was a higher order of being that disabled this impending doom. Feeling now even more at ease and at peace, he turned off his reading light and drifted back into unconsciousness which he preferred.

He thought, "Was this mechanical problem intended to KILL ME?"

When Nikko awoke, a pitch black sky was displayed through his window and a redheaded green-eyed flight-attendant sat down another brandy on his tray table. Nikki waved his hands, as if to say, "No more." She left it with him before he could get the response out of his mouth. She smiled and left. He swirled the brandy around in the sifter, perhaps looking for something subconsciously. While doing this, he noticed a liquid that looked incoherent with the rest of the brandy in the sifter. It seemed as if it were a heavier substance, almost like an oil, or a poison. He became horrified, staring at the two liquids that didn't combine well.

He smelled the concoction and quickly poured the entire substance into the magazine pocket on the back of the seat in front of him. He filled this with papers and tissue to absorb the insidious liquid. He thought this a better way to dispose of it, rather than to spill it on the floor, for all to see. He wasn't aware of what was to come, however.

Immediately after pouring the liquid down the cloth pocket in front of him, he heard a strange noise, like threads ripping. It was the cloth pocket on the seat in front of him being eaten up by the extraneous liquid. It bubbled, then ate small holes in the otherwise durable fabric.

"This WAS an attempt to kill me," Nikko concluded, as he scoped the plane for the redhead who served him the potion. "They couldn't do it the first time, so they tried it a second time," he told himself. He scoped the jet but saw no one but brunettes everywhere, as they had just departed from Greece. No redheads were in sight. Frustrated, he resorted to flagging down the male attendant to ask for his help.

"Can you ask the red-haired flight attendant to come my way? I have something I need to ask her, please," Nikko politely uttered.

"There is no redhead with the flight crew. You must be mistaken. Sorry, but we are solely an Athens based flight crew on this plane. Do you know her name?" he interrogated Nikko.

"No, but I wish I did," Nikko replied. "This red-haired woman poured me a brandy and set it down right in front of my sleeping body. She left. Then, I noticed and smelled a strange liquid, like maybe I shouldn't drink whatever it was...And look, it made these lovely holes in the fabric here, see?" as he pointed out the tears.

"I know nothing about this, but we will conduct a full investigation upon landing in Amsterdam. Can you stay for a few moments after disembarkation?" the attendant worriedly asked him.

"Of course, but just for a few moments," Nikko sternly replied back. He tried to go back to sleep, but was unable. He felt like a hostage, with no control. He was a prisoner in the air and had to patiently wait.

"The authorities would find the person who perpetuated this act, or would they?" he wondered. "This had to be the work of the Irish again," he thought. "What do they want from me? It had to be because of Francis, this whole thing. I have to take it from here and separate good from evil and make good prevalent, unlike what Francis did."

More and more he felt like meeting Francis at the bar in Santorini was the WORST thing that could have happened, and the BEST.

After five more hours of turbulence, which Nikko never felt because he was now sleeping like a baby, the jet started its descent. Startled, Nikko awakened when the plane dived. He gazed out of the window at the morning sky and the morning traffic and felt glad that he was headed to the supposedly calm, vacation state of Florida, after one change of planes.

Nikko had been in the United States only one time, when Maricela and he went to visit his great aunt. He was four years old. For now, however, he really felt excited to be in the US, for what he considered to be his first time, as he did not remember his previous visit at all. His first visit had been to Detroit. He had never been anywhere else, not even to change planes at an airport, as it had been a non-stop flight to Detroit.

Upon arrival in Amsterdam, all passengers began to shuffle their belongings and quickly retrieve items stored underneath their seats. Nikko remembered that he had to wait for authorities before he could exit the flight. Impatiently, he did.

Five minutes before officers got to the gate to investigate, a petite woman, wearing stilettos, a mid-length black chiffon skirt, and a transparent ruffled ivory long-sleeved silk shirt came waltzing by with a very small dog in hand. He looked at her well-formed legs, upward to her face, and her hair, and that's when he saw it. Two or three straggly pieces of hair were not tucked into her black beret, and they just happened to be rosy red pieces. Nikko was sure she was the one. She grinned at him, winked, licked her lips, and exited with her puppy, and her long white mink wrap, draping it over her high firm shoulder with every step she took. She looked back at him, walking past him from the flight's coach section. She left the jet and walked down the terminal hallway.

When the investigators arrived at the scene, she was gone. Nikko could only tell of the situation and describe the perpetrator. Fabric spots were cut to take to the lab for investigation as to chemicals used.

After this scenario, Nikko was given a card as to who to get in touch with if anything else should occur, or if he should remember any more facts that would attribute themselves to a case history. This case now was assigned its own number. Nikko was impressed, but frightened. It seemed as if he could no longer trust anyone. He felt that he must quickly get into the confidence of the girls, if he were even able to track them down, so that they may work as a team. The three needed to straighten out this mess of high- stakes' death benefits, payable to everybody and to anybody, and he was anxious to get started on the project.

The next terminal's departure to Tampa was extremely busy, a sold out flight. Passengers were getting mean, as it was also getting very hot in Schiphol Airport and agents didn't seem to care about any problem these passengers were having today. These workers just wanted to go home and get away from all of this corporate garbage. They still needed a paycheck, however, and that was why it seemed, they hung around. Nikko was last in line in boarding his next flight for Tampa, since he got off his previous flight later than expected. He did not care. He had his seat assignment and knew he was headed down to find his girls, *wherever they might be.*

Once on the flight to Tampa, settled in first class, he was seated next to a younger gentleman who had a seemingly curious nature. This young man kept asking questions, which turned into an all-out interrogation.

Nikko asked the flight attendant for a brandy, and then asked the gentleman, "Why all the curiosity?"

He simply replied, "I have nothing else to do." They both continued innocent chit chat, of which Nikko could not stand, but he persisted, regardless.

"I need to catch some shut-eye," Nik finalized, before closing his tired, limp eyelids.

"Sure, I will talk with you when we land," the irritating passenger noted.

When the plane landed, Nikko remained asleep. Nikko never spoke to the young man again.

Finally, the flight attendant woke him and said, "You need to leave this flight. We have passengers embarking in about five minutes. Talk to the official first at customs."

"Okay, I will. Sorry that you had to come to get me up, but it seems that I was so tired from flight."

"That's alright," the attendant remarked. "You can sit and wait until all of the passengers have disembarked."

"I have places to go and important people to meet," he replied, and he left the jet.

He passed through customs with his expedited Greek passport that the Dutch police gave him. He quickly went outside to flag down a taxi to carry him to the inn, near Ellenton, the one that Francis had always talked about.

"Boy, won't the girls be surprised?" tired Nikko asked himself, as he entered his room, ready for a good night's sleep. He couldn't wait until tomorrow.

Chapter Five

Ty's Underworld

Coming from a rough protestant family, who later became the backbone of the IRA, sixteen-year old Ty was not at all surprised when he was asked by the European Terrorist Group, to kill two French men, as they exited their homes in the south of France. The Basque father of one of his numerous girlies had asked Ty if he could do this for his cause, the ETA, and that he would get paid quite handsomely. Ty, of course, said "yes", and that proved the beginning of his quench for power.

After traveling back to his homeland of Ireland, he became acquaintances with several chums, who hung out at the local pubs near his family's flat. They were uneducated, mean, dirty, but clever...very clever. The young men took the sixteen year old under their wing and taught him everything that he ever needed to know about how to survive as an IRA member, and how to do his job extremely well.

Ty went with the men to every beating, intimidation, "knee-capping", money-laundering and drug-trafficking event in Ireland. Ty's mum and pop were thrilled when he wasn't around. They wished he had never even been born. Ty was too "'boring" and "expensive", they said to him on many occasions, while fighting hysterically with one another about Patrick's numerous affairs, while drinking their nightly four pints of ale. Ty was glad that he had not been an only child and had two brothers who also had to endure some of this treatment.

Unbelievably, there had always been a tiny part of him that was unselfish and generous. He just could never let that side show, not if he wanted to succeed in the exciting and profitable underworld that his family had exposed him to.

Ty quickly became embodied in the culture of hate that extended to new immigration, not just religion. He had become no better than a terrorist. There was also surmounting rivalry between the Irish and the still-existing bit of Italian Mafia.

One of Ty's Irish Canadian clan spoke of the clash in terms of "Only silk suits will be topped with blood." This Irish Canadian was a member of the West End Gang of Montreal, a huge city underworld group. The Irish Mafia and the IRA were now seemingly everywhere. This was exciting to Ty, as he intended to head both organizations.

During the ceasefire in Northern Ireland, military gangs of delinquents continued robbing, money laundering and drug trafficking, as well as performing simple homicides in the streets. It was a turbulent time.

The so-called "Irish Mafia" began to rise in the states, particularly in cities like Boston, New York, Chicago and New Orleans and take the place of its cohorts of criminal European organizations, in terms of significance and radicalism. Ty wanted to be master of all the entities found throughout the entire world. He even began to dabble in studies of the Muslim and Hindu religions, as a means of getting these worshipers under his thumb, and having no conscious besides, he was well on his way to reaching his unscrupulous level of worldly-ranking.

In 2004 the IRA stole 26.5 million British Pounds from the Northern Bank in Belfast, which was considered the biggest bank robbery in European history. Ty had been in charge of this entire operation. He had made a total of 1,215 hits during his twenty years of crime up until now. He felt that this was not enough. He needed to take out anyone who stood in his way, no matter what. Time was getting short, in his eyes. He was almost forty and had to go for the gusto. Ty thought that now was his only chance.

After the 2004 hold up at the Belfast bank, he concocted an elaborate plot, as he sat along-side his date, bored to death, and watched the Dublin City Ballet.

He had heard of Cynthia Tidwell, the great ballerina, and of her father, Jack Tidwell, US. Ambassador to Iraq. Ambassador Tidwell was a millionaire, owning several companies and many acres of land developments in the Northeastern US, as well. Ty knew that he was now about to score. This was the moment he put his charade into full swing, for the purpose of money, power, drugs, and terrorism...and did it ever work.

He eventually married one of the most moneyed, influential, and powerful young women in the world, who just happened to hide herself as a simple ballerina, not earning any of the lavish attention which she so adamantly deserved, and most vehemently despised. Cynthia was a sweet, quiet, simple angel of whom anyone could easily take advantage due to her naive ways, especially a man as evil as Ty, her husband.

Ty's relatives were now on their way to Dalanzadgad, by way of Frankfurt. Dalanzadgad was the largest airport in the Southern Gobi desert. The two would disembark from the plane and embark on a journey of smuggling, bribing, and death.

First, they were to pick up many microscopic explosives and many ounces of expensive and exotic drugs to be transported to an undisclosed czar for purchase, then distribution. The journey back would go from Dalanzadgad by motorcycle and continue down to Ekhiingol, an isolated oasis of about twenty families who grow cucumbers, watermelon, tomatoes and peppers, only for their daily consumption, as there were no flights in and out, and only very rough dirt roads by which to travel.

From Ekhiingol, the transporters would then be given their next assignment. Ty and his players used Ekhiingol as their first pick up in this escapade, since it was so quiet and virtually vacant and had a thriving agricultural research center, used in communist times, and it always grew very healthy produce. Now, it was used for producing healthy plants which produced bountiful drugs of all types.

Ekhiingol was Ty's gold mine and could provide him with world domination, along with his plan of receiving a one billion dollar ransom from Cynthia's father. The ransom was to be sent to an address in a vacant area in Northwest Turkey, and which only held a buried mailbox and a pad lock. The mail carrier had rehearsed going in and out of the mailbox quickly without ever being seen, in the early morning dark hours.

Ty was to fly to Varna, Bulgaria and drive his awaiting car through a quiet, unmanned northeast border back road to the unpopulated area, about fifty miles from Istanbul. He was then supposed to pick up the cash inside the designated mailbox and drive to a nearby private air field to catch a small plane to Lucerne. Here, he would deposit the cash in one of his banks, then head back to Belfast. He always had IRA Matters to attend to there. He had also rehearsed this scene many times *for himself.*

When Ty first arrived in the Southern Gobi, he found it to be breathtaking. He thought that the gravel desert was such a compelling sight, with its underground city remains, buried long before the Roman Empire was ever formed. There was even a smattering of dinosaur fossils found there.

"Tomorrow, they should be on their way, and all shall be well…. *for me anyway,*" Ty chuckled, as he entered the locked basement of the pub where Cynthia was being held. Ty glanced around the dark, wet and humid basement, until he found the tall and very slender Cynthia groping at the ropes which held her arms together, placed behind her. She looked at Ty in disbelief, with hate seething out of vengeful eyes. Her lips were bandaged with tape. Her ankles were knotted tightly together with sturdy anchoring rope, which rubbed holes in her fair skin.

Ty said to her, "My sweet, this will soon be over." Cynthia grimaced, as he stroked her entire body, and especially her belly. He then tore a shirt sleeve off one of her frail shoulders, slowly unbuttoned her dress, and had his way with her. His helplessly-bound wife was now too weak from undernourishment, much too weak to ever fight back. She had only enough energy to spit on his feet.

Ty planned on keeping his wife downstairs for the entire nine-month maternity cycle. Of course, he did need to get a "yes" from a doctor who was a member of the group, that she was indeed pregnant. With Robert's heavy male sperm count and Cynthia's ovulation date, Ty knew he should be good to go. After the birth, the pub was to have a gas explosion, with Cynthia inside. Her body would be burned to a crisp, unrecognizable, but Ty would have his baby boy in arms, *along with lots of dough on his person and power flowing throughout his veins.* It had been Ty who was not able to produce a child, not Cynthia.

Chapter Six

Nik meets the girls

The day at the ranch started with much commotion. The three dogs that Jude had just adopted from the Pinellas County shelter were trying to get out from the property. They were not used to their surroundings yet. The shelter was located only three miles from Jude's office. When she drove by, something made her want to turn in the driveway and check the dogs out. She hadn't been in this establishment for quite a while. It was so very disheartening to see the sweet things in cages, awaiting their fate. Only this time, fortune for three animals was to override doom. Jude asked the animal control officer if there was any behavioral problem or medical condition that caused these ten dogs to be quarantined here.

He answered, "Not that I know of. They were all just strays, with no tags, chips, or collars. We have five more being processed upstairs. They were just dropped off by two families who couldn't afford to take care of them anymore. Would you like to see these five?"

"No, I'll take these three," she replied, pointing to a black and gray terrier, a beagle mix, and what appeared to be a tan Belgian Shepherd. She would check this breed out later at home. Jude was very content.

She had done her good deed for the day, maybe for the year. If she could, she would adopt all of the strays and unwanted animals in the Tampa Bay area and keep them on the ranch. She knew this could never happen though. It was just a humanitarian dream of hers.

One of the workers was at the gate trying to keep the three dogs from escaping their new yard.

"They just have to get used to the place," Jude shouted out the window, as she put on her robe and flip flops and woke up Kimmie who was sleeping in the next bedroom. They both ran out onto the huge front lawn, yelling the newly-given dogs' monikers. "Monte, Bella, Jazz.... Come here...now!" Jude demanded, in her strict, maternal voice. They all came toward her, wagging their tails.

She cuddled them and said, "Don't you ever do that again, ya hear".

The dogs ran with Jude and the still sleepy Kimmie up the rolling green hill that rambled on, across the entire front acreage. When they got inside, Jude put on some coffee, so that they could plan their attack on the corruption that had been put on their plate. It was going to be complicated to sort out, but with an honest, intelligent lawyer, of which there still are a few, the ranch would remain theirs. They did have contracts for both cattle and citrus products. Kenneth would have never left them to deal with all of the problems that they faced now.

"We still know very little about what really transpired, especially with the sale of the property. The main thing is that my uncle did not sell his property. I'm sure that he did not actually sign the contract. He would never do such a thing and leave us homeless. We have to investigate everything that we have heard that occurred and all of the so-called players in this charade. We have to come up with a solid plan on how to secure this property, this business, and my uncle's good name," Jude stressed, as she poured another steaming cup of coffee for the two of them to enjoy. Kenneth had taught the two girls to fight for what they wanted and believed in and that was what they both agreed to do.

At that moment, the phone rang. It was a Tampa number. Kimmie ran to answer it, thinking that it might be one of the lawyers whom she had left several messages with their legal secretaries.

Instead, a strange, foreign accented gentleman greeted her on the line.

He asked, "Is this Kimmie, or is this Jude? I have mny thngs that I need to shar with you too."

His English had been getting better, but now, it seemed to be at the elementary stages once again. This was, perhaps, because of fright, and being excited and very wary from the long flight, and of course, these past few months of facade and criminal escapades. He felt that it was now time to come clean with the girls.

Even though Francis had willed everything that he owned to Nikko, he could not take the girls' assets away from them. He had an overriding sense of moral obligation within him, still, but he also knew that the assets and this money that he now possessed had never belonged to Francis in the first place, even though Francis did stand to get a piece, being Kenneth's only brother and his twin besides.

"We have no time to play games," Kimmie yelled and slammed down the receiver.

The phone rang again and again.

Kimmie yelled into the receiver, "Don't call here anymore."

The phone rang soon after that, but caller id displayed "Gimpie". Kimmie answered the phone. Gimpie was just checking on the two girls and the situation at hand. She had recently found another job as a manager at a discount department store in Bradenton. She was scheduled to start tomorrow. Her husband was doing fine, just traveling a lot on business, the fertilizer trade.

Upon hanging up with Gimpie, the ringing began again. This time, Jude answered. Nikko was on the other end, begging for her to listen to him.

Hurriedly, he stated, "I am at the Tampa Airport. I just flew in from Athens. I want to help you get back your claim back to your property. I will tell you everything that I know of this whole ordeal. Please, let me come see you today. I know where you live and how to get there. We will battle the courts to take back the estate....together. Francis did not do right by you. He was a greedy pig. I despised him. Well, I can be there in a few."

He was now showing off perfect English phrases, as he knew that he had to. He was simply on his best behavior.

"Interesting," Jude muttered. "But will we be able to trust him?"

"Your guess is as good as mine," Kimmie replied. "We'll just play it out and see what he says before we call our lawyers."

Forty minutes later, a beep was received through the front gate. The dogs began to bark. A man was there. He stated that his name was Nikko and that he appreciated being seen at such short notice. The girls jumped up from the breakfast table and ran to the front door, only to let in the most handsome man that either one had ever seen.

"Hi ladies. Nice to meet you....my name is Nikko," he said, extending his hand out to each of them.

"Hi Nikko. My name is Jude. I am Kenneth's niece, and this is Kimmie, Kenneth's goddaughter."

"Is there any place where we can sit?" Nikko asked. "What I have to say may take some time."

They showed him into the living room, turned on the soft jazz channel and offered him some coffee, which he accepted. He asked the girls if they had any anisette liqueur to mix in with his coffee. He was so used to this combination having lived in Greece where drinking its counterpart, ouzo, occurred daily. Jude shook her head and told him that there was only brandy remaining in the house.

"My uncle worshiped brandy," she interjected, with a disapproving smirk.

"No thanks, I will just have some strong, hot coffee, please," he decided, being tired of brandy.

Once the coffee was served by Kimmie on a big platter with small cookies alongside, business was in order. Nikko began to describe the blustery day that he met Francis on the main pier in Santorini, where Nikko was fishing. Francis was disembarking from a cruise ship, three large bags in hand. He flagged Nikko down for help and paid him well for his efforts. From that point on, he said that they were inseparable criminals. *Nikko had been his lover, his cohort... his confidant.*

Nikko stated, "We just made things happen…everywhere we went. Francis looked different and sounded different, whenever he needed to. He did this for fun….and for money. It was strange. He was strange, but…."

"But who is Francis, and why…?" Jude frantically broke in.

"Francis was supposedly your uncle's twin brother…that's what he said." Nikko continued to explain, "He played his twin and his twin inadvertently played him, so that the Irish mobsters could get loaned money back. Francis said the mob even gave him a share for doing this, but he scammed them, really scammed them. He was getting out of control with me and everyone. I had to do it. I had to. He would have destroyed everything and everybody!"

"What did you *do?*" Kimmie inquired.

"After his nightly intake of brandy, which he guzzled and got quite used to, as the Irish boys had funneled the stuff down his pipes for many nights…Well, you see…Francis had impersonated Kenneth in their plot, so he had to be like him to the 'T'," Nikko spoke.

"Tell me more," Jude butted in.

"Well, I slipped a lot of codeine pills down his throat, so he wouldn't wake up," he started. "I couldn't take it anymore, the sex, the lying…the scheming. He had no morals whatsoever, so…I did it, and from that point on, I paid…I paid dearly. A little while later, I was shot in the Athens airport by a mobster named Hugo. He's dead now. Pop shot him later that night."

"Hugo? That must have been the man who came to our house not too long ago," Jude announced to the room. "We all passed out because of him. He's bad…*real bad.*"

"He came here?" Nik asked in amazement, and answered himself, "That figures."

Then, there was silence. The girls were dumbfounded.

He went on, "The bullet did not hit any organ. He must have been a bad shot. I lived, but my father, who inherited everything from me, by way of Francis, by way of Kenneth, is dead…shot by the Irish gang a few days ago in Athens. He lived in a mansion which he was to inherit from me, but I lived after all. I inherited the mansion from Francis, who had been portraying your uncle and godfather.

Francis became so bold that he scammed the Irish Mafia and took all profits with him to Santorini. It is now time to destroy anyone involved who is still alive and before they have the means to get our fortunes into their filthy hands. Nobody does that to my father and gets away with it. Nobody should do that to you girls, either. My father did nothing but good...his whole life. They will now pay, and you will get your property back, too...I promise," Nikko adamantly stressed, as he carefully laid his cup on the tiny saucer that was placed in front of him.

Chapter Seven

The Grand Escape

ikko told the girls that he had in his possession the numbers that Francis had left behind when he passed away, numbers of important Irish mob connections and locales.

Jude demanded excitingly, "Let me call one of them up and give them holy hell, those bastards."

"No, I'll do the honors. I kind of know them, by way of Francis," Nikko replied. "I'll call the pub that Francis had called once or twice in Shannon." Hugo told him that this was one of the IRA aka the Irish Mafia headquarters, where all European business was decided upon and far enough away from Belfast, so as not to create any suspicion. He phoned the establishment on the house phone. It still had on its caller ID, "Kenneth Redman". He didn't care now. Besides, he had no more minutes on his cell phone. It was dead as a doornail.

He rang and rang again, until a soft-voiced man answered, "Hello, *Pub of all Pubs*." Nikko quickly hung up the receiver, not knowing what else to do, and he quickly phoned the next number on Francis' list of Terrorism.

A funny, high-pitched voice answered and asked, "Hello. You are Kenneth Redman... one of Ty's friends, I presume? Is Ty okay? Do you want to see me tonight about anything? Tonight's as good as any night. Anytime you say, I'll be there."

This time, Nikko slammed down the phone and belted out, "How disgusting!" With what she said to him, along with her subservient Middle-Eastern accent, he knew that something was up, something big time was about to transpire with these clowns.

Nikko decided, "We are going to the pub, all three of us. We need to find out more. I am your friend. I have nothing to gain. I have money that was given to me by Francis, but I don't want your property and will do everything in my power to get it back for you."

At that minute, he got on the internet in the entry hall and booked three first-class tickets to Shannon, by way of Atlanta. He was ready to go and tackle the misfits and the *ignorants* of the world. He always had had no tolerance for these types of people, even though for a long while, he could barely speak the English language. Nikko had natural smarts and savvy, however.

Upon hearing the ringing of Ty's cell phone that he had left behind in the basement of the pub, Cynthia began to stomp, squirm, and throw a fit the best that she could, being bound and gagged.

She knew that she had to get someone from upstairs. It had been a whole day and nobody had attempted to even enter the basement. She thought to herself, usually during the day, Jon, the young naive bartender works. She thought that he would be the perfect one to get herself out of this dark and dank, smelly dungeon. She continued stomping with her long, but graceful, muscular feet, until low and behold, Jon entered the darkness. He turned on the light switch, saw her tied up and gagged, and ran in her direction to help her.

Jon was a very nice boy who had always secretly had a severe crush on Cynthia and had always loathed Ty for having married her. Jon had adored Cynthia since before she met Ty, when she was just a gorgeous and talented ballerina on tour in Ireland. He saw the beautiful Cynthia and thought that she looked drastically different than she had a few days ago. He knew that something was wrong.

Jon said, "This will hurt, but I have to do it," and he ripped off the bandage which was covering her mouth. Cynthia could now speak, but she thought it better to simply keep quiet about the whole mess, for her sake. She didn't know who exactly to trust. Jon quickly untied her hands and ankles from each other and let her catch her breath, before asking her what had happened.

"Oh, nothing," the quick thinking Cynthia uttered. "Just had some kinky sex before Ty got an urgent call, and he left. He said he would be right back, but didn't come. It must have been important." She convinced him, totally playing a used and abused feminine fool. "Oh, Jon, could you get me some of Ty's Prozac from the medicine case down here. I really appreciate it. Thanks."

"Sure," Jon responded.

Jon came toward her holding the Prozac bottle between his thumb and forefinger and slipped it to her. Cynthia uncapped the bottle, grabbed Jon's wrists from behind with her very capable grip, held them together while she retrieved the cloths which Jon had removed from her own ankles and wrists, and she proceeded to tie his wrists and ankles tightly together and to secure the cloths to a long extension coming out of the wood wall. She then stuffed many Prozac pills down his throat and gagged him with a scarf she had pulled out of her hair.

She then said to him, "I don't know if you are the enemy or not, and if you aren't, sorry I had to do this to you, but this is now a game of survival for me, hon."

Cynthia quickly grabbed Ty's cell phone, stuffed it into her huge, long jacket pocket, which she thought the perfect thing to do, now that her mind was working overtime, and she left the establishment through the small, thin, almost rotted-out back door. This exit and entry was rarely used, thus she had a hard time even opening it.

Cynthia ran into the fresh, clean, cool crisp February air, feeling so free and full of life. She would never act like a "bimbo" again, as she now felt like she had portrayed herself for many a year with Ty.

She stopped far enough away from the pub, about three blocks away, and looked at the phone number that had called the earlier, when she was tied-up. It said "Greek Nikko" on the screen. She pushed his number to send the call through.

A hard to understand voice answered the phone. It said, "Hallo, this is Nikko. Is this Ty? Where are you right now? I must talk with you."

After a few moments of silence, the new *brave heart* Cynthia answered, "No, Nikko. This is his wife, Cynthia. You called when I was tied up and gagged down in the basement of our pub. I am out now, on my own, never to return to him again, never to reveal my whereabouts to anyone again. I prefer to live in seclusion now."

"Yu a…you annda many people who you are close to are in danger," Nik stuttered. "I was Francis Cranford's best friend. He told me many things before I killed him. Ty's dangerous, even Francis was scared to death of him, he once told me. He is planning to rule the world with his money and criminal and terrorist contacts. Ty has his pawns scattered throughout the globe. They will do anything for him, as of right now. He controls the IRA and most of the drug trade in the world, especially in the opium and cocaine-producing regions. He also controls most ammunition and missile production.

He is a very powerful, manipulative man who can get anything that he wants through his massive illegal profits, his huge array of whores, and his amazing oratory abilities. He is a slick man who will never be brought down, unless somebody kills him, and that is almost impossible with all of his armed hoodlums that constantly surround him, I have heard."

"I'm scared, real scared. I don't know where to go or what to do," Cynthia blurted out, trembling.

"The girls and I are coming to Shannon tomorrow. We are leaving tonight. Just tell me where you are going to be and what time you want to meet," Nikko assured her.

"Who are *the girls*? Do they know Ty?" she asked.

"The girls are the main players in the game. They're good players. We'll tell you the whole scenario when we see you," he reassured her.

"Okay, I'll be at the Kilpatrick's diner downtown at 4 in the afternoon. I will be wearing sunglasses and a black scarf wrapped around my head, with a straw hat and a long black dress. See you then," she informed him, in a hesitant manner.

"Oh, what will tomorrow bring?" she asked, as she flagged down a bus for her sister-in-law's home.

They had always been great friends.

She had no money on her but ten Euros. She thought that should get her there. The driver asked for seven. She heaved a huge sigh of relief. She hoped to find some refuge for the night and change her appearance. Cynthia was excited about her scheduled meeting tomorrow and very frightened and non-trusting, at the same time.

When the bus stopped at her sister-in-law's corner, Cynthia climbed out and trudged up to the white farm house door. It felt like such a welcome change for her, being in the green countryside. She fit her hands firmly through the door knocker and began to bang.... and bang....and bang.

Then she yelled, "Susanna". No one came to answer.

"Oh well, they must have gone into town to shop. I'm sure they'll be back in a jiffy," she mumbled to herself, as she stumbled through the garage, looking for the hidden key, which was supposed to be under a stack of papers in the back, underneath the heavily-packed shelves.

"Ah ha, here it is," and she proceeded to unlock the back door and go inside.

In the kitchen, she found scissors in the junk drawer and ran to the bath down the hall and whacked off her long blond locks. She found some henna in the closet, which Susanna used occasionally when trying to look more sophisticated, and less like a farmer's wife. She left the henna on her head of hair for a total of twenty minutes. She was now a darkish redhead. Feeling kind of creepy, yet comfortable, Cynthia put on her sister's flannel robe, prepared a cup of hot black tea, sat down on the sofa and turned on the tele, awaiting the arrival of her in-laws.

After watching two short black and white British detective films, her eyes became heavy and shut, not opening until the sun glaringly shined through the sheer curtains at dawn.

"Where am I?" she confusedly asked herself, as she awoke from her deep sleep on the chair. She looked around the room and remembered where she was.

"My God, they're still not back!"

At that moment the house phone rang. Cynthia answered it. It was the US State Department asking to speak to Theodore or Susanna.

"They are not here now, but this is their sister-in-law, Cynthia. Can I help you in any way?"

The official on the other end was silent, then he transferred the call.

"Cynthia my baby, is that you? How did you get away? What happened? I didn't know how to get a hold of you, so I..." The phone then went dead.

She phoned the number back on her Ty's cell. *She found it to be already programmed in his phone.* Cynthia knew too well the voice on the other end was that of her distinguished father. He was living near in Washington DC, where he served as Ambassador to Iraq.

"Hey dad, sorry about that. Listen, tell me what's going on."

Cynthia had grown up in the political and social circles of Annapolis, where she was born and where her father had been a scholar at the Naval Academy, which led to his eventual rank of Admiral in the United States Naval Corps.

Cynthia had been used to getting everything she wanted in life, even though she never acted like a spoiled brat. She had always loved to dance, ever since she was a toddler. Her parents sent her to a boarding school in the countryside of Virginia. She made mediocre grades, didn't like it, and asked to come back home. She told her parents that she never had time to study, because she was always stretching and trying new ballet moves. They knew what she was destined to become, so they enrolled her in a private school in Annapolis and got her a private ballet instructor who was recommended to her father by one of the Supreme Court Judges. She had never been so happy in all of her life. Her perfecting talent was blatantly showing.

At fifteen, she was asked to audition for a touring version of the Nutcracker. She landed one of the starring roles which she performed for one month, having a private tutor all the while. Cynthia was widely received in ballet circles now. She continued to perform in starring roles in Washington DC and Baltimore.

After she received her high school diploma, she was asked to understudy for a star who had a leg injury. This was for a holiday version of the Nutcracker, for only a two week stint in Boston. It was here where she was asked to work for a premier ballet company in Dublin, and the rest is history.

"They said I had to give a lot of money to a specific ISIS leader. They also said that the United States had to free all Islamic prisoners for your safe return. I wouldn't have been able to do that, *no way, no how.* I'm just so glad you're safe and unharmed," her father blurted out before the phone disconnected again.

Two days ago, the Ambassador had received an urgent call on his cell. The caller ID said "private". A male voice spoke quietly and slowly, and stated in an unrecognizable Irish accent, "You have a mission, chap. You must deliver us one billion dollars, plus maps of all your ammo depots and underground bases, but most importantly, we must have the release of all Muslim prisoners being held in the US and its military bases. This way, your family will all stay alive, your capital building will remain pretty and all in one big white piece, and your national banking system will not default. You understand? Put money, plans, and strategies in a black briefcase and place it in the hands of a turban-wearing Iraqi gentleman, who has on a pin-striped black suit and who will be leaving the train station main exit at exactly eight-fifteen tonight. Do this, and the world will remain calm. Don't do this, and you won't be able to fathom what is to come," the haughty caller warned the Ambassador. "The world is in your hands now." The caller had been Ty.

Since Ty had been informed that Cynthia had escaped, new strategies were in place. Aware that now there was a manhunt for her... shoot to kill was the spontaneous order given by Ty.

The Ambassador hung-up the phone, then realized he had not asked for Cynthia's number. He asked his aide to put a trace on the last international call to come into office suite. After four cups of strong coffee, one of his busy staff members came to his closed door with the news he awaited. The young blond girl efficiently laid the piece of paper in the center of his ornate desk. This paper contained even more numbers to reach his daughter in Ireland, if needed. He dialed the last number that called him.

Out of breath from excitedly running to her cell, Cynthia answered with, "Hi again." She proceeded to tell him how Ty had had her drugged and tied-up in the basement as a hostage.

"I do not know why, where, how, or anything else. I don't know anything about Ty...I don't know anything about my husband. The whole thing has been one big charade. I miss you so much, dad!" she revealed.

"I'll be there, hon. Just wait for my call tomorrow," her father frantically requested.

It was at that point that he realized how much he truly needed his daughter in his life, and how he had never been there for her during his rise to power. "I'm going to stop this ridiculous gerbil run that I am on and go see my little girl," he shouted to his aide. "Bobby, book me a flight to Shannon for tonight."

"For what purpose, sir?" his clever assistant questioned, nosing his way to the answer.

"Personal, Bobby. It's Cynthia," he quietly muttered, and grabbing his briefcase and jacket, he left the premises for his home, ready to stuff casual shirts and pants into a small duffel bag that he could carry on board. He did not want to exude any diplomatic charms on this trip. He had to remain incognito. He rammed his Porsche into first gear and sped down the interstate from DC towards Alexandria.

Since Cynthia's mother had died two years ago, he had no one to answer to, nor call...had no agenda whatsoever...but oh, how he missed the answers, calls and agendas. He missed his wife so.

In the meantime, Cynthia quickly showered and changed into a calf-length gray linen skirt that she found while rummaging through her sister-in-law's neat closet. She slipped over her head a cream-colored cardigan, squeezed on some penny loafers, put on some rouge and mascara, and twisted her hair into a French twirl and secured it in place with two silver ornamental hair combs and a scarf. She quickly put a hat over top her head and began to walk to Kilpatrick's to meet the trio. She didn't know who to trust, so she grabbed the pocket knife that she saw lying on the coffee table, put it over the top of her skirt and underneath her cardigan, locked up and left, with raincoat in hand. She was still bewildered as to where the couple might be.

"Oh well, maybe they got hammered at their chum's place and stayed there until they sobered. That's probably it," she said to herself, as she kept on trudging through the sparsely-filled streets.

When she finally reached downtown, she was greeted with sprinkling rain. She quickly wrapped her raincoat around her and briskly walked in the direction of the diner. No one seemed to pay any attention to her, as she looked like just another tall, slim, Irish woman struggling to get in from the rain that was growing incessantly louder and faster and wetter.

At four o'clock, Ty's cell rang. "Hallo! Cynthia, are you at Kilpatrick's yet? We just landed in Shannon and are on the way right now! Can you please wait? We are in a taxi, as we speak," a pleasant sounding female American accent verified to a panic-stricken Cynthia.

This scenario had all been all too much for her to cope with. She laid down her head on the table and quietly sobbed, praying for a solution to her dilemma.

At that moment, a woman's glowing, sparkling shadow engulfed Cynthia's presence. This glowing shadow wrapped around her entire being, picked her up for a split second, when no others were around and consoled her, reciting the words, "You are strong. You will survive. You are strong. You will survive." Then, the friendly low octave female voice added, "I was once like you. You'll be okay. I'll make sure. Trust in me. My name is Camille."

In the next moment, the shadow left her existence, and she was dropped back onto her seat, just in time to be intact, as several patrons entered the diner. They wanted Shepherd's Pie, of which they had none, so they just ordered chicken platters.

After the final cup of coffee had been served to this rebellious young couple, and they had left the establishment, Cynthia glanced up toward the main entrance and spied a dark-haired man entering the diner curiously, along with two overly excited fair-skinned maidens by his side.

"Cynthia?" he yelled down the aisle to her.

"Over here, Nikko…over here," she confirmed her identity.

He and the girls raced over to her.

Nikko was obviously enchanted with Cynthia, as he scoped her every move with precision. The two girls remained silent, as Nicholas gave all details of what had been a methodical and strategic plot by the Irish mob, of which her husband was chief instigator. Cynthia was devastated with all of the horrid details.

On the verge of collapse, she remembered what her seeming angel had said to her earlier, *"You will survive. You are strong."*

"I am Jude, and this is Kimmie. We are relatives of both Kenneth and Francis. We have just learned about this plot as well. I don't think we quite understand everything about this dirty, ingenious plot of greed and devastation. We will do everything possible to prevent your husband from controlling this planet, as Nikko seems to believe he has been planning for quite some time. We need your help. There are most likely others, many others involved in this plot of *New World Order*, where the public acts as subordinate subjects to world-wide domination of evil forces and terrorism. We will not stand for this, and I am sure that you will not, either,"

"And my father won't either," Cynthia blurted out harshly. "My father is the Ambassador to Iraq and definitely has something that they want, I'm sure having to do with National Security issues. He should be in this town by tomorrow. He'll inform us of their desires then. He supposedly left tonight for Shannon."

"Is there any place we can stay for a night or two, until we determine what has to be done," Kimmie asked Cynthia.

"You know something strange is happening right now at my in-laws' farm house. They are not there, as of yet, and I don't know where they are, but they have three small bedrooms and a couch. You can stay there for as long as you need," Cynthia assured the three, hoping she was believing the "right" side, while hoping she was doing the "right" thing.

When they returned to the farm house, it appeared to still be vacant. Cynthia assigned bedrooms to the three, while taking the couch herself.

She had ulterior motives with this strategy, however. The couch had the only phone lying beside it, on an end table, clear access to the front and back doors for emergency exit, and access to all kitchen weaponry, which she moved to a drawer underneath the coffee table right in front of her. She now felt safe.

She made sure that everyone was in his or her respective room before she finally plummeted herself on the comfortably quilted sofa and embarked on an exotic dream, in which Camille played the starring role. Camille had encompassed Cynthia's being from the start of this ordeal, and Cynthia had let her, because she herself was in such need.

Cynthia awakened with a start fifteen minutes into her dream state and went into the kitchen to make a quick cup of Darjeeling tea. She heated water for one minute in the microwave, found the remote on the table in front of the couch, and turned on a British spy flick. She continued to hear silence upstairs, where her guests were sleeping, which was a good sign....a very good sign. She thought more and more about how really naive she had been, letting strangers stay in the same house where she was sleeping.

Once again, she drifted off into her dream sleep and met Camille for the second time, but this time with vengeance.

"Help me. Please help me with my head, so that I find a way to get Ty, dead or alive, and straighten out all of these wrong doings all over the world. I need an angel to guide me through the turmoil that I have and am about to encounter. *Please...please...please,*" she dreamily whispered to her Camille.

Camille replied, "You have no reason to worry for long. I am here for you, forever. Just have faith in me and your future will be bright... very bright. Mischief may be minimal, fortune may be fierce, and happiness may be abundant, but you must believe me, and hang on. Please dear, don't give up."

Camille's angelic insight inspired Cynthia to rise into a higher state of being, almost like in *Maslow's Hierarchy of Needs*. In these dreams, she now felt able to handle anything, in this *Self-Actualization* state that few humans ever reach.

Her insightful snooze was rudely interrupted by the sound of the clanging tonal ring of Ty's cell.

Cynthia lifted her body to reach the phone which was lying on the coffee table. She picked up the receiver and looked at the caller ID, which displayed "Theodore's cell". She excitedly greeted him.

"Hey Theo! It's Cynthia. Whereabouts are you two?"

The phone went dead.

It sounded once again.

This time when Cynthia answered, she simply said, "Hi."

Theodore, who was on the other end asked, "Is Ty around? I need to speak to him."

"I don't know where he is. I thought that maybe *you* would. He almost killed me, Theo. Is Susanna with you? When are you coming home? I have three people staying here. They say, we have had a big problem in our past, have it now in our present, and will have a world-wide epidemic in our future, if certain powers remain intact. I need your help and advice," she commanded him.

''Later," was all Theodore said, as he pushed the frigid button on his cell phone to end the call.

"Something's definitely wrong," Cynthia sounded out loud, as she visually searched the meticulous farm house, in hopes of finding an out of place clue, but nothing showed. She pulled up Theodore's cell and called it. No one answered, only the recording. She did it again, and the same response.

She laid back down on the sofa, but this time, she couldn't go to sleep. She had to meet with Camille. Cynthia hoped down deep inside her being that everything was going to be alright. She just didn't know how.

She watched a world news network until morning arose.

"Time to make coffee," she said to herself, as she scrambled six eggs she found in the fridge, and poured a box of corn flakes into four bowls that she spied in the cupboard. "It's time to awaken and 'roar'!" she screamed to her upstairs guests in her new, rather masculine-sounding, heavy-laden throat of intent, rather than with her otherwise, soft and mild and charmingly feminine vocal chords.

Camille's strong sense of purpose, as well as her deep voice, was definitely having an effect on Cynthia's being. The tired ballerina pulled out a chair and sat down in it to await the arrival of her waking guests.

Chapter Eight

The Czar

Upon arrival in Dalanzadgad, the largest airfield in the Gobi, and after two changes of planes, one in Frankfurt, the second in Budapest, both with long layovers, Theodore and Susanna were exhausted. They had extreme jet lag for the fairly short distance that was flown.

The couple was met by two Mongolians whose legs were covered in faded blue and holey jeans, with heavy long, black leather jackets covering dark, snug, turtleneck sweaters engulfing each of the two Mongolians' massive physiques. These physiques could not speak English well, so they used minimal words and phrases and a lot of sign language to get their messages across. They both suggested to the Irish couple, by pointing outside, that they were to get on one of the cycles parked by the terminal exit. The couple followed their orders to the hilt.

Theodore was given a map of the route that he was to take, and which happened to be located near the beginning of the old Silk Route, the renowned trading road of bygone centuries. He revved up the motor and looked to his back to make sure that Susanna was situated properly on the seat and that she was comfortable. Luckily, Theodore had been a "motor head" all of his life on the back roads of southern Ireland, so he knew how to drive, how to drive anything well, very well. Race cars, snow ploughs, trains, buses, tractor trailers, choppers-it didn't matter. Theo could drive anything like a professional, even on ice, even in Dalanzadgad. He was very confident, and Susanna felt secure knowing how competent her talented husband had been in the past, when attempting these feats.

The couple took off with the two Mongolians close behind. The map was given to Theodore, only as a precaution. The two Mongols were to be close...very close to the couple. Parting from them would prove to be a terrible inconvenience in tracking them, as there was no GPS system on the cycles, and there really didn't need to be one installed. They didn't need to accrue more cost to their mission. Besides, there were only so many roads that were able to be traveled on a day like today, so the Mongols were not too concerned.

The two hour ride through ice patches and blizzard conditions proved life-threatening, as Theodore skidded several times, nearly throwing the bike over on its side, as they were cruising at too high of a speed, as what was demanded by the leather-wearing Mongolians. Theo wasn't expecting such dangerous conditions. He was almost thrown for a loop, literally and physically.

The four cycle riders finally arrived at their destination of Ekhiingol, only one hour later than expected, and only because of a blizzard white-out that lasted for two miles. They had to stop and wait on the side of the thin two-lane road until conditions got better, so that they could at least find the path in front of them. The Mongols had to keep a watch over their "cargo" until their "cargo's" deed was done. Theodore and Susanna thought that perhaps a ride through the Southern Gobi Desert in February might be a little crisp, but still bearable. They were not expecting this.

When they arrived in the oasis town of Ekhiingol, the Irish were whipped with hunger and fatigue, not mentioning their frost-bitten state. The Mongols directed the two to a small inn. Here, the couple got off the cycle and proceeded to check-in after paying their respects to the Mongol boys.

"Hold up," the taller one authoritatively said, as he displayed a shiny pocket knife. "The first batch is with us, boy." He threw him a medium-sized bag of what appeared to be "dust", but Theo knew it was no "dust". He remembered the agreement that he had with Ty. They must deliver whatever was given to them, in order to bring Cynthia back. He caught the bag and stuffed it into his duffel, ready to proceed to the next stage, wherever he needed to go to get his sister-in-law back.

They both bid "adieu" to the two "leathered-up" boys and walked inside to ask for a room. The workers, both with slanted black eyes and very high cheek bones, said that there was one room already reserved for them, located down the hall. It had been prepaid. They quickly carried their bags to the small, clean, efficient, and best of all, warm room.

The couple went back out into the lobby to relax and catch even more warmth from the rustic, roaring fireplace, surrounded by sparse furniture and few windows, but plenty of vodka at the bar. This was how the people of the Gobi Desert survived these harsh winters, with vodka, bread, and huge fireplaces. Theodore ordered Susanna and himself straight ones with bread.

They sipped and ate at the bar, not saying a word to each other. Theo then pulled out his cell phone, brought up Ty's number and pushed to connect. Dumbfounded he was, when Cynthia answered Ty's phone. He hung up his end.

"I thought she was supposed to have been kidnapped," he crazily gestured to his tired wife. "She just answered Ty's phone. Someone is playing us for fools."

At that moment, the two Mongolians appeared from out of nowhere, came up to the bar and "suggested" that the couple get some rest.

"Tomorrow a car will be here at nine in the morning for a ride to our next destination, and please, don't be late!" the burly one of the two suggested, after yawning profusely. The couple staggered to their room, now for sure not saying one word to each other, as Theodore thought the room to be bugged.

The next morning the couple was up at six, ordered a light room service, checked out, and was met by three well-dressed Slovak gentlemen. The leader gave the couple airline tickets to Damascus, Syria, and said to them, "A limo is to pick you up in less than one hour. Make sure you have all your stuff, because you're going to the 'hotbed' to pick up a shipment for us, so don't be late. *Please*....don't be late," the healthier looking one of the three muttered, before he knelt down, down into the ground, seemingly of heart failure.

"No one is ever safe around here," the limo driver said to Theodore and Susanna, as they got in. They believed what he said. "I will transport you to a small Learjet air field close to town to board a small aircraft." Those were the last words he spoke. In ten minutes, they got out to board the plane.

Unknowing to the couple, this flight was supposed to be destined for Damascus, but now that Cynthia had been found alive, flight plans had changed. The couple was told they were now to be flown to Haifa, on the Northwest Coast of Israel, not too far from the Lebanese border. Haifa was beautiful, a serene paradise, with majestic mountains and sea coast abounding. It seemed to be one of the few places in the region where all religious sectors acted humanely with one another.

"What are we to do next, and why are we traveling to Haifa?" Susanna asked.

"I have an Israeli taxi driver to meet you dockside. He is going to pretend he has only met you to bring you up to the exotic garden area, but it is a lie, an intense lie. He wants to give you more ammunition for you to take to our American confidant."

The two boarded the small glider for Haifa. It was such a bumpy ride. The two never believed that they were going to make it to this beautiful Israeli city alive. They did however, descend and land, and were eventually met by three dignitaries, displaying suits, briefcases, and a fancy Mercedes Benz. They were asked to follow one of the Israeli officials, who led them into an awaiting limousine for the airport in Tel Aviv.

"First, however, we have a stop to make in the Baha'i gardens. We need to pick up exports from Luther," the official said. "He said that he would be waiting by the locked gate."

Luther was at the entrance when they drove up. The three discreetly and nonchalantly exchanged briefcases, as though nothing had occurred. The three Arabs, as Theodore and Susan soon came to believe, were impersonating three Israeli dignitaries, in order to get this shipment from Luther.

"Otherwise, why would the Baha'i have been part of this obvious arsenal and, or drug exchange?" they asked each other in barely audible groans, moans and whispers.

After a seemingly endless sun set, traveling through arid coastal regions, the entourage arrived in Tel Aviv, where they traveled to a landing jet in a field near the airport, then were escorted up a short staircase which led to the small, luxurious jet. They all hurriedly climbed on board the aircraft. The female attendant placed all briefcases underneath the seats, intermittently shoving them amongst seats that were vacant. The flight already had its passengers boarded in the ten rows of its passenger section and was ready to roll, as the engines blasted. This seemed to have made for the perfect getaway, as was suggested by the smiles and gestures given among each of the three, who were watching from the runway upon take off.

Things were evidently going as planned. The couple was now to bring all "cargo" into Syria for payment. Payment was expected at several locations, and at several times of the day. This way, nothing or no one could be tracked or traced. This was all that the bad boys wanted. After that, the two Irish countrymen would be disposed of by an ISIS terrorist, in one way or another...no questions asked.

The couple boarded the lavish and expensive forty seat Learjet, with drinking delicacies being offered to them at every turn. They ate a gourmet meal, drank a bottle of vintage wine, and then fell asleep on the plush leather seats of the airplane. When turbulence started to set in, both arose from their slumber.

"Fasten seat belts. The landing strip is approaching," the pilot informed the few passengers who were on board.

"Syria, here we finally come," was all that Susanna could interact before landing abruptly on a runway that was in great need of a new concrete job.

The other passengers, who included an elderly East Indian woman and her son, and a handsome turban-wearing, middle-aged gentleman, wearing a loose-fitting gray linen suit, all remained calm on impact. They appeared quite used to an event like this one. Obviously, they had all flown on these jets many times before, as immense wealth was wreaking from their pores.

Upon further detection, Susan became aware that these East Indians were from a higher cast, judging from the handsome facial dot and gem seen on the woman's face, as she had learned in high school. The Arab was of course, super rich, as jewels were abounding from his fingers, arms and neck, as he showed off graceful moves and bends with no modesty.

Once in a stationary position, the jet's door was opened and a staircase pulled up to the narrow opening to greet the passengers. All of the passengers proceeded very cautiously down its slick steps, as it was sprinkling rain on the runway. Stored briefcases were given to each of the ticket bearers.

The couple walked slowly to the inside of the airport, cleared customs and proceeded to baggage claim, as they had been advised to do. They waited for what seemed to be fifteen minutes.

Suddenly, an old man bumped into Theodore. Theo fell to the ground, when he lost his firm stance. The old gentleman apologized and handed him a note. It advised, "Give the briefcase to me, if you want to live."

Theodore handed the heavy, rather worn-out brown case to the older man, who now appeared to be an American FBI agent, perhaps with double agent credentials. Theo did not know who to trust anymore. Even his own brother he was becoming skeptical of. At his first convenience, he knew he must call Ty's cell number again to see if Cynthia answered, or was it only a game. He was baffled.

The older gentleman, who now spoke with a Midwest American accent, was advising the couple to stay put.

"A black limousine will soon be on its way to pick the two of you up, so we can transport you all the way to Istanbul, by way of Kusadasi, the Turkish Riviera port town.

There, you are to meet with two government officials from Turkey in the ancient town of Ephesus. They will do the exchanging, talk for a while over Turkish coffee, then say good-bye. I will be with you the whole time...no worries."

This never happened, however. Once in the vacation town of Kusadasi, their limo made a sharp right onto a narrow, hardly-paved road. This was the less traveled route which was to take tourists to the ancient city of Ephesus.

Upon arrival in the ancient Roman city, the supposed seventy year old gentleman, who was sitting quietly in the front seat, got out from the limo. He was quickly gunned down by two persons wearing black ski masks, and who had been awaiting the limousine's arrival in the bushes.

The limo driver put the car in reverse and shouted, "We are headed to Istanbul."

"Okay," was all that horrified Susanna could utter.

The couple was already super worn-out and didn't know what to expect minute by minute in this horrendous game of chance. As soon as the two were alone, Theo knew that he must make that call to Cynthia to see if they hadn't been played for fools, which he was now sure that they had been all along.

After stopping at a rug store to receive another package and drink a cup of apple tea, stressed-out Susanna and Theodore soon fell asleep, arm in arm while riding down the coast in the limo.

When the limo remained at a complete stop for five minutes, possibly more, the two awoke and asked the driver where they were.

He said, "Our last stop before we get to the city. One last shipment to contend with. Probably, the most important overall. You take this box," the driver demanded, handing it to Theo, "to that house on the hill. Ring the bell. When he answers, give him the package. Come back to the limo as fast as you can. You will be at the home of one of the czars of the world. This ruler must be stopped, by bomb, knife or bullet. It is up to you to decide whenever you get to the door. This is the most important piece of the puzzle, deciding how this imbecile will die, slowly and painfully, or quickly and methodically. The only thing is, you will be carrying the bomb that we detonate. Oh, and by the way, he's American," the driver laughed, as he gave him a gun and a butcher knife.

Susanna waited in the limo, while Theodore walked up many flights of stairs before reaching the elaborate front door which was hand carved in ivory and mahogany. Theodore knocked at the door. No answer, so he rang the doorbell.

Finally, a long-haired gentleman opened the door, angrily, and told Theo to "get inside", which he obligingly did.

He was escorted to a huge carpeted glass atrium, where files upon files were being stored, and disc upon disc were being warehoused, for some reason, or reasons. He could "smell money reeking" from the meeting room which was laden with elaborate Turkish carpeting.

Nobody here had any decency, principles, or morals. The more power one had, sufficiently enabled him to succeed in whatever he had desire to spend time manipulating. This seemed to Theo to be a rather boring, but current practice in twenty-first century life. This was why Theodore was so pleased that he had always had the "simple life". Nothing could ever take the memories of this peaceful life away from him now. "What was he to do?" he panicked, as he waited for conversation, still holding the mystery box.

"Was this scenario real, or simply an outright lie, designed to engage him in the plot, while disengaging him from the world-wide leaders who plan on reducing the number of inhabitants on the planet, by means of genocide, poisoning, and inoculation?" he wondered. "It is a well-thought out, highly-strategic plan, involving numerous people, famous and not, designed to see this plan come to fruition," he thought to himself, as he began to feel terribly weak. His balance was failing him. Theo threw the box over to the corner of the room. It only produced a small "bang".

Theo was thrown down the hill by a black-hooded terrorist who proceeded to behead the czar.

Ty "Silky" Riley was traveling with Sunny and her influential Middle-Eastern long haired and bearded brother along the ancient Silk Route, picking up cash, ammunition, and drugs that were exchanged by Theodore and Susanna, for others of the same type. This was how the wealthy terrorist-smuggler kept his game alive, with no one ever knowing anything about him, never where he is, nor where he came from, nor who he really is. A terrorist keeps all of his plans and his "pledge" for destruction abroad to himself for a while, then "POW", he unleashes his secrets on the Western world.

Sunny and her brother, Med-hi, retrieved Ty at the sidewalk by baggage claim at the Alexandria, Egypt International airport. There happened to be a lot of commotion that morning, with many important looking shiny black cars and sedans which were obviously waiting for royal dignitaries and International Embassy officials. Med-hi informed Ty and his sister that there was an important meeting scheduled in one of the banquet rooms, located in the hotel beside the Royal Palace estate. There was business like this conducted on a regular basis in the city, since Alexandria served as the second capital of Egypt, Cairo being the first.

Most of Alexandria was a gorgeous, moneyed, Mediterranean city, with magnificent views abounding from every angle. Parks were filled with pedestrians, Muslim-attired women, jean and sweatshirt wearing Catholic women, who lacked a veil, and of course, gads of men dressed in Islamic fashion, even some displaying no particular religious belief.

On the other side of town, the impoverished side, was where the other half lived, with virtually no utilities and run-down, insect-ridden small accommodations. Trash was piled high on either side of most streets, piling up over the part cement and part dirt sidewalks where the children happily played, not knowing there were better forms of living that were found in the world, even in their own city.

These people had no means of transportation, except for a very dirty bus that came into the poor neighborhoods of this section of the city, only a few times each day.

Two young men sat on a rotted bench on a side street in this section of town. They were dressed very shabbily and asked everyone who walked past for coins. They appeared very poor, poorer than most of the people who lived in the district. Some non-district dwellers flipped a coin or two into the men's hands, only as a good gesture. Others cursed the two men and glared at them.

When the three left the airport grounds, they headed for the wealthy district. Their first stop was at the hotel were the oil barons were staying, so that they could check in for the night. This was the only way that they could even enter this prestigious hotel. Room keys, familiar faces, money and power had to be shown to the hotel door staff, of which all three possessed. Med-hi left the hotel saying that they would return very soon, before the meeting began. They all scurried to their waiting car, because they had to get back before the other oil barons sat down at the conference table.

"Now, this business has to be done first," Med-hi stressed.

Med-hi put his car in first gear, floored the accelerator and charged through the sleepy streets of Alexandria's corrupt residential community. Proceeding along *there*, he knew all of the police and knew he would never be stopped for speeding.

After about fifteen minutes, the area started to change drastically. Ty had never seen living conditions like this, not even when he was a tot, living in rural Ireland, before his family acquired wealth and status. It was a dirty and degrading existence here. He actually felt compassion for the people who lived here, but would never let that emotion show on his rugged and confident face. Med-hi sped up to the front of the shop where two young men were sitting on the curb collecting money from stool pigeons. With his tight-steering column, he spun his silver Jaguar into a 360 degree turn in a split second. No one saw or acted as if he had seen a thing.

"Mum is the word," Med-hi would always say when handling these transactions in this part of the globe.

The two men got up from the stained curb and hobbled over to the Jaguar with hands extended, waiting for coins to be placed in each of their hands. Several coins were placed in both of their hands, along with paper money. The young beggars put their hands into the pockets of their worn-out jeans and discreetly pulled out bags, filling up each of the men's hands.

After this exchange, another coin was given to the right hand of each beggar, which was placed again in the pockets of each. When both men's hands came out of their respective pockets, the hands contained microscopic, pin-like devices, which laid alongside four very small detonator-looking devices. Everything was packaged in tiny plastic bags, like the type they used in their hashish sales. The young men began walking to their rooms, located in the better part of the still impoverished zone. The two had their cash and knew they could survive yet another month, or two. This was how the two young men had survived adequately for so long.

Being intellects in science and electronics, they started making all types of deadly devilment when they were teens, thus becoming fast and furious friends. They knew that manufacturing these chemical concoctions was the only way out of their hell hole and into glorious, rich freedom.

The young men knew that they were holding the key, having plenty of both mechanical and electronic knowledge and devices that few held. They were ready to excel.

"It is finally going to happen Ty, my boy," Med-hi interjected, after the transaction was done.

Chapter Nine

The Miscarriage

*O**nce** back in the sedan, Ty felt the bulge in his side trouser pocket where he had always placed his cell phone, which was his life. It had all of his contacts' information and dates, times, and places for secret meetings. He always felt safe when he put his hand on that bulge. He reached into his loose-fitting pants pocket, wrapped his medium-sized hand around the medium-sized rectangular object. He pulled it out and gasped in a panic-stricken manner. He was holding in his palm, not his cellphone, but instead, the thin dark green remote control for his small black and white television in the basement of the pub. This television was turned on during IRA meetings, so that no one could hear the goings on downstairs with the sound-proofing that was added to the back of the door which led up to the bar. Ty patted down his entire being, trying to find the lost phone, but nothing. He climbed out of the parked car, screamed to Med-hi to unlatch the trunk and searched his small bag of luggage.

With clothes and other personal items strewn across the once immaculate trunk, Ty shut it and held his head in his hands and yelled,

"Dammit! How could I have left it? Med-hi, give me your phone. I have to make a call."

"To whom? Wow, you really are an unorganized son-of-a-bitch, aren't you?" the French Moroccan calmly stated.

"To whomever answers my phone. Hopefully, it will be Ron at the pub, where I left it. Dial my number for me, fast," Ty dictated to Med-hi. Med-hi did as instructed by his cohort and handed him his cell.

Back near Cobh in the farmhouse, the trio was getting ready for their day of waiting and wondering. Cynthia's father was flying into Shannon later on, so they would have to drive a fairly long way to pick him up at the airport. After that, Nikko suggested they have dinner at her mansion and search for clues that may be lurking around.

Cynthia agreed and decided to surprise the staff and "pop-in" on them. She told the three that Ty's driver took her to the pub, fed her drinks, which she was sure were drugged, carried and raped her downstairs. He was responsible for her being locked in the basement for two days. She told the three that Ty was not at all happy, when she revealed to him the news that she was probably not going to ever conceive, perhaps because of her age and frailty. The doctor did not know why for certain, but advised her that since she had not gotten pregnant as of yet, she probably shouldn't count on children. *Cynthia did not realize yet that she was now pregnant, not with a boy, but with twin girls, and not by Ty.*

"Well, he became like a maniac, totally changed his demeanor, then did this to me," she said.

"I know now. He will pay for his deceitfulness. I was good to him, too good." *Camille smiled to herself.* "Nikko, you take my phone, and you answer all calls. I think it's safer that way. I don't want anyone to know anything about me now, or that I am even still alive. You see, not being able to have a boy, I am no longer useful to his plan. I see the whole morbid plot now. I just want to leave them guessing," Cynthia dictated, then she daintily picked up the cell from the coffee table and threw it to Nikko. She wiped her hands clean of it. Just then, the cell played an Irish chant, which Ty used as one of his songs when signifying the caller's importance. It was one of his important rings.

Nikko answered with a deep throated Spanish accent, "Hallo!" Then, he questioned the caller intimidatingly, "Who IS this?"
Ty didn't even flinch.

"Hey, is Ron around? This is the new cook, right?" Ty asked in a rather demeaning manner to the other voice coming out of the receiver. Nikko hung up.
Ty called back without hesitation.

"Hey, don't you ever hang up on me. Do you know who I am? I am your paycheck."

Nikko hung up again.

Ty kept on ringing and ringing until finally the ringing stopped. Feeling very worn out and tired, Ty finally got the presence of mind to call the establishment directly to see who indeed would answer. He rang and rang, and nobody answered there, either.
"This shits bricks. What is going on?" he frantically asked himself. "My cell rang. I don't know who answered."
Irritated, Med-hi rolled down his window and yelled, "Get in the car. We've got places to go, men to meet, and exchanges to make."

Ty fell into the back seat of the car where two brutal blows struck his head from behind. He never even saw them coming. Ty was slipping.

First off, leaving his phone, his "bible" in his hostage's quarters, then letting himself get pummeled by Med-hi's thugs from behind.

Ty always preached to all of his people, "Never let your guard down for nobody. Always be aware and don't let your anger get the best of you, not ever."

The terrorist organizational head who was working with the Irish Mafia, aka the IRA, was now getting tired of Ty's forgetfulness. It could provide for ruination of their plan. Med-hi started the sedan and drove to the port where a small cargo vessel was waiting to take them to Istanbul. There could be no more risks. Means of transportation had to be changed on a constant basis now, knowing that all pertinent information was located inside that phone, and if the wrong person got hold of it, Med-hi's quest for world-wide domination would be denied. He knew that he had to force Ty to call his cellular company to get all areas where calls had been recently placed from and received from, before doing anything else. He also had to stop Cynthia and her Ambassador father from progressing any farther.

It was late afternoon back at the ranch house near Cobh, and Cynthia was ready to move. She couldn't wait to see her father again. It had been nearly eight years, since she married Ty. Her father never approved of Ty, thought he was a ruffian and didn't particularly treat his daughter as well as he would have liked her to be treated. It was because of this that Cynthia knew she was going to hear it from her father. She was ready for what was to come, the truth about the flaws in her character, of which she had many.

"*You are just too ideal and trusting*," Camille consoled her, as she quickly straightened up the house. Cynthia knew Camille was over her. She always felt secure and whole whenever Camille was around.

Jude and Kimmie grabbed their purses and summoned their new friend, Nikko to come downstairs, away from the computer, from which he had been investigating many facets of Irish gangs, the IRA, and the Russian and Italian Mafias.

The web also provided the names of several terrorist organizations that worked alongside this corruption.

"Alright, I'll be down in a minute. Just let me comb my hair," he pleaded, as his black locks had become super frizzy and curly, because of the constant dampness outside.

"I will have my staff prepare a huge array of 'quick to fix' foods, once we surprise them," she advised. "What kind of wine do you prefer for starters with cheese?" she asked the girls, while waiting on Nikko, who in her estimation, was taking longer to prepare himself for the world than any woman she had ever known.

Cynthia had to sit down. She suddenly felt faint.

Nikko came running down the stairs at that moment, two steps at a time. Out of breath from non-exercise, he vehemently said, and demonstratively motioned, "Come on, or the plane will be there before we are."

The three girls just looked at each other with their jaws on the ground. The four sauntered out and climbed into the Toyota that Nikko had rented at the airport for three days. He realized now, it might have to be for longer.

Over the rolling green hills of the immaculate Irish countryside, the Toyota turned onto a small seaside road that led to the airport, near the mansion on the coast. The waves were whipping the coast and the birds were singing and fluttering around the nebulous cloud formations in the sky. Cynthia couldn't believe that she was finally going to see her father after almost eight years, in just a few minutes.

After the bumpy coastal ride over semi-rough terrain, the four arrived at a side entrance of Shannon International Airport. They had to wait for the Ambassador in the lobby, because of world-wide airport security measures. Cynthia informed the others that the exact time of supposed touch-down was 4:46 pm. The group waited until five, thinking that he should be there at any moment, then when it was 5:30 and still no sight of him, even though the plane had disembarked at 4:50, they knew something smelled rancid. Cynthia forced her way through the line of ticketed passengers and went up to the unoccupied first-class counter. There, she informed the agent of the situation with the utmost urgency. The agent said that there was no record of him ever being on the flight, or reserving it in advance.

"I know he didn't reserve it. He just decided to come over yesterday. He must have been a walk-up. There is no record of the United States Government sending one of their officials to Europe?" she questioned nervously.

"No, not a thing," the ticket agent replied after searching her screen.

Cynthia ran back to the others with tears in her eyes and told them, "He never even bought a ticket for the flight. Something must have happened to him." She fell to the tiled floor. An ambulance rescued her and took her to emergency, where they found out she was pregnant. They did an ultrasound. She was to have twin girls. *Robert's "magical genes" had not paid off for Ty this time, Camille concluded to herself.*

In a National Airport janitorial closet, the Ambassador awoke. The intense aroma of cleaning potions jogged his memory. He had been tasered on his back in an airport lobby restroom urinal. He never even had a chance to purchase a ticket. His body was dragged into a janitorial closet by one of the supposed night crew janitorial staff and left there, deprived of food and water for hours.

He knew he now had to gather up strength to holler for help, or simply rise and start walking to safety. He pulled himself up to a vertical position, looked for his phone and wallet, which had both vanished, and began to calculate what he was going to do now. He called his office for cell phone records of all incoming calls for the last two days. He knew he would get her number.

After about an hour of sitting and gathering up strength, his assistant phoned the pay phone he was kneeling in front of to give him the only Irish incoming number. He had it! He phoned. The operator message stated that the number had been disconnected, and to please check the listing again.

"It's over," he surrendered to the powers that be.

The Ambassador headed to his home in Alexandria to freshen up before going back to the Embassy. He could not let anybody know what was going on.

After secretly leaving the hospital by taxi to go the airport to get their car, Nik revived Cynthia by quickly pouring a shot of brandy down her throat, which he always had on him now. She began to unwind slowly, drinking another shot of Nikko's brandy.

Suddenly, her eyes got huge and she jumped up from the chair, searching for her cell phone. When she found it in her purse, she hysterically interjected, "I have to call dad."

After she hit one of the recall numbers to connect, a tonal melody sounded with a computerized voice stating, "This line has been disconnected. For more information, please call 611."

"They disconnected Ty's service. Damn it! Well, I guess I'll call my dad at the Embassy when we get to the mansion, while dinner is cooking. Let's hurry," Cynthia suggested, having an unknown sense of confidence, *all due to Camille.*

They went to the car parked in the short-term parking lot, paid the fee, and Nikko sped along the beach route straight to the mansion, of course with the help of Cynthia's great navigational skills. She really was such a wise woman, and with such common sense. Ty had called her "boring" on several occasions. Everyone in the vehicle wondered how Cynthia could have fallen prey to a devil like him. Nikko thought it the right time to disclose the truth to Cynthia.

"When you fainted, the hospital found out that you were pregnant, and with twin girls." Cynthia couldn't even speak....Bu...ho...how? She then knew that even with all of this turmoil and chaos, everything was going to be alright. She just didn't know how.

Camille whispered in the ballerina's ear, "*Just hold tight, my pretty one. Everything's going to be alright.*"
Cynthia became calm immediately, upon driving into her now-haunted house. She felt different about the place now. It was not the charming small palace that it once was, and that came with an honest, hard-working husband, who turned out to be a complete turncoat. Nikko pulled into one of the three spots, which undeniably had had no other cars parked there recently, as it was completely oil free.

Robert, the chauffeur, and Ty's "right-hand man", came racing out of the house, screaming, "Who are you, and why are you here? You are not permitted on this private property."

"Oh, but I am, my dear Rob," Cynthia interjected.

"How, I mean...Why are you here?" Rob asked.

"We have a problem, Robert. Do you remember that night when you fetched me a Bailey's and coffee, and I passed out? Well, it was drugged, and I remember being raped when I was put down in the basement of the pub by you, and tied up, simply left to die…until I got an idea, a great idea. You can never pull anything over on me."

Just then, she began to feel a little light-headed, and she took a seat.

"Well, I know nothing of what you speak. I have been here with the staff for one full day waiting for Mr. Riley. Do you happen to know where the master is, my lady?" the chauffeur condescendingly asked his "mistress".

"I have no idea. Where are the servants?" she asked him, wearily.

"Brittany, Jezebel, come out," he said. "The mistress wants you. It is time for dinner."

Med-hi had arranged for one of the secret agents from the Iraqi Embassy to drug the Ambassador into unconsciousness, so that he could not proceed to Ireland to visit his daughter.

"No chance is a good chance," he told the agent at the Embassy. "We need more time. Take him out for now," was all he advised, after taking back Ty's borrowed cell phone. Ty was still knocked out. The plan was now in effect and would stay that way. The secret agent was the Ambassador's assistant. Until now, he had been a stellar employee doing more than expected, with longer hours, and not asking for more salary. Maybe this should have drawn a red flag, but it did not. It was not supposed to, in the cover-up.

Med-hi had a huge ego. He wanted everything that Ty had and more, much more, and he was determined to achieve these goals. He was just that sort of a person. He had no feelings for sorrowful situations and no guilt tendencies. He admired himself from top to bottom, so he was ripe for the asking, the perfect egomaniac.

The table was being set for Cynthia and her four guests, whom everyone idled in curiosity.

"I have missed this place so much while on my trip," Cynthia said, lying to her servants, not telling them anything. "I appreciate this being made for my guests and me on such short notice. You are a marvelous crew and always have been," she acknowledged them wholeheartedly, while putting down her teaspoon after hot, strong Colombian coffee was served.

The meal was of a light fare, soup, chicken salad croissants, and lemon ice box pie. Coffee was served with the last plate, and it was scrumptious.

After their last sip, three rough males barged through the front door, as if looking for someone. The tallest said, "Soory for the intrusion. It's just our Russian blood and need for Borscht.

Do you have some, or at least some of Ty?" directing his question to Nikko. Where is the man now? He is your hubby still, ain't he, sweet stuff?" he was now directing his attention onto the still beautiful face and body of the aging ballerina.

"Who are you? Why are you here?" she asked the intruders, as the heaviest of the three grabbed her from behind and held her in a head lock.

Jude, Kimmie and Nicholas tried to run, but were blocked at the front door and side door by the mobsters. They were taken downstairs into the large, but drab and cold basement. Cynthia was thrown down the stairs with the rest of the victims and left unconscious. The others passed out.

When Nikko awoke, he paid strict attention to make sure they were still alive and continuing to breathe. It appeared to all three conscious victims that they were now trapped in the locked-room, with no solution, or exit in sight.

The now clever Nikko rationalized, with head in hands, pounding his skull to come up with a plan. He was never going to let these brutes take out Jude and Kimmie, and especially not Cynthia, the woman whom he was becoming so enamored with. He wasn't used to this feeling, a feeling of utter contentment, every time she was around him. She was all that he could think of now, and he was utterly worried about her being in this horrible unconscious state, with no medication, and the beginning stages of ugly black and blue bruising across her forehead and right eye....but most importantly, a baby in her womb. *The Russians were more than pleased.*

"Cynthia, dear, sweet Cynthia....please, please awake," Nikko whispered into her cold ear.

Her eyes never opened, never even fluttered. He felt her pulse. It was mildly beating, with worrisome tendencies, but she was still alive. Nikko glanced over to the corner of the room and noticed an antiquated sink, with copper handles from bygone days. He motioned to Kimmie who stared at the wall in front of her, sitting cross-legged. He suggested that she find *something* here in the dark to fill with water from perhaps the sink in the corner. Kimmie got up peculiarly, as if in a trance, and found an almost demolished plastic cup on the other side of the dingy floor, picked it up, and walked to where Nikko was pointing.

It was so dark that she could hardly find her way. Once over there, the moon shone brightly that she was able to now find a long, skinny, red candle in an ornate, brass holder with a sturdy handle. This holder was alongside a large box of big, thick matches. The now intense moonlight shining right into her deflective brown eyes, enabled her to snap out of her trance-like sense of being and into reality. She quickly struck the wood match on the box and lit the long candle. Kimmie shrieked into the darkness. Her ornate holder with lit candle dropped out of her hand and onto the damp cement floor, as she stood, look-ing at Jude, who was strung up on the side of the wall looking like a puppet, with a child's jump rope wrapped around her scrawny neck. The rope was attached to one nail in the ceiling. Her feet were gently gliding in the cool wind, which had been entering through one of the slightly opened windows that had not been tightened by its crank. She dropped the candle on the cement floor and ran over to Nikko in desperation.

Aghast, when he saw this display, he swiftly untied his faithful new friend, hoping to save her, but when he did, Jude fell like a ton of bricks, non-responsive.

"How and when could this have happened? It was too quick, just too quick," Kimmie sobbed, as she returned to her former state of disbelief.

"I think that they drugged us. We don't know how long we have actually been down here honey," Nikko gently rubbed her shoulders. "They are maniacs and should be annihilated."

At that moment, Cynthia fluttered her eyelids and wiggled her nose. She awakened and felt inside her side pocket where she usually placed Ty's phone, but now she felt a dull pain. She felt a prickle on the tip and sides of her fore and middle fingers. She pulled out the rather sharp object, or objects, she didn't know which yet, and she found a pine cone stuck to her hand. The phone was no longer there... and neither were her twins. She held her stomach and screamed.

Chapter Ten

The Setup

As Theodore and Susanna left their transportation to wait in the first airport security line at the Istanbul Airport, the two terrorists removed the microscopic detonators, ammunition, and drug assortments which had been all attached to the inside of the couples' boots. Before they entered the airport lobby, they first had to clear an immediate batch of sensors, then clear security again after checking in at the counter, and finally, again at the gate. They whispered to each other, "Nice security."

Theo said, "I wish we had it like this in Ireland."

"I know Theodore," was all that Susanna could say, before the guard motioned Theodore to proceed through security.

"Take everything out of all your pockets, and leave your bags here," the Turkish official advised, while pointing to a black conveyor belt on the right hand side.

"Certainly," Theodore blurted out in jest, as he pounded the large suitcases on the belt, thinking he was now finally safe, out of harm's way.

"How can I get a message to someone in charge?" he asked. "I have to be cautious though, very cautious," he thought.

Upon feeling the inside of Theo's left worn-out leather boot, which he had been forced to remove, the official started screwing up his face in disbelief. He motioned and spoke in Turkish to another official at the other conveyor belt on the right-hand side of security, motioning him to come over in a very hurried manner. As soon as the second official arrived, he too squatted on the ground and felt the inside of the boot, squinting his eyes, as in a severely concentrating manner. He was feeling the heel of the boot.

"Hey, chaps. What's going on here? I have nothing, only sweaty feet inside these boots," Theodore blurted out in an angry, blustery fashion.

The second security guard who wore a navy coat on top of his neatly pressed silver uniform attire, pulled out his worn-looking cell and called an unknown source. Now, holding his hand out, he let Theodore know who was in charge, and for him not to take one step farther.

His unknown source had evidently been the police, who arrived as fast as lightening. They brought Theodore to the side of the security offices and hand-cuffed him.

"What did I do? What did you find on me? I have nothing illegal, now," Theo told authorities.

The most forceful of the four officers repeated his last word in question form, "Now? What does that mean, *now*? It means that you once had contraband and reinforcements on your body, did you not? But NOW you do not? So what does that mean? What is this all about? What are you planning on doing with these?" he slyly smiled, as he slowly pulled out security's monumental findings.

The ugly, huge and twisted nosed thug of the terrorist who drove Theodore and Susanna to the Istanbul Airport was now far from sight, as they walked Theodore from the meeting room to the ticket lobby. Theodore was still within the terrorist's perfect vision, however. The thug looked more evil than the devil himself and seemed to be angrier than a raging rodeo bull.

When Theodore's eyes finally met the bull's square on, this terrorist displayed the cutting of his own throat, using his own forefinger.

"Sick, sick people," Theo muttered.

The "officials" proceeded to escort the cuffed and now very miffed and bewildered Theo through the lobby to divert the "real" security's attention.

The terrorist "thug" was sitting in the far lobby, watching and waiting to make his bold move. He had already been cleared through the first security check point, with microscopic weaponry adhered with epoxy to his wide brim and opium attached in the same manner to the inner lining of his porous white turban. He continued waiting until Theodore had exited the airport before then clearing the second security check point. This was supposed to be a less enforced stop than the first one. He would then proceed down the hall to his departure gate. He was aware that terminal gates were to have the least surveillance of all three check points.

"I AM finally going to rule this world, as Allah intended for me to do," Med-hi thought to himself, smirking all the while, as he calmly walked down the corridor, toward the second "danger" point.

He walked straight through, taking off his slip on soles and laying down his small case on the belt beside him. Everything looked clean in the pictures. Nothing shown on the film through his thick turban fabric lining. His gate was only a few yards up on the left.

Again, he quickly walked through the sensor machine, after plopping down his small black bag for viewing.

"*Tout est bon,*" Med-hi quietly uttered in his native tongue to a fair skinned German blond flight attendant who had been nudging him, trying to make her way through the line behind him, as if she was in an extreme hurry. She arrogantly grinned back at him, pursing her brightly colored pink lips, which displayed the perfect contrasting tone to her spiffy peacock blue jacket, garnished with small white buttons, and her mid-length matching skirt. She possessed slender, toned legs that carried her medium-heeled pumps fashionably.

"You are quite a well-groomed specimen," he replied back to her arrogance with dominance. She batted her eyelids in a subservient manner.

"She is now under my control," he assessed the situation with strategy.

Med-hi was a French-Moroccan born in Marrakesh who became an Egyptian strategist, having worked as Captain on a Mediterranean cargo vessel, moving at a snail's pace through the Suez Canal on many occasions. He made friends, as well as underhanded deals, in order to get him the money and power that his ego and lifestyle needed.

"I have to have these things so that I can have the world all to myself," he wrote in his diary that he kept in a securely buttoned fold in his bag. He wrote in it every day, not giving any information as to what he planned to execute and where, but scribbling plenty of tributes to himself. He worshiped and treasured himself, only himself....his sister...and Allah.

Once inside "Airport Police Headquarters", Theodore was read all of his "Turkish" rights. "I have the right to call my Irish attorney in Dublin, don't I?" he asked the officials nervously. He was flatly denied by each of them.

"Not when you are caught in Turkey, sir. You are our slave now," the heavier one of the six militia screamed and proceeded to ask him about the American Czar.

He slapped Theo's face from cheek to cheek several times, trying to get him to divulge information. Theodore never did. He just stared at the blank wall which was directly in front of him. This lasted for almost four hours, until he could take it no longer. He broke down and gave the Turks a summary of what he was asked to do by his brother, in order to get his sister-in-law out of harm's way, and everything that he had done.

"The reason that I said I don't have anything on me now is that they were supposed to confiscate it all from me to use for their own ambitions and fortunes. I guess they forgot some of it. I don't care. I just want my wife back. Where is she?" he irritatingly asked.

He was now beginning to realize what his future fate was to be and the game that was being played on him and Susanna, and probably Cynthia and her father as well, judging by the prior phone call.

"My brother, Ty, is obviously in with the bad guys for profit and world domination. Is there any way you could you please ring a special number for me in Ireland, so that I may prove our innocence? It's my sister-in-law's, really her husband's, my brother's, cell phone. My brother held his own wife as a prisoner in the basement of his pub. He told me she had been kidnapped by terrorists and taken along the Silk Road to the Gobi Desert. She had indeed been kidnapped, but held only in Ireland, never in Asia, like we were told. We were forced to go there, however, held against our will, and forced to haul whatever those demons wanted us to bring into the selected countries for them. They were using us for this purpose. We were led on a wild goose chase, one that almost killed us with intense weather. Ty's phone had been left behind by him, inadvertently, inside the basement of his pub, which was used as the indiscreet headquarters for the Irish Mafia.

When Cynthia finally escaped, she took Ty's cell with her and called me. However, there was interference on the line, or a low signal, and or charge, and we got disconnected.

Yesterday, when I tried to phone her again at Ty's number, the same number she had called me from, I got a recorded message saying the number was no longer in service. Could you please, please try to call again? I beg of you. I have the number stored as the last call received in my phone. It's in my jacket's right pocket. Can you get it out for me?" he asked, pointing to one of his leather jacket pockets.

The silent officer who sat across from him simply gazed attentively into Theo's light green eyes, making no movement or verbal interaction.

Finally, one of the other Turkish officers who sat by the door, stood up and retrieved the phone from his pocket. He pushed the number of the last received call and got the same recording that Theo got earlier. He threw the cell down on the concrete floor. They all watched the phone shatter into millions of pieces, millions of pieces of important information that could never again be used to prevent the ensuing annihilation of the planet. Theodore now knew this was being orchestrated. There was no one on his side. No one would believe him. Ty had made sure of this. Theodore felt like such a fool. At that moment, Susanna was brought in without handcuffs to be questioned as well.

"Say goodbye to each other, give each other a hug and a kiss. This will be the last time you ever see each other again," the officer who had been silent the entire time finally dared to utter these commanding phrases of sentiment. Susanna kissed Theodore on the lips one last time, as they dragged her crying body into another room to be sentenced by their make shift courtroom.

After a five minute hearing, she was given a life sentence in solitary confinement. When they finally got Theo into the court, it took the powers that be all of one minute to sentence him to death. The officials could perform the action right in their "precinct", where body bags were stashed and plenty of ropes, guns, and knives were hidden in drawers and wall safes, along with all of their other inhumane devices that were designed for intimidation. The most forceful of the six patrol got out a stiletto from his desk drawer and placed it on its sharp edge. He aimed it straight at Theodore's pale throat.

He maniacally told Theo, "Ty just wanted you two held in prison forever, but Med-hi now wants you dead, and Med-hi is MY Allah. I do EVERYTHING he says. Susanna is a woman. Yes, yes, and a very nice looking woman at that. It doesn't suit Med-hi to have her removed right now. No, he has other plans for her, very sexy, sexy plans for her in her solitary confinement cell, where he is the only one with the key."

With the knife still at his throat, Theodore yelled, "You are not real, not real police, not real courts, *not real anythings*. It's all a set up. It has all been one bleeding setup."

"And you just now figured it out? The real police and security officials were knocked out.

They're inside my cargo van in back. And these so-called ammo's and drugs are…." he crushed the ammunition pieces under his thumb and forefinger. They turned to dust. "nothing…fakes…

And the drugs…well, watch me now," the terrorist demanded, as he took one of the opium pills that Theodore had transported into one of the respective countries and threw it with placebo vengeance down his knotted throat. "You see, nothing. It's a placebo given to us by one of our medical friends at the university. We got the goods we needed. And you killed our main target, you know the American Czar who lived on the side of the hill. You really made him squirm in misery when you *slashed* him. One of our men *saw* the whole thing. He said you were *terrorist* material," the actual terrorist laughed.

"Wait," Theo yelled. *"I didn't do anything..."*

"Did you really think that we were even going to leave one piece of ammo or drug on your person that will help contribute to the funds that Med-hi needs to rule the planet? He will now make the perfect human race, presiding over all. We will succumb to his every need and his every whim. He is the second Allah, and this Allah wants your wife alive, *and you dead*," the enemy chanted, as if in a mosque.

"Why, you...," Theodore softly said, as he couldn't talk that well, because the sharp knife was being thrust closer and closer to his throat. All he could do was angrily spit at the so-called official, which he did with force.

The fearless young terrorist asked, "You really do want to die, don't you?" and he slashed Theo's throat.

The Turk got out a body bag, stuffed the body inside, wrapped it up and shoved it into a parcel post canvas bag. Next, he tied it up, cleaned the room, and himself, and left the premises, down the dark, back hallway into the awaiting armored cargo van. The authentic police and security officials were still drugged, so they were easily thrown out into a field by the parking lot. The van drove nonchalantly away.

Miles away in the Turkish hills, near the Bulgarian border, Susanna was taken to an underground jail cell in one of Med-hi's many country estates. This one he had always used for women. He used women as sporadic slaves, one batch at a time, until he got tired of them. Then, after several months of loneliness, he would have his dominions gather a new batch, until he became bored again. He had constructed an elaborate gold-plated tunnel which led from Med-hi's enormous bedroom into a red satin-walled room that possessed a large water bed with statues on either side and all sorts of orgasmic devices electronically attached to the bed and placed on top of the foot board. There was a movie-sized screen with a DVD player and a movie rack of triple X-rated flicks. She had never before seen such a horrid and immoral sight. Susanna was to become only a sexual entity now.

She knew that she would soon lose her mind, maybe even in a matter of weeks, being in isolation with Med-hi as her only companion and with sex being her only activity. She had never really adored sex and wondered how she would ever handle this predicament without going insane. "Would she fall in love with him eventually," she wondered, as she had read of these things happening when the enemy is one's only contact.

"I can't stand this. What a dreadful existence!" she screamed. "Where is Theodore?" She was given a glass of water and a sedative to help calm her nerves.

"This will help you sleep," the nicer of her two escorts assured her.

Med-hi had heard the scream and soon came running through the tunnel to the elaborate bedroom.

"Your husband is dead, and now you are mine," he brutally pinched her, as he held her forcefully in his strong and dark muscular arms.

As she stared at him, not believing what he had just told her, she began to feel woozy and faint. She then knew who he reminded her of. He looked like *Rudolph Valentino*.

At this revelation, she fell to the bed. He raped her, then told his boys to continue administering drugs to Susanna on a daily basis.

"I won't get tired of this one for a long while," he told himself, as he fixed himself a scotch on the rocks.

Chapter Eleven

The Investigation

After phoning his turncoat assistant at the Embassy to tell of the terror situation at hand and of his dilemma in the airport, he emailed the top Iraqi officials in Washington and Baghdad and the CIA and FBI to urge them to start investigations into dominant terrorist organizations. He also reprimanded them strongly for not bringing any concerns to his attention, if there had been any indication, which he felt for sure there had been. He advised them of the current situation with his daughter and the Irish Mafia, aka the IRA.

They sent him back an immediate email which advised him to remain at his assistant's abode in Georgetown, leaving his car behind. An agent would pick him up in a brown four door 1970's Ford in two hours, take him to a rental car office in Arlington, drop him off there, then continue on.

The Ambassador was to wear black glasses, a ski hat and a ski vest with very baggy sweat pants and tennis shoes. He was to be given a driver's license by the FBI which displayed a nonexistent street address. The Ambassador was forced to be incognito.

"No restaurants, no clubs, and no correspondence with anybody, not even friends of your daughter," was how the slim balding FBI agent instructed him to live. "At least for a while, everything has to be private," he insisted, when he called the Ambassador back a few moments later on his land line. "We will save the world, day by day, piece by piece, if you continue to help us with the situation, sir".

"I will be obliged to do anything and everything you say in order to find my daughter and get her back to safety and away from that maniacal murderer, her husband, Tyrone Riley. Please get that son of a bitch for me...and our country."

"We will sir. We're leaving tomorrow morning for Shannon, then Belfast. In these two towns, as well as the others in between, we should get to know more about Ty, his cohorts, and his operation... will let you know by an untraceable cell phone left in your aide's home, in his desk hear two rings, then nothing, then two rings again, then nothing, answer on the next ring. It is us with information," the clever assistant stated. He seemed to be the more aged of the agents, with much knowledge and expertise under his belt. "The airlines will be the only entity who knows who you are. They must know, for your safety."

"Aye-aye," Cynthia's father ended the call quickly, so nothing could be traced or retrieved by anybody, then he walked over to his bar area, grabbed a crystal decanter and poured himself a shot of gin to calm his frazzled nerves and soothe his aching skull.

He slowly walked back to his messy bedroom to retrieve an overnight bag. He stuffed it with a couple of warm jogging outfits which he wore when running through Centennial Park on brisk days. He also threw in undergarments, heavy socks, shampoo and other hygiene products. His sturdy "Chuck Taylor" basketball shoes, which he had always used for jogging could sufficiently serve as his only pair of shoes during his hibernation. He changed into a pair of Rough Rider black jeans, a Redskins sweatshirt with matching ski cap and walked back behind the bar. It felt good to him to dress casually, at least for a bit.

He poured himself another shot of gin, so that he would feel comfortable and content while waiting on the couch across from the front door, his bag alongside him. "All of the doors and windows are locked?" he asked himself again, "and my money is put away in my wall safe? I will need a little, so let me go into it and take some out. How much do I need?" he mentally asked himself. "A thousand should be plenty. If I need more than that, I will just have to go to the bank. Ohhh........ they would not like that! Everything MUST be under-cover," he sternly told himself. He could not slip up in any way.

Just when he was finally getting comfortable and relaxed in his own home, he saw the Ford as described, stopping first at the front window, so that the Ambassador could obviously recognize it, then slowly pull-ing through the narrow gravel alley in back, which had on it a line of garages up and down the block. The Ambassador gathered his belong-ings and left through the solid white wood back door of his colonial home and through the well-manicured and flowered small back yard.

Upon reaching the tall fenced gate, he pulled out a pad and keyed in a code to secure it with locks and alarms, just the same as he had done when he left his house. He was ready for anything bad, or nothing but good, of course he hoped it was to be the latter. He leaped into the Ford.

"Hello my friend. How are you?" the Ambassador smugly asked.

"Ahhhhh," was all the driver replied. He stared at the Ambassador during the entire ride to Arlington, without uttering another sound.

The Ambassador became slightly nervous with the silence in the vehicle. He then reached in his bag and pulled out a half-filled plastic bottle of Kentucky Bourbon, which he treasured. He threw some down his node-ridden throat.

"Maybe one day I'll give up the bottle and never worry about hid-ing my addiction again," he thought to himself, as the angry driver hit another pot hole.

After what seemed like a twenty minute drag race, they arrived at a no name car rental lot in Arlington. Older, slightly damaged vehicles filled the parking spaces, ready for insured drivers only. The Ambassador climbed out of the low-riding Ford and carried his belongings with him inside the rental office, never saying thank you or goodbye to the "mute" driver, who had planted a new driver's license firmly in the Ambassador's hand.

Once in front of the rental agent, the Ambassador requested the best vehicle they had available. The agent slapped down a set of keys and pointed outside. "Number 16 is where you will find it."

"Where is the paper I need to sign? Here...here is my license." The Ambassador showed him the fake license.

"I do not need a thing. It's all been taken care of, sir," he informed him. He turned his back and walked into a far room where the Ambassador could hear him locking the door and phoning.

"Well, I'm out of here," he squealed in glee, as he walked out of the stuffy office to find car slot 16. He was taken aback when he found the number. It had a 1972 red Pinto parked on the space.

"This is the best you had, yeah, right," he said to the Pinto, as he opened its driver's door. He zoomed out of helot towards his assistant's condominium in Georgetown. He couldn't wait to get another drink under his belt.

Recently, the Ambassador had become quite the eccentric, ranting and raving absurdities at international events, all due to his excessive drinking habits. He knew what the consequences would be if he were found to be a drunk, but now, he didn't even care. He didn't care about his position, if he did not have Cynthia in his life. He had disregarded her like one does with a worn-out chum from grade school. He was never going to do that again. She was his life and always had been. He was just going to have to accept the pain associated with his wife's death and challenge it.

"*Maybe one day*, I'll give up the bottle entirely and never have to hide myself again," he commented to himself, as he threw in his bag.

When he guzzled more and more, he became more and more belligerent. His behavior was becoming more and more frowned upon in political and social circles.

After his distinguished and lovely wife of thirty-eight years died from complications due to a heart bypass, he had never been the same. He had alienated his daughter because of the pain of remembering their wonderful days. He drowned his sorrows in the bottle. He felt that this was the only way he could act like and function as a sober diplomat in the day, by getting smashed at night. He was so depressed. He was an insomniac. When drunk, he stared at the ceiling at nights, instead of falling asleep. He started each and every day with coffee and rum. He didn't know how long he could exist living this lifestyle, and he hadn't cared....not until now.

"I will change, if you give me my daughter back. I can't lose her, too," he pleaded to the heavens as he drove into the city.

Camille's spirit glistened all around his body and the vehicle. She had secretly been with him since Arlington. The rental car establishment was located across and down the street from the National Cemetery where Kenneth had been supposedly buried.

The Ambassador thought that he must be dreaming. He thought that he heard a soft whisper say, "*No, you won't. You can never change your ways. It's too late.*"

"I need some sleep," he said to himself, shaking his head. He soon pulled up to the parking garage of his assistant's condominium complex and entered in the code for the gates to spring open. He parked in a spot very close to the elevator, got out from the battered inside, pushed the third floor button and zoomed up to his refuge for the next few days, or until he received orders from the FBI.

The Federal Bureau of Investigations, along with the Central Intelligence Agency had both concocted an elaborate plot to find the Ambassador's daughter using undercover agents who were hooked up supposedly with terrorist gangs, so they could weed out enough information via recorded telephone conversations to put a plan into motion. They needed to have a starting point first. Federal agents discovered that Cynthia's husband, Ty, was not a pharmaceutical salesman, as the legitimate crowd believed, but rather a razor-edged Irish Mafia boss, also the strident leader of the Irish Republican Army headquartered in Belfast. Now, he had all secret meetings, plans and documents downstairs in his pub in Shannon.

He had two residences, one which was a shabby one room apartment in a small store in Belfast, which served as IRA headquarters in Northern Ireland, but where he rarely conducted business. He stayed there only when Sunny came in town. He liked it down South in his castle. He enjoyed the southern surroundings.

He had used his pub front as a hideout and meeting point, where the boys involved would discuss all illicit plans for world domination. No one knew about this office except for the underworld. His main residence was a small castle on the Southwest Coast of Ireland, near Shannon, which he shared with his wife, Cynthia. Both governmental agency heads involved in this maneuver thought Shannon to be the most logical place to start an undercover investigation.

Two FBI agents who were of Irish decent were sent on this mission to pose as criminals, trying to worm their way into this deceptive Irish manhood organization. They flew on Aer Lingus from Baltimore to Shannon dressed in scruffy attire, with unshaven faces and perfect Celtic accents and phrases which they had studied for several years, along with several Eastern European dialects. These men were the top agents and the most prepared to handle international affairs by impersonation and discretion.

The more handsome one of the agents got the acting scene underway by asking an Irish flight attendant if she were married. When she answered, "No," he went in for the kill.

They flirted off and on for over an hour. Then, she slipped her home number into his hand, as she shook hands with him. She whispered to him to call anytime, just not too late.

"I have a baby sister who I am taking care of and who cannot be disturbed. She has a severe asthmatic condition." The attendant left, glancing back at him, as she made her rounds down the aisle.

"I've often heard that stewardesses can give you the scoop on anything and anybody. They meet so many men, even sleep with them, and a lot who are in the underworld," he told his buddy who was sitting to his right. "I bet this damsel can lead us to who we need to know. I'm keeping her number for insurance sake. We've got a lot to do in a little amount of time."

Just then, the pilot made an announcement over the loud speaker that they were starting their decent into Shannon. The plane rumbled and rocked, as it made its way through the turbulent gray clouds which felt as heavy as concrete when flying through them, but appeared as light as cotton candy.

After clearing customs, the undercover agents left the terminal for their car, supposedly waiting for them in the short term parking lot. They were told the vehicle was a small 1990 BMW with Belfast tags and registration. It was registered under the name of the infamous Irish thief, "Pattye O' Henry". Pattye had fled the Isles years prior and was never apprehended. Two Irish license cards were found in the glove compartment, with the names Pattye O' Henry and Thomas McKnight. Appropriate photos were displayed in each card's corner. The agents were off and running, headed toward the couple's estate on the coast nearby. The two men were well-seasoned and knew they had to play out every move, one minute at a time. Planning strategic endeavors was not an option here. They knew not where they were entering.

Pattye and Thomas, as their identification cards suggested, sped along the coastal two-lane road until they reached their stopping point behind a large, barren hill that had an Irish flag in its soil, blowing in the blustery wind. The two men trudged up, took out the flag from the soil and retrieved the planted weaponry necessary to carry out this maneuver. FBI agents were permitted a firearm on board the Irish jet, but no rifles, or AK 47's, which they now possessed.

"We are going to need these, not just for our own protection, but to take down and destroy," the handsome, newly-named Pattye declared. Once again, his insatiable appetite for success was making him feel invincible.

"Think of what you're saying," quiet, sensible Thomas said to his cohort, as Pattye swerved on the seaside mountain road, one tire on and one tire in the air. He couldn't wait to get to their first stop, the small castle in Shannon.

Loaded with ammunition, guns, and knives, they both proceeded down the long, gravel drive towards the massive front doors. Pattye used the door knocker to announce their arrival. The boys at the Federal Bureau of Investigations had devised a scenario for the two to play act by. As soon as the door was opened by the butler, Pattye was to place his hand on the butler's shoulder and ask in a Celtic slurred street dialect, "Hey, my good fellow, I need to see Ty. Is he occupied?

And yes, I have had a few pints. Tell him Pattye is here to see him. I know the old bloke's heard of Pattye O' Henry. Why, I have held up so many currency exchange houses in Dublin and Belfast that it would blow anybody's mind away." It worked. He struggled to make it over to a comfortable chair to wait.

Thomas followed after him, apologizing the entire time, as he was instructed to do. The butler invited the pair to dine with Ty's friends, who were now occupying the castle, supposedly awaiting Ty's arrival.

Several of Ty's friends came, one by one, dressed very slovenly, through the back door and sat at the dining table waiting for food.

Having no manners, they never asked who the duo was, or even greeted them properly. They were introduced by the butler, as the Irishmen scarfed down their meal.

It wasn't until Pattye asked, "When is Ty returning?" that the Irishmen stood at attention.

One asked, "Do you know Ty?"

The other asked, "What's your name?"

"I am Pattye O' Henry of Belfast. I was the leading jewel thief and bank robber in Ireland. I know that you've heard of the name. I have come to see Ty about something he might be interested in. It has to do with world domination, terrorism and money. I know Ty loves all three."

"You can tell us. We'll give him the details. He hardly sees anyone," the older thug informed them.

"Well, I only want to speak with him. Where is he?" Pattye asked again, as Thomas sat quietly, awaiting action.

"Look, you are not our guests, were never invited here. You boys have to EXIT," the butler nervously requested.

"No, James. Let them be. Just reach inside their pockets and give me their wallets," the roughest of the four said. "I want to have a look at who we are dealing with."

"Here, sir," and the butler threw down two wallets on the table in front of the ruffian.

"Okay, everything seems to be in order. These two are Pattye O' Henry and Thomas O'Leary, both of Belfast. As far back as I remember from being a kid, these two were cocky swindlers from the old school. I don't think these two could ever make it in today's world of espionage, terrorism and lies," the ruffian joked, with the other Irish and Russian dirty looking dudes who sat beside him, displaying devil tattoos and Third Reich emblems on their slightly developed and girlish-looking forearms.

"Those days of heisting jewels and currency are over. Those days were for our fathers and grandfathers. Where have you been?" he smirked, "And what century are you from?" the Russian asked.

A big clank sounded from down below in the basement before that question could be answered. Pattye ran to where the sound came from, the basement door. Four dirty-looking Irish thugs and the two Russians followed, awaiting an altercation. Pattye tried to open the closed door, but it was locked. "Where is the key to this cellar?" he asked.

"Don't have it, chum. Don't know where it is," the ruffian smugly replied.

Another loud noise and faint scream resounded from down below, and the FBI knew it was time to show their real sides. "Pattye" pulled out his gun which had been concealed in his jacket and blew the lock off. As he ran down the slippery cement staircase, he felt an object being wedged in his back. It felt like a gun.

"Slow down partner. You ain't going nowhere, but to hell," said the indistinguishable voice coming from the ruffian on the step above him. The other three held Thomas with his arms behind his back at the door opening. It seemed to be doomsday for the two seemingly prepared and well-trained FBI agents.

Suddenly, Thomas decided to use his college kick boxing to pay off in a big way for the both of them. He kicked and grabbed each larynx and proceeded to throw them all, one by one, down the long flight of hard, jagged cement blocks, which acted as stairs.

The biggest of the bunch crashed his skull on one of the steel footers which was positioned in the ground to help support this massive structure. Blood seethed out in abundance and momentarily covered the entire cement floor. It was apparent he was dead. The other two were simply unconscious.

"Thomas, throw all weapons on the floor. If you do what I say, Pattye will not be hurt. You may be surprised who you are about to see," a new voice blurted out from down below, as he pushed blindfolded and gagged Cynthia in front of his body. "Here she is. Is this what you came for?" he questioned. Thomas threw down his weapon, careful to note where he had strategically placed it.

At that precise moment, Kimmie lit her candle with a long match to catch everyone off guard. She made the room glow with light. Thomas, with his incredible reflex action, dived down onto the rifle of the mystery gunman and forcefully angled it straight at the enemy's face. With both hands on the gun, the Irish thug proceeded to fire two novice shots which landed in the wall behind him.

At that instant, it was over for the Irishman. Three shots plummeted into the thug's nasty brain, causing all of his menacing organs to ooze out onto the concrete block wall.

The agents were more than satisfied. It was a job well done in their own eyes and would be as well as in the eyes of the bureau, they were certain.

Cynthia, Kimmie, and Nikko were set free by the two agents. The three were later taken to a shelter near Dublin to be questioned the following morning. Jude's body was scheduled to be cremated, as she had desired, with her ashes to be thrown into the Gulf of Mexico. Her body would be flown back to Florida soon.

All of this had been too much for Cynthia, almost as it had been for Camille. Camille vowed to hover over her for as long as she needed strength to cope and stand tall. Cynthia retrieved Ty's phone from on top of the dead man's briefcase. Cynthia felt like she finally held the power to defy the odds and get revenge on her husband through his cell phone numbers. He had one hundred fifty stored numbers in his phone, and Cynthia planned to go through each and every one, until she found the missing piece to the puzzle, just like Camille so desperately had wanted to do, before she died at the hands of HER OWN husband, Ty's brother, Hugo. The two had had so much in common… and they had become sisters-in-law.

Camille knew she had to stand over Cynthia, making her presence known to her at all times, especially in Cynthia's weak state.

First and foremost, however, the two agents had made sure to stop by a local clinic to have Cynthia looked at and receive medication, if needed. The physicians that attended to her said that she was out of immediate danger, and informed her that she had had a miscarriage.

Cynthia flipped-out and went into hysterics.

Chapter Twelve

Ty's Assailant Lover

With the information given to the FBI, as well as Scotland Yard, arrests were soon to be made. Secret warrants were issued for certain pub staff who had helped in Ty's scheme, his three remaining right hand boys who survived Thomas' powerful defensive moves would also be charged with premeditated murder, and of course, the infamous "Tyrone Silky Riley" himself who gave the order, and whom they couldn't retrieve any information as to his whereabouts, and or condition. Ty had vanished from radar. His cell phone number had not been re-connected either, so no traces could be made, unless Ty called in to the castle, or to the pub, which was proving to be their sole hope.

"This IS the only way," Thomas advised Scotland Yard, "by staging a thriving pub business and home life that is meeting the needs of Ty's plot. This way nothing will seem out of place, no red flags will be raised, and we can wait and wait until we nab him. The newspapers and networks must never know the truth. They must still believe that

Cynthia is being held somewhere and by some group for a ransom to come from her Ambassador father. More importantly, no one must ever say one word about these arrests that we have made this evening. Can we keep this to ourselves, dudes and dudettes?" he jokingly asked the British Lieutenant, who stared at him blankly.

"You can always depends on all of my men and women to do the right thing," the chief constable smiled and affirmed.

"Good,"Thomas sighed. "Then, all stages are set. I have employed several women to masquerade as friends of Ty and of his already arrested crime boys, in order to get more information. It's kind of flimsy, but it's all we've got. Somebody WILL squeal. I know it, and the lively staff that has been arrested shall give us MORE pertinent gab. I'm sure of it.......I am confident this plan will work. I have my neck out on a limb for this, so it must. Talk to you chaps in the afternoon, after I have cleared my head from this pounding jet lag headache I have. I really must snooze, but first, I need to confirm with Pattye's stewardess 'girl-friend',"Thomas jokingly said, and noted that the plan was in full swing to begin tomorrow morning.

"This scenario should probably only play out for a few days. Ty's ego won't be able to stand it, with none of his boys even bothering to call him on his new number, that I am sure that he already has ordered and no one is even answering his office, bar, or home phone. He should flip out, not having any control. No one now seems to care about him. He WILL be back to Shannon to see what's wrong. We will just wait it out."

"It sounds like a great one, Thomas. We're all professionals and we'll see it through," FBI agent, "Pattye" said in a serious tone.

"With any luck at all, we should wrap this up quickly and become super heroes in the bureau," the now braggadocios Thomas added.

Hold up in a room in a hut in Afghanistan in the backyard of Sunny's brother's house, Sunny began to question Ty, "When are we to get married? Are you really on my brother's side, or just in it for yourself? When are you divorcing your wife?"

There was no response from Ty. He kept twiddling his thumbs.

"I want to fly up to Ireland with you...to your precious castle. I want to meet your wife," Sunny announced.

Up until now, she had no idea to suspect that Ty was manipulating the United States Government with threats and ransoms. She still thought he was rather ignorant and good, and she knew that he had a whole lot of money from jobs that her brother had given him and that had all been well done by him and his boys. She also knew the combination to his stash safe down in the basement of his pub.

He had given the numbers to his boys over his phone one night after he hung up from her. He thought that he had pressed the red disconnect button, but evidently, he barely pushed it in with all of the commotion that arose from one of his men who had made a near fatal mistake earlier that evening. She quickly pulled out an old piece of paper from her diary and began writing the combination down. She thought that it might come in useful someday, and it may be soon.

"I cannot ever marry you, Sunny. You're a great girl....super sexy, but I'm not in love with you. I'm not in love with anyone, not even my dear, sweet Cynthia. You get it? And we can't fly up there just yet, not until I know what has happened. I'll phone them when I can," he tried to pacify her.

Sunny, getting belligerent and bold said, "No, you won't, sweetie. What do you think I am, a doll you can play with until you get bored, using me and abusing me the whole time? Well, think again. You know

Med-hi is not happy about what you've become. He says you are not the same, or you have been playing with him. He's also not happy about how you are treating me. One never disgraces a man's family in the Middle East without paying the consequences.

This evening you will board a plane with me for Shannon where you will get a quick and very expensive annulment, and then, we'll get married ourselves. Maybe, we could have a wedding on the rocky coastline right underneath your house, where we are soon to spend eternity. 'Til death do us part, as they say in the United States of America.

I know that I can provide you with at least one boy. Males run in my family. Just ask me, and we can set the date....NOW, honey, baby....you know that you DO love me. You're just getting nervous... that's all," she spoke in a motherly fashion, stroking him all the while.

He had had about all that he could stand when he grabbed her wrist and started twisting it.

Sunny screamed, "Help, help me, Med-hi." Her brother was outside with a business associate when he heard the cries and came running inside his small, dark, but very comfortable home in the outskirts of Kabul.

"Ty! Get your hands off my sister!" he screamed furiously.

"He won't get an annulment from Cynthia, and he won't marry me either," she cried out hysterically.

"My sister has been your supreme being ever since I have come in contact with your piece of shit warped mind and infertile body. Sunny was told how Cynthia finally got pregnant through a gang buddy. She said she was drugged with Bailey's, then escorted to the basement down below the pub, where this man's semen was pumped into her womanhood, then he tied her up. In turn, she got pregnant, and you believed that since your boy had been "blessed" with five boys and no girls, that he was sure to "bless" you with a baby boy to take over where you left off. If this didn't happen, you obviously planned to "snuff" Cynthia out. She would be of no use to you with girls.

Well, her twin girls are a thing of the past... but not Cynthia. I just heard this from the Russians. You never cared about my sister, or me neither. It's all just a chessboard to you, a mere chessboard. Sunny and I would have done anything for a strong friend, as you were proving to be. We would have died for you. Ty, on the other hand, you are a wimp and a failure. You will never succeed in anything you do, maybe in Ireland, but not down here, in the bowels of society, the Mid-Eastern world. So, you won't marry Sunny, eh chap?" Med-hi spoke as intimidating as Ty. "Well, it doesn't matter whatsoever, not whatsoever. I am going to make you pay, before Sunny kills you," he announced.

"She would never do such a thing, Med. She loves me," Ty proclaimed.

"That may be so, but pride and dignity are more honorable to our culture than romantic love.

She will do it. She has done worse in the past," Med-hi spoke in a monotone voice, while getting the lock ready for Ty's stay of seclusion, then execution.

"I love you Sunny, so much. I know you would never do this to me. You will find me a way out, won't you, dear? Then, we will be married, for sure. You are all that I want, no one else.

I've just been scared to admit it. You trust me darling, don't you?" Ty asked.

"Of course I do," Sunny angrily spoke.
She could not hold back her emotions any longer. She cocked her gun back and plunged a bullet into Ty's upper chest. Ty clutched

his shoulder region in agony. A second shot was fired, but hit the wall. More gunfire sounded and proceeded to his strained heart muscle region. Then, the final shot rang out. This went straight into the middle of the medulla section of his brain. It was now over. Ty, the wanna be ruler of the universe, was now dead at the hands of his assailant lover.

Chapter Thirteen

The Disposal of the Body

Sunny raised herself up from the pool of blood in which she was wadding and kissed his fair cheek one last time. Med-hi got out a plastic body bag. He carried it on his shoulder, as the two walked down the small lane. He then met up with his sheik neighbor friend who lived in one of the most exclusive homes in the country. His neighbor, Samar escorted Med-hi and Sunny to a large courtyard that had ponds and lily pads and gorgeous flowers strewn throughout the imported sod lawn. It thrived day in and day out in the summer months because of the heavy duty underground sprinkler system. Samar lived like a king in this poor, downtrodden country of Afghanistan.

Going against Muslim ways, he offered his cohort and neighbor, Med-hi, a shot of black market scotch, which Med-hi vehemently refused.

"We need to light the fire as soon as we can," Med-hi suggested. "We need to get ready of him....of all of his lies and promises..... NOW, RIGHT NOW!" he screamed in the purple, newly-starred evening sky.

Then, he struck a match with the greatest of ease and sent it flying to the top of a pile of dry leaves and sticks, which were placed strategically in the middle of the back yard to collect breezes that would spread flames, making bodies disappear much faster. He then pulled Ty out of the bag and put him on the fire. It had become their fastest means of disposal yet, for their non-loyal countrymen, and business partners, and non-subservient wives, of which all three categories were escalating. Sunny cried and ran home.

"The plastic disintegrates like magic. No trace anywhere, just smoke. I never liked him anyway," Med-hi admitted to Samar. "His own boys in Ireland had it in for him. He was scum...and how he treated Sunny....."

Forgetting what he stood for, Med-hi broke off the conversation with tyrannical gestures and said, "I will take that scotch now," as he waved to Samar. "I need a shot before I see Sunny."

He received a shot which he poured down his throat, then another and then another.

Samar invited Med-hi to stay for a quick dinner of chicken and rice which Med-hi loved to eat with his hands, as he was accustomed to, growing up in Morocco. Med-hi declined.

He said he had to go back to his place and comfort Sunny.

"She is a strong, strong lady," Med-hi said. "I wish that I could be like her sometimes," he said admiringly.

It was rare that a brother felt that way toward his sister in Afghanistan. He attributed that to his French Moroccan influence.

His mother's family had traveled to Morocco from Afghanistan, and his father was born in Marrakesh. The family had been happy for twenty years until a French woman from Avignon entered the family's life. His father ran away with the thirty-year old woman to her vacation home in Marseilles. She had a boat for him docked on her private dock. She had inherited the sea-front property from her late father.

Becoming more and more bored at a moment's notice, she flew off to the cosmopolitan city of Marrakesh, in French Morocco, every chance she had. It was after one of these flights of insanity when she met Med-hi's father, cleaning his fishing boat one evening, as she stumbled up the path to her hotel. She had not one sober bone in her limp body. The two talked and agreed to meet later that evening for drinks and dancing in the lavish disco of the well-staffed American 5-star hotel at which she was staying.

Med-hi's father never returned home again. His entire family life was shattered. Both teen siblings had to go into the city to find work, so that the family could eat. They found it at the grand bazaar in the heart of the metropolis. They sold merchandise for several vendors for two years, then they began buying spices, fabrics and rugs to sell at their own shop they rented in the bazaar, and eventually in that same 5-star hotel. They were becoming well-off. Their mother was proud, but didn't live long enough to enjoy the luxuries of an unsuppressed lifestyle. She soon died of kidney failure. The two siblings thought that she had actually died from her heart being broken so tragically. They had her remains flown to her home country of Afghanistan.

Med-hi and Sunny flew with her body and went with her ultimately to her final resting place, which was a quiet, unoccupied plot of land 100 km North of Kabul, where she was born and where her parents had been buried as well.

Med-hi and Sunny never left the area. They started a life there. Med-hi got involved with the Taliban immediately. He liked its way of thinking, of standing up to anybody for the rights of its own country, displaying the rights of each man, and for its way of thinking and perceiving how females and family should coexist.

Med-hi had a terrible grudge against women, all due to that French woman who had abolished their secure family structure. He would never feel the same about women again, except of course, for his deceased mother and his angelic sister. He was the perfect Taliban member. Med-hi had often thought about moving to Syria, as two of his new friends were linked with ISIS. He felt especially drawn to these men, as he thought them to be the strongest group in the world, more deadly than the Taliban.

Med-hi felt that he was definitely a supreme being, perhaps the strongest being on the planet, just like Ty had once thought of himself. Now, Med-hi was definitely it. He had planned this action from the start, only Ty, with his immense ego, had not surmised that Ty's scheme would ultimately bring him and his plan down...down to the ground and that Med-hi would be the one to soon reach Allah, and he couldn't wait. He was more than ready.

Med-hi felt like he had no more use for this planet, other than to rectify it for Allah, which he felt he had mostly accomplished by killing the main vermin of civilization. He had killed so many countrymen and political figures from around the world who wanted to obstruct the Taliban way of life. Med-hi felt that he had done his duty. He could hear his God whisper in his ear, and in his figment of momentary imaginary ecstasy, he picked up a revolver that he had lying on a nearby glass table, asked Samar to look after Sunny for him, and he blew his brains out, with a smile on his face.

Samar added Med-hi's body to the flames and prayed to Allah. He then went inside to calm his nerves before going to see Sunny in person. He didn't know how she would take this, after all that she had been through. He had to look after Sunny and cherish her, even though she was only a woman, a mere bearer of a man's children, but he had to, and wanted to do this for Med-hi. He left his home and walked down the small cobblestone walkway which led to the former home of the mother of Med-hi, and where Sunny lived now. He bent down to his knees in a weak moment and extracted wet drips from his, up until now dry, unsaturated sterile eyes. He realized at this moment that he was possessed with feelings...real feelings.

Samar composed himself and started up the dirt drive. That was when he saw Sunny standing motionless by the window sill.

Samar gently knocked on the window, which she was looking out of, and waved. She came barreling out of her quarters, clothed in a light pink silk dress, with a transparent cloth wrapped around her nicely-shaped, tan head. Wearing no make-up, as was custom with her culture for females, made it easy for her beauty to shine through, without being masked. Sunny had almond-shaped, golden-brown, and heavy-lashed eyes, which displayed her every emotion. This made her seem child-like and naive, the quality she possessed, and which captivated most Middle-Eastern Muslim men. Her thin, but naturally red-plum luscious lips, with the beauty mark placed right above her top right lip, tantalized every man who ever stood near her. Her slender, slightly freckled, exotically proportioned nose, wrapped up her sweet, serene, gorgeous package. When and wherever her long garments were to blow in the wind and wrap around her body in a tight fashion, men thought she to be a sight to behold.

One Arab who had been walking through the littered streets of Kabul, with two United States Army officers by his side, told Sunny that Allah would be "proud" to see her naked. The officers scolded and hit the man for speaking to a young innocent girl that way. At that time in her life, she definitely was innocent....very innocent. Sunny was an independent thinker, and always had been as independent as she could be, being female, in an Afghan world. Her brother always looked after her, from baby until now. He was never going to let her be unhappy, or become used and abused by any man, "no way...no how", was his motto. Sunny was Med-hi's angelic sister, and Med-hi was Sunny's heroic brother who would never let her down in any situation. They had been through a lot together. Sunny always wondered how she would get along in life without her brother by her side. When she asked herself this question, Sunny would simply look into the sky and pray for the almighty to keep her brother alive. She never knew exactly what to call her almighty. She had heard many references to him as Jesus, Allah, God and Buddha, to name a few. She was confused as to what to call her almighty, so she just called him "the almighty", because he was so evident in her life and had helped her through so many tumultuous situations that he was her best friend. Her "almighty" was all that she ever needed. She had always felt blessed, that was until Samar came to her with the bad news about her brother.

"Sunny, do you have a moment? There's something really important that I have to tell you.

I know how terrible the day has been with Ty being such a traitor and all, but he's gone now, never to be heard from again," Samar informed Sunny. "Can I come in?" he timidly asked her.

"Okay," she said. "Come in. Samar, where is Med-hi?" she then asked in a panic state.

Samar just stood quietly in front of her, waiting for the strength, and the opportune moment to tell her why he had come to her bedroom door.

Sunny knew something was up, due to the silence in the room. She grew increasing anxious awaiting Samar's response, which never seemed to come.

"No, Samar. He cannot be gone. Tell me the truth," she screamed, pounding her fist on his chest.

Keeping her from breaking into hysterics, Samar took off her head scarf and started massaging her scalp and shoulders. It progressed into something more, a sweet sexual encounter she had not again expected with her brother's best friend.

At the height of his orgasm, he quietly whispered into her small, daintily, pinned-back ear, "Med-hi is dead. He killed himself with my gun, the one that's lies on the patio table in the courtyard. He said that it was time for him to meet Allah, and that Allah was making him do this, and the gun went off. He's dead. I'm so sorry sweetheart for your loss of Med-hi, even for your loss of Ty. You're so strong, like

Med-hi always said. He was right. He asked me to look after you forever, before he pulled the trigger. I will do that for him. Sunny, have you ever thought that we could marry? I would treat you right, letting you have the independence you desire at home, of course, not in the Taliban world, but between us. Please girl, I will take good care of you and give you a fair fortune, which Med-hi and I acquired through our oil dealings. You have no more hopes of grand fortune through Ty.

You don't know where he kept his money, or how much he really had, so come with me, please," he demanded again, as he began gently caressing her slim body and kissing her lips, until she could hold back no longer.

"I can't do this anymore. I have to leave tomorrow, after a short burial service with just us present, no one else. I can't stand the people in our world. I have to get back, back to my once peaceful refuge of Ireland," she professed to Samar, but really knowing that she could never part from her world there.

"But, you can't. I promised Med-hi that you would become my wife...that I would look after you forever. I can't turn my back on his wishes, now can I?" he questioned her, as he became more violent and roughly pulled her hair back from her face. "I want you to be mine."

Sunny jumped up, socked Samar in the jaw and rammed her knee cap into his testicles, so that she could escape his hold.

Flying out her door, she ran down alleys and secluded streets, until she got to her best friend's home. She told her best friend and her husband what had transpired earlier, and that she needed a disguise--a beard, glasses, pants, and a long, and a white male garment. She was carrying Med-hi's turban. They searched the small two room dwelling until they found the rest that she needed.

"This is good...Sunny. You get out...no problem...and don't come back....it's no good for us here," her best friend warned her. Sunny looked more like Med-hi than ever before. There was no way she could ever fail at this attempt. She hardly spoke, only mumbled now.

The couple drove Sunny to the airport and escorted her to security. Holding identification from her dead brother, Med-hi, when she uttered a word, it was always in a soft, monotone voice, barely audible, using sign language more than anything else. She had cleared Afghan officials to board her flight to Shannon.

The flight was sold-out. She was forced to buy last minute first-class passage, which she felt that she needed anyway, just to relax and think about how she was going to conquer her fortune, the fortune that was due her, the fortune that Ty had promised her so often. And now that her beloved brother was gone, she didn't care about any consequence.

Sunny cried off and on, as she waited for the flight to ascend. She blotted her handkerchief over her once feminine eyelashes, which she had snipped off with scissors back at her friend's home, and she proceeded to read her inflight magazine.

She was petrified for what she was about to do. She had written down a combination to the basement safe of the pub in Shannon. The same combination that Ty had blurted out to his employee while on the phone with her. She was not stupid. Sunny knew that this combo might be her salvation one day. Well, this happened to be the day, and she was off to his castle in Shannon, boys, or no boys, and the safe in the pub.

After a six hour bumpy flight to the Irish hub city of Shannon, Sunny's jet laid its wheels down on the runway, headed for safety. Sunny had never liked flying much and had to have several glasses of sweet wine to get through any mischievous cloud formations. She talked on and off with her aisle mate, a young man of twenty, who was from Shannon and knew of Ty and of the castle where he lived. He had never met Cynthia, but he had heard a great deal of her, and of her talent. Sunny had never wanted to meet Cynthia...always hating her, but now she truly felt sorry for her, for having had to live a lie for all of these years with a man whom she hardly knew. Her good side wanted to be friends with her now, but knew this would never happen.

The jet landed in Ireland. Sunny, dressed as a man, retrieved her carry-on from the overhead bin and walked into the busy terminal. At the baggage claim area, she picked up her large case and headed outside to flag down a taxi. The castle was awaiting her. She had no idea who was there, or what was in store for her, but she couldn't wait. She was mad, revengeful, envious, but most of all...resourceful.

She knew she was going to leave Ireland with a bag of money in her hand, because she had the combination....the combination to Ty's safe, in the basement of his pub....the combination to Ty's life...the one that held his fortune....she loved it.

Chapter Fourteen

The Turban

*S*unny climbed into one of the awaiting Town Cars outside of baggage claim. She spoke gruffly to the skinny, fair headed lad and told him that he must carry her to the small castle on the cliffs of Shannon where "demons live and devils play". The young chap stared back at this supposed Middle Eastern gent with a blank expression on his pasty white face, which was slowly becoming flushed with anguish and anxiety.

"I don't know where you mean, sir," was all the boy could utter. "I have lived near the cliffs all my life and never knew that a place like that ever existed sir," he babbled on nervously.

"And I don't know that you ever should have heard of this place. Its evilness and corruption kills, thus creating sadness," she replied crazily.

"I still don't know where you want me to take you, sir. Maybe, I could ask the gent up there in that car if he knows the location, 'cause I sure don't," the boy said. "Let me pull up here to ask…"

"No, you don't have to do that. Just tell me, do you know a man named Ty?" she questioned him.

"Why, sure. Everybody has heard of Ty. He pours a mean scotch and soda, from what I have heard, and he has a stunning wife, too. I have seen her two times, once on the stage, and once walking through town. She makes my knees go weak. She's so bloody beautiful!" he announced.

"Yeah, I know where they live, but why did you call them demons and devils. They are no such beings. They are wonderful, upstanding citizens that would never speak a cross word to anyone, and they also help the needy. They have lots of cash and are not selfish at all. Everyone loves them here."

Even though she had gotten the boy in a defensive state, Sunny knew she had just scored. The boy quickly revved up his engine and took off following the shabby sign that said "to beach", remaining to himself for several minutes.

Breaking the loud silence, Sunny asked where Ty's pub was. The driver said that he didn't know.

"I hardly ever go into town, just stay by the water, or by the airport. I like it that way. No demons nor devils where I come from..... Maybe in town....but not here," he said.

"Hey, why do you need to go to the castle up the road for anyway? Do you know Ty and Cynthia? Do you have business there?" he asked in an investigative manner. He got no response back.

Suddenly, he stopped the car in the middle of the road and shouted, "Get out...I want you out...now...before I call the authorities, sir."

Sunny secured her carry-on from the back seat, quickly unbuttoned it and pulled out her toothpaste.

"What are you doing now? I said to leave...you know...skedaddle," he stated, finally sounding very confident, as he pulled out his phone to dial the police.

"You, my boy, are not calling anyone. You, my boy, are never going to see anybody else your entire life, which by the way, is about to end." Sunny slid out a stiletto from inside the tub, which was covered in green paste, but nonetheless razor sharp, and she stuck it in the naive boy's eyeballs, to show his inept servitude toward her, then she slashed his thick throat.

With blood pumping from his face and neck, Sunny tore off two pieces of cloth from her head dress and stuffed them inside the wounds to stop the bleeding. She had seen her brother, as well as Ty perform these kind of tasks to great avail. She had watched so many instances, but still could not perform the feat as well as they could. This showed in her work. It was sloppy....very sloppy. It looked so amateurish. She made sure that no other traffic was coming for miles, as she looked down the long, narrow, totally straight road in both directions.

When she felt sure that she was safe, Sunny pulled the chubby body from the car, walked with it to the side of the cliff, and straining her muscles, she sent it plunging, plunging down the steep, jagged-edged, rocky and sandy cliff which tried to mask the serenity of the ocean down below with its awesome and majestic beauty. It was if these two elements of nature had eternal competition with each other.

Once her duties with the young man were over, she sat herself in the driver's seat and motored on. She knew that she was on the correct road. There was no other coast, and large houses were beginning to multiply with every hundred yards that she drove. She was headed away from the airport, towards the water. There was no other way to go. She drove like a speed demon, along the now twisting and turning narrow cliff road. Soon, she saw a sign that read "To Town" with an arrow pointing to the left. She smiled, knowing that she was about to find his castle at any moment. Ty had always referred to that sign as a directional reference to the location of his castle.

"I have to find out where the stinkin' pub is as soon as I can, so that I can get my money out of that damn safe, and quick, before anyone hears of Ty going 'bye-bye', but I seriously doubt anyone ever will ever find out. How could they? *Most nations are stupid. They are not supreme beings, like our people.*" She knew that she could never change her attitude.

With laughter coming from her gut, she slowly drove through the open gate and onto the gravel drive. She then heard a voice blare out of the box attached.

"Who's there?" asked a slurring, rough-edged male voice. "Do you have business here, bloke?"

"You might say so," Sunny answered, projecting the most masculine tone that she could muster from the insides of her flat, well-built and boned chest. "I need to see Ty. Is he here, or at the bar?" she asked quickly and demanding.

"Well, he sure ain't in this dive," the irritated voice shouted. "You can ask anyone in town where Ty is. They'll tell you." The voice spoke no more.

Only knowing Northern Ireland, Sunny assumed that town was most likely just straight up to the right, remembering what Ty had always preached, "a good location for a man's empire should always be a distance away, but still a straight shot to civilization, for sanity and security reasons."

She slipped inside the Town Car, peeled out of the driveway, and headed north. At the stop sign, she turned right. She evidently had made a wise decision to trust her instinct. The road was becoming more populated with every mile. She knew that the town was soon approaching.

Once at the town square area, she found an out of the way parking area with only one spot left vacant. It became hers. She jumped out of the town car with enthusiasm, awaiting her monetary triumph. Her new masculine eyes darted around, under dark sunglasses until they came upon a spot in the distance where she remembered Ty talking about the excellent breakfasts served, and that it was so close to the pub. She ran to the entrance, stepped inside, sat at a newly-cleaned, ammonia-scented booth and ordered a cup of coffee and rye toast. She was accommodated almost immediately.

After putting warm milk and brown sugar in her weak British coffee, of which she was not accustomed, she buttered her thickly-sliced toast and motioned for the waitress to come over. The medium-built young brunette hobbled her way over, grunting and gesturing profusely the whole way.

"Do you happen to know where a typical Irish pub is around here? I need to throw back a few," she whispered, almost inaudibly.

"What'd ya say? I couldn't hear ya," the waitress screamed into her ear.

"Is there a pub around here, ma'am?" she asked in a polite and soft, but deep-pitched octave.

"Why, sure there is. Everyone knows it around here. It's called "Silky's"...the best of the best. The biggest guy in the world owns it. Made a lot of money at it, besides. Used to come in here all the time... and bring his dandy wife. His tips were lousy though. Anyway, it's just a block up, on the other side of the street. You can't get lost around here," she flirtatiously commented, after unbuttoning another one of her buttons on her white-laced smocked uniform.

"Pardon me, but where are you from?" the server asked. "Did you just arrive?"

Sunny said nothing.

"I could show you around after I get off work, okay?" the waitress persisted.

The server then paused, and went right back to her spiel. "Hey, you are one of those oil guys from way down there in those sandy lands, ain't ya love?"

"Yes, ma'am. That is I, and yes, I did just arrive," Sunny spoke in her most allusive voice yet.

Not knowing when these great sounds were soon to give out on her, she asked for the check, paid it, and exited.

The frustrated waitress was yelling obscenities through the doorway the whole while. Sunny could hear them and turned away. Then, she looked back at the server in the doorway, smiled and waved.

Trudging down the narrow, cobblestone road, Sunny felt like a medieval queen, even though she was dressed as a man. She could not wait to take off her costume. As soon as she could flee with the money, she was becoming herself again. She was finally away from Afghanistan. It had been hard, very hard for her to take being a servant to males, but she did it. She had to do it. She did it for six long, gruesome years. She had always wanted to attend a university and study engineering, but of course, she never was able to. She had never wanted to marry and have children, until that is, she met Ty. Then, all bets were off. She would have succumbed to slavery to be with him. She had been enthralled with the man for years, until one day she woke up and asked him when they were getting married. He said that they weren't, and it was all over in her eyes. She didn't feel a tinge of remorse for what had happened to him. She had actually enjoyed watching his flesh flake-off with each spark landing on his sun-tanned skin. She was finally at peace with her existence and ready to enter the bar, as she stood before it. *She knew she would always remain as faithful as a puppy to Afghanistan. She could never be anything else.*

"Hmmm...Not a very good looking establishment and not very cozy either," she thought.

"Nobody could ever drink in a place like this...probably used as a front, since he stored all his cash inside."

When she entered the shabby pub, she was amazed. She had never before seen so many men sitting at a bar in all her life, with an inter-mingling of scantily-dressed young and middle-aged women.

Everyone was laughing, with not all of their senses in high order. It had been a long, hard work day for most of them. Sunny stepped right up to the bar and took a seat.

"What may I do you for, mate?" the pub manager interrogated her.

"A pint of Guinness," she muttered.

"Coming right up sir," he acknowledged.

She now thought that it was going to be harder than ever to find out how to get to Ty's basement safe without anyone seeing her move. She glanced around the dark brown painted room and noticed red curtains, which when pulled back, led to a narrow, rickety stair-case, making its way down into the ground. She watched as several employees marched their way down the muddy steps. They always came up with something of significance in their hands, a file, an add-ing machine, receipts, money. She knew that they were coming from an office below the bar, a secret back entrance, which was most likely where the safe was cemented into the concrete slab, but she had to be sure.

Sunny talked to the pub manager, while supposedly becoming slightly intoxicated on her third beer. She had spilled a lot of the other two jugs under the counter where she was sitting, when no one was looking, so that her faculties would remain intact. She asked where the toilet was, and when she was shown, she was horrified at the thought of having to look at men urinating. This was not her place, she keep thinking to herself.

"I have got to get to the safe, rip it open, and leave…for good," she whispered to the thin air, on the way to the toilet, where she had already decided, she was not even going to step into.

Her eyes speedily scanned doors, exits, windows and entrances to see what she could find. At that moment, an intoxicated worker came out of the water closet. She bumped into him, and said that she was sorry.

"Too bad there isn't some type of underground facility in this two-story establishment in case there was a bad storm, being so close to the sea and all, ya know lad?" she dryly questioned him.

Slurring his words, he came back with, "Well, of course there is, just around the corner and down the hall. *There is the door to the basement,*" he pointed to it and proceeded to stumble, then he caught himself.

"Well, I knew there had to be something," she chuckled, pushing the water closet door open momentarily, until he was gone from sight. Now, she was gone for good, never to return to finish or pay for her brew. It was over. This had to be the right place.

She skulked around the decorated corner and down the dark, dank barren hallway, leading to an almost rotted door with a silver hinge hanging from its side.

"Good, and no one will see me here. It's not like the other one that's in the center of the pub."

She tugged at the door knob. "Oh, thank the heavens it's not locked," she said rather loudly, as if in shock.

So far, everything had been going according to plan, and she hoped that it was going to continue in the same manner. She looked from side to side, down the hallway and down the stairs. It still appeared that no one was around, at least not in sight. She had learned long ago when going out with her brother in town that what is apparent, is not always as it really is and vice versa. She had learned to be always conscious of her environment.

She tiptoed down the creaky, almost rotted staircase, which showed holes of frayed wood chips and pieces, ready to give splinters to any bare foot that dared step on it at any given moment. Her long, white head gear was definitely getting in the way of attentive survey of the situation at hand.

Frustrated, she took it off and threw it. It landed in a dark, dusty corner of the room, not readily viewable to anyone coming down the stairs. That turban had been giving her problems the entire day in which she had been wearing it. It was rubbing a hole in her forehead, and needless to say, causing immense sweat underneath its tight, soon-to-be money-laden brim. It has and will serve its purpose even more, she thought. It happened to have been Med-hi's, and he had a very long, slender head, and she a rather round head, with lots of thick hair to make it fit even tighter.

Once completely down the non-supported staircase, she ran over to the safe which was hidden in floor by displaying a Persian rug on top of it. She walked over to a particular dark corner of the room and pulled out the slip of paper from the hole inside her brim, and on which she had noted the combination to the safe the afternoon when she mistakenly heard the secret conversation. She had been speaking with Ty on the phone a month ago, when he had called her in Kabul. He evidently was in the basement of his pub talking to a worker. He said that he just had a situation come up and that he would have to call her back. She waited for the phone to go dead, however, it never did. She kept hearing male voices chuckling and rambling on and on about certain patrons at the bar and a certain woman of which Ty shouted to his workers, "Ohhh...I want her so bad".

Then, all of a sudden, his conversation got serious and changed to that of the floor safe. Ty whispered to his "right hand man" what the combination to the buried safe was, in case Ty was ever detained by anyone, or anything. The safe was said to hold the Pub's, the IRA's, and Tyrone Riley's every dollar from fraudulent criminal and terrorist activities, and these dollars were said to be mounting high.

"Every dollar is traceable.... every dollar is recorded strategically and methodically....every night before closing....every worker is expendable," Ty loved to warn his new workers, as they entered his place of business.

Sunny pulled out her piece of ratty paper that held the combination to the safe, as well as her flashlight. She began to feel revenge and justification, which she had hoped she would during her entire flight to the Emerald Coast.

She began to turn the dial to the left, then to the right, and back again. Her heart was pumping fast, faster, then faster, like it was about to pop out of her sweat-laden skin. "Only one more turn to make with the dial....come on...come on..."

Just as the safe lid loosened, then sprung open, the door up above flew open, and a faint light turned on. Sunny reached for her stiletto, which was hidden inside the band of her long, white draping turban that she quickly picked-up in the corner. She was petrified now and dripping with cold sweat. She reached inside the "bank" and quickly and quietly began to pull out her future. She heard footsteps slowly descending and coming towards her.

She had pulled out all of the stash and put it into her cloth carry bag and began to run, when she tripped on an uneven concrete block.

"Stop right there!" a well-dressed man in a navy silk suit demanded, as he lit a long match in the moonlight, and which also lit her pretty round face, in such a way that she now looked like a girl, even with the professional disguise and makeup job that had worked considerably up until now.

Chapter Fifteen

Hijacked

The Ambassador was immediately called at his assistant's condominium after two days of worrying, sleeping, eating like a gluten, and of course drinking…a lot. His assistant was "closed lip" about his habit, as bringing it out into the open would only nullify his position with the United States Government, which he had worked his whole life to attain. He knew he would never again be a paid again so handsomely for transporting secret data from the United States Government to *other* sources.

His assistant drove the Ambassador to Reagan National Airport where he was to catch the first flight out for Dublin, scheduled to depart at noon. He was to be retrieved at the airport in Dublin by officials and escorted to where his daughter was being held for questioning. The two stopped at a drive-thru window for coffee, near the airport grounds. His assistant let him off at the departing flight entrance, holding one carry-on piece of baggage in his hand, then sped off himself to the office.

The Ambassador showed his credentials and was quickly escorted past security and onto his awaiting airbus. He ordered a tall Screwdriver, as he sat in first-class, preparing himself for his reunion with the daughter who was like a stranger to him. He felt awkward and uncomfortable, yet excited about seeing her again, and of course, all in one glorious piece. He downed his cocktail, then ordered another, and another, until his flight attendant, whom he found out was based in Washington DC, warned him that he might be drinking too much for an Ambassador of his status.

He nodded in agreement and asked for orange juice only. As soon as she was gone from view, he reached into his carry-on bag and pulled out a tiny bottle of gin, which he had placed inside his sock. He poured the gin into the orange juice and began drinking it with a huge smile on his face. As soon as the jet was well-stationed in the altitude, a big meal was served to the first-class passengers of either, scallops and shrimp over rice, or beef tips and gravy, again over rice. He ordered the first selection, served also with salad and broccoli and chocolate fudge cake. He had so diligently been trying to lose ten pounds for three years on a diet which had never seemed to produce any result for him. He thought, "With all the booze, there's no way I'll be able to loose even ONE pound."

After he filled his belly with the last morsel of the chocolate fudge cake slice, he felt guilty and wondered why he even took one bite of the cake. "I am the United States Ambassador to Iraq, and I can't even abstain from a piece of cake. If I did, it would ultimately be for the good of our country. And the drinking…I've got to stop," he muttered to himself. There was nobody within earshot from where he was sitting, so he could vent. The first-class section was virtually vacant.

There was one other gentleman who had a long, black braided beard who kept turning back to look at the Ambassador. The Ambassador thought this odd and obtrusive, but just smiled at him, every time he looked back at him.

At that moment a loud raucous was heard coming from the rear of the aircraft. Women started screaming and heavy footsteps starting running up to the front of the jet.

Two seconds later the nylon drape which separated the first-class and coach sections was pushed back violently by a dark, nervous man who entered with gun in hand. The bearded man raised up out of his seat and gave a signal to the dark man to sit down beside the Ambassador. The dark man pulled out cloths from inside his pockets and wrapped them around the Ambassador's head and eyes, so he could not see. The bearded man went into the cockpit and demanded that the pilot fly back to Washington.

"There is business to take care of there, matters of state, regarding the Ambassador, his daughter and money," he told the pilot.

Then he shouted to the passengers, "The Ambassador's daughter has escaped.

Now, we want a ransom from your government of one billion dollars to insure the safe return of your Ambassador, the safe return of every person on this aircraft, and another safe day in the city of Washington DC, with no bombs detonating. Pilot…radio to flight control that we want the President of the United States to greet us at Reagan National, with money in briefcase. Can you do that?" he shouted butting the pistol further into the pilot's white skull.

"I can do that," the pilot replied, as he lifted his device that enabled him to speak with flight control. "Flight control, we have an emergency…." the pilot could not finish, as he was then thrown from his seat. The bearded terrorist had fallen and his head was now lying face down in a pool of his own blood, bloody gun at his side. The co-pilot scooped up his gun and realized that he was dead. He had knocked the back of his head on the flight control board, as the co-pilot headed into the massive clouds of turbulence and wind-shear, which jets would have been warned by flight control to avoid, at all costs. He felt that he must execute this move. He could not let these men bring the plane and the country down, which he thought might have happened had he not opted for this strategy.

Once inside the whirling cloud, the co-pilot proceeded up through more battling clouds, as diligently and calmly as possibly, in order to prevent more catastrophe, of which he was certain there had been farther back in the aircraft. He continued until he saw blue air and sunlight in the horizon and placed the craft on auto-pilot and headed back to Washington. Flight control began radioing him, incessantly. He just let it be for several minutes. He wasn't ready to talk to anyone yet. He couldn't believe what had just occurred and that he was still alive and not even hurt.

The co-pilot wiped the sweat from his eyes and climbed over the terrorist's body to pat his pilot's back.

"Good job, Don."

He got no response. Don's body keeled over and fell away from the flight desk, onto the floor.

"Oh, my God, Don…I'm sorry….so sorry," was all he could utter, as he got up enough courage to open the flight door and see what had happened to the passengers, crew and the other terrorist.

When he opened it, there was a stillness in the air, except for an occasional moan and groan. There were no passengers in first class at all, only one sore flight attendant who had fallen in the small sink at her station.

He remembered there to be some government official supposed to be seated in first class. "Could I have been mistaken? No one's here." His head was so rattled, he had no recollection. That, plus, he had an excruciating headache. He thought that he needed to be checked-out at the hospital once back in the states, just for a precaution.

He walked down the aisle way and saw dead people, bleeding and hurt people, fearful and quiet people, and one hurt terrorist, with a broken leg and a gun that had been seized by an injured military man seated near where the terrorist went down upon impact with the severe wind shear. The US Marine had reached down and grabbed the gun from on top of the floor, while grunting, as if in severe pain.

The co-pilot calmly informed the survivors that the jet was headed back to Washington.

"All victims will be taken care of, and the sick and the hurt will be transported to local hospitals." He consoled the survivors, "We have to move on with our lives, to create meaningful existences for our children, our mates, our siblings, and our parents, and for our country."

At the close of this statement, he realized that Jean and Bern, the two flight attendants serving the coach section were not anywhere to be found. He continued to stalk up and down the aisles, searching for the attendants, and for the American diplomat.

The co-pilot checked everywhere, except in the galley down below. He looked down the spiral stairs and saw a trail of blood leading to it. He looked inside and threw-up all over the nicely-scrubbed galley floor. There were three bodies, all with throats slashed and eyeballs cut out, two were Jean and Bern, the other was Cynthia's father, the Ambassador to Iraq, he found out, as he pulled his authentic credentials and passport from his left jacket pocket. The co-pilot was horrified. He made his way back to the cockpit and proceeded to radio flight control.

"We have an emergency situation on our hands and are flying back to Washington. We have dead, hurt and wounded. They all need assistance. Please notify family members of all passengers on this flight. It was a hijacking. One of the hijackers is dead, the other is wounded. The US Ambassador to Iraq was on this flight and is dead, killed by a terrorist. Jean and Bern, two of the flight attendants on this flight are dead, as well as the pilot, Don. That is all. Be on the ground in about an hour...over and out," was all that that co-pilot could muster up enough strength to say after this harrowing experience.

The co-pilot guided the jet to a safe landing. He told flight control upon landing that he did not know how he was able to maneuver the aircraft under such circumstances.

"I just thank God. It could have been worse...much worse," he cried, not being able to hold back his tearful voice any longer.

Ambulances, hearses, and camera crews were all stretched between the runway and the arrival gate. The co-pilot realized that this had been a world-wide incident and was a probable world-wide disaster.

The surviving passengers were sent down the slide to safety, while the dead were carried off the aircraft in large plastic bags. The co-pilot was taken to a hospital, as soon as he stumbled through the interviews, as he climbed down the stairs, walked the runway, and entered the terminal. Dozens of news crews' lights were all around his being. He suddenly felt like a star. The Ambassador's body was taken off the jet by four United States Army Lieutenants. The Ambassador had been drafted into the army as a teenager. Everyone saluted, as the casket came past them. The body was carried to a hearse that was awaiting it near the terminal entrance. Flags in the city were lowered to half-mast.

Still answering questions by Scotland Yard officials in Dublin, weak Cynthia was getting tired and fed-up. "How much longer do you think that you will be needing us?" she asked the flirtatious official.

"Unfortunately, your pretty face is soon to depart from our view," he responded, with a gleam in his steamy, blue eyes.

"I don't know where to go, since they say I cannot go back home. It is supposed to be under investigation for quite a while," she said.

"Well, that I can't help you with. You could stay with me at my flat, but my wife might object," he ridiculously suggested.

Kimmie spun her chair around and looked Cynthia square in the face, as if she were blessed with a revelation.

She shouted, "Hey, you can stay with us on the ranch in Florida. All you have to do is get your passport, some cash from the bank and clothing from your house. Can you send an officer with her to pick everything up, please?" she questioned the official. "And Nikko, you are welcome to stay there too, for as long as you want. We are a team now, have been through an awful lot..."

Nikko butted in, "No, a HELL of a lot is more like it, sweetie." He felt worn out and took her up on the offer."

At that moment, the officer's phone rang, and he grabbed it. His expression changed, as he continued listening to the other party. "Yes...yes...I don't know...amazing...amazing. Sure, I will tell her."

The officer hung up the receiver with his head lowered and eyes staring at the desk beneath him.

"I don't know how to tell you this, Mrs. Riley, but your father is dead," he told her.

"Oh, my God!" she cried out in shock. "How...when...where... why?"

"It seems that he was a victim of a terrorist hijacking. Their motive was obviously to get the Ambassador for some purpose. It might all relate to you and Ty and the world dominance and ransom issue. It is being investigated, of course, quite heavily. No one will rest world-wide until this is resolved. In the meantime, please take Kimmie up on her advice about getting all needed personal items and absconding from this place...to a place where no one would even have a notion that you would ever go. You must...for your safety," the officer warned her.

"Ohh... Can't I go to see his body? Is it in Washington, or had the plane made it over here yet?" Cynthia asked in a panic. "I wanted so much to finally get to know my father and be a real daughter, for the first time in my life, oh God, what is happening to me?" she looked up and asked the heavens.

"Now, now, we fully understand how you feel. Pull yourself together in that back office over there, have some tea to settle your nerves, and take the *bloody* plane over to Tampa. You will have a new name, new identity, and basically a new look. Give me an hour. Relax back there, get freshened up. Even pour a drink. A beautician will be in straight away to attend to your new look. Remember, you have only one hour, and chin up, it's not that bad. I mean your dad was a bloody drunk, you know, and soon to be booted out of office. We all surmised that here in the Yard," he blurted out in a cruel matter-of-fact tone of voice.

On that note, she grabbed her belongings and marched straight to the back room, where she plunged a tea and Irish whiskey down her feminine throat. She sat in silence for fifteen minutes, as she let the whiskey take effect. She washed her face in the sink and freshened herself up in the mirror of the dimly lit room. "What was the beautician going to do with my look?" she wondered.

The jet-black headed beautician who dressed herself as an eighties new waver, came prancing through the door with bag in hand, chewing gum and blowing bubbles the whole while.

"I am going to truly make you look brilliant. You will look and feel like a beautiful porcelain doll," she exclaimed. "I will show you, love." She pulled out pics of the bobbed-spiked hairdo and platinum hair color that was soon to be Cynthia's. Also, she showed her pictures of makeup techniques that would make her nose look wider and her eyes smaller. She definitely was not going to appear as refined as she once was.

"But I don't want to look like this!" Cynthia stated in an uproar.

"You will if you want to continue to live," she replied back in a stern fashion.

Cynthia glanced around the room, as if in dismay, as she decided, "Okay, do it." She remained in silence with her beautiful eyes shut tight as the process took effect and was eventually completed thirty minutes later.

The beautician whispered into Cynthia's nicely-shaped ear, "It's all done. You look great, a little different....but still great. See for your-self, honey." She handed a small mirror to Cynthia.

Cynthia opened her eyes and gasped. She did not know who this person was. She kind of liked the look, but had never seen this spiked-haired, platinum-blonde woman before.

"It'll work, don't you think?" the beautician asked the once classy ballerina, who now looked sleazy.

"I look so different. Of course, it will work," Cynthia stated, as the door was pushed in by officials.

"Your car is waiting, Mrs. Riley. You are now Miss Eleanor Buchanan from Rochester, New York. You were on a tour of Ireland with your cousin, Kimmie. Nik is your fiancé, so act like he is such," the now serious official demanded of her.

"You'll clear customs in Tampa, and everything should be fine from that point on. We will keep tabs on the situation. If any element arises that you are unprepared for, notify us and the local authorities, as soon as possible. It's always better to be safe, rather than sorry, ya hear, me girls and boys? Now get out of here. It's time to put our strategy in motion. And, by the way, we will send to the ranch all newspaper clippings and videos of the funeral for you to keep. There will be news segments about it as well on all of the networks. You'll feel like you were at the funeral."

Cynthia, Kimmie, and Nikko hopped into the minivan that was to take them to the Cynthia's bank, then to her coastal estate to pick up some of her wears, and finally onward to Shannon International Airport, where freedom awaited them.

With her new bleached-blond bobbed hairdo, fake nails, and heavily made-up face with gaudy, loud clothing besides, she was sure she was going to pull off the scheme. The car stopped by her bank first, where she withdrew the two accounts, after she had put on a beret to hide her hair. On the way to the exit, however, she was stopped by a customer service representative.

"Oh, Mrs. Riley, we have tried to contact you, regarding your home loan for several days now, but have been unable to reach you. It seems that your account has not paid for four months now, and of course, we will soon be starting bank acquisition procedures. We just wanted you to be aware of the dilemma. All that we need are the four mortgage payments, along with the back taxes on the property. This should amount to a little over one hundred-thousand pounds."

Cynthia said nothing. She ran outside to the awaiting car that had the others inside and put down her head between her legs to quietly sob.

"Ty didn't pay the mortgage or taxes for four months. The bank wants possession. What am I to do now, and where is Ty anyway?" she frustratingly smirked. It didn't even matter anymore about Ty's betrayal. To her, he wasn't even worth fretting over anymore.

Nikko put a strong hand on her shoulder to rub the tension out.

"You will put it up for sale at a great price. The home should sell instantaneously this way. It seems to be a special piece of property, so don't worry. I will take care of this matter," he assured her.

Suddenly, Cynthia felt strong, whole and sure of herself.

"Okay, Nik, and thanks, thanks a lot," she said. Then, she closed her eyes and rested and waited, until the car pulled up to the gates of the estate.

"Here we are, folks," the Inspector rumbled in a bass voice, waking Cynthia from her new state of slumber. Irritated, he asked, "Does anyone know the secret to get into these gates?"

Cynthia told him the combination, and they slowly cruised through, up to the empty, lonely- looking mansion, once full of life, now in disarray.

Nikko now gazed at the mansion and its grounds thoroughly in the sun light and stated, "This should sell in no time, especially at the right price. They always do at a great price...No, I don't see a problem whatsoever. I'll phone a realtor from the airport, and they should be able to get it ready to market by tomorrow evening," he was beginning to feel very close to Cynthia, almost as if he was falling in love with her beauty... her charm and wit, and most of all...her money. His demons were back, and they felt like he must snag her...and soon.

All three walked inside the massive home. Nikko and Kimmie were aghast at the beautiful decor found in every room, from the fancy woodwork, to the sculpted ceilings with diamond-studded chandeliers. These features made the home feel more luscious and full of worth than it really was. The three sauntered upstairs gazing at every masterpiece portrait placed on the walls.

After the long, steep, winding staircase, they finally reached their destination...the master bedroom. This was truly a sight to behold, with its twenty foot ceilings, equipped with polished silver chandelier and two massive French doors, leading out onto a huge covered wooden deck which overlooked the most beautiful part of the coast. This time, they saw and felt every naughty breath this castle exhaled.

Cynthia grabbed a small suitcase and started stuffing her clothing into it, the most flamboyant of her clothing, as she was instructed to do. She filled it until she could hardly zip it shut. She sat on it to fully close it.

"Let's get out of here," she said to the others, as she walked with them to the car, never dreaming she would not return to Ireland for months.

When they got back to the vehicle, the Inspector told them that no one had seen hide nor hare of Tyrone and that that was a *very suspicious thing.*

"One of three things has happened to the chap. He either absconded with all of the money from his safe, he's doing secret business abroad, or he is simply DEAD," the Inspector stressed the third possibility quite heavily... "But we will soon find out for sure, or at least scratch off at least one of the three possibilities from the list... Driver, let's change course...*to Silky's Pub.*"

Chapter Sixteen

The Safe

The deep-voiced Inspector pulled up to a very small, shabby and dirty Irish pub, displaying devil ornamentation on its signage. The Inspector raced inside the establishment and asked the unattractive young man if Ty was working there, and if he could see Ty and the safe. The Inspector was told that Ty was not around and no one knew when he was to return.

"I need to look inside the safe of this pub please," the Inspector insisted.

"Here you go sir," Ty's driver and bar worker said mockingly, and he threw him the keys to the basement. "Have at it." The Inspector opened the pub door and motioned for the three to go inside. Cynthia was amazed that this worker who was Ty's "right-hand" man, did not recognize her at all.

"Watch yourselves going down these rickety steps," the Inspector advised the three, as he was unlocking the basement door. Once done, he pushed the heavy steel door ajar and entered wearily. The others followed close behind the officer.

"I wonder where the stupid safe is here in this dark, smelly basement. There seems to be only one light in this place, and its here." He flipped up the wall switch that he only found through feel. There still wasn't enough light streaming in from up above to see much of anything down below.

The Inspector, the girls, and Nikko felt around the walls, looked behind tables, in closets, and behind a bookshelf. Still, no signs of a safe anywhere.

The official yelled upstairs to the help, "Hey you bloke, get your ass down here to tell us where to find the bloody thing."

No response at all. He went up the stairs to ask again and found the door to be locked, with no sound coming from the other side. Probably, no van was waiting outside either. The hoodlum evidently had wanted to take them as prisoners all along, they mentioned to one other.

The Inspector felt stumped and foolish, and he did not like the feeling. He circled the floor of the basement, calling out on his cell phone to the yard...no reception. He paced the floor with hands clutched around his head, as if asking for answers to this obvious insurmountable task. He kept their inescapable predicament a secret, so as not to create panic. He must come up with a solution.

Just then, his shoe slipped on the flimsy rug which looked as if it were placed there to show cheap charm.

Kimmie came running to the rescue as soon as she saw the inspector slip and fall. She helped him up. It seemed that he wasn't severely hurt, only shaken up, and a little bit embarrassed by the incident. His upper thigh was sore from falling so hard on it, and he began to feel an immense throbbing sensation from his hip to his foot on his right side. He let out a muffled yell each time the pain occurred. Kimmie pulled him away from the cheap rug and carried out a folding chair from in front of the small television at the side of the room. She eased him over to it and placed the hobbling inspector in a sitting position on the seat.

While executing these humanitarian duties, Cynthia scooped up the rug so that no one else would trip on it. It was on the slippery, concrete floor, and the rug was not anchored down by anything. She felt safer for everyone to take it away.

Cynthia was awestruck, as she stared at what appeared to be a floor safe underneath this rug. She couldn't move, and she couldn't even speak.

Nikko, still searching frantically for the safe with all of the money inside, asked Cynthia how she was doing in her search. No response was given to him.

"Hello, Cynthia…How is it going?" he loudly asked her, and still no response. He glanced at Kimmie who was tending to the Inspector, and then at the back of a motionless Cynthia. He came up behind the immobile and speechless Cynthia and spun her around, stirring up the quiet basement, as he stared at an amazed face and long, slender arms pointing to the ground.

"Cynthia, my angel, you've done it, you've found it!" he could hardly form audible words in his excited state of being. He picked her up and smacked her with dozens of kisses.

The Inspector limped over to the spot of interest and said, "Good work Cynthia," and patted her on her sensuously feminine back. "It's all over. We'll take care of the rest from here.

One of the three possibilities might be scratched off the list, like I told you it would be. Ty is gone with the money, conducting monkey business in distant lands, or he is dead. I personally prefer the latter of the three. Cynthia, take all of the money from the safe and put it in one of those plastic bags in the corner as soon as the safe is opened."

She ran over and snatched one of the bags off the floor. As she walked back to the safe, all three were asking, "What's the combination? What are the Numbers? Let's open it."

"What combination? I never had it. He never told me anything about having a safe...I had no idea that he was hiding money...anywhere. He was so distant and so secretive all the time. I just never questioned anything. Oh, how I wish I had," Cynthia cried out.

Nikko then scolded Cynthia, "I can't believe you would ever let him do this to you, and you never wondered...?"

The inspector butted in, as he thought this to be an appropriate time to disclose the truth.

"Girls and boy, we are in trouble. There's no way out. The front door is bolted shut, and we have no reception to call out from down here. Unless someone from the Yard figures out where we are and wonders why we have not returned or called in, we're screwed. Oh, and our driver has left the scene, either through abduction, or he is one of their men. I don't hear the van's rattling engine out front anymore."

"Wait one second mates...just one second," Cynthia excitedly blurted out, as if in a theatrical performance. "I do seem to remember something, something that kind of caught me off guard. When I was being held against my will down here, one night, late at night," she could hardly make a complete sentence, she was in such deep thought.

"I remember Ty's driver," she said, "as he was coming into the basement that night. He shouted up to the pub workers, 'Where are they?' He walked to the right of the cubicle they had placed me in, gagged and bound, and came walking across the room to what seemed like the location of something, maybe a safe. He had what sounded like a set of jangling keys in his hands. He then yelled upstairs, 'Got the lute for Ty. Where does he want me to meet him?' Then, the voice trailed off.

There must be a hidden key to a drawer on the safe, somewhere near that cubicle," she guessed, pointing to it.

The Inspector painfully got up out of the chair to look and feel thoroughly behind furniture and on the walls where she described the incident taking place. He found a small ring of keys on the wall, behind a small refrigerator. On this ring were two minuscule keys, and one large door key. He knew he had to search for a small lock. He found this on the upper right hand corner of the safe. However, it appeared that this lock was not to open the safe, but rather a small, thin compartment located above the opening. He turned the key and found a piece of ratty paper folded on top of a notepad. He opened it.

"Yes, I knew it…the combination to the safe, here it is," and he waved the piece of paper in front of everybody's eyes in glee. The gang's initial state of felicity quickly changed to despair when the inspector opened the safe, only to find it empty.

"Well, that's it. The first possibility must be the one. He's gone with the money. Ty has left his former life for good…and with that much cash, *death is always at his door*. My dear, he's gone from your life forever, one way or another." the Inspector boldly stated. Cynthia took the news on the chin.

"Our next problem we must solve is…. *how to get the hell out of here*," the Inspector demonstrated with flailing arms.

Cynthia looked at him sheepishly and simply shook her pretty head, motioning for the others to follow her. She led them to a secret opening in the dark, camouflaged walls of the dungeon, with another muddied, rotted staircase leading up to red curtains, which opened out into the pub's back doorway. They turned the bolt and exited.

Once outside, within range of cell towers, the Inspector phoned Scotland Yard for the minivan to be sent back to the pub. The Yard said that they never sent a van to begin with. "They sent a Town Car from the station," the Lieutenant declared.

The Inspector certainly did feel like an idiot now. He would probably be reprimanded, or even dismissed. He knew that now was not the time to be thinking of downfalls, no it was time for rectification.... and he was the man for the job. He flagged a cab for Shannon Airport for the three, and himself. He was soon to be on his way back to London to do his duty and bring back this vicious, egocentric and manipulative Tyrone S. Riley, *dead or alive.*

Chapter Seventeen

The Flight over the Atlantic

*S*unny left for Shannon International Airport after visiting five different banks on the western and southern shores of the country. She was able to diversify, so that no one would question the extreme amount of money that she had locked up in each of them. She had most of her money hidden in eleven secret deposit boxes in each bank. She also had a few medium-sized certificates of deposit due to mature in six months, and five rather small checking and savings accounts, all in her name. These gave her the breathing room she needed. She would be back to collect everything she left in the banks in six months. She now had time to devise a strategy, one like her brother would have most likely concocted.

Sunny kept $100,000.00, all in large currency, in the band of her stylish turban, acting as extra padding. No one would even have the foggiest notion of what was being carried under her heavily-garbed head gear. In a detector, it would appear merely as a mixture of paper and cotton padding.

"This amount should hold me for six months easily. I have a lot to do, a lot to see and lots of people to meet, but I should do fine with this amount for that long. I plan to make a whole lot more in the months to come, if everything goes according to plan, and I know it will," she whispered to herself in the minivan she had hired through her inside agent at the Yard. It was the same van that had transported the Inspector, Nik, Cynthia, and Kimmie to their impending doom, she thought, earlier that day.

Sunny found out later, however, through this same agent, that all four had escaped. The driver had put Ty's man, Roger, in his trunk while the crew was locked in the basement. Locking them up downstairs had been Sunny's doing.

She had been informed through her spy at Scotland Yard that Nikko, Cynthia, and Kimmie, along with an Inspector, were headed to the pub to collect what was inside the safe. All that they needed was a large, dependable vehicle and quickly. Plans were momentarily set in motion, with the help of Med-hi's double agents in London. They had been the ones who met her in the basement of Ty's pub earlier.

Afterward, these double agents informed the Irish gang when she was supposed to be flying to Tampa, dressed as a man. Sunny's inside connection in Scotland Yard was one that her brother had used frequently, and this informant transferred information to Sunny's being about where the three were flying this afternoon from Shannon. Sunny arranged for the same flight. She had been informed as to how all three were dressed and what their faces, hair, and bodies looked like. She felt like she had been well-provided with essential information for her plot and couldn't wait to be seated near the three on the aircraft. Her informants, however, were not on her side.

Sunny knew not what anyone looked like, except for Cynthia, and that was only through photos and newspaper clippings that Ty had showed her in the past. She couldn't wait to finally *kill* them at the ranch in Florida.

She laughed and said to herself, "And I am sure that they are going to enjoy being seated next to an *Arabian Oil Baron with so many interesting fables to share.*"

Her driver idled the van in the departure terminal area, collecting a big sum of money for all of his work, then whisked away.

She first made sure with the ticket agent that she was still booked in the first class seat, 6D, before she retrieved her boarding pass from the machine.

"I wish you the best Mr. Hassan, and have a nice flight," the representative spoke at the counter.

She boarded the plane at once, then began the wait... wait for money...money and world domination...what her brother and Ty each wanted for themselves. "I am doing this for you, my dear brother...to bring down Ty, YOUR NEMESIS."

More first-class passengers boarded the plane and pretty soon, it was full, for the exception of three vacant seats. The three remaining first-class stragglers soon boarded the jet and sat right in front of the coach passengers' bulk aisle seats.

"They were late," Sunny mumbled to herself and the vacant seat next to her. "Better late than never."

She greeted the three newly-boarded passengers who were seated across from her, one handsome man who looked Greek, a cute boyish girl, and a cheap-looking blonde wearing high heels.

Sunny looked the last one up and down, and maliciously thought, "YOU are MY nemesis. You wait and see for yourself... just wait and see for yourself," she whispered, while continually smiling at Cynthia.

"Ty, I'm going to bring the ranch so far down that you won't even know what hit it," she quietly said to herself. "You know my love, the one you and Hugo talked so much about and couldn't wait to take over one day. Yes indeed, now it definitely is MY game of revenge," her now frazzled mind promised her ex-lover. "And I guarantee you, I WILL GET MY RANCH....once and for all."

Camille yelled in the wind, "*Oh no you won't...not MY ranch, sweetie, NON JAMAIS........ma cherie.........NON JAMAIS.*"

The flight took off, lights were dimmed, and all parties slept, not to wake until landing.

Epilogue

*I*t has often been said that Atlantis sank into the Atlantic Ocean after a failed attempt by an Athenian invasion, "in a single day and night of misfortune". It was a naval identity which laid in front of the "Pillars of Hercules", which was larger than Libya and Asia sized together. Travelers could cross to other islands from Atlantis. Here existed powerful and great Kings who ruled over the entire island and over many other islands and parts of the continent.

Socrates mused about what is a so-called perfect society. According to Socrates, ancient Athens seemed to have the perfect society, while Atlantis, on the other hand, represented the supposed antithesis of this ideology.

According to Plato's dialogue "Critias", the Hellenic gods bequeathed the island of Atlantis to Poseidon. The island was huge, larger than Asia Minor. Soon after receiving his massive island, Atlantis was unbelievably swallowed up and sunk by an earthquake.

> "But at a later time there occurred portentous earthquakes and floods, and one grievous day and night befell them, when the whole body of your warriors was swallowed

up by the earth, and the island of Atlantis in like manner was swallowed up by the sea and vanished; wherefore also the ocean at that spot has now become impassable and unsearchable, being blocked up by the shoal mud which the island created as it settled down."

And so the legend continues...

Some ancient writers thought of Atlantis as merely fiction, story-telling in Hellenic times, while other philosophers believed it to be an accurate account, like Cantor, the philosopher, who professed that prophets testified by the Egyptians are written on preserved pillars.

Where is this lost continent? Is it truly in the Sardinia, Santorini or Crete regions of the world? Is it, as some speculate, in the middle of the Atlantic Ocean, where Bermuda is today, or is it closer to Europe itself, like in the Azores or the Canary Island region? Is it the now non-existent island of Spartel, near the Strait of Gibraltar? We can only surmise. There is no documented proof or evidence.

So then, the question is simply, "Is this a real tale, or just some entertaining and enchanting legend which has been passed down since the beginning of beautiful time?"

Will we ever know of its reality?

Subterfuge

PART THREE

Introduction

eople are not always as they seem. They can change in an instant, or in a decade, but they can change, and often do. Perhaps, the one who you thought to be so kind and brilliant, is actually cunning and clever, possessing a demonic soul. These are the facades that turn a helping and trusting mankind into a blood-thirsty and need-driven, scavenger society. Keep your ears up and your eyes zeroed in.

Chapter One

La Dona Cecilia Hotel

The touch down at Tampa International Airport was as smooth as it gets. Sunny gathered her few belongings from overhead and underneath, smiled at her three aisle mates, and left the airbus. She exited the building downstairs at baggage claim, after a long shuttle ride, and kept walking, until she found a taxi cab. It was a hot, muggy spring day, so she thought to herself, "Maybe all the taxi drivers are at the beach." She asked how much.

The driver said, "Sir, I need to know where you are headed."

Because her masculinity was soon to become a thing of the past, she asked the driver in rather a homosexual sounding melody, "Take me to the classiest hotel around here, and it has to be on the beach, with places I can walk to. Oh, and I have to be rather close to the Ellenton area."

The driver replied, "Well, there are two places, one in Sarasota, and the other on St. Pete Beach. They're both the same distance from Ellenton and are both top of the line places to rest your head."

Sunny asked him, "Where would you stay if you were arriving here for the first time and wanted some fun and sun, and of course, rest. Which is closer to us now? I don't want to drive that far today. I'm tired and have plenty of things to do tomorrow. I need a hotel that can get me a sporty rental car too."

Without hesitation he said, "I am taking you to La Dona Cecilia Hotel on St. Pete Beach. Its close by, lots to do, without being too loud and harsh, and very beautiful besides. You know, it even served as a hospital for those wounded in World War II. It has quite the Spanish flare, too, and it has one of the most beautiful beaches in Florida. And they can call from the front desk to have a car delivered to you anytime, great restaurants, bars, and shops besides. How about it, my man?"

"You've sold me. Let's go," Sunny said, still able to keep her masculinity in check. "What's the fare?" She pulled out her gem wallet so that he wouldn't see it and retrieved a fifty dollar bill from its pocket.

"Will this do?" She was glad that she had received such an over-the-top exchange rate from one of her banks in Ireland.

"Yeah, that's enough," the driver acknowledged, as he sped along I-275 South towards St. Petersburg.

It was a beautiful day, a bit muggy, with a front coming in, and it was getting a bit breezy. The palm trees were even beginning to sway. They soon arrived at the hotel after passing by an immense array of beautiful homes and gated condominium complexes, complete with parks and fountains. Sunny spotted what looked like a big, ornately-decorated, Spanish-stucco hotel, as they came over the bridge.

"That is the place," the driver said, as he pointed to the structure in the distance.

"That's exactly what I am looking for. It's perfect. Driver, do you happen to long it takes to get to Parrish, near Ellenton?" she asked him.

"I'd say about twenty-five minutes from the hotel. It's just over the Skyway....the bridge that connects Pinellas County to southern Florida. Why do you want to go to Parrish? There ain't nothing there but cows and oranges," he looked back at her, with a curious scowl on his face. The driver went up the driveway which led to the fancy main lobby entrance.

"Here we are. I'll get your stuff out for you and take it in for you."

He walked up to the marbled lobby counter with her bags and set them down. Then, he asked her if she needed anything else.

She replied "no", and handed him a five dollar bill for all of his troubles.

"Thanks a lot sir, and you have a real nice time here. Welcome to Florida," he said, as he shook her hand. Then he walked away.

"Oh, driver....come back for a moment, please," she requested. "I forgot to ask you if you know where this ranch is located," as she pulled out an address from her large robed pocket. "Do you know what exits and roads I should take?"

He put on his reading glasses to view the small, almost unreadable print.

"This must be the huge ranch off of 301, near Main Street," he rubbed his forehead with his fingers, as if to try to bring more brain power to the region.

"Leave out on the Bay Way towards Bradenton. At the split, take the Parrish exit Hwy. 301. Continue on that road until you see an old general store and a fire station. At that street, take a left and continue for about one mile. Large black rod-iron gates with 'The Ranch' should be your target spot. It's a big place....hundreds of acres. They give fruit to the big juice company near there. It's a big business.

Why do you want to go there, if you don't mind me asking?" He demanded.

"A private business deal, involving oranges for export," was all she could think of to say.

He acted like this was a valid reason, so he wished her "good luck" and left the scene, calling the boys immediately to tell them of the place he took her.

After checking in at the front desk in the elegant lobby, where they gave her an ocean view suite that they had available for the same price as a standard deluxe room, she felt like a victor. She took the elevator to the top floor, where her room was located, found the room, and entered it. She fell on the feather-down comforter with the greatest of ease. She rested there for about fifteen minutes, gazing at the one-of-a-kind objects which were displayed around her suite, antique furniture pieces, as well as the objects on the teak wood book cases which lined the walls.

She opened the French doors to her fifth floor balcony to let in the ever-growing fragrant breeze, while she took off her manly clothing, only to dress herself in a modern western female garment....a black satin fringed mini dress, with sewn-on pearls on the mid-length sleeves and around the scoop neckline. She took out a silver pair of high-heeled sandals, but painted her toenails pink first. She grabbed from her bag the costume jewelry which she could never wear and wrapped pieces around most of her exposed body parts. She now felt like a real woman and was ready to start conquering the world. Not until, however, she put her clothes, shoes, jewels, cosmetics, and hygiene items away in drawers and in closets. This was always a very important aspect of her life....cleanliness and order. She couldn't stand to live in disarray, and that was another reason why she secretly hated living in Kabul. She loved it in Florida, already.

Sunny put her brother's turban and robing in the closet, so as not to mess it up. She would have to fly to Europe a couple of times within the six month period before her certificates of deposit matured in different banks in Ireland. She would have to dress as her brother then, as his name was on every CD.

"I have to figure out how to get US Citizenship, and in a hurry!" she exclaimed.

Sunny did her final freshening up, as she turned on the recessed lightening over the two sinks, the bidet and Jacuzzi-tub area. She layered on her Parisian make-up that Med-hi would bring back into Afghanistan for her to wear, but only at home. She was ready to go downstairs.

"Boy, do I look great," she screamed into the frosted mirror, as she gazed at her curvy figure.

When the elevator doors opened into the lobby, everyone stared, even did double takes. Sunny set her eyes on the bar to the right and down a short flight of stairs. It was full of patrons. There was one empty bar stool, right in the middle of the "L" shaped mahogany bar. She pulled out the stool to take a seat. After she ordered her usual sweet white wine, the gentleman seated to her left immediately began to converse with her. He was a tall gentleman in his late fifties. He was very distinguished and most likely very moneyed. He asked her if she wanted to dine with him later that evening, after he met with his client whom he was waiting for at the bar.

"I had originally been saving this seat for him, but when I saw you come near me, I forgot all about my work," he complimented her.

"Thank you so much. When and where do you want to meet?" she questioned him, thinking that this might be the answer to citizenship for her.

Looking at his Rolex, he answered her with, "Say around 8:30, since its 5:30 now, and let's meet over there at that table." He pointed to a small table underneath a Rembrandt copy.

"It should be quiet there. Until then, and I am truly looking forward to it, my dear...by the way...I'm Berton, and what should I call you? What's your full name? Mine is Berton James."

"They call me, Sunny," she responded to the interrogation. "Sunny...uh...Smith." That was the only western world name she could think of that quickly. She was not expecting that question to be thrown at her.

Staring at Sunny, as she stood up with drink in hand, ready to leave her "already taken" bar stool, he commented on her last name.

He pried, "Smith is obviously your father's surname. What was your mother's?" he cleverly asked her, trying to wiggle out information as to Sunny's ancestry. She definitely looked like beautiful Middle-Eastern woman through and through, and he wanted to know who she was.

"Excuse me," he responded to Sunny, presumably walking to the restroom. Around the corner, however, he phoned his contact.

"Everything is going as planned. I'll get your information for you."

All he heard from the other end was, "You better. Where is she staying?" he questioned Bert.

"Your *taxi driver* called and told me that she was checking into La Dona and was acting very stressed, in need of a drink, so that's where I found her, at the bar," he assured the contact. "Don't worry, I'll handle everything," and Bert turned off his phone.

Chapter Two

The Enchanted Garden

Sunny just smiled at Bert and laid it into him with, "And wouldn't you like to know. I'll be here at eight-thirty. Don't keep me waiting," and she darted off, wrapping her long cream silk scarf that matched the border of her elegant, sexy dress, around her neck even tighter.

"What a tiger.....rrrrrrhhhh....," he told his client, whose head had turned and was following the now departing Sunny. "I like my women like that. They're better in bed when they are that way, you know."

"Now, now Bert. What about Mel? I have never seen a woman who is more devoted to a husband than she is to you. You are such a lucky man, and you better not forget it. Why didn't you bring her up with you, anyway? It could have been a special weekend. You know what I mean? She's great...sweet...pretty....and she's Melody, my sister," his client stated in a cold manner.

"Ralph, we've been married for going on thirty-three years. It gets old after a while, no matter how great your partner is. We just live an hour away. It's no big deal. Hey, I don't see you winning any award for perfectionism, either. Do you remember you gave up a four year marriage in grad school for a man? You became gay."

"I have always been gay. I never became gay. I just didn't show it. In graduate school, I couldn't lie any longer. I fell in love and had to get out of my marriage. At least we had no children."

"How could you? Did you ever do it with your wife, or any girl? Or didn't you like it?" Bert asked him smiling the whole while. He liked to dig into people's personal lives. I guess that what comes from being a news reporter in Sarasota.

Bert didn't keep Sunny waiting. He and his brother-in-law sat and drank at the bar until she sauntered down the spiral staircases which wrapped around a panoramic view of the Gulf of Mexico. She was surprised to see the two "boys" still sitting in their exact locations as before, and she was even more surprised to see how they looked, with eyes half shut and ties hanging down almost to their waists.

"What has happened to you guys?" I must fix you two up before anyone sees you like this, then it's safe for you two to be on your way. I need my beauty rest tonight, anyway," she seriously stated, draping two silk veils tightly around her neck and her small waist. She was an enchanting sight to behold to anyone who glanced her way.

"Please pour us some coffee, and you can give me a shot of brandy to go along with the coffee," Bert slurred. "And don't worry, honey. I'll make it home okay." Bert knew he wasn't going anywhere.

"Only coffee for the gents," Sunny shouted to the bartender. "And we will be sitting at the table over there," she pointed to the painting.

Steaming hot dark Italian roast coffee was served to all three. This seemed to do the trick. The two men were like brand new.

It was now eight forty-five and time to eat and say good bye to Ralph. The two thought this at the same time and simultaneously rose from the table.

"It has been a pleasure meeting you Sunny, and it's always a blast being with you, Bert," Ralph stated, pulling away from the two.

"Are you sure you don't want to join us for dinner?" Bert asked him, in an obligatory manner. "It might do you good. I still don't think you are in any shape to be driving anywhere."

"I'm fine. I'll just grab a bite up on Gulf Boulevard," he stated.

"Well, alright, if you insist," Bert ended the conversation, as he was ready for a night of lust and *information*. Sunny and Bert called over the maitre d' to provide them menus. He ordered Chateaubriand and champagne for them to relish, in that dark corner.

In Bert's line of work, he was always approached by numerous characters, some braggarts, some bogus, and some real, *very real*.

Two weeks ago, Bert was working on an investigative piece about a drug cartel from the British Isles, by way of Colombia. Its leader had been apprehended on Venice beach, partying it up to the max, flirting with all of the girlies and telling them about the Independent Republican Army, or the IRA, as it is more commonly referred to, and of which he happens to be an important member on its ladder. He had supplied the cause for years with funds from his drug trafficking, etc.

Ten days ago, a suspicious man quietly walked out from behind a large bush in the WORK parking lot, stood before Bert and handed him ten one thousand dollar bills.

"This is your reward, and only if you keep your smacker closed about all escapades involving this story. You don't know anything about this drug cartel, or the IRA. You don't believe anything about a drug cartel being mixed-up with the IRA, and you don't even care about it....*you understand?*" he commanded Bert to answer. Bert simply nodded his head.

The thug asked him again, "*Do you understand?* There is more money to come. We need your help. You can either make us, or *break us*."

The Irishman told Bert, "Get info from the Middle-Eastern girl at La Dona on St. Pete Beach in two days....*We need it*....Read your instructions thoroughly."

He did not look at the man, only listened to his the rhythmically-accented voice dead ahead.

"Good. We'll be talking and we'll be watching.....everywhere," the heavy voice warned him, as it walked off into the foggy evening beach air, handing him a note with instructions first.

Bert then nervously searched for the key which opened his black Lincoln. When the locks went down inside the vehicle, he finally felt safe, that was until the Gaelic gentleman rammed him from behind and two more vehicles encircled his Lincoln. Bert got out of his car. The other drivers remained inside their vehicles with their windows wide open, as he read what they wanted from him.

"Now you know we mean business, right?" the top dog said to Bert. "Read it," he demanded.

"Uh huh," was all he said, with his arms covering his face, as the bright headlights blinded him.

"Good," he said, and he motioned for the two cars to leave, then got in his own car and left.

One week ago, Bert got an urgent phone call at the station. The hoarse-voiced, heavy-accented man on the other end told him, "WE now want to meet with you at the diner up the street from the station. We'll be waiting. It is OUR turn now." Bert left the station straight away, after his broadcast, and hurried to the diner for the confrontation.

When Bert arrived, he was motioned over to a four-seat booth that held three fat men already in place. He squeezed his trim frame in amidst the heavy-laden atmosphere. He felt cramped up, but he waited patiently for their verdict. "What do they want me to score for them?" he nervously wondered.

"We have big plans for you, my boy. We hope you can pull them off, and well...because if you don't...." he simply paused as if in thought, then he continued, "but if you do...maybe your news days are a thing of the past."

"I love my job though and make great money," Bert revealed.

"You'll like this even better...*guaranteed*. All you have to do is hustle, be innovative and intuitive, and most of all, be *heartless*. I don't know if a pretty boy like you is this sort, but I hope so, for your sake, and the sake of all that money sitting in our vaults awaiting a home."

"Ya know, it's kind of sad boss, when you think of it that way," the smallest of the three blurted out.

Bert simply stared at each of them, straight in their black, brown and hazel eyes, and professed, "I am not this sort of 'pretty boy', as you call me. I agreed to suppress a news story for a bunch of Irish people, but I can't go farther than that. I'm not a violent person."

"Oh, but we are not asking for violence in any way. No, we take care of all that. What we want is that you nurture an enchanted garden for us, one that is full of prosperity. It will feed hundreds of poor people in our homeland, and in yours," he mocked. "We want you to go to a certain five thousand ranch and citrus growing plantation and start us a worthy enterprise---growing hundreds of marijuana plants. We have a multitude of buyers that like our damn good shit and are willing to spend a fortune to get it…that is…if it is nurtured well, and if it provides the effects they like and they *need* in their powerful and moneyed existences. Are you in bro? There'll be plenty of cash for you my friend, plenty of cash for a job well done."

"If I get lots of dough, I'm in for anything. I can pull off anything. I do it on a regular basis, every day at the station. No one really knows me, or who I am. I prefer it that way," Bert acknowledged.

"Okay then. We'll start tomorrow. I will bring you plantation renderings with designated planting areas outlined in red marker. You get into the property at night and begin your cultivation process. I'll bring you over some soil nutrients that are very good for the product. I really do hope you can handle this. Remember, one word out of your trap about any of this to anyone, and you are done," he stated dramatically.

"I do anything for money and am as quiet as a mouse," the anchorman reassured this bully from Palermo in a subservient tone. "Cross my heart."

"Good. Come on boys," he said to the other three goons who squeezed out of the booth after Bert.

"We have work to do and money to snag. Snap to it."

The other three robotic goons did whatever the brute insisted, perhaps for the coins, as they called it, perhaps out of faithfulness, or perhaps out of humanly fear.

Bert ran to his coupe, hopped inside, and put the pedal to the medal, then peeled off, toward his dream of freedom from his bondage at the station. He felt like a great absconder from justice, that was, until blue lights started flashing behind his shiny yellow antique coupe that had a white rag top overhead for protection from the elements. As he turned his head back, he saw these blue lights reflected from his super clean, almost transparent convertible top, and began to pull over.

"Why are you going so fast, son?" the officer blurted out, as soon as he was within eye range of Bert.

"I don't know officer. I just have places to go and babes to meet.... sorry, sir," was all that he could think of interjecting at a moment's notice.

"Well, I have places to go too. So, I'll write you a ticket for speeding in excess of fifteen miles over the limit.

Hope you have learned your lesson," he grinned, as he slapped a thin white rectangular piece of card stock in Bert's boned hand. "See you in court," the officer stated, as he sped off to catch another speeder, so that he could achieve his daily quota.

Chapter Three

The Murder

Even though Sunny had really wanted to go to sleep early that night, she still pursued the night. She thought that it might be fun and a bit relaxing to unwind with a stranger, before setting her mind on what was to come tomorrow. Sunny began to flirtatiously talk to Bert, as he poured her champagne, one right after the other. She became very loose-lipped. She had not yet been able to keep every secret to herself. Sunny found that she was not able to do this at all with alcohol, because she had had no real experience with it, due to her Muslim upbringing.

Sunny began talking about a ranch in Parrish which she hoped to find easily after breakfast. She asked Bert if he had heard of this ranch which grows citrus products and raises Angus beef.

Bert nearly choked on his tender beef with Bearnaise that he managed to balance on his tongue, while sipping on his bubbly.

Bert quickly responded with an answer that came out of the blue, "No, I don't know Parrish well, but I do have a colleague who lives there and knows everything about the place. I can ask him in the morning and drive you down there. Hey, why are you going there anyway? It's a strange place for you to want to go."

"I have a friend that I must see. I really need to go there alone," she nervously replied to him.

"No problem. I can give you directions tomorrow, that is if you still like me in the morning," he smilingly remarked to Sunny, as he touched her champagne glass with his. All Sunny could do was meekly smile and laugh. She felt not as worldly as she thought she was and definitely was unable to handle what was about to transpire.

Bert paid the tab, left a mediocre tip and went up with his soon-to-be lover for a night in her suite.

"I wish I had been trained by Med-hi how to handle these types of situations," Sunny thought to herself, as she watched the floor numbers illuminating, until the elevator doors opened wide.

It was show-time.

Once up in her glamorous suite, Sunny became a tiger. She didn't know where it was coming from, but didn't question her mood. She was happy…very happy. A flash back appeared in mind of a prudish fifteen year old that had never even touched a boy. She acted up until now, almost in the same realm.

She was not a virgin anymore, however. Her only lover had been Med-hi's slovenly fat cohort in terror and crime, Samar. He had always been entranced with Sunny.

During the night two years ago, he entered her unlocked bedroom, after visiting with her brother in the meeting room area, on the pretense of going to urinate after their hot apple cider beverages. The low-key rape took place in only a five minute period, and she swore to him that she would never tell anyone, if she knew what was best for her and her family.

"I never wanted to hurt you my dear Sunny, but I needed you so badly and probably will again. Remember, you're mine on a silver platter for the taking...Don't forget it," was all that Samar said to Sunny after the incident.

She never spoke to Samar again, until the day that he came to see her to tell her about Med-hi's death. Sunny surmised that he must have been secretly ashamed for belittling his best friend's one and only sister. She had been shy and very subservient, letting anybody do anything to her, until then. She slowly came out of her cocoon and spread her wings. Sunny knew that she could fly to the moon, if she so desired. She had paid every bit of dues imaginable.

"Now," she thought, as Bert squeezed one of her breasts, as she provocatively undressed herself, "I am about to get what I deserve. I have put up with so much humiliating, degrading behavior, but no more...no, no more. I'll be the star. Everyone will do what I say... what I demand," she began to laugh out of the blue, during their prelude session.

"What are you giggling about my sex pot? Oh....I wish my *wife* looked and acted as hot as you do. Where'd you learn how to turn on a fellow so much? Just let me stick it in you...just for a second. I can't hold back no more," he spoke softly, but with a gravel voice.

At that moment, Sunny threw up her arms, away from Bert's hairy body, and ran to the bathroom to grab the robe, which was placed on the ornately-shaped gold hook by the walk-in shower stall. It had scripted letters on its white terrycloth pocket which read, "*La Dona*".

Becoming unglued, Bert began to play his fairly new criminal role halfheartedly.

He yelled out, "Hey hot chick, I spent a lot of big ones on your sweet ass tonight, and I want some payback, ya hear?"

"I am not your or anyone else's hot chick, you hear?" Sunny repeated back to him.

"*You have a wife?* You're just a loser, a real loser. You don't even take me to your own room. No, you have to come and use mine.

The card you used to pay for dinner is probably used for company expenses.

You see, I may be what you think to be a third-world Arabic citizen, and maybe I was once upon a time, but no more. Now, what I say goes, and I want your flabby ass gone...gone from my sight. Now... right now," she yelled in a medium-pitched voice.

"I'm not gonna do anything you say, until you give me what I am looking for," Bert brutally insisted.

"And what may that be," she shockingly asked him.

Bert ran over unexpectedly to Sunny and held his hand over her throat and around her skinny neck.

"I need all names of people at the ranch, all their bank account information, and access to land at the ranch. I have a money making operation that should begin to prosper tomorrow, with the right soil and sun. Parrish should be perfect for it...a very unsuspecting place."

"Only if you split the money with me," she suggested in her least cowardly tone of voice. Sunny felt that she was finally entering the big time, playing with the so-called "big boys." She wasn't going to take any "shit" from any one of the players, so she violently pushed him off of her with as much strength as she could muster.

Then, she froze in mid-step, as she touched the hotel room door, watching him pull out a long, sharp dagger from a pocket inside his classic-tailored white linen jacket.

"You can't. I'm still too young...have no children yet. Okay, take all the money. I'll tell you where it is. Just walk out of my room before my brother hears of this. He will kill you," she pleaded.

"Your brother's dead...and *you know too much*," Bert quietly said, as he planted his long feet in front of her quivering, disrobed body. Sunny's face and body parts turned ice-cold and blue when Bert aggressively stuck his dagger in her unblemished abdomen.

"This was not how it was supposed to end for me," Sunny choked on her words. "I was supposed to rule the planet, put Ty in his place.... get....the....girrrls," were the last words she muttered.

She closed her eyes and drifted away to a demonic existence, never to return to grace. She had become no better than her now nemesis, Tyrone Riley, and had also accomplished nothing for herself, nor any of her people. Sunny had died a complete zero, and she felt it during her last beat of life.

Chapter Four

Russian Roulette

Trying not to cry, as she again mourned the murder of Jude, Kimmie busily straightened the inside and outside of the once lively plantation house, as soon as she awoke from her much needed slumber of the previous evening. When the three of them felt the jet touch the pavement the afternoon before, they each realized that he or she was still exhausted, slightly inebriated, and ready to hit the sack again, that is as soon as they arrived at the now infamous ranch "headquarters". The house had been like an oven when they first entered. Kimmie wondered why somebody had turned the temperature up so high.

"I mean, we really can't afford it now," she thought to herself.

She guessed that there must have been so many people inside and outside of the ranch house while she and Jude had been gone.

It was at that moment of enlightenment that Cynthia came out from the small guest bedroom upstairs wearing nothing but a teddy. Kimmie had given her from a stash of guest wear. Nikko was still sleeping and could be heard snoring from the bedroom down the hall.

"Where is the coffee?" Cynthia asked, as she tried to inhale oxygen from a series of yawns. She glanced at herself in a mirror and felt glad she had returned her appearance back to normal.

"The coffee is brewing. The pot is underneath the microwave, and the mugs are already on the counter. Sorry, but you have to drink it black. The milk's gone bad, of course, and the sugar is old and sticky from all this humidity. Boy, I sure would like to wring somebody's neck for what they did to this place. There was so much mold and mildew in the bathrooms and kitchen from the heat. It took me two hours this morning to scrub it all off. At least I have the 'sanity' that the house has been 'sanitized'," she giggled halfheartedly, as she sat at the breakfast bar with Cynthia.

The two girls looked at each other in silence for over five minutes, simply drinking their java, still trying to believe what had just happened. Kimmie could not stand it any longer, as her mind would not let her stop contemplating about why this immense amount of pain had been placed upon her. She instinctively made herself busy, which she had forever done to prevent her from using "too much negative energy". This was how she had put it on several occasions.

Kimmie tried to be an optimist as much as possible, but she never could reach the level of optimism that Jude had. Jude was and always had been Kimmie's heroin and role model.

"There will never be another one like her," she broke out of her silence and loudly cried, waking Nikko, who came in the kitchen bleary-eyed and half-naked, but when he saw the beautiful physique of Cynthia's scantily-clad body, only with a still slight protrusion of belly, he stood at attention, eyes wide open. Unable to utter a syllable, he moaned and pointed to the orange juice pitcher.

"Does that mean you want some juice," Cynthia questioned him using her most sexy tonal qualities.

"Uh....yeah. I mean....I do," Nikko replied, unable to return to normalcy, as he got a slight glimpse of Cynthia's long, dark red nipples protruding out of her almost transparent thin rag.

She got up real close to him, almost as a way of teasing him, as she waited for Kimmie, who had blotted her face with a paper towel to dry up the tears, to come to the table with the pitcher and the glass. Cynthia laughed at him hysterically, but still worried, as she hadn't had her period for over two months.

"Do you think this body could ever be yours? Well, dream on, because it never would, or could. Unfortunately, it belonged to a deadbeat hubby named Tyrone, and because of that, it can ever and will never belong to anyone again, only myself," she commented sullenly.

"Honey, I am sure he will get what he deserves. What goes around, comes around, you know?" Kimmie asked in a serious voice. "Now I need to call Scotland Yard about flying Jude's body home. I want her ashes thrown in the Gulf of Mexico, not the Atlantic Ocean," she revealed, pointing in the distance.

"Jude loved the Gulf, so her body must have eternal life underneath these waves and rays. She would have wanted that," she said, breaking into tears again.

"I will call Scotland Yard," Cynthia suggested. "You're in no shape to handle the matter at hand," Cynthia consoled Kimmie. She forlornly stared in Cynthia's mesmerizing greenish-blue eyes, thick with dark brown eye lashes, and she nodded.

Nikko quickly brought Cynthia the receiver of the land line, as he looked at her gorgeous, almost naked body through her tight, see-through, extremely short nightgown. Her dancer frame was incredibly appealing to him.

"Here you go, my dear," he sweetly said, putting the receiver on her long, thin fingers and palm. She kissed him in the air. Kimmie was sitting quietly the whole time, watching the two of them get more and more out of control.

Finally, after fifteen minutes of flirting, with phone still in Cynthia's hand, Kimmie jumped up and stole the phone from her palm. She went upstairs, got her purse with the Lieutenant's number written on a piece of paper from the yard that a secretary had given to her upon leaving, and she ran downstairs and into the backyard patio area, glaring at the two "love birds" the entire time.

These "love birds" were becoming more and more enthralled with each other, as they played a "cat and mouse" chase. Neither one really wanted the other. It was just for this chase, and perhaps other sexual fantasies. Cynthia never wanted to have another serious relationship, and Nikko had never even had one, nor wanted one. He was strictly a player on both sides of the fence. He loved his noncommittal existence. He thought of himself as an independent loner. Cynthia was also beginning to feel about herself in this way. It was because of these shared qualities that the two were becoming inseparable.

Kimmie paced back and forth on the short walkway leading from her back door onto the brick patio, with huge grill, red wood Jacuzzi and bar, all sheltered by a classic navy blue and white striped awning. Finally, she got her call connected. She spoke to the Lieutenant who was handling the case.

"Could you please fly Jude's body to Tampa, so that we may throw her ashes in our Gulf, and as quick as you can?" she pleaded with the soft-spoken British gentleman. "Of course, we will pay all charges."

The British official replied, "Right away, Miss. I will email you at the address which you provided to us. It probably will not be until tomorrow morning, though. You know it's close to four o'clock here now. I can guarantee that Jude will be on a flight tomorrow....Will let you know, Miss," was all that the British gent said to Kimmie, before she heard a dial tone.

"He didn't even let me say goodbye to him. What's that about?" she asked the phone, as her perplexed look turned into temporary lines of wrinkles. These soon vanished, as soon as she walked onto the ranch grounds and looked at the white fence and at the horse jumps. She remembered the good times she had there. It had been too short, she thought.

"Now that everyone's gone but me, I have to take control and become stronger than I have ever been and take down anyone who gets in my way. This ranch is my legacy." A squealing car sounded in the distance. Kimmie ran to the front of the house and peered over the white fence in the distance.

She saw a truck with a television camera mounted high on top, with the letters WORK, and the italicized slogan underneath that read, *We WORK for you in Sarasota.* The truck pulled into the long driveway, and stopped at the ornamental gate, displaying *The Ranch* in beautifully written manuscript. Kimmie ran over to question the driver of the truck why he was there.

He let down his window and answered, "I have permission from the lawyer of the development company that you are suing, for us to enter this property to film a story. He says that you are obligated to oblige. He says that this actually is nobody's *legal* acreage right now, until the suit goes to court....if it ever does, and then there is the appeal factor...Well, you're lucky the courts are even letting you stay here. Please now....please let me in the gate," Bert demanded smugly, not even batting an eye and tapping on his accelerator to stake his claim. He was growing impatient.

"You may enter on one condition: You are out of here in thirty minutes, otherwise, I will get my lawyer on the phone, come what may. I'm timing, starting NOW," she stated, staring down at her silver and gold thin-banded, high-priced Swiss watch that Kenneth had purchased at a Munich jewelry store many years ago.

Kimmie cherished this watch. She had never removed it from her strong, thick wrist, especially when she rode and jumped horses, since she treated this watch as her security and her good luck charm.

Bert was wearing a slight disguise when he entered the property. He had longer than normal hair, a pasted on gray goatee and a cane that he used, as he was now walking with a limp. Nobody would have ever put two and two together to come up with an accurate conclusion, that Ernie, as he called himself, was not just a camera man like he stated, but rather the prestigious, glamorous, and the most well-known person in Sarasota, possessing a great voice, great jaw line, but having "used-car salesman" ethics. He had everything he needed to get him to and keep him up at the top.

Kimmie wondered what the two "infatuated ones" were doing inside. She didn't even want to think of what was probably going on, as she was fending off prey on the outer lawn. She glanced at her watch. She said to herself, "Ernie has two more minutes before I find him and throw him off this property." She was really getting tired of scoundrels. It seemed like they were everywhere. She got into the ranch pick-up and peeled off in the direction of the Gulf.

"I love you, Jude. I miss you, Jude," she screamed in the blustery wind conditions. Then she saw the truck in the distance, traveling towards her in what seemed to be a great hurry. Kimmie put the pick-up in park and waited for "Ernie". He pulled up alongside her, maybe two minutes later, and announced that he was sorry. He was right on schedule.

He stated, "I got all the dimensions I need for the piece. Can I be here again next week? Your number's in the book under Redman, right?"

"Of course," Kimmie answered the slovenly television station employee, with a demeaning glitch coming from her throat.

"Talk to you later," he said to Kimmie, before swerving out of the white gravel driveway at a fast speed.

"Oh well," she said to the wind. "I should go inside now and start making calls to plan for Jude's cremation. I have to close up her practice and have all medical records transferred to another clinic."

Bert found himself speeding to his home on Siesta Key. He dialed the number of Frank, the mobster who he was to answer to.

"Hey Frank, my friend," Bert greeted him in a cool manner. "I went to the ranch today and got it all planned where I am going to plant the stuff. And how much is my percentage again? I need to know, before I can plant anything. How often do I have to water? Do I need nutrients? What kind? I want to sell, sell, sell, you know...I want the money. No raises in this economy, and I've got an expensive lifestyle that I can't give up, not for my image, anyway."

"Hold up, sonny. First of all, you need to call a short blonde massage therapist named 'Fate'. She'll get the seeds for you tomorrow and tell you all about growing them 'the right way', so that we can all make the money that we need.

The mob has an image it needs to keep up. You better do this for us, 'the right way', otherwise, you never know what or who might be lurking around. Just remember, we're not friends, just business associates. You don't know anything about any of us. We know everything about you, though. We know where you live. We know what hours your wife keeps at work and at home, where she shops and where her friends live. We also know that your two dogs are kept in the side yard during the day and there is an unlocked gate there.

Oh, by the way, we have just found out that you have two concurrent mistresses. You see each once a week, one on Tuesday evenings six to nine at her apartment in Bradenton, and the other in a rented motor home in Palmetto on Wednesday morning from nine to twelve. Tuesday you broadcast at noon and Wednesday at six."

"Wow," was all that surprised Bert could interject. "You are a bunch of hoodlum spies, and I am not standing for it. You guys will suffer the consequences, not me."

"Do your job, and do it well. Trust me. Do what I say," Frank warned Bert.

"I don't want to play Russian Roulette. Okay, only this one job… no more," Bert sheepishly stated.

"We'll see about that," the Italian mobster replied. "And you know, we do work with the *Slavic Syndicate*, the Russian gangsters. "Sometimes, you know, you WILL have to play *roulette* with them."

Frank just chuckled in the receiver and said, "You just won't learn, will you Bert. Now get started. Here are some large bills for you to pick up the seeds from Fate. You need to plant them tonight, when all lights are out and everyone is in bed. No one will ever know that anything has been planted on that plot of land. It's completely vacant, insignificant acreage. What I would give for even a small piece of the pie and here they are throwing acreage in the garbage. Well, not for long. All of our troubles are soon to produce a fortune for us all to share, in Parrish at the ranch, and on Pelican Isle, across from La Dona Cecilia Hotel. I will tell you about that next time. Right now, let's concentrate on this venture."

All of a sudden, there was a click and a fast busy signal. Bert had never seen so many people in all directions staring at him through their car windows. He was becoming paranoid about everything and everyone. He surmised what the battling underworlds had in mind for him.

"I simply have to do what is requested by them all, otherwise everything in my world will change, and not for the better," he concluded to himself.

Chapter Five

Massages of Fate

Bert headed back to his wife who had just gotten off work later than usual at a law firm, in which she was its newest paralegal, and in which she worked very long hours seven days a week. This made it very easy for her husband to be unfaithful on a weekly basis with the two very young and firm girls that he had become enamored with. Both were exceptional in bed, but lousy conversationalists. They knew nothing about the world, its people, its creation, its food, its geography, or its terrain. All they knew about the world was Central Florida, and its shopping malls. He had met both young ladies six months prior when he gave a sales talk about the benefits of obtaining a communications degree at Central Florida University in Orlando. They were both in the same beginning speech class. They were freshmen classmates.

Alicia and Victoria, as they introduced themselves to Bert, were very pleased to make his acquaintance. They invited him to a plush hotel lounge nearby for happy hour Margaritas. He accepted, being one of Florida's leading drunks and womanizers. They all three drank together for two or three hours, then walked Bert to his SUV. The petite blonde, Alicia, pushed him in the back seat, then climbed in after him with aggression. A more meek and meek Victoria squeezed her brunette locks in between the two heads who were passionately going at it.

They ended up having a wild threesome in the back of his vehicle. The two girls climbed out after the fun was over. He handed them each one of his cards and asked for their numbers in return. They excitedly recited their numbers and emails to the attractive middle-aged anchorman who felt so on top of every other man because he had scored with these hard bodies, who were virtually children.

"And they were really turned on by me," he said to himself on the drive to Siesta Key, where he was supposed to meet his tired, worn-out, but still pretty wife of fifty-two, with her salt and pepper hair always flying wild in the wind.

They never had any children. Melody had spent thousands on fertility treatments, but none worked. They had Irish Setters, Babe, Ruffles, and Pete. They were all three great watch dogs, so Bert knew that he could never sneak out, or in their home without their "alarm" barks going off.

He called both girls the following day and arranged the set-up that the three have now, one on Tuesday after class and one on Wednesday before class. His naive wife, Melody, from rural New Hampshire never suspected anything.

"Honey, I'm home," he chanted to his overworked, responsible, loving wife who greeted him with a gigantic bear hug.

"What a day," she said.

"Yeah, mine, too," he added, kissing her soft freckled cheek.

"Is there anything in the freezer to microwave? I'm starved?" he asked his wife, as he pulled out his cell in which Frank had programmed the massage therapist's number.

Bert fixed himself a whiskey and soda and went into the study to take care of business.

When he dialed the number stored in the cell, it rang and rang and rang, with no recording.

He was about to disconnect when a rehearsed sophisticated voice answered, "Hello, Massages of Fate. Can I be of assistance to you?"

He got the immediate sense that this was not only a cheap-ass massage parlor, which was located on a seedy stretch of Highway Forty-One in Sarasota, as he could tell from its address, but it was also a bordello and drug house, in other words, a sin-city retreat, or any preacher's worst nightmare.

"Hello Fate. We have a mutual friend who gave me your number," he rambled on.

"Ah yes. This must be Bert, my favorite news man in the whole bay area. You can have a free massage… and more… anytime you want," she notified him.

"Okay, but first, I need to buy seeds, the easiest, most fertile, and most profitable seeds you have," he weakly demanded. "I am ready to buy tonight, if I can."

"Yes you can. I do have plenty of Afghan marijuana seeds which are sold in bulk at a better price. They will grow pounds and pounds for you in about eight weeks. They are very easy seeds to grow, both inside and out. Afghan marijuana is a popular plant, because it has a taste much like hashish, and some say it produces effects like it, as well," Fate informed him in a most business-like fashion.

"Sounds like what I want. Is there a money back guarantee?" he laughed, but was actually very serious.

"No, there's nothing like that here, but since it's not your money in the first place that you will be using, it really doesn't matter. I don't sell trash to any of the organization's people. My life's at stake, just as yours is, and will always be….. You want to meet in an hour? I have a client in fifteen minutes, and I'll be free after that," she stated.

"I'll be there," he whispered so that his wife would not hear, as she was sauntering down the hallway toward their bedroom.

Bert returned to the kitchen and took at a frozen dinner, cooked it in the microwave for eight minutes, then sat down to peel the box lid completely off and dig into the "scrumptious" delicacies found inside the card board lining. He could only stomach half of the dried out mashed potatoes, which were lacking gravy, and two bites of the Salisbury steak which was surrounded by stale broccoli florets. He threw the box away, still hungry, and screamed to his wife that he had to pick up some booze and cigarettes, which he did almost nightly, anyway.

Melody was still in the bedroom, cleaning and paying bills, which she also did nightly. She was a super-efficient mate and a clean freak besides. Bert found these traits of hers calming and caring, but still rather boring. Sometimes he felt that he would rather have reckless excitement in his life, than intense organization.

He slammed the side door behind him, looked in the eyes of his dogs who were staring intensely at him from behind the fence, and said, "I'll be back in a minute boys. Guard the property." The dogs barked, as if to acknowledge his message.

Bert drove for ten minutes, once he got off the key and onto forty-one north towards Bradenton. Bert spotted cop cars hidden around every turn.

"I didn't know this stretch had gotten so bad. And so is the way of the world," he said aloud, as he looked for a sign representing the name, "Massages of Fate". Bert spotted the address, but it was vacant of signage.

"I hope this isn't a set-up," he prayed, as he stumbled out of his car in fear, looking at all the run-down, seedy establishments filled with hoodlums which were now lining the block.

Upon seeing Bert through her peep hole, Fate unlatched the "fortress door" and told him to come inside.

"No one can ever break in this place. The boys built it that way. It's safe. Don't worry. I don't feel threatened in any way, anymore. By the way, my name is Fate," she said, as she stuck out her hand to shake with his.

"Nice to make your acquaintance ma'am. I have the cash, if you have the stuff," Bert acknowledged.

"Of course I do," and Fate lifted the top of the coffee table near the front door and pulled out a rather heavy small brown canvas bag.

Bert opened the bag and looked inside at the hundreds of seeds and the assortments of light bulbs *"for indoors, just in case,"* she added, as she winked her sly slanted golden brown eye at him.

"Okay then. I'm off to plant. See you later," he smiled, as he walked towards the door, intrigued with watching her buckle her hipster jeans.

"Don't forget. Anytime you want that massage....well you know," she hinted, as she shut the door.

Bert climbed up into his vehicle, shaking his head in disbelief, "Wow," was all he could say to himself, as he started the ignition. He would be home in a fifteen minutes, if he floored it. A series of red lights and party animals made the ride home a sheer impossible feat.

"Melody's gonna be so mad," he thought speeding fifteen miles over the limit.

Now making good time and almost at the Bee Ridge intersection, he felt pretty safe from all outside interruptions, that was until he saw and heard the flashing lights to his side, coming out of a book store parking lot.

Scared to death, he pulled into a strip mall lot, then quickly folded up the brown canvas bag and stuck it under the seat beside him. The officer slowly got out of his car and sauntered over to Bert's car with paperwork in hand.

"Well, hello again fellow," the officer said, flashing a light in his face. "Hey, aren't you the man on the news? Yep, you are for sure. Why are you goin' so fast anyway on a nice calm night like this?"

"I had to get home, so my wife wouldn't worry. You know, I was meeting with friends and all that."

"You don't have to explain any more. I've been there and done that myself," the officer smiled and winked at him. "And just for that, and who you are, I'm gonna let you ride with a warning this time, okay? Just try not to let it happen again, ya hear?" and he patted the utility vehicle, as he walked off.

"Whew," Bert said, as he wiped the sweat off of his brow. ''That was so close. Slow it is."

In five minutes, Bert was in his driveway with dogs barking and trying to lean over the fence to kiss him. "Soon, he whispered, would be the moment of truth." He unlocked the front door and stepped inside. Sweet Melody threw a pillow and blanket at his face and slammed the bedroom door. He knew the moment of truth had arrived.

"I'm sorry it took so long," he shouted to a locked door. "Lots of traffic, lights, parties, and not a lot of booze or cigarettes. I had to go from one place to another, and still....nothing. Oh, and by the way, I got pulled over by the police for speeding, since I wanted to get back home so bad. He only wrote me a warning though," he pulled that one only out of his pocket to show her, and he knocked on the door.

Just then, Bert heard his bedroom door opening slowly. He looked up and saw Melody coming towards him with puffy pink, but dried up eyes. She threw her arms around him and suggested that he came back to bed with her. "I'll make it worth your while," she said.

"No, honey. I'm so tired. I'll just stay right here." He barely got those few words out, when he passed out with fatigue. Bert knew that he had to wake up before the sun came up in order to plant seeds. He would have to wear his best athletic gear in order to climb over the fences and jump the streams found throughout.

He was awake at four o'clock in the morning. He put on his old track uniform from high school, which he kept on a shelf in the hall closet, and slowly and quietly made his way to the driveway. The dogs were still asleep, so he tiptoed to his vehicle, opened its door super quietly, jumped into it, turned the key, backed up and drove the speed limit all the way to the Parrish exit. He turned left at the first stop sign, and this time sped past the country store on the corner and all the way to the entrance of the ranch. He parked away from the drive, so as not to call any attention to his vehicle, pulled out the bag of seeds from underneath the seat and began his trudge.

In the foggy moonlight, he jumped over small picket fences, balanced himself on jagged stone walkways, holding two bags, and jumped over brooks and even small ravines. His days of being a high school runner were saving his life now. There were no lights in sight, nothing but peaceful solitude, except for the occasional garden snake making its way out of the bushes to freedom and safety in the night, and the rare trogon bird that kept his nest in the low growing palmetto trees making humming noises that floated in the stiff wind. He finally felt at peace and not tired one bit.

"The acre should be straight ahead, maybe 100 yards, then to the right, at the edge of the property line," he recited to himself, as he remembered the trial run he took yesterday.

After twenty minutes of wiping sweat from his body, in this more humid than normal night, he arrived at the spot where he had put a large black piece of wood in the ground, by which to remember the exact location. He unzipped his small duffel bag and took out his apparatuses that he would use during the planting procedure. His most important tool right now was his effulgent flashlight that he pulled out from his pocket. He poured the seeds into his sweaty palms and dug spaces in the fertile field to pop in each seed.

After a little over an hour, the entire acre was filled and ready. Now all he had to do was wait for the impending storm.

Bert looked up at the gray, murky sky and felt a large drop of rain on the back of his neck. He wiped it off, but another landed on his head, then another and another, until it was coming down hard, like pebbles. Then, lightening flashed, illuminating the still cloudy dark sky, but it did not matter. His work was done.

The local news station said it was to storm just before the sun rose, but it wasn't supposed to while it was still dark.

He galloped, dodging raindrops with his speed. He ran and ran for what seemed like thirty minutes, until Bert spotted a light coming from upstairs. He was glad he had worn dark clothing, just in case anyone happened to be peering out their window. He jumped over his final stream and raced up to his final barbed wire fence, which he skirted over recklessly. These feats, however, only produced a thin cut on his hand, and a slight twist in his ankle. He knew that he had to get used to this activity, as he would have to tend to the crop on a bi-weekly basis.

When he finally made it to his SUV parked down the street, he stopped at the driver's door and sprawled his long, aching arms on the side of the vehicle, drawing in deep breaths all the while.

"This is really hard work for a man of my age. I never knew how good I had it at the station."

Bert finally caught most of his breath, but he remained outside his vehicle, soaking up the much needed water from the sky.

"How am I gonna explain this one and the others to come? Oh, it's time. I have to work at my real job tomorrow and try to become the polite, well-mannered imbecile who everyone has come to love and admire, on air anyway. They don't even know me," he laughed out loud, as he started his engine and turned up a heavy metal station until he became almost deaf. He didn't want to have to think about anything, just look and listen.

"I wish that was all that we had to do in life, just look and listen. It would be so much simpler," he thought to himself, as he laid his head back in the seat rest, his muscles aching terribly.

When Bert returned to his unlit house, the dogs were still asleep, presumably in the shed, and Melody was snoring in the bedroom. He unlocked the front door and entered the marble corridor.

He stripped down to nothing in the dark. At least he was now dry, he thought. He turned on the ceiling fan and snuggled under the quilt on the sofa. He quickly fell asleep.

Before he knew it, light beams were reflecting from his now violet-colored eyes. He woke up to find Melody standing over the sofa, frying pan in her hand.

Chapter Six

The Crop

Nikko and Cynthia were becoming quite the couple. Cynthia had totally forgotten about ever being in love with Ty. Nikko was so kind, gentlemanly, and as she thought, intelligent. Yesterday, they walked around the ranch, rode horses and barbecued in the lawn. Cynthia was falling in love with Nikko, and Nikko knew it. He liked Cynthia, but could never fall in love with any woman. That just wasn't his make-up. He had to have at least one occasional fling with a man, or even a boy. He hid these bad traits well, even from himself. He was a first-class flirt and love maker, but could never make a commitment to anyone, woman or man. Nikko had enjoyed their day together, however, and he wished that he had been born different, more normal.

"Oh well," he said aloud, as he sat down to drink the already brewed coffee, evidently prepared the night before and timed to start this morning, as both girls were still asleep. He reached in the fridge and pulled out a bagel and some cream cheese. He found some Spanish olives in the corner top shelf. This was as close as he could find to the Greek and Spanish breakfasts that he had grown up with. He ate in silence, as he wondered what he was doing in this place. "Would here be here for long? How long?" He poured himself another cup of the potent black coffee that the girls knew he liked.

At ten o'clock, Kimmie woke up and soon after, Cynthia did too.

"Where's Nikko?" Cynthia asked Kimmie, smiling, and remembering last nights intense love making.

"I don't know," Kimmie acknowledged. "Oh, there he is walking far out there in the horse field. Look, Rainbow and Julian really seem to like him," she sweetly said to Cynthia, as she saw the horses leaning on Nikko with their heads and noses.

"Oh, he has that effect on everybody," she laughed quietly, and walked out onto the front porch.

"Here is a cup of java with a splash of fresh milk I just bought yesterday evening at the general store at the corner. I've had no time to go into Ellenton to shop since we've been back," Kimmie said. "Maybe today. Do you want to go with me on a food and drink run?" she politely asked.

"Why not?" she asked Kimmie. "Nikko will be fine for a few minutes on his own, I'm sure."

"Hey, he's a grown man. What trouble could he get into?" Kimmie nonchalantly asked Cynthia, as they both glared at each other, with dumbfounded expressions, after hearing this ridiculous comment.

✳ ✳ ✳

Bert was not yet totally coherent when sweet Melody raised the frying pan over his head and demanded answers.

"I know you left in the wee hours of the morning and didn't get back until just now. I was so mad. I just let you leave. The dogs told me you were gone when they came to the slider crying. I knew something was up, so I went to the driveway, and low and behold, your car was gone. Where were you, darling?" she chanted, as she held the pan closer and closer to his skull.

"I had to go for a drive...to clear my head...that's all," he replied.

"That's all?" Melody asked.

"Yes, that's all," he restated, as closed mouth as possible. "You know how stressed I have been at work lately. I didn't want to tell you this, but I am thinking of leaving the station...."

"And going where?" she abruptly asked.

"I don't know yet, but what I do know is that good things are yet to come. I know it. I'm just planning for our future, baby," he tried to coax her with kindness, but it was not enough.

"Get your things together and go, and don't ever come back!" she stomped down the hallway backwards, pointing to the front door. When she reached the master bedroom, she went inside, slammed the door shut and screamed, "And I mean it this time."

Bert was sure that she meant what she said. He had never heard her speak that way to him, not ever.

He packed some of his belongings and headed to his blonde girl-friend's apartment to the North, the one in the low-rent district of Bradenton. He banged on her door for what seemed like five minutes, until the door finally opened. A young man of about twenty-two stepped out, bleary-eyed and with a tongue.

Bert said, "Fuck you," and walked very suavely down the apartment outdoor staircase, until he reached his vehicle, which he had parked in a handicapped spot. He did this whenever there was a space available, as he carried a handicapped decal with him at all times. He found this decal one night in the television station parking lot and picked it up. It had been his ever since.

"I'm getting out of here. I'll tell the station that I'm returning next week. I have a personal dilemma, which I do. If they don't like it, they can kiss off," he screamed out his window with the radio blaring.

He drove for miles over the Skyway and onto St. Pete Beach, where he grabbed a room, as quick as he could, and for as cheap as possible. He found one with a great Florida residency rate of $475 per week, since it was slow. Tourists were scarce, because of small oil spill in the gulf, near Central Florida. It was not fully expected to even get to St. Pete. The media had been hyping it up so much that hotels and restaurants up and down the coast from Clearwater to Sarasota were suffering monetarily.

Bert got a call from the station, as he was entering his tiny, clean, adequate room, carrying his suitcase in one hand and his cell phone in the other. He threw his bag on the queen bed, so that he could be receptive to the ring.

"Hello," he irritatingly answered.

"So, you will be back in one week?" his secretary asked in an irritated manner herself. She had put Bert in his place, over and over again, in the eight long years they both worked at WORK together.

"Stud says he'll get the new understudy, Joe Corbin, to take your place. Says it'll be good for him, but he definitely wants you in his office in a week. He says he can't handle these last minute schedule changes and said he 'ain't gonna tolerate it no more'."

Stud, who was the producer of the evening news, didn't have the best of grammar when it came to talking with his fellow workers and friends, but when it came to impressing strangers, he most definitely put on the air. That was how Stud got the top position he held today.

Melody continued to hold her ground and not contact her "beloved" spouse.

Two days later, however, after getting drunk on the Beach, Bert called Melody. She could barely understand his slurring gibberish, except when he apologized near the end of their short conversation.

"I'm sorry for being so cruel to you with my lies and schemes... and my two girls...my two girls who I thought worshiped me...but they're whores...just like the whole lot of you. Oh, not you...my sweet. I didn't mean to include you with them. Ohhh, babe...I was a bad cheat...bad...bad...bad," and he dropped his phone and his body on the fresh, damp sand.

He woke up as the sun woke. He had forgotten what he had exposed around midnight the night before. He trudged back to his motel to get freshened up.

After ten, he thought it late enough to call Melody at home. He got a recording that the number had been changed to a non-published number. He tried her pay by the minute cell phone, of which she hardly ever used, and got no answer. He tried and tried again until she finally answered, "You are never to come back into my life again. Contact my lawyer, James D. Balastine in Sarasota. Divorce papers are to be served to you at the station on grounds of adultery... and to think, all I've done for you." Then, there was silence.

He never called her again, or her lawyer. He returned to station the next week and picked up the divorce papers. Bert was to live in his motel room on the beach for the entire three months of the growing season. St. Pete Beach was near the Skyway Bridge. This provided easy access to Sarasota and Parrish.

He continued broadcasting at WORK daily and tending to his plants on a bi-weekly basis, depending on the amount of rainfall, and there had not been a lot of rain this entire winter. This was getting to be such a reflex action for him, never having to think, an easy routine. Bert loved his life!

He watered his crop late at night, most of the time, using his flashlight, and on occasion in the daytime when he was to be "busy" at night with his other abundant crop of female tourists who he would buy for a dime a dozen on any given night of the week. Bert was really enjoying everything. Bert would party all night and work a wee bit in the afternoon, still making a sizable pay check every week, even without the crop being ready yet. He was so looking forward to being in the big money.

"Then, I will be able to have everything I want, anytime," he said to himself as he drove over the Skyway Bridge.

He did not know, however, that his glee was to take a turn for the worse with his pending divorce. Melody was asking for half of everything that he made, plus pension, plus the proceeds from the house she was putting up for sale. Melody was going back to her roots in New Hampshire, where she had met Bert for the first time, when he worked as a news reporter in Concord for one year.

They met at a fancy bed and breakfast inn there, where Bert was living. She was working her way her first year of paralegal school as a cocktail waitress. She served Bert his traditional whiskey and soda, with a squeeze of orange, in what he thought to be a very sexy way. He was hooked from that point on. They started dating, got married two years later, and moved around the country like gypsies, until he landed a stable higher paying news anchor position in wealthy Sarasota.

Melody had always been an excellent paralegal in every city he had ever worked, but she loved her position in Sarasota the most. She hated to leave it, but she felt she must. It was just too painful for her to stay.

Bert agreed on everything she wanted. He simply wanted the divorce to be over.

"I will never marry again," he told his lawyer. "Why would any man? It's just too fun out there. Why would any man nowadays settle for just one broad when he could have thousands? It's just so easy. They're ripe for the pickin'," he haughtily chuckled, as he signed the last document.

"So when will it be final, counselor?" Bert asked sarcastically. "I have things to do and money to make and clients to please," he boldly laughed.

His lawyer disappointingly put down his head and answered, "Probably in another month." He grabbed his document case and departed from Bert saying, "Call me if you need me."

"Sure shootin' I will," Bert abruptly remarked to his long-time friend.

One week later at dusk, Bert was ready to check out the "bud" on his three-week old, lush marijuana crop that was doing extremely well with the nutrient found in the soil at the ranch, the watering Bert did, the almost total sunlight during the day, the tips that his woman dealer suggested to him, and of course, the marvelous Afghan seeds. He knew he was going to be part of a big money racket when he saw the size of these plants.

"And this is only the beginning," he spoke out loud, getting out of his now dirtied, sea salted vehicle. His gut feelings told him that he should have waited until later on in the night, but he had a super-hot date with a super-hot, fiery, auburn-haired chick of twenty from Spain at ten that night, on the beach.

Women were definitely his top priority, so he didn't go with his gut. He parked in his usual secluded hiding spot which he had found two and a half months ago when he turned off the two lane road that bordered the back property fence onto this pot-holed dirt road, seemingly dug out for pedestrians or cyclists. It was so narrow. His vehicle had begun to really resemble a wrecker lately.

As soon as this business was done, and his money was collected he would get himself a clean, straight, smooth, black, vintage cigar Jag. He climbed out with the hose. He always hooked up to a spring water source in the ground to water the plants and always had the tools necessary for a good job of picking the "bud" off the plant, so as to keep the plants healthy. He put the "bud" in a sturdy plastic bag.

When Bert walked over to the small field in an out of the way part of the estate, he was greeted with, "Hello. May I ask what you are doing on the girls' property?" as Nikko unequivocally waited for a reply with his arms folded and legs in a firm stance.

Caught off guard by their unexpected meeting, Bert dropped all of his gear and ran toward his vehicle, with Nikko keeping up the pace, until he reached Bert.

"Oh no you're not," Nikko declared, as his strong grip held Bert's arms together, in back of Bert's body. "Tell me, what you are doing here?" he asked Bert.

Nik looked down at the bag and at the plants growing in the land. "This shit looks like weed."

Bert hung his head low and revealed that it was. He told him that he had stumbled upon this road and noticed a small piece of empty land, hidden from the world. Bert knew better than to tell anyone about his ties with any mob. He knew he wouldn't last too long on the planet, if he did.

"I just thought that I could make it work this one time, so I could put some food on the table at home. I'm broke...lost my job," he lied. "I wasn't gonna do it again, I swear. I'm sorry...sorry. I didn't know who's property this was, or even if it belonged to anybody. You're not going to turn me in are you?" he asked in a subservient, almost begging way.

"I won't only if you cut me in on half of your earnings. I don't know if you're working by yourself or not, but I want my half," Nikko demanded.

"Okay, that sounds fair," Bert said halfheartedly, knowing he would have to find a way out of this mess. There was not going to be a split of money. He knew the guys would frown on him for letting this scoundrel into their existence. He did not know how to rectify the situation.

"When, where and to whom do we sell this load of jewels," Nikko asked in a take charge manner. He was ready for anything, being an ambitious fellow, just like he was back in the Mediterranean. "Now, I don't have to depend only on charming Cynthia's money," he revealed his plot to Bert, laughing aloud. "Let's take some 'juice' from the 'vines' of some of these babies, and I'll follow you home so we can plan our next move."

Bert knew he wouldn't be able to stretch the truth any further. He had to disclose all information.

"What is your name?" he asked the dark headed and skinned young man.

"My friends call me Nikko, for Nicholas," he replied casually.

"Well, Nikko, how 'bout if you come with me to my new home over the Skyway where we can talk it over this evening and have some drinks and fun with Spanish babes?" Bert asked.

"Sure, you know that's where I'm from originally, before we moved to Greece," Nikko said wild eyed.

"Okay, then let's harvest. Just follow me and do what I do," Bert showed him every move to make with his fingers and wrist, so as not to damage any part of the plant, and he showed him how to retrieve the best pot. He learned this from the girl who gave him the seed in the bad part of town. Fate had been rather eccentric and always relied on her intuition, which is how she suggested taking the marijuana off of the plants...using intuition.

"Fate says that this seed may produce buds in only three weeks," Bert revealed.

Their hard work lasted over two hours in the stifling hot sun. Now, Bert was actually glad that Nikko was here to help him with the project. They bundled their first small harvest into a large plastic bags, which was to be divided later into smaller bags for sale. They put the clear plastic bags into cloth sacks and began their journey to the motel.

Bert told Nikko nothing but lies about his personal life, as he crossed the water to get to Pinellas County. Nikko told Bert nothing but the truth, starting from his birth, up until the time he met Francis. Thereafter, however, he told nothing but lies. They both were con artists...both the same...in every way.

Chapter Seven

Luciano

Their talk that evening turned into both a loving friendship and a rivalry full of hatred. Bert called his contact who was located now in Tampa, as the mob was investing in a hotel downtown near the bay. Franco told him to drop the bags off at a specific location underneath the front desk located on the partially built ground floor of the soon to be luxury hotel. Nikko and Bert both drove down 1-275 and got off at the Ashley Exit, where Bert was instructed to go. He followed the precise directions until he arrived at his designated spot, near the city center area, navigating through a series of one-way thoroughfares.

Nikko stayed in the vehicle while Bert carried the heavy burlap bags, one by one into the shell of the hotel and deposited them where he was instructed. He walked swiftly back to the vehicle. Then his cell phone rang.

"Bert, you have done an excellent job for us so far. Please continue the good work. You will be rewarded soon...very soon. We have a series of important clients whom you will be meeting. We will give you instructions on when to pick up the 'gift' bags and where to deliver them. They will all be prepaid. It's fast, and it's easy. After your delivery services this whole week, you will be presented with your share of the 'pie' and yet another set of instructions on where to plant more and where to stash excess cash for us...I believe it's near where you are living now, by the way.

Oh, and I was very sorry to learn about your divorce finalization today. But now, she's not a part of you and not in harm's way anymore," his contact spoke softly, but directly.

"My divorce went through today? I'm officially single," he said with slight remorse. He wasn't expecting to feel this way when it happened. He was actually kind of sad now, and all the games and chases didn't matter much now, because there was no deceit. He was a true single player. He no longer felt that mischievous sense that he had felt ever since he had married Melody.

The two men had a late night rendezvous with the Spanish girl and her average looking acquaintance who she managed to snag for Nikko. Attractive Nikko had not wanted any part of this "kid", as he called her. He remembered waking up with pretty, sweet Cynthia that morning and now he was subjected to this crap. He walked back to Bert's motel. He wondered what the girls must think of him vanishing, without even saying goodbye. He couldn't see them for a while, until this was all over. He didn't want them to be involved in any of this.

"It's too dangerous," he whispered to himself, as he heard the door slowly opening, and a big brown figure whose face was hidden by a bandana and beard, was standing in the doorway holding an envelope.

This figure said nothing but, "Give this to the man." Nikko simply nodded his head, then he heard the door slam shut.

About two hours later, Bert returned soaking wet, sandy, and intoxicated. It appeared to Nikko that Bert was back to his normal self again. He handed him the envelope.

Bert asked, "What is this shit for," as he stumbled into the desk that was placed by the television set. He opened his letter and quickly sobered up upon reading it. The letter had all delivery locations and amounts, all to be picked up at the same location downtown, and all to be delivered in the Tampa Bay area tomorrow.

"We've got to sleep…got lots of things to do in the morning. We'll grab a bite to eat on the way. There's no time to waste. We've got lots of deliveries tomorrow," he reminded Nikko, as he pulled off his pants and shoes, kept on his t-shirt, then turned off the small lamp by his bedside.

In two minutes, Nikko heard him snoring. Nikko turned off his small lamp and got into bed with his shorts and stayed awake thinking about his future for over an hour. Once asleep, all he could dream about was Cynthia.

At six in the morning, the Boss called. "Rise and Shine. Your day begins right about now. I am your human alarm clock," he said in a matter of fact way.

"Oh, fuck," Bert exclaimed. "We have to get the shit out of Dodge, and quick."

"I took a shower last night. I am ready to rock," Nikko professed, slipping into his tight and faded denims and rubbing deodorant under his arms every time he took a step. "I'm going to grab a bite next door while you're getting ready, okay?" he asked Bert.

"Fine by me. Just be at my car in thirty minutes," Bert stated.

Nikko didn't respond, only shut the motel door in his face. Plenty of beauties were at the beach bar, even at seven in the morning, drinking hot coffee and sipping on potent Bloody Marys. He decided to have one of each, then two of each. When he met Bert at his car, Nikko was fairly zonked, and it was only seven-thirty in the morning.

"Oh, I cannot believe you!" Bert exclaimed, feeling like running Nikko over.

"Let's go. I'm not too bad off. I just had some early morning fun. That's all," Nikko exclaimed to Bert, flailing his arms over his dark brunette, square-shaped head.

"Get in and buckle up…got many places to go…first of course to the hotel…to pick up the gift packages," he informed the deadened senses of Nikko.

They traveled for almost one hour, in heavy rush hour traffic, until they finally reached their pick up spot. Bert confiscated the "gifts" and got back in the vehicle to proceed to his first drop. He was ready, but still nervous.

He drove from Tampa all the way up to Hudson, in a northern county of the bay, over to Haines City, near Lakeland, then down to Punta Gorda, where his last big drop was, and where the boys were to meet him with his pay.

He waited at the convention center near downtown Punta Gorda for over thirty minutes. Finally, the big navy Escalade pulled into view. Bert heaved a sigh of relief when the Boss stepped out.

"I believe this is for you, my boy. Nicely done. I hope it's like this every time. Then, you will always be our star player. And who is this?" the Boss man asked, staring accusingly at Bert.

"This is my good friend and cohort, Nikko," he proclaimed to both of them. "He is working with me…has worked in a number of 'sticky' situations," Bert laughed, "all over Europe."

"I think I might have heard of you through our grapevine, or maybe through the Greek grapevine," another man commented in a Slavic accent, getting out and pulling something from his coat pocket.

Nikko was now getting very nervous, realizing that these men might be associated with Francis' underworld dealings. He started backing away, as if ready to hit the high road.

"Come back here," the Slavic man demanded. Nikko stood still. "Come back here I said!" Nikko inched closer to the heavy-handed, plump, fair-skinned man. "When I say move, you move. You always DO what I SAY…you understand?"

Nikko and Bert looked at each other in disbelief. Then, Nikko nodded in agreement. He did not want to cross this vindictive man who reminded him of a sandy haired Dracula.

"I don't want you both to try any funny stuff. If you do, it'll be a quick 'game over' for the two of you. You understand. We don't play. Now, what I want you goofs to do is drive over to a quiet neighborhood in front of La Dona. In the water in front of it, there's an island.

It's a small island we call 'Pelican Island'. They're the only inhabitants there.

Take a raft, or a small boat, or swim. I don't care how you get over to it....just get there. The only problem is, there are many houses lining the street which faces the island, with big windows looking out onto it. I would suggest going over at night...late at night. It has to be when everyone's asleep. You must be equipped with shovels, strength, and strong flashlights. It is pitch black over there at night, even with stars and moons. There is so much damn bush over there, that we thought it best to leave it to you, Bert, and now your *compadre*, I assume. I want you to dig...I want you to dig until you reach China. That way, nobody... or no bird, will be able to abscond with our belongings," and with that, the Slav went back to the car.

"Do you have any further concerns before I head on out to kill someone and make some more money," the Boss man dramatically added to the finality of the scenario.

"What do you want us to bury in that bird-ridden island?" Bert asked, as if he were crazy.

"Oh, I am sorry. I did forget to tell you cream puffs that, didn't I?" he surprisingly added, as he headed to a blonde-haired beauty, wearing an almost non-existent bikini, and who was awaiting him by his Ferrari. "Oh, this and that," he said, as he threw two burlap sacks with hundred dollar bills ripping through the seams toward both men.

Then, the Boss squatted down to climb into his low car which possessed striking black leather seats. Nikko looked in and noticed that each seat had the name "Luciano" embroidered at the top. The car then sped away.

Nikko had caught one of the bags, and Bert the other. Nikko opened his and out dropped bundles of cash, each banded together. When Bert opened his, cash also came bounding out, along with a few small plastic bags containing unsealed quantities of expensive marijuana, perhaps by mistake, or maybe as a way to show gratitude and promise for things to come.

"Well, I suppose we should head up north and wait 'til the sun goes down. We could have a few shots at La Dona, then head on over to the isle to perform our duties," Bert smirked at his cohort.

"Sure shootin'," Nikko replied. He was used to hearing that expression from Francis' "Tex" days on the island of Sardinia. "Hey, Bert. Did you notice the leather seats in his Ferrari?"

"No, what about those damn ugly things?" Bert impatiently responded to Nikko in a jealous way.

"On the tops, in a half-moon shape, were sewn the name, 'Luciano'," Nikko revealed.

"What?" he answered, already half-drunk, having just pulled out a beer from his trunk and downed it already. He put the bags of "goodies" in there as well. Bert felt now at his masters' beckon calls. He knew he was trapped and would never be able to live a normal life again.

At that moment, he prayed for salvation. He was so glad that Melody was not a part of his life anymore, strictly because of this.

"If I go down," Bert told Nikko, "I'm just glad that Melody won't be along with me to enjoy the ride. I wonder what she is doing right now. I wish I could call her to find out, but I can't. I could never get her in the line of fire, all because of me. I could never live with myself."

"I hear you bro," was the only coined expression that Nikko could use to display his overwrought feelings of past guilt and current sympathy. He had heard this phrase so many times on television and in the movies, that this was the only way he could think of to display his feelings of remorse for the things that he had done wrong in the past, and what he was attempting to do wrong now... in the present.

As Bert drove up I-75, then I-275 to the St. Pete Beach exit, he thought that the name "Luciano" was of course, Italian. Was there any way possible that three mobs, the Irish, Russian and Italian could be playing this gig together, or even against each other, for ulterior motives? They must want to collect billions with other marketing ventures too, not just millions from the estate and its grounds.

"We are playing with a full deck of cards now and three rival mobs. Be careful. I will. Let's defeat these bloodsucking gangs that have taken....oh my God, have they taken... and never returned nothing to no one," Bert said to Nikko, in a grammatically incorrect statement. He was always taken aback by abhorrently incorrect statements like this one, used by "illiterates" of society, as he referred to them, but on this occasion, he used it himself.

The two insidious men arrived at their motel and went to their room to deposit the cash and weed in the safe deposit box. Next, they walked the beach to the pool bar at La Dona, then paraded through the infamous ornate lobby, which had all of its eyes on the Gulf of Mexico. When both took their seats at the bar, one got high on liquor and became out of sorts. The other remained coherent and on schedule, ready to "stash" all the "cash" in the ground tomorrow.

At ten, it was still too early to swim to the island without being seen. They both had to be very inconspicuous so that no visitor or family living in one of the very comfortable houses that bordered the street across from the island would see any sign of movement.

At twelve, it was time to go back to the motel and pick up the shovels and plastic bags. They both needed to gather some wits about themselves. Nikko had become a slight bit tipsy with persuasion, but Bert, on the other hand, was out cold. Nikko ordered hot coffee from the bar maid to revive Bert's spirits.

After three full cups of black coffee, which Nikko made him drink quickly and carefully, Bert was now ready to "take on the world", even to "glide" over to the island in the shallow water. They found this to be their only means of getting there. They had to carry bags and shovels in hand.

"This should be *interesting...very interesting*," Bert said, as Nikko drove the car out of the lot and down the street to park in front of one of the houses that was located across the street from the island. They both got out of the vehicle...*silently...very silently.*

Chapter Eight

Pelican Island

They parked next to the curb of the house which lay directly across from the uninhabited isle. It was a small home, but it had a large marbled Jacuzzi in the front yard, along with green-striped awnings hanging elegantly over each of the front windows. It had its own dock, with its own sailboat, of course. The people who lived in this neighborhood came equipped with money, and they had to have the best, at all times.

Nikko got out of the vehicle first, scoping out the situation. "The sign here says we need a parking pass to park here. It says its patrolled twenty-four hours a day, seven days a week," he advised Bert.

Bert got out, glimpsed at the sign, and said in an irresponsible manner, "Who cares? WE'VE got bigger fish to fry. I'll TAKE the chance." Changing the subject, Bert blurted out, "I'm ready to dive in if you are. We've got to start sometime." He put his toes into the water.

"Come on...it's not cold...no sharks in the waterway, either... hopefully," Bert assured his newly-found best friend of three days.

Being an expert swimmer, Nikko decided to show off a bit and add some flare. He ran from across the street as fast as he could, diving into the fairly shallow inlet, holding one of the burlap bags and a waterproof flashlight that he had found in a compartment in his vehicle. Nikko reached the island in one minute flat, with unparalleled swimming strokes that he had learned both in Palma de Mallorca and in Mykonos.

Being a little bit of a wussy, scared of everything, and incapable of just about anything having to do with water, Bert walked to the end of the land and looked into the waterway fearfully. He made the sign of the cross and jumped in, holding his nose. Bert could barely swim and used dog paddles to get over to where Nikko sat in the dark, waiting... and waiting. Bert was being weighed down by the load he was carrying, and which he found in that same compartment...the compartment for emergencies, like this was. He managed to stay afloat, inching closer to Nikko with every paddle. Nikko shined the flashlight at him in jest, laughing all the while. At that moment, the front door to the house across the way slammed shut, and they both could see a tiny young woman, dressed in a long, simple brown dress, sneakers, and a white bonnet, not yet tied, come running over to the boat-less dock which faced the island.

"Keep the light off until we need to use it, you fool," Bert reprimanded Nikko in a whisper.

They walked as softly as they could in the huge weeds and half worn fossil shells of the bird island. Nikko, leading the duo, stopped and turned to Bert, when he reached a certain part of the island.

"I feel that this is where we need to stash the dough and the goods. Nobody will ever come out to this island, especially this part, right in the center, right at all the birds' droppings."

"Sounds plausible. Start digging. I'll shine the flashlight...I'll shine it just a little," Bert warned Nikko. He turned it on, and Nikko started digging in the sandy soil, perfect for hiding belongings that is, until the tide changed and water invaded the land in this high flood zone neighborhood. He knew nothing of the geography of the land, had no training or background in anything that diverse and cumbersome. All he had ever wanted to do was get by in style...and live well...super well, which is what he always had managed to do.

As Bert illuminated the small area of ground in which Nikko had already started digging two deep, spacious holes for both stashes, using his already blistered hands that showed no pain whatsoever, a Quaker woman sat on a bench built into their dock. She sang a haunting melody and prayed, staring straight out, onto the island.

"Are you done Nikko? Bert hurriedly asked.

"Yes I am, and thanks for your assistance," he mocked back to him.

"I can't believe that wench came out right when we got here," Bert whispered and not in a calm manner.

"Believe it, and get ready to swim. We've got a long way to go to get to the other side of the neighborhood," Nikko pointed out. We can't go anywhere near her. She's already seen us and your car."

"I'll be ticketed and towed for sure. I know it, and with her seeing a glimpse of us tonight, we sure got problems. I might never see my car again," he said, as he got in the frigid water. "What have we got ourselves into Nikko? You know, now there's no way out of this."

Nikko nodded.

Changing moods, as he began to swim for the other side, in the deeper, colder, choppier water, Bert laughed and declared, "Well, Nikko. Maybe it's time to buy that Jag I have always dreamed of. Let's go count our cash in the room." With shovels and bags left on the isle, Bert managed to swim swifter and steadily, in order to catch up to his counterpart.

Once back on dry land, they each took showers and changed into dress shirts. Bert had a couple lying on his bed, so he threw one over to Nikko.

"We've got to go to the mall in the morning to get you some clothes. It's like I kidnapped you, with only a shirt on your back. Sorry," Bert let down his guard. He had always been pretty transparent to folk anyway, and a little naive.

"That's okay. Hey, let's meet in the lobby at La Dona. They have a jazz piano player there right now. Didn't you hear him? He sounded magnificent, from the notes I heard, as we were walking in. Now, count your money," and he opened up the safe and threw him his share.

Nikko left the room, with cell phone and money in pocket. He headed up to the grand entrance where he could get some reception, and he called the girls.

Cynthia answered crying and hysterical, "Nikko, where are you? What happened to you? Oh, I'm so glad you're alive and that you called me. I have been so sick. I don't know why, maybe because of the miscarriage. I guess it's just my luck."

"I am so sorry dear. I will explain everything when I will come down tomorrow. I'll call you later," he said as pushed the end button on the phone when he saw Bert staring at him through the windows.

Bert came racing through the lobby and out into the sub-tropical cool night air.

"I thought I told you not to call no one. Who'd you call? Was it the girls?"

Nikko nodded his guilty head, "I had to Bert. I was so worried about them that it got the best of me. Hey, could you do me a huge favor. No one will get hurt...promise. I have a good plan."

Bert stared at him with piercing eyes.

Nikko stumbled on, "We don't need to go the mall tomorrow. All we have to do is make our way down to the ranch, pick up my clothing and see the girls. I will introduce them both to you. They're great... you'll love them. I will tell them I met you recently, maybe at the general store up the street in Parrish. You said you were a gardener/landscaper who lives in St. Pete Beach. We had a few drinks at your place, slept them off...and here we are now...and by the way, a whole hell of a lot's been goin' on, so the Ranch really needs some cosmetic fix-ups, really the whole area around the house, you know, bushes, flowers, trees."

"We can take a leisurely stroll around the grounds, particularly over to the spot where our Mary Jane plants are growing," Bert was now getting excited. "How brilliant."

"Wha...whatever you say...cause you're the landscaper now...but why do you call them Mary Jane plants?" Nikko asked in a goofy way.

"I didn't make it up. Somebody way back did. It's an expression," he told the still muffled looking face of Nikko. "You know a phrase... how do you say it in Spanish...oh yeah...*frase*." Nikko shook his head up and down and was satisfied with the explanation. He had always had a thirst for knowledge, and would not settle for anything less than having all of his questions answered, trivial or urgent.

"Let's just make it one night cap, okay Bud?" Bert asked Nikko. "I'm wiped out."

"Me too," Nikko said, as he yawned. The two strolled back inside, ordered night caps, requested three songs, then they paid for a bay view room, so that they could enjoy a peaceful night of slumber there.

Before they were passed out on their respective beds, Bert remarked, "Hope our car is there in the morning. We've got business to tend to."

He heard no response. Nikko was already dead to the world, and Bert was not far behind him. Bert turned off his light, shut his eyes, and began to snore heavily. He dreamed not of mystical things and places, but of the malicious and violent situations that had occurred recently. He had never even struck a woman before that night of passion with Sunny, yet alone killed someone. However, it had proved horrific and delightful to him, at the same time.

He awakened with a startle, as he remembered the police prancing up and down the interior corridors of the same hotel in which he now slept, remorseless. They had asked questions of all the guests in the hotel. Luckily, he didn't have a room there at that time, and he had dressed incognito which he did on numerous occasions when venturing out into the public's spotlight. There was no way that anyone could ever link him to the murder, he lied to himself, not even with the car registered in his name parked by the nosy Quaker's residence and her recognition of sound in the distance, coming from the island. He hoped that they had not found any Afghan marijuana seeds like he had the night of Sunny's stabbing.

Bert had cleaned the room, using one of his driving gloves that was stuck in his pocket, ransacked the closet and drawers to make it look like a robbery gone bad, and that is when he found it, another stash, in one of her two large, deep pockets of her linen beach blazer that was in her closet. Bert had grabbed the seeds, put them in a white plastic beach bag he found in the bathroom area and left. No word of this murder had ever reached the press. The authorities were keeping it hushed for some reason. That scared him. Her turban, and all other garments, remained with the authorities.

"I am afraid they could link this to me. If you get a guy who wants to move up the ranks, he'll go out of his way to piece things together. I am a celebrity which makes things even worse. I just hope that the parking lot at the station was empty that night they wedged me in. That's it," he said to himself, "Before going to the station later on, we have to stop by The Ranch to see how the new seeds are doing, then I'll call Tampa, where his goon's now living to tell him what's going on. He'll help me. I know he will. He's gotta...he's gotta...he's just gotta," and he drifted back to a state of slumber. This time, he was more at peace, because he had made the decision to call the Boss.... tomorrow.

Bert would be a cheapskate until he died, no matter what king of money he came into. It came from his upbringing. His parents were Pentecostal missionaries, traveling throughout Central America. He, of course, went with them everywhere. He learned Spanish fairly well having acquaintances and friends of Hispanic descent. Most of his buddies, however, were sons of his parents' fellow missionaries. They lived communally.

Bert was never particularly a church-goer, due to what he saw going on down South, some unorthodox, like the many rapes he witnessed at the commune. The rapes involved male missionaries and their Central American victims, usually very young girls, sometimes boys. Bert had been, nonetheless, a spiritual boy, believing everything that transpired in life was meant to be.

Wanting to break away from his roots, he ran away from home in St. Paul, Minnesota when the family returned from El Salvador. He was sixteen. He ran as far as he could go with one hundred dollars to his name, and that was to Chicago. With his good looks, smart wit and fabulous vocal qualities, he got a low-paying job as a "gofer" for a large network news show.

When his parents got wind of this through the station, they prayed for his safety...and prayed that his prayers would finally be answered. They trusted him in every way to survive, but they did send him money from time to time. Whenever, they came to visit him, they praised him, bought him a good home cooked meal, and they were on their way. They had no time to waste. They were off to rescue another family in Central America who was in harm's way.

Bert stayed at the Chicago network for fifteen years, advancing slowly, but surely, to senior news correspondent, then host of his own current topic show. At twenty-nine, he was offered a stout yearly income being an anchorman in Concorde, New Hampshire for the same affiliate network. He took it, eventually meeting, then marrying Melody. They were married for ten years before moving to Sarasota for his work.

This was another well-paying job, a warm location, with good hours, thus providing fringe benefits for him, he surmised. His parents were probably squirming in their graves, as he thought about all of his infidelity, but he could not stop. It was like an addiction to him....not the sex...but the power....the fight...the glory...then onto the next challenge. He simply loved to win.

Bert ordered coffee and eggs to be delivered to their table on the veranda, overlooking morning traffic coming from the drawbridge toll up the road. Once brought to them, the tray of food was placed on an end table, while an elaborately embroidered cloth was placed over top the round table. The waiter then took each plate and each cup off of the tray and presented them to both of the guests. He took off the silver cover which was put over each entree, poured the steaming hot coffee into each cup, gave them all condiments, then waited politely for a tip. Bert arrogantly said and demonstrated with his hand, "scram." The waiter bowed to the table and quickly departed.

After a few bites of perfectly cooked scrambled eggs, Bert picked up his cell from inside the room. He plopped back down in his sturdy lawn chair and punched Luciano's number. No answer. He tried again. This time, it was a different scenario.

"It's about time you called me," the boss answered his cell. "How'd it go last night? I hope well...without a hitch."

"There were no hitches, however I do need to talk to you. Do you have a minute," he submissively requested of the Italian.

"Sure, shoot...the ball's in your court, sonny."

"We...we...well," Bert nervously stuttered. "I might have a problem. You see, the Irish boys told me to come to La Dona to meet a girl...a girl from Afghanistan who was to check into the hotel after her two in the afternoon arrival from Ireland. She did come downstairs. We did have a drink at the bar. We did go to her hotel room. She did threaten me. *I did kill her*......She did give me *no* information."

"No need to worry your novice head about this matter. We know all about the episode. We have top police officials over there who are in the organization and a couple taxi drivers," he chuckled. "They kept it quiet...that's all."

"So you think I'm okay?" Bert asked. "Even though we planted seeds I snatched from the girl's room on the island last night?"

"What!" he exclaimed. "You guys were only supposed to bury some cash for us, so that it couldn't be traced....that was ALL...You had seeds from her this whole time and you didn't even..."

Bert broke in with, "And that's not all. This woman saw us, I'm sure and stayed in her front yard the entire time we planted. It wasn't for that long, but my car was parked outside her house...on the curb... too long...I guess...It's gone...I'm scared..." he whined like a baby.

"I'll get someone to remove your vehicle from the tow lot. In the meantime, why don't you boys get away for a few days, like down to Ft. Myers for some fun, sun and broads. There's someone I want you to meet there. He's a handsome guy, plays in a band down there, and works for us. But I don't want to tell you again, don't ever go against the mob with your own ventures. Thanks for telling me about this new enterprise. I'll give you one-third to split amongst yourselves, and I'll take the rest, but you have to take all the chances. Remember, the seeds must be tended to constantly, like down in Parrish. Only this time, they're in the middle of A NEIGHBORHOOD. HOW COULD YOU HAVE BEEN SO STUPID? Hey, I like you, Bert, and I don't want to see anything bad happen to you, so watch your back, okay, and let's keep this conversation private, only between the two of us, you hear?" Luciano pleaded with Bert.

"This conversation's only going in my ears and nobody else's," Bert reassured him. He ended the call, then informed Nikko, "Even the boss is on the take." He told Nikko all about the call. Bert had never kept one promise, not in his entire life, and he was feeling extra confident, like no one could take him down. He was now playing dangerously out of his league.

"There will be hell to pay for Bert. Only Bert doesn't know it yet. He doesn't know what's in store for his psycho-driven, foolish, egocentric, head of worms," Camille told the other angelic beings that were gathered around her, listening to her goodness... to her remorse... to her revengeful plans.

Chapter Nine

The Landscaping Business

The underworld entities were not going to let a chump like Bert take them down with grievous errors in judgment. They also knew that he was a liar and a cheat. From every situation viewed where Bert was involved, the consensus was that he was not to be trusted. Luciano planned when and where they were going to knock the socks off of the boy. His contact got in good with him over the phone. Bert thought he had won Luciano over and that the Italian mob trusted him. In two days, however, they planned to kill him at midnight, when the first harvest of the plant would take place on the isle.

They were supposed to go over there by boat, pick him up to take him to dry land, then continue out into the rough Gulf of Mexico, knocking his person from the vessel and leaving him there to drown, to be eaten by the incoming sharks from Texas. No trace of him whatsoever. His co-workers called him the "malady of the world". No one had truly liked him for years, not even his wife, and the mob knew this. They knew that nobody would be searching too long and hard to find the most rudimentary soul of existence.

After a silent breakfast, they each took quick showers, got dressed into jeans and rugby shirts, which Bert again loaned to Nikko, and they were off, off to look at the new crop at the ranch, and of course, to meet the girls. First, however, they had to stop downstairs at the counter to purchase a rental car for the day, until he had enough time to purchase the car he really wanted.

Bert drove down the same stretch of interstate he was so accustomed to driving, day in and day out. He turned off toward Tampa, then made his exit to Parrish and wrapped over the interstate. Finally, he was in the country town which usually made him nauseous. Today, however, it made him feel serene. When he headed down the narrow two lane barely paved road towards The Ranch, he really felt excited. He didn't know why.

After pulling up into the gravel driveway and speaking into the system at the entrance, two luscious and scintillating babes, who were not too terribly young, but in great shape, came running out barefoot, in shorts and t-shirts. They ran up to the car, Kimmie on Bert's side, and Cynthia on Nikko's.

"Where were you? I missed you so much. I was so worried about you. Oh, I'm glad you called me last night. What were you doing anyway?" Cynthia demanded to know, as she put her head inside the passenger seat window and stared at Bert. "And who are you?" she questioned him.

"I'd like to know the same thing myself," Kimmie stated firmly.

"Nikko and I are best friends and soon to be landscaping business entrepreneurs," he informed Kimmie, with a hint of boyish sarcasm.

"Well, come on inside. I'll make put on some apple cider," she said in a distrusting manner. "It's good for the heart muscle." She ran back to the house. Cynthia waited until the vehicle was parked and Nikko jumped out and into her awaiting arms. Bert knew why he had looked forward to arriving here. The girls were beautiful.

"Nikko, how did you get a girl as pretty and sweet as all this?" he asked, patting him on the back.

"I guess it's my charm," he said, as he winked at Cynthia.

The men walked inside the massive manor estate and climbed into comfortable chairs. The two girls sat side by side on the fringed couch, after Kimmie distributed cups of cider to everyone.

"You have a grandiose place here," he stated, looking at Cynthia.

"Oh, it's not mine. It's hers," she informed Bert, nodding her head in Kimmie's direction. "That is, unless the Irish boys manage to take it away from the only surviving heir in court. It really is horrible what we've seen...what people have done. I live in a small castle near Shannon, Ireland. I have it up for sale. We all have been through a lot...and had to leave...you understand, if we are not the best company right now. We don't know who to trust and probably never will know ever again."

"Well ladies, you can trust me. Now, I don't know about Nikko," he said jokingly, grabbing his head in a jovial manner. "I am here to clean things up, and in a literal sense as well. I'll get my supplies and look around the property to advise what should be done. Are you coming Nikko?"

"No, I think I'll just stick around here and talk with the girls. I'm pooped out Bert," he replied.

"Come on," Bert demanded in a stern voice, pulling him up from his sitting position by his small polo collar.

"I've been ordered to the front...must go," he told the girls, as he gave them a salute.

The girls stood quietly, watching the men trudge into the now heavily weeded field. Cynthia spoke quietly, in a perplexed manner, "You know, I can't help feel that there is something strange with that guy. He's attractive and intelligent as all get out, but there is still something."

"You have one of your overwhelming bad feelings about him?" Kimmie asked.

"You could say that, and I don't know why. He seems to have a mystique to him. I see it when I look in those beautiful eyes...lots of pain, covered up by bad morals. It just gets people through sometimes, like when they are taking intense drugs for life-threatening diseases, it gets them through the difficult moments. Maybe that's what he's had to go through. I don't know what his circumstances are, but I will find out...one way or another. He is VERY intriguing though, wouldn't you say?" Cynthia questioned Kimmie, batting her eyelids, as she walked over to the fridge to grab the orange juice container.

"But I thought you were getting along so well with Nikko!" Kimmie surprisingly exclaimed.

"Oh, he's great, but we're not married. I can still pick and choose as I please. I have to be sure from now on. You know, I too have a lot of pain that I have hidden, using 'good morals only.' Well, it hasn't got me anywhere. Maybe I should dive into the wild side for a bit, then come up for air and live the righteous life once again. Who knows, Bert may be the one," she laughingly told Kimmie, as she took out oatmeal packets from the cabinet and began making a light, healthful breakfast.

Bert and Nikko staked out the top soiled areas around the house. It seemed that they all were in bad need of clean up. Bert jotted down a figure on a pad that he pulled from his pant pocket. Then the two began walking farther and farther towards their target, acting like they were surveying the situation at hand. They laughed and walked and walked and laughed until they reached their destination. They found even more plants beginning to bud. They each possessed a very distinguishable aroma, which made the weed extra special for patrons. Bert had been over just a couple times in the very early morning, before arriving for the AM show at the station. He hadn't needed to swing by much at all during the past two weeks, because of the daily rains showers that were known to Florida residents in the summer months, and this summer had been no exception. It had been hot, humid and rainy every day...good for the crop and good for Bert.

Bert took his pint out of his pocket and had a swig of bourbon to keep him going.

After the two made the "gardening" rounds on the property, they went back inside. Bert gave the estimate to Kimmie for the work around the house. He included weeding and mowing all acres and stated, "It really needs it. Since there's not that much planting being done here anymore, the weeds are beginning to take over the property." He didn't know what he was talking about, but thought that it sounded good. All Nikko could do was laugh under his breath with a closed mouth.

"Okay," Kimmie confirmed. "I'll ring you in a few days to set up a schedule, when I know what's going on around here."

"Whenever you're ready. I'll be here...at your convenience," Bert slurred in a melancholy tone.

"Let's go Nikko. Got more work on more properties. He'll be back soon, very soon," Bert promised.

"I'll call you every night and every morning and every afternoon that I am away from you," Nikko lied to Cynthia to keep her satisfied.

Cynthia, however, had changed her feelings about the Spanish-Greek. She now was into his friend, who appeared as if he had come from some kind of Scandinavian descent. She turned and walked away, but first grabbed the piece of paper that Bert had given Kimmie. She placed it on the kitchen counter.

"And where are you living?" Cynthia asked Bert before he left.

"Oh, here and there, around St. Pete Beach. I look forward to hearing from you," he responded graciously.

As soon as the men left the house, Bert jumped for joy and said, "YES." They screeched out of the driveway and began their journey back to the motel.

"Everything's mint now. I will never have to sneak around the property late at night ANYMORE," Bert screamed. "Yes!"

As they traveled over the bridge and back to civilization, as Bert would always comment, Bert told Nikko an array of dirty jokes that he had heard at the station, and they both laughed hysterically, almost to the point of missing their exit. Bert had to swerve off the interstate and into the next lane, in order to make his turn off.

Once on the Bayway, he heard a beep on his cell. Bert exclaimed to his partner, "Well, I guess we need to think about going to Ft. Myers in four days....that's what the text says from Luciano. He says he has business for us down there. He's putting us up in a two-story bungalow for two weeks so that we can talk, walk, rest and eat, and of course meet beautiful babes, as he put it. First of all, I definitely do need to get a new set of wheels. This rental car thing is not going to cut it, and especially not traveling down all the way down there. This, dammit, is a piece of crap!" he huffed, remembering how the subcompact car shook the entire time they rode on the interstate, anytime it went over fifty-five miles per hour.

"I'm going to order a pizza from up the street. Are you okay with that?" Bert asked.

Getting bored with his situation, as Nikko had always been in the past due to his short attention span, he was ready to move on...and perhaps stay in Ft. Myers for a while. Cynthia was already disappearing from his mind, but not from Bert's. Then, Bert's cell phone rang, showing a Manatee county area code on the screen. He got excited and answered it at once.

"Berton James here."

He always hated his name. His parents thought it up for him after watching an old Spanish western flick, up in the mountains of Honduras on their last trip before flying back to Minnesota to have their baby delivered at home. Berton James it was, and he had to accept it. He did, however, shorten the oddity down to "Bert".

"Bert! Hi, this is Cynthia. Kimmie asked me to call you to see if you could come over next week sometime...morning...afternoon... it doesn't matter to me...just come on out," the words slipped out of her mouth. She never asked to speak to Nikko. She felt the flame had died on their short-lived romance. Cynthia was now enthralled with another, Bert.

"Something has come up that requires my immediate attention," he told her. I have to meet with a client down in Fort Myers, so I can't come over 'til after that." Bert was deafened by the silence on the other end of the call.

"Are you still there?" he asked.

"I don't know what to say. You'll have to set that up with Kimmie. You see, I am thinking about heading back to Ireland to see how my castle's doing," she told him in a matter of fact tone.

"You really *do* have a castle, or were you just kidding?" Bert asked her.

"I have a small castle, or manor, as some refer to it, on the coast of western Ireland. It's for sale, and I haven't been able to get in touch with anybody at the real estate office in Shannon when I call from here early in the mornings. I've left many messages, and nothing.... it's troubling, so I feel I must leave very soon to see what's going on. I may, or may not be back. I haven't told anyone else, so keep it to yourself, please."

"Silence is the word, Ma'am," he solemnly stated. "I can't let her just walk out of my life, and especially not now....she has a castle that could be mine," he thought long and hard to himself. It took him all of five seconds to ask the girls to join the two boys on their mission.

"We've got plenty of space. We're renting a two-story bungalow right on the beach," his words lied. "It's plenty big enough for the four of us...just a get-away...are you and Kimmie game?" he asked her nonchalantly.

"I'm ready if you are, even if Kimmie can't leave...I can," Cynthia excitedly stressed to him.

"Let me see, today is Monday night...let's say I pick you up at seven, Friday morning. How does that sound?" he asked. "And listen...I know you don't know much about me, but you will soon... and you'll like it...a lot." She felt her heart beating like a jungle drum.

She calmed down to conclude the conversation, "Okay, at seven it is."

"What's all the hysteria?" Kimmie asked, as she heard Cynthia shrieking in glee and trying to catch her breath to regain her composure.

"You're not going to believe this, but Bert wants us to go down to Ft. Myers with him and Nikko...for TWO WEEKS...a lot could be accomplished in that time," she informed Kimmie, as she took out a notebook from a kitchen drawer to make a list of clothing she was bringing with her.

"You are not going with that man, are you?" Kimmie asked. "*I* certainly am not going," she revealed to Cynthia.

"Oh, everything will be alright. It will be fun...loads of fun. You know Nikko's going with us, don't you?" she asked.

"I'm still not going. I don't even know Nikko that well, and for that matter, I don't really even know you. If you leave, consider it permanent. All I was doing was doing you a favor by letting you stay here, so don't act like a slut around my grounds. I won't have it," she spoke in a chilling way.

"That's fine," Cynthia affirmed. You know, I thought we would turn out to be special friends, but the lord works in mysterious ways. I'll get all of my belongings and head to the inn that I noticed up on the main road."

"Great, and the sooner, the better," Kimmie spit out her words furiously. She had escaped from her realm of tranquility, into a survival of the fittest mode. In addition, high morality had always been an important standard for the horseback rider.

It took about one hour for Cynthia to collect all of her belongings and fold them neatly into her large suitcase. She had always been a clean freak, just like Melody. She tried to have everything organized and in its place every minute of the day. Ty had always thought this very irritating, and he told her on numerous occasions that it was a "horrible trait" that she had come equipped with. She wasn't spontaneous at all. She always had to have everything planned out. This bored Ty immensely, which was the main reason he needed to find other women soon after they were married, and he had had many. Cynthia knew, but didn't want to admit it to herself.

Cynthia left the estate without saying one word to Kimmie. She walked with rolling suitcase down the street, about a quarter of a mile, towards the main road.

A farm hand who drove a beat up old pickup asked her if she needed a lift. He said extending his hand to hers, "Hi, I'm John, Johnnie people call me. Hop in. I work just up the road...the next farm over."

"Hi, my name is Cynthia," she said, displaying a hint of a British accent. "I appreciate this. My bag is more cumbersome than I ever imagined it would be," she giggled. "If you could drop me just up and over on the main road. There's an inn…"

"Sure, I know it…behind all the trees. You can barely see it from the street. They use it as a trucker's motel too. You know, hourly rates and all that. Just be careful," he suggested.

"Oh, I will. It's only for a few days 'til I go to Ft. Myers. I was thrown out of *The Ranch*," she blurted out, as they pulled into the driveway of the motel.

"What?" he asked. "Well, it's probably a good thing, in my estimation. All of the damn things that have happened o'er there, and all of the *strange*…I mean *really strange* people. We've been given strict orders by our owners to stay away from it and its people." He laughed, "They'd probably fire me on the spot if they *seen me* give you a ride from there to here, but no worries. Our secret is safe with me," Johnnie smiled as he slowly drove off into the sunset, thinking about the beautiful girl he just met.

After she checked into the one room they had vacant, she went to the convenience store across the street to get a sandwich for dinner. She was starved. After she ate, and after she had cleaned up any crumb that she found hanging onto to any thread of fabric, she phoned Bert to tell him the situation and the new plans.

"No problem. It will be more fun with just you anyhow," he recast his mental plans, as he had done so many times before, for survival sake. "You know, I didn't really like Kimmie from the moment I laid eyes on her…something about her reminds me of my ex," Bert interjected.

"She didn't like you either. Isn't that funny?" Cynthia interjected. "I DID like her…A LOT. We've been through A LOT, in a short period of time, and I hate to see our friendship end, but she is acting like a class 'A' *bitch*. I must go now…a funny movie just came on the TV. I just want to relax some, so I'll see you bright and early Friday, at Sharpe's Inn, right?"

"I'll be waiting with bells on," Bert animatedly replied, saying this coined phrase with expression and glee. However, he mixed it with a little bit of deception. "Until Friday," he boldly uttered.

Chapter Ten

The Fort Myers Trip

Friday came and went with no one coming into the inn's gravel entrance to pick her up, not at seven, not even at three. She called Bert's cell several times and got only his recording. She watched television for another whole day, bored out of her wits. Cynthia got out the phone book to dial her favorite Irish Airlines on the antiquated black phone, seemingly from the 1970's, when she heard the screeching and squealing of petal to the metal, coming closer and closer to her window, which finally parked in the spot right outside of her door. It was a striking four-door, black jag, long and lean and very shiny.

"Why would someone who owns this be staying here? This is basically a truck stop," she said to herself.

She had seen many truckers during her stay, some were gentle, some were harsh and mean, some flirtatious, and some very religious. This line of work encompassed all types. That she surmised. Only on a few occasions did she see one of them carry a girl to his room. Mostly, they were there to get the sleep they needed and so much deserved.

She kept looking out her foggy window at the luxury vehicle that had just pulled up in front of her room. "Who are you? Won't you hurry up and get out?" she thought to herself. To her surprise, the door opened wide, and out jumped Bert carrying a bouquet of roses, with a grin from ear to ear on his chiseled face. Cynthia screamed and opened the door.

Bert came bounding into the room and said, "Sorry I'm late. My new car wasn't ready to be picked up from the dealer. They had to detail it before handing it over to me, which is a good thing. I don't want to be seen in a pile of crap. I'm leasing it. I'll trade it in, when I get bored…but right now…hop in. I'll get your bags."

"There's only one. It's right over there," she said sweetly, pointing to the other side of the dresser.

He loaded the suitcase and said, "Okay, we're ready to roll. Fort Myers here we come."

Cynthia got in the fancy car and exclaimed, "How nice…great tan color of the leather," then she saw Nikko lying on the back seat, waking up from his nap. "Well, good morning chap, or should we say bloke?"

He rudely replied to her, "Don't ever say that to me again!"

"I didn't mean anything by it. What's wrong?" Cynthia asked.

Nikko sat silently. "No worries, dear. Nikko has just had a bad dream. But we are embarking on a great dream, filled with great fun, on a great beach. I'm really psyched. Can't you tell?" Bert asked.

Cynthia giggled and gently rubbed her sensuous strawberry blonde hair on his shoulder and said, "I can't wait either."

The two up front hadn't heard a peep out of Nikko who was lying on the comfortable back seat with his eyes wide open, as in thought. After the earlier comment that had been uttered from Cynthia's thin, red lips, he couldn't get his father out of his mind, and how he was killed. He was sure the hit had come from the Irish gang. They had controlled his existence ever since he had met up with Francis and were more than likely still doing it, tracking his every move.

Nik asked himself, "Was it merely a coincidence that he had received a call at *The Ranch* about a possible prowler who was spotted on the outer boundaries of the property? They had wanted to speak to the man of the house. Why does the *Italian mob* want to be so heavily involved with Bert now? They all knew that Bert worked at a Sarasota television Station."

Bert had revealed to Nik late one drunken night that the Irish cornered him in the parking lot there and demanded that he take part in all requests of the mobsters, primarily to drop the story on the IRA, which was a leading revenue story for the programming at WORK for a bit. WORK got the scoop before anyone else did, so Bert had followed through with the story. He had also been fascinated to finally get to meet Kimmie, as he had read so much about her in all of his research. Upon meeting her, however, he wished he hadn't. There was no rapport between the two of them. They were both as different as oil and vinegar.

Cynthia, on the other hand, he hadn't known about in his research, as he was just beginning to track the suspects and events which bound Parrish and Ireland and the rest of the world together...and how the Irish mob that had already purchased the property from Francis, using an undercover business name. They were to grow fruit products for the large packaging plants that paid phenomenally well. Now, Ty and his stooges stood to receive the entire ranch, and all of its assets...and all of its product. It was still tied up in court, however, but the boys had the best lawyers that money could buy. They were very confident. There was one obstacle in their quest that they had never perceived, however, and that was Cynthia.

Cynthia was once sweet, quiet, and very innocent, never wanting to start a raucous, but no longer. She had been scorned. Her facade of niceness was peeling off, showing her armor underneath. She had been the wife of the "King of the World", as the European and Middle Eastern gangs had called him. All proceeds from his business dealings were to be given to the ballerina upon his unforeseen death. These underground organizations were all very aware of this.

Bert had been more than enchanted to meet Cynthia from the start, not even knowing about all her worth. She disclosed to him that she stood to inherit billions....and billions. Now he felt....she was *Treasure*.

Chapter Eleven

The Sabertooth Shotguns

Once the troop arrived at their bungalow on a magnificent stretch of beach in Ft. Myers after a grueling two hours of slow traffic, accidents on the highway, and *loud, loud* southern rock music, which Bert had adored since his youth in Minnesota, Cynthia and Bert got out. He hugged her, then kissed her, and said, "Oh, home sweet home...paradise, and he bent down as if to smack the sand with a kiss, but instead he planted a luscious wet one on Cynthia's already puckered red lips.

Waking up from his two-hour nap in the back seat, Nikko caught view of the kiss, got out of the luxury car and said, "You whore... you are nothing but a sophisticated whore...you go from one fellow to the next. At first it was me, now it's Bert. Who will it be tomorrow? I'm so sick of you. You turn my stomach." He grabbed his bag and swiftly walked up the stained wood stairs to the half-moon glass entry.

Cynthia just watched him, mortified by how he had spoken to her. No one had ever said those things to Cynthia, not even Tyrone. She thought to herself that maybe she deserved those words. She had never behaved liked this, always being so pious.

"I'm sorry Nikko," Cynthia screamed up to him, as she waited for Bert to toss him up the key. "I don't know what has come over me. It has to be all of the stress. I have a terrible sense of bitterness that I must vanquish. Please pardon me, hon."

Nikko caught the key, unlocked the door and stepped inside saying nothing to the girl. Two seconds later he walked out of the wooden home empty-handed, and in a huff. He walked in the opposite direction of the couple who was approaching the stair case. Cynthia glanced backwards as she climbed the stairs and saw Nikko trudging through the thick white sand, not knowing where he was headed, and not really giving a hoot. He had defamed her, and his body tingled... but still, it was full of remorse.

Cynthia was frazzled by the whole scene, and Bert knew it.

Once they got into the living room and set down the three large bags that they had been struggling with up the warped, weather-worn steep steps, Bert went over to her to stroke her neck and shoulders and promised, "Don't worry. I'll be very good to you my dear. Nikko could have never supported you like I am going to do," and he proceeded to lay the scantily dressed subservient Cynthia down on the sofa. He always had liked subservience. He knew he had finally been presented with everything he had ever wished for on one large silver platter. He was not going to let his enrichment leave him...no, never.

"What about love?" she blurted out, as she pried herself away from his forceful grip that was keeping her locked down, beneath bitter-sweet love.

He said nothing. He was shocked that she would go against him.

"I'm asking you, could you love me, or am I only another one of your toys?" she confronted him, finally taking charge of the situation.

Again, there was no response, not even an utterance of a breath from him.

"I need some fresh air," Cynthia remarked, as she took out a thin wrap from her suitcase, grabbed her small purse and left the bungalow in her very short shorts, tank top, "strappy" sandals and sparkly black wrap. She looked like a million dollars. Bert frenetically pondered as to how he could stop her from leaving. He decided to stay in the bungalow alone...to think...plan...reason. He needed some alone time...some quiet time.

He drifted off, as he lay on the couch, calculating designs for his sterling future. He was out for the duration of the night...no lights... no television...silence and darkness....no window shades open to reveal the full moon.

✳ ✳ ✳

As Nikko combed the plush beach in the dusk hour of seven. He became very withdrawn, not even saying hello to anyone who smiled at him in passing.

"I've got to get home, but how?" he lambasted himself in his mind, as he thought about all of the money he had spent like a fool on women, men, and drink. He needed more of the take that Bert said he would give to him in a few weeks. So far, he hadn't received a penny. He had to split everything with Bert fifty-fifty, even though the takes were generally miniscule, and he hadn't brought much cash with him from overseas. He didn't know the laws about bringing cash into another country. He had been in such a hurry to depart, having been through so many heavy ordeals, in such a short period of time. He sat down in the sand and put his hands over his head. He sat there for over an hour watching an amazing St. Elmo's fire demonstrating its brilliance directly in front of him. He thought this to be a sign. Something important was going to happen very soon...good or bad. He couldn't wait. Malicious activity had become an addiction to him. He just couldn't get it out of his blood, once he had tasted it. Anxious tears flowed out of the pockets of his eye ducts.

When Nikko was wiping the salty water which flowed out of his wild eyes, having misted his face from the Gulf, he was startled by an overwhelmingly shrill, harsh, and annoying Irish-accented voice. Nikko gazed up into a breathtakingly handsome, animated face with light brown hair and penetrating large round hazel eyes that were almost transparent. Nikko felt very comfortable with him, almost as if he had seen him before.

"May I help you?" Nikko asked in a curious way.

"How are you doing my *Greek God*? Haven't seen you for quite a while. You do remember me, don't you? I dropped off the supplies for the projected mishap on the boat, which never happened to you... thanks to Francis.

We have new plans for you my boy. We've gotten word that you have recently planted a lot of in demand, high dollar weed. Where is it? Oh yeah," the outlaw smirked, thinking and sitting down beside Nikko, Guinness in hand.

"It was on that small island near La Dona, right? The one that is surrounded by trees and nobody can see that huge sunny plot of land right in the center...it's the perfect place...can never get caught...not if you do it right. I think you have what it takes...you do so far, anyway. I have five thousand in cash right now and the rest later, if you pull this off for us."

"I really do need the money right now. What do you want me to do on the island? Haven't been there lately...it's been raining every day. I suspect everything's going as planned. We're scheduled to harvest in about a month and a half, then I'm going back home to Greece. I'll play the racket where I belong, in my homeland," Nikko rattled on.

"I want you to harvest the batch for us...for Ireland. We need as many proceeds as we can for our righteous organization," he jealously stated, using an angry tone of voice.

"We have many more hungry mouths to feed than our Italian counterparts," the Jekyll now laughed. "They have the climate for free nourishment down there in that sweat factory. We only have the climate for cold, embittered political pain. Simply aforesaid, we are requesting your cooperation. Remember, our gains are far more plentiful for you than those from the others, and our reputation is far less dubious."

Nikko sat there looking as the sun made a swift "ploop" underneath the ground where he sat contemplating life momentarily. "I said I would do it, and I will. You'll have to wait at least one more month for the crop to be decent enough to sell. I just need to harvest before Bert does it for Italy."

"We can wait, and we will. Just see that it is delivered within a month and a half to this address in Clearwater," the mystery man advised Nikko, handing him an address and a name which was typed on a computer. Nikko looked at the paper dumbfounded, "This is a Russian name!"

"Yep, the Russians are working with *us now*. Together, we will defeat our boys to the South. Harsh winters keep the brain and muscles in shape. We don't and won't get lazy…never," the stranger commented very seriously. "The Russian keeps in touch with me daily. For your own good, don't let us down." He put on his thin shades and trotted off, never looking behind him, only staring at the couple who was making out and taking off their beach garments in the sand.

Nikko made his way to a small Polish tavern. He walked inside and ordered a dark beer and proceeded to get hammered, ordering one after the other, as he felt more and more relaxed by the harmonious music that resounded from the small Bavarian orchestra. "I think I've found my calling."

Meanwhile, Cynthia, who was getting more and more independent, and less and less fragile, took a seat at the most male dominated saloon for miles. This was so because of the more than adequately-sized drinks they poured and because of the great sounding original bands they had on a regular basis. Tonight was no exception. The bar and the tables had become completely full, as the moon began to wane. The owner of the club introduced the band that was about to perform as "The Sabertooth Shotguns". Cynthia thought that was a very weird name, but unique in its own right. She ordered a Cosmo which she always drank as a celebratory measure for each well-received performance, of which there had been many. Her ballerina feet showed off their high insteps when she slid out of her sandals and placed her sexy feet, along with expertly manicured toenails, on the ledge of the bar stool.

The band came on and began their first number, "Love does not always last forever." She liked the sound of the band, but especially the sought-after singer.

Most of the girls in the bar room were hooting and hollering and running up to the stage to kiss Willie, as she found the lead singer's name to be. Cynthia just sat there, shrouded in a rag of confidence. She hardly looked at the singer, but his eyes perpetually drifted her way. It intrigued Willie to see a woman who cared nothing more about him than to hear some good lyrics and singing. He wanted to talk to her. He sang his next number in his mind to her, "I'd never let you go."

After the first set, Willie came over to the bar, right where Cynthia sat, and he ordered a straight whiskey. He smiled at her. Cynthia smiled back and said, "You sing well." He asked her if she minded if he stood beside her during their break. She said, "Of course not."

They talked about everything in their lives during that brief fifteen minute encounter. He told her he would come back beside her during their next break, if she didn't mind. She repeated, "Of course not."

After another set of fantastic originals that sounded as hit songs often do...very catchy, he came her way and bought her another Cosmo, which she accepted. This charming man had such a great speaking voice and such sturdy hands. She supposed that it was from having that perfect resonant vocal tone and from playing lead guitar so well. She was charmed again, but this time, it was different, different from the other times, and definitely different from her courtship with her now dead husband.

"Are you staying around here...on vacation?" Willie softly asked.

"It's a very long story. Maybe I'll get to tell you sometime, once my crackerjack box finally has the right ring in it. It's a killer novel... everything that has happened to me," Cynthia let loose with her tongue, feeling no pain after two stout Cosmopolitans.

"I'd like to hear the story, maybe after the show...?" he asked her.

"Yeah, I'd like that, but only for a walk on the beach," she told him, still full of composure.

Willie put his hand on hers and said, "Last set. After this, I'll take you for a walk on the coolest stretch of beach in Ft. Myers that leads right up to a New England style diner. The chowder is awesome there. Sound good?"

"Sure does...Now go play...work for your money," she ribbed him. "I wish I could have taken three long breaks during MY performances, you lucky fool." She felt like it was meant to be. She could say anything to him without him taking it the wrong way. That's how he was...she was sure of it.

"Your performances...what did you do?" he interrogated her.

"Well, my man," she flirtatiously batted her eye, as she puckered her lips for another sip and continued. "I was a premier ballerina overseas, in Europe, mostly in the British Isles and France. Can't you tell?" she asked her new acquisition, as she showed off her arched feet and rubbed on her beautifully sculpted legs.

"I really hadn't noticed to tell you the truth. You just looked so sweet and kind of lonely all by yourself...not at all like the other dregs that I see here...bothering me all the time. You seem happy with yourself...and that's a compliment coming from me...I'm definitely not a womanizer...but I like what I see. Hey, that's neat about you being a ballerina...and in Europe. I've never been over there, and I've never known a ballerina before. Well, I guess I better get back to work... See ya," his words trailed off, as he made his way back onto the stage.

Bert was snoring away, having sexual fantasy dreams, as he always did. Nothing could wake him now, not even the clanging ring of a telephone right beside him. The caller left a cold message:

"I hope you are there already, and I hope you are not snubbing us. Tell your boy to be careful whose side he's on. It could get him in a lot of trouble. Remember, we're everywhere."

Almost out of change and becoming bored with the place and its patrons, Nikko thought he would head back to the bungalow to get some shut eye. When he walked through the back exit and onto the crowded beach, he heard loud music and lots of voices coming from the left. He headed in the direction of the party to have a shot.

As he stomped through the wet sand with his flat feet, he began to think, "Maybe I'll find a rich one…woman or man…it doesn't matter. It's like the old days with Francis."

When Nikko needed money, he got it…no matter how, and this evening was no exception.

Cynthia sat staring with infatuated eyes at her new interest, when her ex-infatuation entered and walked up to the bar. Not noticing that Cynthia was sitting two stools over from where Nikko was standing, he started flirting with a young, well-dressed preppie who opened his wallet to display a large wad of large bills. Nikko always had his built-in telescope on standby, and it zeroed in on this boy as soon as Nikko saw him in the corner. The attractive young man asked Nikko if he could buy him a drink, which of course, he accepted readily. Just when his brandy and ginger ale was served to him by the seasoned bartender, Nikko glanced over and met with Cynthia's guilty eyes.

Willie's band had just finished the last number of its last set, so he came over to be with his new found friend one more time before he left for the night. He never took girls home with him after a gig. It wasn't professional, in his estimation, and he was an ethical man besides. Very upset, Nikko left the bar.

"Nikko!" she screamed and went running out the door as fast as she could, through the hard packed white sand until she reached the dark bungalow with no sign of life. She went up the creaky stairs, opened the door and saw Bert sleeping. Cynthia went over to him and kissed his sweaty cheek. She walked over to the thermostat to lower it, because she felt awfully hot inside. She saw a red light flashing on the phone receiver, showing that there was a new message. She played it….and commented.

"What the hell…? Will this game ever stop?"

Just then, Bert awakened with a throbbing head and saw Cynthia. He asked, "Are you still mad at me?"

"Not really. I got it out of my system, as I walked on the beach. Oh, by the way, I saw Nikko at a bar." Her sentence was cut off due to the stupefying bang of the front door hitting a large glass-framed picture in the narrow hallway as it was thrown open in anger by Nikko who had entered the condo in a mean drunk state of being.

"Flirting again I see," he reprimanded her. Then, he sank onto the large armchair and drifted off into total unconsciousness.

"What was he talking about?" Bert asked her.

"Oh, nothing. He saw me talking to the leader of the band who was performing there, and he got jealous. We were just talking about ballet...stuff like that...you know?"

"I don't care. I just want to make love with you...right now," Bert sensually whispered in her ear, as he carried her slender body into the largest bedroom and began undressing her, then himself.

He kissed her passionately and caressed her erotically. He laid her down on the plush comforter and went straight for the kill, into found paradise. Cynthia couldn't take it any longer.

"I can't do this. I tried...but I can't," she started to sob.

"We'll try again later," was all Bert could utter, as he walked out of the room, upset as could be.

"When will I be a woman again and get over my pain from the past? When? Oh, when?" She hit herself in agony, knowing she would not be able to sleep a wink. She wondered if Willie would be the one to do it for her. She stared at the ceiling for the entire night...thinking....just thinking.

Chapter Twelve

The Tea Room

And so the three stayed at their pad, Cynthia and Bert in one room and Nikko slept on the large sofa where he could make nightly runs to the fridge without being seen or heard. Life was good for those two weeks. Nikko got over his jealously, due to a sexy package he met on the beach trying to take her top off. He ran over to her screaming, "You can't do that. It's not legal here."

"But it is in Miami, and this is Florida too, sooo..," and she proceeded to undress her upper half.

"Well, don't say that I didn't warn you," he commented as he took a seat beside those lovely bosoms.

"My name is Sasha. What's yours?" she asked, as she squirted lotion all over her bare chest.

"Nik," he answered, staring up and down at her voluptuous, firm physique of hers, just lying there, wanting to be fondled. He rubbed her shin, and she slapped him hard.

"Keep your filthy hands off of my superbness," she yelled, as if in a film.

"I can see you don't take shit from anybody, and...I like that quality," he clarified to the girl.

"I don't mind them looking...I'm used to it, but *touching...get outta here*" Sasha stressed loudly.

Nikko never left, and the two ended up meeting there every morning at eleven and stayed the entire day in the sun except for the hour that they grabbed a bite and a cocktail. She bought everything. She was loaded and owned a Victorian three-story manor on the main Street. She had received the property in the will of her elderly ex-husband. Nikko surmised that she had been a gold-digger. He didn't think that was any worse than what he had become, a sexual piece of trash for both women and men, even boys. Thinking about some of his shenanigans literally made him ill. Sasha liked their friendship, not getting *too* close mentally. That was safe to her, yet getting close enough physically to feel a sexual tingle in her groin area. That was all she needed during the day...no lifetime commitment. Sasha had been there and done that and had been bored out of her mind with this humped back, overweight old man, even though he furnished her every whim, triple-fold.

Bert and Cynthia still had not been intimate, but he could wait he told himself and her, every night. When he would go shopping for groceries, he would pick up some sweet young thing who was looking for action, and she satisfied his needs. This was sufficient while he was waiting on ecstasy.

At the end of two weeks, the three were ready for another vacation. They had partied and sunned so much that they were all worn-out. Nikko knew what the Irish mob expected, and he also knew not to give wind of who came to see him on the beach. It was for his best interest. Bert had called his Russian connection during their first week there.

Hearing mostly silence, proved very worrisome to Bert. He met with a biker wearing a bandanna at a prearranged rendezvous where written maps were given as to where to deliver the new batch with included names and dates. The biker informed Bert that they would soon get back to him as to when, where, and if there was to even be a new seeding.

"The Italians seem to have other plans for you, Bert. They want you for a bigger dig. They want to meet with you next Tuesday at three. They have reservations for tea on Central Avenue, near 66th Street. It's that small British place, supposed to be awesome. I'll be there myself. I'm part of the dig."

"Right-o," the usually smug Bert yelled, as the biker revved up his engine and took off at top speed, doing wheelies until he hit the interstate. Bert sat in contemplation on the park bench after the biker departed. He was getting tense and uneasy feelings throughout his being, those which he had never had before. He knew he had to do whatever they had in store for him. This had gone on too long. He simply knew too much. He had played right into their hands as a premier stool pigeon. He went back to the bungalow and put on a happy face and faked a carefree attitude. He didn't let any of his stress show for the entire last week of their vacation. Nikko was virtually separated from the gang now. He met with Sasha every day and every night for sun, libations, and sexual encounters. They sometimes had orgies, when she so desired. Most times, however, they just had three-somes with locals, and occasionally, a one on one session, where she yawned most of the time. Nobody, or nothing could excite her. She was perpetually bored. Actually, because she was a perpetually bor-ing soul herself. They had nothing to share mentally with each other. They had basically used each other for "exercise" the entire week. That was enough for Nikko.

Now after a two week jaunt, they were all ready to go home, to their temporary home at the small motel on St. Pete Beach where Bert had negotiated the good monthly rate. Bert raced back, dreading a speeding ticket, but he took the chance anyway and came out a winner this time.

Once back at the motel, Bert asked for a larger room with perhaps two bedrooms. They found him an adequate one with two very small bedrooms, one and a half baths, and a decent-sized living area with kitchenette. He paid double the rate of the other one. He didn't quibble. It was a comfortable room, they could buy groceries, and cook where it fronted the Gulf.

"Who could ask for more?" he whispered to himself. All they had to do was relax as best as they could, and wait for the harvest on Pelican Island, wait and wait for further instructions from the Boss man. It was going to be a long month for the lot of them.

Monday and Tuesday came and went, and finally, his big day arrived with a fiery yellow gleam. It was a scorcher from the start. Bert knew from these signs that he was to be given a very important, and perhaps evil agenda. He got dressed and waited impatiently on their patio, eating nothing and saying nothing. Cynthia knew by now that when he was in one of his "funks", just leave him be. Bert appreciated their communication sometimes, and lack of it, all the time. He hated yapping women. He was happy enough with his ballerina. He was surprised he hadn't wanted to look elsewhere yet. It was two-thirty, and Bert was off.

Nikko asked, "What's the rush?" Cynthia just shrugged her shoulders. Those two had a love-hate relationship going on. When Nikko wanted money or things, he always went to generous Cynthia, not miserly Bert. Cynthia put up with a lot and always had. She was trying to stop though. Nikko picked up his cell from the coffee table to make a call.

Walking into his efficient bedroom, he loudly verbalized, "Hey Sasha, Give me a call when you are able," and he locked the door.

He wasn't mean to Cynthia now, just cold and standoffish. She did not care. She finally had an opportunity to call the club down South and leave her number, so that they would give it to Willie. She kind of missed him and hoped that it had not been for not. She pulled out the business card of the establishment.

"Rocks on the Beach, how may I help you?" an authoritative voice greeted her. She thought this must be the manager, or the owner.

"Yes, I met a gentleman there the other day...he was the singer. Willie was his name, and I had to leave so suddenly that I never said bye, and never gave him my number. Could you give it to him for me? Please tell him it's from the ballerina." He scribbled down the number.

"He doesn't play until tomorrow, but I'll give it to him then," he informed her.

"Thank you so much," she said, as Nikko entered the living area once again, half naked and eating some kind of junk food.

"How's your belle doing?" Cynthia asked in a light manner.

"She's not there. I haven't talked to her since we left…so I don't know…don't really care though," he replied with a pompous attitude.

"Where did Bert go off to so huffy?" Cynthia asked Nikko.

"I don't know…never asked…and really don't care about him either," Nikko stated with the same attitude as before.

✳ ✳ ✳

Bert found the English tea room with ease that afternoon. He parked his car under a shade tree and trotted inside to see what he was in store for, dressed sloppily, in beach clothing, he did not care.

"Hello my friend. Please sit down," the biker dude told Bert authoritatively, as Bert glanced at the other members of the table. He had only seen one out of the three. The other two were mobster-looking gents wearing black silk suits and vibrant colored ties. They were hefty besides.

The mobster with the orange tie spoke first, "We've ordered tea and scones for all. Is that okay? Don't have a lot of time, maybe thirty minutes to hear what I have to ask of you…or may I say what the Boss expects of you…To put it short and sweet, he wants you to wed this ballerina dame as soon as you can. That way, you can still keep the castle in your family, thus putting it in ours. See where I'm coming from?"

Bert nodded in obligatory fashion.

"She put the estate up for sale before she came to Florida…couldn't pay all the back taxes and payments on it. Her Irish-ex was a swindler, but he couldn't swindle it back, and the wife wanted out. Who could blame her? He was a complete jerk, no 'ands, ifs, or buts'…he was head of the Irish Mafia and IRA in Belfast and a part of several terrorist organizations in other countries. To make the story even juicier, you know that broad that you?" he implied with whispers, "Well, she killed that ballerina's hubby in a jealous rage. Isn't that something? Are you beginning to see the whole picture now…and see our whole plan?"

Bert nodded again politely.

"We could have used her in the end, but who knows, maybe she would have been proud and smart. Maybe she would have been arrogant and dumb. All we know is that you had no idea of her worth to our network…I hear the leprechauns aren't smiling about it either. Anyway, the ballerina is our focus now. We hear she has docs, photos, and letters that could bring the boys, their toys, and their hidden Republican Army down…and I mean down to the ground. It's now up to you to find these things for us, plus a whole lot more.

We are going to get the dough to purchase this mansion and fix up the property, which is now in bad need of repair we understand. If you sell it, and make a fortune for us, some of it will go in your pocket. Get married after the harvest. We'll be in touch and have tickets waiting…that's all…you know your place…now go…," he talked very softly throughout the whole conversation. This orange-tied mobster remained sitting still, waiting for Bert to stand up and depart.

Bert left the tearoom with his tail between his knees. He felt like such a loser, a real nobody…when he was amidst those guys.

"What side am I really working for? It seems like I'm playing with fire. What have I gotten myself into?…you fool…you fool…you fool!" he said to himself over and over again out loud, hitting himself in anger as he drove to a nearby bar

Chapter Thirteen

The Arrest

I t was a long, hard month waiting on the chance-filled harvest.
The rain had stopped. It was now rather dry, which was a good
thing. There had been so much flooding on the streets of the neighborhood which made Bert worry about the excessive water in the
island soil.

After this boring, sleep-filled "eternity", having no contact with
enemy nor friend, Bert finally got out of his lazy and drunken stupor
one morning and woke to find Cynthia gone. She had been gone for
the entire day. They had really nothing to say to each other anymore.
He knew that he must change the whole feel of the play now and get
back into Cynthia's good graces and marry her soon.

Thinking of what needed to be done before it got too late, he
banged on Nikko's room where Nikko had been laid up as a virtual
hermit this entire time, only coming out to get a bite to eat, then off
into his room again, like a rebellious teenager trying to hide from
authority. He was wasting away to skin and bones, but didn't care. He
wanted to go back home. He was depressed.

"Nikko, hey. Get out here. I need to talk to you. It's time to do it to it, boy," Bert insisted. He got no response, only the sound of a razor becoming electrified. "You have to swim over when it turns dark."

"Yeah, I'll be right there," Nikko replied in a monotone voice.

Bert waited and pondered about where Cynthia could have gone this early in the morning.

"There's something suspicious about where her head has been these last few weeks. I hope that I can pull this plan off!" he thought to himself, growing more and more nervous.

At that moment, while he was staring out at the quiet Gulf, Nikko came bounding out of his room.

"I'm ready for whatever…got my trunks and flippers on. Let's go to it. I'm going home after this," he told Bert.

"Nikko, do you happen to know where Cynthia went, or when she'll be back?"

"I haven't a clue…was trying to get a hold of Sasha all day. I guess she's busy with someone. She's been very cold, you know distant to me this past week. I think she's tired of it. I KNOW I am just so bored."

"Why didn't you hone in on a young thing on the beach? You know you can just look out the window here and see dozens of almost naked girls all day long. Doesn't that excite you man?"

Getting irritated with all that Bert was spouting, Nikko grabbed his knife and stuffed it on the side in his wet suit. He now had a pretty sufficient bulge in the middle of his right side, so he covered it with his hand, which was stationed on his hip now and spoke in the most playful, feminine way.

He laughed and spoke in a mocking voice, "My dear man, don't you get it yet. I've been with all makes and models of girls and boys, and right now, I just want to get back home and try to start as normal a life as I can. You know, I still have the right to Francis' estate. I was never dead. Upon my death, it became my Pop's… and now he's dead, so it goes back to me. It was kind of like willed to me twice."

"What are you talking about? You must be punch drunk, or mental. But I tell you, you've got a great creative streak in you. You're one to be reckoned with."

"I speak only the truth, as weird as it may seem," Nikko rambled. "I was a grade school drop-out who couldn't even speak or write English. I couldn't even understand it. But now, it seems so easy," he concluded, as he stared at the door in silence for a couple of minutes. "I'm through," he stated, as he went through the motel room door, leaving it ajar.

A gusty breeze entered the room upon his departure and scattered the money that Bert had been counting all around the sitting area. Bert kept his proceeds all to himself, hidden in the closet wall safe. He changed the combination weekly for security reasons. He hadn't seen where Nikko was keeping his money, but he surmised it was in his locked suitcase, since Nikko was so trusting and naive. Bert was right. He found Nikko's small key in the front outer pocket of the case. He reached his hand inside its inner pocket and felt it lined with fifty dollar bills. He stuffed a few into his own pocket and announced to himself as he straightened up his mess, "This is to fund the celebration dinner at the Grill tonight, with plenty of champagne for plants well harvested," he spoke excitedly to the telephone, as he picked it up to make a reservation for later that night.

"Ten o'clock's fine, thanks," he said, glancing at how much time had passed between now and when Nikko had left the room. It had been fifteen minutes. "Perfect timing," he uttered, as he shut and locked the door behind him and got in his car to drive to his motorboat rental that was waiting for him, moored to one of the small piers facing the isle.

He drove to an empty parking space which had to be rented by the hour with coins. He put four quarters in the meter, thinking that it should not take more than two hours for their escapade.

"And if it does, who cares?" he thought, walking to the pier to untie his boat.

The ropes were wrapped around the mooring so snugly that he couldn't tear them away from the post without ripping off his fingernails and causing rope burns on his hands and fingers. He finally managed to, then horrifyingly stared at the unsecured craft.

He had never maneuvered a piece of machinery, other than a utility vehicle or a sports car. Bert was and had always been very cowardly behind the curtain, but in the public eye, he courageously led the way. That was how he beat all of his colleagues to win the anchorman position, by ripping them to shreds, making them seem like fools, liars, and incompetents.

He had a following that would make heads spin, from movie stars and authors who had their winter homes in Sarasota, to Wall Street tycoons who spent time on this coast every chance they got. He was true blue, in their eyes…a trooper who would do anything for anyone. That was his persona on air and in public…but inside himself, he never truly felt like that, never felt how he strangely projected himself to be. He didn't know why.

He had tried so many times to be good and true, but those trials never matured into anything much, maybe goodness for one day, but after that, back to his degenerate way.

"Oh well, at least I tried. Maybe I'm not SO bad after all…just a little chicken right now," his brain admitted to his body. He started the feeble motor with his feeble key and hauled ass, not really being sure how to stop the thing. He just had to let nature take its course.

Meanwhile on Pelican Island, Nikko was still trying to get his wind back from the horrendous swim in high, choppy waves. It wasn't super far…but far enough in inclement weather. Even though he knew his strokes well, but he had never had much physical endurance training in his life. Everything he knew, he had learned by trial and error. No one had ever mentored or coached him in anything…not even his "Pop". His father had been a decent man, a good provider for the family, but he had had a weakness for craps, that he didn't pass down to his son. Nikko was very happy about that. He was also very happy that no one appeared to be outside after the sun set. It had been a rather hot and sticky weekday. He thought that was probably the reason.

"It makes my job a whole lot easier, not to have that religious woman snooping around," he uttered taking out his blade.

Just then, the sound of a motor in the noiseless hour resounded through the densely populated palm, mango and banyan trees and inside Nikko's ringing ears. Nikko gazed out into the unlit water and saw Bert waving his hands and saying nothing. Nikko remained quiet and ran over to lead him to the crop.

Not saying one word, Bert acted as a look out, as Nikko slashed what he needed off of the plants and blindly stuffed it into large, dark plastic bags. After about one and a half hours went by, the deed appeared to be done. Nikko couldn't see, nor feel any more *treasure* on the plants.

With three full bags of just-picked weed which smelled to the high heavens, Nikko announced, "It's time to celebrate. Let's get on the boat. Here, help me with this stuff," he gave the heaviest one of the bags to his cohort and trudged along carrying the other two himself. They each threw their bundles in as gently as they could, then boarded the cheap motor boat as carefully as possible.

Bert was preoccupied about how to put the boat back in the same position in which he retrieved it, when Nikko asked, "Hey asshole, aren't you going to drive out of here while the coast is clear," not seeing the four awaiting police cars hiding behind the lush greenery that surrounded the pier area.

Bert started the motor, and being a perpetual conceited jerk, he said to the Greek-Spaniard, "Hey Nikko, it's time you started to pay your dues around here."

Bert jumped out of the boat and untied it, laughing all the while. "I hope you know how to stop!" he screamed, as he laughed wickedly.

It didn't phase Nikko one bit. He thought it funny to get the last laugh.

Bert knew nothing about Nikko, nor his background. He didn't know that he grew up near a harbor and piloted his first boat when he was eight. Since then, he had become very skilled in the maritime realm and even thought about becoming a captain on a cargo ship when he was younger. This never panned out for Nikko, however. There just weren't enough zeros in his father's meager, but stable bank account.

Bert couldn't believe how well Nikko handled the craft, and with such skill. "He should have been piloting the boat the whole time, not me," he announced to a pelican that just flew down and landed right beside Bert, in search of eats.

A sense of eeriness was in the still night air. Nikko felt like something was not right. Something was about to happen, and that's when it did. As Nikko drove the boat up to the ramp, radiating lights blinded him.

"What the hell?" was all he could manage to say, covering his squinting eyes with his forearm, a natural instinct which prevents blindness.

"Stay where you are. You are under arrest and have the right to remain silent under a court of law," the skinny moustachioed officer advised Nikko.

"You've got the wrong man. Somebody set me up," he replied to the officer.

"It don't matter who we got. You're the one who has weed on him. Now explain that," the officer demanded.

"You said I have the right to remain silent, so I'm remaining silent. Can I call someone?"

"At the station, buddy. Wow, you've got a lot of expensive shit here. Ya grew it over yonder?" the officer asked Nikko, as he pointed to Pelican Island, trying to illicit a response from the outlaw.

"We got a call a few weeks ago from around here. Someone said they saw people swimming over to the island...said they stayed there for a long while. We took a boat over the next morning and found nothing growing, but the car we found parked illegally across the way, well, it was registered to a well-known Italian hit man. Today, we got another call. We want to talk with you," the policeman requested. "Who are you working for?"

Nikko remained silent. He couldn't wait to get his hands on his former "buddy" who obviously set him up to take the rap. He spied

Pelican Island to see where Bert might be. He saw a movement in the brush and screamed, "Look over there. He's in the bushes!"

The police didn't even budge. One of them nodded in agreement like Nikko was a lunatic and said, "Sure, sure, he's over there. We'll get him tomorrow."

"No, no, really, I'm not fooling…you've got to believe me…I took the fall for everyone," Nikko restated to the cops, as they escorted their handcuffed victim to the squad car. "Hey, where are we going anyway?" he asked the two who climbed into the front seat.

"We're going for a fancy ride, boy…to Clearwater….to your new home…the Pinellas County Jail," they promised him, with grins on their sun worn faces. Then, the car was silent, except for two notifications of a robbery and a purse snatching. It had been a relatively calm day, crime-wise.

Bert was scared shitless back at the island, hiding in mosquito infested banyan trees with pelicans stationed over his head moaning to one another. Finally, the police drove away. He did not know what to do next.

"One thing is for sure," he thought, "I have to get the hell away from here before I get some rare disease from all these insect bites."

He gathered up all of his mortal strength and tried to wrestle with some weird "immortal" feeling that he received from above.

All of a sudden, he felt very cold and alone. He got an overwhelming feeling that his days at the station were numbered and that his days on Earth were as well. Camille was breathing venom down on him from her spot high above civilization letting him "feel" what evil he had caused over the past six months.

Bert thought that he was a good "fit" for the Italian mobsters, and what's more, he felt comfortable with them. He couldn't give up this easy life now, and he wouldn't continue with his legitimate career anymore. It was getting too time consuming and stressful for both. One of them had already waned in his mind and that was working at the station.

After waiting on the sub-tropical island for all activity to cease, and still infested with insects, Bert gathered up his lack of courage and swam as quickly and quietly as he could to shore. Neighbors had come out of their homes near the landing to revel in the excitement of the night.

"They all seem to be nestled in their large homes right now...enjoying the good life," Bert muttered, as he tried to keep afloat over the choppy waves. Bert had never been a good swimmer, really not even an adequate one. He was a poor one to be blunt. In his early teens, he had to be rescued by a friend of his father's, who was a former Navy Seal, when the boat they all were on hit a stump in the lake, which threw Bert off the bow. Bert was gasping and calling for help, as he used dog paddling strategy to stay afloat. The Seal came to his rescue.

Bert had always been rather mean and lean, which made him a decent runner, and of course, an outstanding "bull-shitter". He constantly got everything he wanted in life, no questions asked. He extended his long, non-muscular arms in front of him to tread water and kick his long legs softly behind him. He learned how to survive water through a short series of swimming lessons that his parents enrolled him in, after the boating mishap. He still wasn't any good at it, and just got by. He always just got by with everything in life. He wondered, however, if things were about to change. He had a bad feeling about what was to come, but still wanted to play the scenario out to the end. Bert had never quit a project or a job in his entire life, and he wasn't going to start now.

"Whatever happens, I will survive...I hope...You never know though with these clowns I'm dealing with," he thought as finally pulled himself up onto dry land, onto the same wood deck that belonged to his Quaker friend. It was the closest place by which to get on solid ground again. He didn't realize how much he was a land lubber until now. He wanted nothing more to do with water. He was born in the middle of January under the earth sign of Capricorn. He had a hatred for water and always had.

Dripping wet with nothing to dry him off, he felt mortified. He shook himself off and sat undetected on a hidden wooden bench under a shade tree. He soon walked back to the motel, and still, no Cynthia. He gathered all of his belongings, and Nikko's too, leaving Cynthia's for her to pick up whenever she wanted. He didn't care now. He was about to skip town, buy a plane ticket that night for South America to live the good life with his and Nikko's money. It wasn't as much as he hoped for, but it would do. His now weak body couldn't defeat the stress anymore, that of which his chiseled face had been doing for years.

Chapter Fourteen

A Hasty Departure

The long days and even longer nights were really getting to Kimmie. Without her best friend Jude by her side, she didn't know how to cope. Jude had been her mentor and grounding element since she was a child of about ten, when Kenneth took over in the raising of the spoiled jockey "want-to-be" who eventually did get to realize her dream. She was lost without Jude's older sister-like presence. She remembered Jude seriously scolding her when she did something stupid and without thinking, which was her norm, or on the other extreme, when she threw lavish compliments at her for a job well done, which mostly happened when she exhibited quickness on a horse.

Kimmie was now getting stiff in the joints from lack of movement. She had been laid up in her small second story bedroom for more than one week, not even bothering to go downstairs. She had the perfect set up in her room, a small microwave and a mini-refrigerator, so there was no need for her body to travel any farther than to the bathroom, food area, and television set in her truly depressed state of being.

She thought back in horror to the adventures the four of them had over in the British Isles.

Kimmie had always hated anything to do with Halloween. She hated to watch movies about organized crime. When she was a girl, anything demonic drove Kimmie immediately to the chapel down the street. She was a straight talking, simple, unselfish, and confident young woman who didn't need a "thrill" in her life. She was completely happy with her life, even without a man. Her godfather had caused so much pain and grief in her recent life that she was not ready to take on another one. She wondered if she ever would be ready. She thought about him momentarily.

When she was young, her godfather had such bad coping skills with his life as a Prisoner of War in Korea. He had been subjected to every inhumane punishment imaginable and had seen even worse atrocities. The one that always stuck in his mind was when his buddy, Fred, got caught stealing food from the officers' barracks and he was hanged by his ankles and left to die in front of all of his soldier buddies in the prisoners' barrack. To make matters worse, the enemy fed one prisoner twice a day with a diet of hot peppers and fat. This served as punishment for him waking up late one morning. He croaked on the third day of punishment, having no water. The other prisoners were amazed that he lasted so long, without a drop of liquid on his tongue.

Kimmie was also disturbed out about how she had treated Cynthia. She forgave her, but couldn't bring herself to call and tell her that. To Kimmie, Cynthia had become a very different type of woman from herself, *and she truly had.*

"Oh, I know she's confused…so much has happened to us. I do need to give her a ring. I was a dope. I wonder if she would forgive me?" she spoke to the silent room.

Bert walked out to his car after checking out with the clerk who was dumbfounded that he was leaving St. Pete Beach so soon. He was perplexed by the statement, because he had already been there a little over three months. It was now getting close to July 4th…and now it was definitely time to move on…away from trouble of any kind.

"Whew….South America…here I come. All I need is sun, good wine and a babe to make my life complete," he chanted with his own made up melody.

Just then, a sedan pulled into the lot with tinted windows. The driver's door opened and out walked Cynthia. Bert stood there looking at her dressed up like a fallen angel. Mesmerized, he dropped his keys. She sauntered past him, not saying one single thing.

"Honey, where HAVE you been?" he asked dreamily.

"Around," she whispered nonchalantly.

"Get your stuff. We're leaving. I've checked out…come on… we've got to go…"

"Hold your horses. You have to tell me what's going on? Where's Nikko?"

"That's what I've got to talk to you about. Nikko's been arrested for growing pot on the island."

"Let me get my things…be right back," Cynthia said hesitantly.

She got back in the car five minutes later.

Cynthia's day long lark had ended with sadness. She had met Willie as they had planned for breakfast at a local beach front diner where the two enjoyed a hearty meal of spicy sausage and eggs with numerous cups of caffeine besides. Cynthia was in an especially talkative mood because of this.

They sat there for more than an hour, talking about the dreams of their futures. After that, they took a walk on the secluded stretch of Fort Myers beach, far from any hotel or condo association. Willie ate at that place often because of its perfect location in the sometimes deafening paradise town.

The two "want-to-be" love birds then took up shop in a local tavern near where he played. It was the exact opposite destination from where they came. It was extremely noisy, bawdy and smelly from stale beer.

Cynthia had two lite beers. She didn't want to risk a pound added to her slim physique.

Willie, on the other hand, had four heavy ones, which he downed rather quickly, as if he were in a rush. He glanced at many of the young hotties who walked past him, but he still preferred Cynthia.

He had never been associated with any woman who was such a classic beauty, and so sophisticated, with a head on her shoulders besides. He particularly liked the fact that she didn't have to adorn herself with revealing clothing to be stared at. Her being was enough. He felt proud to be seen with her, like she was hard to come by...and she really was.

After having a fun time at the bar, talking with all the rowdies and singing a couple tunes a cappella, Cynthia and Willie ran along the beach laughing and singing all the way to his rustic one bedroom beach house which he rented during the summer when he played there.

Willie was originally from a small town near Pontiac, Michigan, where he played with another one of his bands for the entire winter. He had a large house in Michigan that he shared with his twenty-year old daughter who attended junior college in the area. She kept it looking nice for him during the summer months.

He was telling Cynthia how proud he was of his daughter, Karen. Cynthia expounded on her wants and needs for a child of her own. Willie asked her why she and her deceased husband, as he came to find out, never had a child, as they sat on his worn tan couch in the middle of a sparsely-furnished sitting room with no windows.

"It wasn't in the cards for my husband to have children. He had a legacy to uphold with male offspring, and so, by means a certain episode of which I was forced to endure, I miscarried twin girls. It was devastating. I can't even tell you the pain. I *need* a baby in my womb... and I *can* conceive."

Willie looked away. "We should be going now."

They didn't speak a word the whole walk back to her car.

"It's been real," he said to her, as he walked away, never turning back to look at her.

"Is that how I am to remember you by...by that panicked expression written all over your face? How can you just walk away like that from me? You know, we shared some intimate moments. I've grown rather fond of you. How do you like that?"

"I don't...really. Honey, I travel around so much playing with bands. It's not the kind of life for you. You're different...a different type than I'm used to. You're a girl I respect, and you don't need to be around this seedy way of living...*It's no good.*"

"Let me be the judge of that," Cynthia blurted back at Willie.

"Well....you've got my number, and I've got yours. Give it some time. I mean, if it's meant to be, and we can't stand to be apart...it will happen," and he gave her a peck on the cheek, before opening her door for her.

"You know....I've really grown VERY fond of you," she added, and she sped off to find the interstate. The sun was setting. Willie just walked away. He was full of relief, yet somehow sadness butted its way into his soul. He was perplexed.

"Oh, I can't think about it now...got a show to do in about an hour," he told himself as he made his way back up the stairs and into his cottage to stretch out for fifteen minutes and get his wits back.

Cynthia came racing back to St. Pete Beach in her rented sedan with a tremendous amount of fortitude and zest. She suddenly felt reborn, like nothing was going to stop her from finally getting what she deserved, peace, happiness, and NO DRAMA. That's all she wanted. That's all she ever wanted...a place to call home, a loving mate, kids and a dog. So far though, she hadn't snagged any of these things. That was when she saw Bert standing in the middle of the motel parking lot.

"Hey you. I'm back," she shouted as she climbed in her car. "Now, where's Nikko? Tell me what happened, and why you are standing outside at night? Hey, what's going on around here, anyway?" she questioned Bert from the window of the car.

"Let me in, and I'll talk to you," Bert demanded, as she unlocked both doors from inside.

"Whatever you say," she squawked back to him, hitting the door in rage.

Cynthia sat looking straight ahead onto the empty four lane road. Her seat belt was left unfastened, her hair was uncombed and her jean skirt was tattered. She was a complete mess. Bert thought differently, however.

"You look cute tonight, Mademoiselle."

Cynthia didn't react to his flirtatious remark and asked one more time for an answer.

"How did Nikko get arrested, and why didn't you...oh....Why didn't you help him? Where were you anyway? You've got to tell me....tell me," she demanded, as she grabbed hold of him by his starched collar that he was never going to need to wear again after today.

"He took all the weed for himself and left me stranded on the island. Serves him right he got caught," he bluffed to her, as she sped blindly down Gulf Boulevard. He told her to continue to the interstate.

"Where are we going?" Cynthia asked Bert.

"To the Airport."

"Why are we going to the airport?"

"We are getting the hell out of this place, never to return."

Cynthia and Bert drove in total silence. They were exhausted.

Cynthia wanted to call Willie, but she knew there was no possible way now. When Bert got his wild hair going, there was no stopping him. She had already recognized the fact that she was falling in love with Willie, but she didn't know how he felt about her.

Willie was strumming his guitar at the bar, when he was overtaken by an overwhelming feeling of bittersweet love. He knew that he was playing Cynthia's favorite of his tunes, and he could think of nothing but her now. His hands froze on the guitar neck. He had to exit the stage. The band continued. In the dressing room he sat, contemplating what he should do, and what he should have done before she left. She was the one.

After his last two marriages, he felt he had finally met up with perfection. He knew he had to call her in the morning. He didn't care what Luciano would say or do to him tomorrow. Willie decided that he was not going to play the game with the "boys" any further.

Not being able to sleep, Kimmie hesitantly picked up the receiver of her bedroom phone to call her former friend. She knew it was late, but pushed in her programmed number anyhow, hoping for an acceptance of the apology that she was about to give.

"How could I have been such a brute? She did nothing wrong. She was just dealt a nasty card," Kimmie mumbled to herself.

"Hallo," Cynthia acknowledged, as the call was connected.

"Please...don't hang up...I am SO sorry, honey, I acted that way to you...don't know what came over me...I'm really sorry...all I ask is that you can accept my forgiveness."

"You know sweetie, I was truly thinking about phoning you today as well. I miss you, and I do accept the apology. What's up? You have to tell me *everything*. Have you been handling things okay?" Cynthia asked Kim.

"Oh, it's okay down here. The property's still tied up in court over this whole charade."

"What's the dilemma with the property anyway?" Cynthia asked.

"Well, I never really had a chance to tell you about the chaotic mess that my godfather's twin brother put us both through. To make a long story short, the courts are deciding what to do...should they keep Kenneth's original will, which left the cash, the property and its belongings to us, or put in effect his twin's will. Francis, his twin, left all his property to the Irish gangsters...But then, Nikko devised an ingenious way to swindle the property from these gangsters. Oh...it's very tricky, because no one knows any of what transpired. It's a very confusing mess.

There is evidence of foul play, however. That's conclusive. My attorney seems to think that I have the overwhelming advantage. Francis took the property over in his portrayal of my godfather, but not legally, it seems. Nothing has been proven. They can't even find my godfather's body. It's pure speculation what happened. Everything is not as it seems and time lines do not match up, my attorney says. For now though, *The Ranch* stays with me," Kim stressed.

"Wow, I'm mind-boggled! And what about the cash? Who does that belong to?"

"No one. There is no more cash. Francis spent it like there was no tomorrow. I have nothing but a small savings, and this property, which is VERY hard to keep up on my tight budget. I guess that's why I was so sore at you that day. I took out everything on you. Again, I'm super sorry," Kimmie revealed.

"Apology accepted," Cynthia replied. Then, there was a gap in their conversation.

Finally, Cynthia broke the silence, "Bert and I are headed to the airport."

Bert shook his head violently and tried to grab the phone. Cynthia knew not to say anything else, judging by his gestures and facial expression. She knew to end the call as quickly as possible.

"Where are you two going?" Kimmie prodded.

"Oh, we just wanted to get away for a long weekend...trying to get some last minute deal....got nothing else to do," Cynthia said, getting flustered and nervous. "I have to go, but let's talk real soon, okay?"

"Sure," Kimmie replied, baffled. Then she heard a click.

Chapter Fifteen

Tickets to Ireland

Bert turned the radio up so loud that the heavy metal rock sent shivering vibrations up and down Cynthia's long, curved back. He performed with his air guitar for the rest of the ten minute ride to the airport. He told her to park the car close to the ticket counter in the short-term lot, not caring about the exorbitant cost of the parking ticket. He was not coming back. The car would stay there indefinitely, or get towed. It didn't matter, 'cause he was off to paradise, with or without Cynthia.

He struggled with two huge pieces of luggage of his, then with Cynthia's one, rather thin and sleek, designer piece. When he spied an empty cart, he loaded all three cumbersome pieces on board and rolled it inside the ticket counter lobby. He spotted an empty counter from which to purchase tickets. He trotted over to it hurriedly. Cynthia mimicked Bert's movements to the "T", as she swiftly moved with him to the vacant counter.

"How much is a ticket to Buenos Aires?" he questioned the airline employee snobbishly.

"Well, when do you want to travel?" the chubby brunette questioned him back irritatingly.

"Well…Right NOW," Bert answered, as he stared at the agent.

Startled, the flustered agent looked at her monitor and quoted fares for both one-way and round-trip, leaving right NOW.

"That is highway robbery…I am not going to pay that much!"

"You have no advance purchase, sir. Now, if you could wait three more days, then the fare would go down significantly."

"I can't wait for three days," Bert exclaimed, looking at an embarrassed Cynthia in disgust.

"And I thought you were different. I thought you were on MY side," he shouted, as he spit on the worn carpet.

Cynthia looked around the lobby at all the people who were staring at Bert. They both took a seat. Bert became quiet, entranced in thought. Cynthia had never felt so embarrassed before in all her life, not even with Ty. Bert had developed a temper that could rival any mad man. It was no fun living or even being with Bert anymore. Her mind momentarily drifted back to those days on the beach with Willie, laughing and talking about nothing…nothing important…nothing at all to do with money, which was all Bert talked about nowadays. It was his new obsession, day in and day out. It had even taken the place of whores.

All of a sudden, Bert excitedly screamed, "Hey babe…look!" He pointed to a large airline advertisement in the corner of the ticket area, on the other side of where they had been standing, almost hidden by the thick lines of now-waiting passengers who were standing in the check-in lane. She looked over and read to what he was referring.

Fly anywhere in the British Isles round-trip for five hundred dollars. No advance purchase.

"That's it. That's where we're going……to…." Bert's speech drifted off, because he was running back over to the counter to purchase two tickets. They hadn't needed to return. There was no reason to, in Bert's mind.

Straggling behind him, always trying to keep up with his erratic state of being, Cynthia shouted to him, "Where are we going…and why?" She managed to get her words out before reaching out to viciously eradicate him. She pulled him close to her by his shirt and demanded an explanation.

"I said...to where? And why?" Cynthia asked in a very serious manner, quiet, yet concerned.

"Honey, we are going to your castle...that's the perfect hideout.... no one will ever suspect that we are there. I have enough money right now to cover the debt. I'll have some sent to a bank of my choosing in Ireland. It's really our only choice. I don't want to spend my money on expensive air tickets. Then, I would still have to buy or rent a place. This way, the property is *ours*...when we marry." Bert thought that his last remark had been a little careless, but hoped that it simply went over her head, or that she hadn't been paying attention, as she seemed to be gazing in the distance, still holding his shirt collar in her hand.

"Fine," she acknowledged to him. "I have been longing to go back to Ireland and straighten out my life, anyway. That's my home now... that is where all of my friends are...and my work. I am ready if you are. Let's go buy the tickets."

"Okay, but these have to be coach, no upgrades. I'm trying to start a new for us. I need to save some money...been too reckless with it."

"Yeah, with all of your *flirty fems*," she affirmed, with a half-smile on her face. She released him from her hold, hit his butt, and said, "Go get 'em tiger." She finally felt excited again. That feeling hadn't come over her in what seemed like forever, but it had come back, because she was about to return...to her abode...where she was supposed to be.

Bert laid down a huge wad of cash to sort out, in front of the astonished ticket agent. He finally handed her the amount needed with taxes for two round-trip tickets to Shannon, along with his passport and Cynthia's legitimate passport. She wasn't scared any longer. The agent told them both how to get to their terminal and where to catch a tram. She apologized for having to give them two seats in back.

"These are the only two that I have open for tonight."

"It don't matter," he said in slang, as he watched the three bags disappear on the luggage belt. He had sealed the bag up with duct tape and locks, so nothing could come apart and expose his zippered clothing, which held some of his money. He hoped that he would be able to transport this legally, without a hitch.

Bert had over the amount allowed with which to travel abroad, he had researched. So, he stuffed it in his knee socks. He knew demons were on his side, and they were powerful...they could win this battle for him...and hopefully, others to come. He smiled sweetly at Cynthia who was staring straight ahead in oblivion.

They proceeded to the first security official, who was there right at the tram entrance. They showed their passports and boarding passes and passed by quietly and quickly, onto their awaiting tram which would carry them to their flight bound for shamrocks, emeralds, and leprechauns, away from these mobster, monster cohorts.

Reckless Bert was filled again with excitement, even though he had had enough in these last several months to last him a lifetime. He told Cynthia that he couldn't wait to have his freedom back.

What he didn't tell her, as it was in thought only, was that he was looking forward greatly to life filled with ease...a castle...servants...a beautiful mate...and lots of cash to spend on whatever, or whomever he so desired. He was psyched.

"One down and two to go," Bert stated with smugness to a nervous Cynthia.

"I hope you don't get in trouble, hon," she commented in a half-whispered voice.

"You don't know me as well as I thought you did," he announced to the empty tram.

"I hope you're right. I have had about all I can stand of this mess. I should have killed myself by now. First my dad, then my scoundrel 'soul mate husband', now YOU. How are you going to interfere in my life? Everybody always does, in some way or another," she uttered, then snickered.

They hurried off the tram when it arrived at the international terminal and found their gate to be located just around the bend. Bert and Cynthia were both apprehensive, as they were told to take off their shoes and walk through the sensors. Cynthia held her breath and walked first. She beeped and was asked to walk through again. She beeped again. A female official took her wand and scanned Cynthia's long frame, up and down, until the area was recognized. It was in the collar area, a pin. They let her walk on.

Now, it was Bert's turn. He was deathly nervous, but never let it show. He walked right through the metal detector with no problem and met up with Cynthia on the other side. They both walked straight up to the noisy boarding area, which was located right around the corner, and took their place in the long, staggering line of awaiting passengers. It looked like there would hardly be any room left for their bags when they finally got on board. The flight was loaded with passengers and carry-on baggage, strollers and wheelchairs.

Five minutes later, Bert and Cynthia were on board, in their seats toward the back of the aircraft, with their two small bags stuffed in one of the rear storage bins of the jet. They both appeared content, as engines were started and seat belts fastened. They each ordered a cocktail from a redheaded flight attendant who knew of Cynthia's reputation on the ballet circuit, and of her husband, Ty, as well as her abode on the waters of the North Atlantic. She offered them both complimentary cocktails to be served upon take off. They accepted, and nodded off for a brief while, in cautious relief.

"Excuse me. I have one gin and tonic for the gentleman, and one gin and tonic for the lady. Would you like anything else?" the flight attendant asked, as she straightened her skirt, uncomfortable of the way Bert was staring a hole through it.

"No, I think we are just fine and dandy...just fine and dandy," he replied, giving her a sly wink.

Cynthia saw this and just sighed and looked the other way. His behavior didn't phase her anymore. She was used to it already.

"Why am I with him?" she asked herself, as she leaned her seat all the way back. "I guess it's because I am so tired...don't know where to go or what to do. God will steer me in the right direction and see my way clear of this mess. I miss Willie. I hope he's the one....*really hope he's the right one.*"

Cynthia still felt she was unable to function totally on her own, even though her independent status was on the upswing. Now, she felt like she simply needed a rest.

"It will happen...*God will send me in the right direction...soon...very soon...*" Cynthia then drifted off to sleep.

The redhead came by to ask Bert if he would like another cocktail. He said, "Not now."

"You know, you are the most appealingly, sexy woman I've seen in a long time, he said charmingly."

"Oh, I bet you say that to all the girls, don't you?" she giggled. "Are you two married?"

"Not yet. I don't even know if she really wants me," he whispered in her sculpted ear. "I don't know if I really want HER. Time will tell."

"I see...I see..." the baffled flight attendant commented. She turned, as she was called by another passenger down the aisle. "I'll be back."

"Well, I'll be asleep, so you can forget the complement," he said in a tipsy manner, bored with the chase.

"Men!" she blurted out, shrugging her broad shoulders.

Chapter Sixteen

Mother of the Bride

Kim tried to call Cynthia's phone several times, and of course, got no answer, because the phone was turned off while flying. Two mobster friends of Bert also tried to call Bert, disappointed that they too had to leave a message. Once the plane landed and fully stopped, Bert ascended from his sardine-like position and rudely stepped in front of the other passengers to retrieve his bag. He left Cynthia on her own. One of the lady passengers up the aisle looked at her in pity and shook her head.

"I know," Cynthia mouthed the words back to the lady, as she thought deeply about when God was going to come to her rescue and show her the way. "It must happen soon," she whispered to herself, as airline workers rolled over the portable antiquated staircase, so passengers could descend from the aircraft. The jet had been forced to station itself in a one hangar old section of the airport, only used when the regular gates were full up, or there was some pragmatic situation. They were there because of the former condition.

As soon as the two descended from the aircraft, they each checked their messages. Bert listened to the Italian and the Russian who were on conference call and hung up in the middle of their question.

"*Where are you? You're not around like you're supposed to be for our deal to...*" Bert slammed the phone down.

"That's bullshit! They're NEVER gonna talk to me like that again... What stupid fuckers...never... NEVER AGAIN....Let's just hurry and get a taxi. I'm anxious to see my new place," Bert insisted.

"I wonder how it looks, who is there, or if it is even still there. This whole thing has been unimaginable...*I'm just glad I'm home*," Cynthia said, as she flagged down a taxi and demanded to the driver, in an increasingly strong and determined voice. "Take me to my estate...I'm Cynthia Riley, Tyrone's wife." The driver suddenly appeared flushed and nodded his head in obedient accordance with the famous ballerina's wishes. He knew that she would not be pleased by what she was about to see.

They drove for twenty minutes on narrow winding lanes, until they got to the turn in the road which dead ended at sea cliffs. The driver turned to the left. Halfway up the block, the almost dilapidated mansion sat, looking as if it hadn't had any caretakers for months.

"There hasn't been anyone around here for a long while. We've had a couple bloody bad storms here lately. It looks bloody bad... bloody bad...sorry," and he held out his hand to take in the cash that was due.

Shocked at what she was viewing, she stuttered and replied to his comment, "Thank you...and I forgot to ask you how much the ride would cost. I only have US currency. Twenty should be enough, right?" she asked him.

"In this currency, twenty is NOT enough right now. It keeps dropping lower it seems. How 'bout another ten?" the driver recommended.

Bert pulled out a ten dollar bill from his sock and replied sternly, "Take it, but I don't want to see you around here ever again, ya hear asshole?"

"Alright by me," the driver answered, as he quickly took his car out of park and peeled off into oblivion.

"What a mess this place has become," Cynthia grieved.

"If I had known it was going to look like this, I never would have come," Bert suggested haughtily.

"Oh, really?" Cynthia asked him in a sarcastic tone.

"Yes, really. I didn't give up everything I had, and everything that was coming to me for this hell hole."

The two didn't speak for the rest of the afternoon, evening, or night. Bert stayed downstairs in the salon with his eyes glued to the tube the entire time...thinking...just thinking...and Cynthia went up and down the staircase looking through each room and straightening up. The inside of the castle she could manage. It wasn't too bad, just dusty. The outside, however, was another matter. She left messages with contractors as to get bids for what appeared to be restoration issues.

Cynthia felt that God was finally showing her the way to go. Seeing Bert's real persona had been a blessing. Cynthia dialed Willie's number that evening, but got his recording. She proceeded to phone him over and over again during her next couple days of solitude at the mansion. Willie still wouldn't answer his phone. Cynthia felt all alone, once again, in the same world that she left. She didn't want to "star" in the same scenario.

After two days of not hearing from Willie, she was beginning to question *his* ethics as well.

"Will I ever know happiness with a mate, or a family?" she asked herself while checking on her flower garden alongside the massive home.

Bert had been gone now for two days and one night. Cynthia hadn't seen hide nor hare of him, not that she really wanted to. She relegated herself to novice status once again. She had never known how to "pick" the "right" man out of a line-up. She had chosen the one that was around at the most convenient time. She had drawn a bad hand, even though they had all been fairly set. Ty had spent more than he had earned over the years and owed many months of mortgage payments and other debts that Cynthia would have to assume. She noticed the stack of bills for auto loans, furniture and clothing loans and "small business" loans in the drawer of his desk. All of these Ty was dead set against paying back to anyone. He felt that money was HIS for the taking, not anyone else's.

"He left me high and dry, and I fell for it...I fell for it with both of them," she confided to a ballerina cohort, whom she contacted on rare occasions. Well, this was one of them. "I don't know what to do."

"Just get your wits about yourself, fix up the place and take control of your life. Remember it's your and nobody else's life. Hang in there, sweetie. I'm with you....all the way," her friend affirmed.

"Thanks Charmaine. I really needed to hear that. My confidence level is way below normal at present." Cynthia hung up the receiver of the land line and gazed sorrowfully out the large picture window.

She stared at a gray, lifeless sky, filled with gloom, pessimism and struggle. She had never been able to escape this dark world, even though she had tried daily, but to no avail.

She fixed a quick snack for dinner in the microwave, a processed food dish and pretty tasteless. She knew her body would regret eating it the next day, but she didn't care. She knew that she had to take back control of her life.

"God, give me the strength," she pleaded once more to an empty house.

Cynthia watched television, while lying in bed, phones remaining silent. She drifted off to sleep. Sleep was her only relief and therapy.

The following morning was blessed with sunshine, birds, and lots of waves. She felt alive...rather happy. She was surprised at how good she felt three days being away from Bert. She now knew what her decision was to be. She called Kimmie.

"Kimmie? Hey, everything okay?"

"Not bad. Glad the court battle is over and evil didn't win. I do need to work though...money's running kind of low now..."

"I know what you mean. It's tight around here too."

"How's your man?" Kimmie asked.

"What man? I haven't seen him for three days now...and I'm rather glad I haven't. You know Kim, I think I just need some space now."

"That's what I've always thought. If you really can't find your-self...you really won't find anyone who's real."

"Well, you were right all the time Kim. I miss you."

"Hey, you're welcome here anytime you choose. You know the door's always open for you."

"I've got to get my life straightened out here first. Then, we'll see. You know you're welcome here too, Kim"

"I'm sorry, but I really have no desire to step foot on foreign soil ever again, if you know what I mean."

"Don't hold what happened against the countries themselves. The entire human race has flaws. Most times we overlook them, because we *have* to co-exist with one another."

"I'm happy by myself, with my horses, of course. They are all that I need," Kimmie proclaimed.

"I feel like that sometimes, but we all do need each other. We need love and companionship. It's a part of humanity. Without it, we crumble, just like society is beginning to do. We can solidify humanity with love, love for one another, not just for ourselves."

"I hear you, hon...a lot easier said than done though."

"At least you can try. You might like it. It's more fun to like and love, than to hate."

"I guess you're right, as per usual. Hey, thanks for calling...I really must go now and pay my new boys who are taking care of the ranch... they're making me go broke...and hey, I *really* miss Jude."

"I know Kim. I'll say a prayer for you...and for me," Cynthia con-soled her before she bid her farewell.

Cynthia had finally come to the conclusion that Bert wasn't com-ing back. "No, he's long gone by now," she realized, as she wiped several drops of water from her mascara-stained eyes, displaying an immense amount of pain.

After a quiet day of gardening, while simmering a large pot of fragrant lamb and potato stew, Cynthia came to an all-important decision. She decided to keep the house and pay off back mortgages and other claims...*slowly...very slowly, because she needed the asset, and she couldn't part with the castle...she truly felt at home here...like no other place on earth...she knew that the show must go on...the party must never end...if he were alive or dead...it did not matter. She wanted her castle.*

Just when her stew started to boil over, and she ran over to turn it down two notches, the phone jingled. She washed her fingers, which were dripping from her recipe, and quickly walked over to the living room to answer it. She sat down. No one or nothing, no matter how important was ever going to make her stumble or fumble, in order to answer a call.

"What happened centuries ago, when there were no telephones? *There was privacy then,*"she complained to herself.

"Hallo," she answered in a throaty voice, not her usual sweet, clear and melodic tone. She projected herself as someone who was extremely worn-out.

"Hey lady!" was the greeting she received from the other end of the wire.

"Cynthia, darling. I need you to star in a production we have scheduled for Dublin next month. The company needs a senior dancer who must portray a middle-aged woman, the mother of the bride, in the production. I can transform you into that woman in a flash with all of my cosmetic techniques. It pays well besides. Can you help me out?

The production is avant-garde and written by a young hopeful. It's very good. You'll be impressed. The name of the ballet is 'Mother of the bride'," the familiar voice trailed off, awaiting a response. Cynthia knew this voice as Ezel's, a director and make-up genius, whom she had worked with on many occasions.

"Ezel, I love you dearly, but why did you call me so last minute. I thought you might have heard of the shake-up in my life, and that I couldn't possibly star in a show like that," Cynthia strongly stated to him.

"You couldn't...or you wouldn't?" he sternly asked, like a school teacher questioning elementary school kids. "I had a last minute illness arise with the current scheduled star, Eugenia Dixon. If you're up to taking her place in the show, I'd really be indebted and would owe you the world! You can dance just as well, I think, maybe even better."

"You know my weakness...my lazy side...too well, Ezekiel, she formally stated. It's pretty tough to take the place of Eugenia Dixon. *My God, she's a legend in Ireland.* Well, when is practice? I guess I had better be there."

"You are a real charm, girl," relieved Ezel broke into laughter. "Thanks a ton! See you at Foyers hall at 8:00 tomorrow morning. You've really saved the day for me, and for the whole cast and crew. Thanks...thanks...thanks. Hugs and kisses, 'til tomorrow."

She ate her stew, while listening to a symphonic radio channel. She felt bored and restless and was almost glad that she got the call. She missed her work, and felt like she needed to get her mind off of her imminent situation.

She stayed up past midnight, thinking, knowing that in the morning, when she was to perform her magic. Suddenly, she began to regret the decision she had made.

Thirty minutes more of soothing relief, listening to Brazilian jazz was all that she needed to calm herself down and slip into an unconscious state. She awoke from the love seat to turn off the music and lights and arm the alarm. Then, she laid back down and went to sleep.

When the programmed clock sounded at six forty-five, she got up and slipped on her shoes to walk to the once ornate kitchen. Now there was barely enough room to walk, because all of the boxes and pilings of dry wall which laid in piles on the once immaculate kitchen floor. She put that on her list of things to do, to call a few local repair guys in Shannon, as soon as she got back from Foyers Hall. Foyers Hall was situated in the suburbs, ten minutes away from the center of Shannon, about the same distance as it was from her home.

She scrambled up some eggs, toasted a piece of five-grain bread, boiled a cup of water to place a tea bag in, and she was off and running...

not confident that the day would end well. She had an intuitive feeling that something was not right...something was awry.

She left her forlorn castle at seven-forty sharp, knowing she would arrive before her scheduled practice time. Cynthia was becoming tougher and stronger and bolder and better every day. She was now looked upon as a super attractive free-thinking, independent character who could and would do anything she so desired. She danced diligently and skillfully, as if she had never missed a day of practice.

Halfway through, a break was called. She decided to dial Willie in Florida to see how he was doing, and what had happened to him. This time, however, the message came from a recording saying that the line had been disconnected.

Angry, she phoned the saloon's number she had programmed into her android. The call showed received, but there was silence only.

Finally, she opened her mouth to start a conversation, "Hallo...hallo."

"Yep. What do YOU want little lady?" the voice clearly questioned.

"Well, I would like to know if Willie is there, or how I can get a hold of him. It seems that his number has been disconnected."

"I know. He don't want to see or talk to you no more. Ya hear." Then, she heard another voice in the distance over her receiver.

"Good job fellow. Here's your dough, and remember...you ain't seen Willie for days and know nothing about him," demanded one of the two presumably flashy-looking Russian voices who were standing alongside the first voice.

After their deed, the two hoodlums strolled their way out of the saloon, four girls clinging to their sides, each carrying a half-drunken Tuscan wine bottle.

She hung up. "What an asshole. It seems that something is still not right. Willie was not like that," Cynthia broke her silence.

Cynthia and troop continued to make beauty on the dance floor, as the music graced them entirely.

After a practice which lasted for over seven hours, and which she didn't know how she ever had retrieved enough strength from within to carry-on, she was more than satisfied with her dancing, but less than satisfied with her stamina. It seemed that she was more fatigued than usual. She popped in a few vitamins, which she always took on occasions such as these, when she was feeling so exhausted.

"I probably should take these on a regular basis, now that I am getting older...almost middle-aged...like my character," she said, chuckling to the younger man who played her husband in the ballet. He chuckled back, and he shook his head in agreement.

"I'll see you tomorrow, love," the male ballerina said to her, as Cynthia left the stage.

"Okay, Charles," she called out. "I must grab some food in town before the grocery closes. Then, I am heading home! I really need a good night's sleep. You wore me out," she laughed from afar.

After she left the market, she took the long way home...to ease her mind...and to just relax.

Chapter Seventeen

The Hits

"WHERE ARE YOU?" the head Italian in the European mobster clan phoned his stool pigeon to ask. "Haven't heard nuttin' from you for three days. That's not acceptable, Roger. Have you seen him at all, and how 'bout her? Speak up. I can't hear ya."

"Boss, I was on the plane with him. I followed him to the castle. He got into a sport's car that was in the garage and peeled out, with smoke coming from his tires...I mean it, boss...I lost him...could not keep up."

"I should have expected that from you. Has he returned to Ty's wife? Are you waiting for him?"

"I'm down the street, back of an abandoned farm house. Nobody can see me here."

"When he comes back, you got to sometime kill him...we don't need him no more...understand?"

"Yes I do, boss," Roger replied, sounding energetic, with nuances of affirmation of delegation by a supervisor in a board meeting of a corporation. "I will get it done."

"I know I can always count on you, son, because you know what's in store if I can't depend on you, don't you my boy?"

"Absolutely."

"Good," the boss said, as he hung up the space-aged receiver of the land line at his mansion in Coral Gables, Florida. He fixed himself a stout Black Russian and proceeded to book himself air passage on the internet to see his "boys" in Belfast.

The boss man phoned for his limousine to take him to Miami International for a red-eye that was scheduled to leave in four hours. He packed a few belongings and kissed his Siamese cat goodbye and waited outside his grandiose palace, enjoying the sea breeze all the while and that which he never has time to enjoy in his scheming, killing, and money-making world. He enjoyed these rare moments, as he thought about how he would miss his sweet cat. His pet was his world.

His cat, which he named "Samantha" could do no wrong. She was the only being that was ever shown tenderness and feeling by her owner. She was his "child".

After a grueling two hour ride, in bumper to bumper traffic, he arrived at his destination. He grabbed his bag and headed in to board the plane and clear inspection. He was totally clean. He only had a check with him for one million dollars. He was going there to present it to the Irish clan at their headquarters, in exchange for possession of the small castle in Shannon. He knew they were going to take the lesser buying price. He had connections...plenty of connections with the Belfast police, and even some IRA members, who were working undercover for the Italian mob, and who were half Italian. There were also some *jihadists*...ISIS members whom he gave profits to in exchange for their "persuasion" techniques. *Luciano was more than confident.*

Bert was feeling drunk and guilty, as he finally came around the bend to head into the driveway of Cynthia's huge estate. He had been on a three day, two night sex and alcohol spree which landed him in several sleazy bordellos in Dublin, with many unscrupulous characters.

They made it hard for him to leave them without having to hand over hundreds more. He felt ashamed and bedraggled and very weary. He just needed some sleep and to be in Cynthia's good graces once again. He headed into his garage spot and rolled up the super slim small windows of the sport's car that used to belong to infamous "Ty". He gathered up strength and courage to get out from the driver's seat and head inside.

He opened the door to the other garage spot where Cynthia kept her small vehicle. It was empty. As soon as he closed the garage door and headed out of his garage door opening, which led to a very long brick walkway near the front porch, a mass of bullets filled his abdomen from afar. Roger did what he had been told to do. The butler was a good "corporate" entity for the clan, and the mob. He worked for both.

"I did it," he phoned the Boss. "It was easy...went out like a light. I stuffed him in the trunk of my car."

"Good. Now, pick me up at the Belfast airport. I should be there in seven hours," Luciano slyly stated and turned his cell off, as he boarded the jet.

Roger always did what he was told, not really because he was scared, but rather because he wanted to be the next in power. This was never going to happen though. Luciano had other plans, plans to kill him too at a "contact's home".

After landing and clearing customs legally, like a good boy, he phoned Roger to retrieve him at the arrival gate. At that point, the deadly deed was set into motion.

Once the two arrived at his supposed contact's home, way out in the clover fields, Roger waited inside the vehicle for Luci to return. He did not return, however. Instead, gasoline was poured on top of the vehicle from a second-story window. The boss man stepped outside of the yellow farm house, lit a thick, dry, frayed rope with a lighter that he used for his high-priced Havana cigar collection and sent it flying towards the vehicle.

Luci ran like crazy, as the car exploded with forcefulness. The wooden frame of the house also got some flames and proceeded to go up in smoke as well. The Boss got into an awaiting car, which was found on the other side of the farm, away from the flames. It flew down the two-lane country road and eastward past oncoming fire trucks which were flying by, "Johnny on the spot".

"It's going just as planned. It's bound to go as good when we meet with the leprechauns. Driver take me to their headquarters...fast...I want to be there first thing...so floor it."

"No problem."

The driver took the Italian to the Irish mob /IRA headquarters in record time. The Italian retrieved his cell from his pocket and phoned Herbert O'Malley, the man who took over Ty's position dealing with the thugs and their money laundering gangs in Europe and in the states.

"Good Morning Herbert. How are you doing? It's Luciano here."

"What can I do for you, sir?"

"I'm out in front and was wondering if you could come out for a drive with me through town, so we can discuss a little business proposition."

"What kind of proposition?"

"I want to buy the castle that's for sale. I have check in my hand."

"*What? It's not for sale, to you guys anyway...and you know that.* I'm coming down."

Herbert warned his boys at the headquarters of the impending threat. He even phoned a couple of police boys who were on the take and asked them to follow the car and be ready for anything, as he put it mildly. They agreed. As soon as everyone was in place, Herbert walked out of the building and into the Italian's vehicle. It had the smell of death in it, in the tobacco-stained, musty interior of the sedan. He squeezed his rather plump frame inside the stale smelling car.

"Nice to see you again Herb. You are looking well. So sorry to hear about Ty, but it's good for *you*," Luciano horrifically mumbled in his scratchy, almost hoarse, deep, scratchy voice.

"Who told you?" he asked the stuffy air. Luci, let's get to the heart of the matter. Why do you..?"

"*Relax... relax my friend,*"Luciano cut him off. "Herbert, I am here today to make a deal...a deal that you won't...or *can't refuse*...get it?"

"Alright...let's hear it," Herbert stated squeamishly.

"I am prepared to offer you one million smackers for Ty's castle. I understand it's been for sale for a time now and you haven't had much luck with it...*and judging from the predicament that you are in, I think that you will take my offer,*"he advised Herbert, as he slowly wedged a silencer into his thigh.

"I can persuade you even more, if needed," he then penetrated the weapon into the fat of his stomach.

"I am persuaded," Herbert stated, looking through the back window.

"Good. Now, I brought an already typed contract for both of us to endorse. Here's a pen. Sign it, before my hand and fingers get tired and unsteady. You never know what might happen then, do youz?"

Herbert scribbled some lines on the document, above the under-line, still looking out the back window.

"What are you looking at, or who may I ask, are you looking for?"

Herbert thought this to be the right time to attempt escape from the stopped vehicle. He flung his arm up, deflecting the pistol away from his body and wrestled his way out of the car, which was stationed for a few moments at a traffic light. He wedged himself in between dozens of cars during morning rush hour. Herbert turned around and flagged his followers to hurry over. It was then that he was met with a bullet in his lower back. He fell on the pavement, torn check dangling from his fingers. The police on motorcycles and the black coupe which carried three of his boys came racing up upon his straddled out, gasping for air, but still alive body. One of the drivers in the car pile-up phoned for an ambulance on her cell, as many people gathered around the wounded body. They each tried to remember the license plate of the vehicle who conducted this mayhem. No one was able to have seen it in the intense fog. The Italian's vehicle found its way out of the pile up, getting and producing many scratches and dents.

The police and Herbert's boys accompanied him in the ambulance to the nearest hospital. They got to Herbert in the nick of time. The doctors were able to save his organs. Herbert had always been a tough, sturdy old geezer, no matter his weight, that's why he was able to take over for the vanished, and now presumed dead, Ty. He was a nicer character than Ty, however, and definitely more decent, but still...a little bit scary. The gang had been told, through the grapevine, that Ty had indeed been killed.

Herbert awoke from his coma hours later and began pointing his index finger in the air, trying to mutter the words, which he finally was able to form.

"*Go to Ty's castle...get Cynthia out...get Luciano.* Get him before he gets any of us. He's bad, vindictive...a son-of a bitch...and *there are others...*" he blurted out, before he fell back to sleep due to bodily shock.

"Let's get out of here. We must do what he says. We've got to get to Cynthia before Italy and *the others* do," Hal, the younger, bigger, and meaner of the two instructed the others. He wanted control of the gang now, in the worst way, and was willing to do anything to get it.

"We have to guess who *the others* are, are they *jihadists...*like the *Taliban,* or even *ISIS* and *Khorasan*? There are so many *others* sprouting up now, and the *Russian Mafia* has to be a part of them too. They have worked with, and against *Italy* and *Ireland* for years."

✳ ✳ ✳

Cynthia awoke with a bang, as the morning sun peered through her large bedroom window, covered by just sheer curtains. She yawned and got up out of bed to make some coffee and get the paper, which was usually thrown onto the brick walkway out front. She slipped on her black flannel robe, as it was a breezy morning, and put on her furry red opened-toed slippers. Her heart was beating especially swiftly, and stiffly this morning. She wondered to herself, "Why?"

Chapter Eighteen

Detriment

Kimmie paced the floor wondering why Cynthia was not answering her phone. Her gut told her that something was just not right. She punched in Cynthia's number once again, but still, the repetitive rings that never gave way to a specialized recording. Cynthia had told Kimmie that she preferred only answering calls and speaking to a human, not retrieving messages and having to call people back. She had always enjoyed living a life of seclusion, except when she was on stage. That was plenty to satisfy her slight needs for socializing.

"Oh well, maybe she'll see that I called and call me later…I hope," she comforted herself with prayer, as she trudged the field to the barn to meet another new student for a barn yard horse-jumping lesson. She loved her new career…and even more, loved her permanent house, the one that the courts awarded her. After strategic deliberations, the judgment was decided that Kimmie was sole heir of Kenneth's property, and of his liquid assets, of which he now had none, because of this infamous scandal, which had just made national news. Producers were even leaving messages, asking Kimmie for interviews on national talk shows. She never returned their calls.

"I don't want to be bothered with that stuff," she said to herself, as she listened to their impersonal messages, one by one.

She tried Cynthia once again. This time, however, she answered her phone.

"Hey Kimmie. I was just headed downstairs to make some coffee and get my paper and try to wake-up. What's up? Are you still teaching horseback riding and jumping? Hey, I'm in a new ballet production that's going really well and giving ballet lessons in my spare time, of which I have none," she laughed and walked over to her old-fashioned percolator.

"Cynthia, I have a bad feeling…a feeling that something detrimental is about to happen. I don't know why…but I do."

"That's crazy…but you know, this morning I had that same type of feeling myself when I woke up. I don't know why, but I felt sort of shaky all over."

"Just watch out, please. I love you. I'm sorry for all of that other nonsense in the past. Be careful, please. Call me tomorrow."

"Definitely will, bye-bye."

Cynthia got the coffee from the cabinet and percolated a delicious brew, every bit as good as one of the many specialty coffee shops found in the vicinity.

While brewing, she walked out front and picked up a damp newspaper which had been beaten by a strong wind. She suddenly felt a forceful grip on her right shoulder as she tried to maneuver herself to stand up, a task that a ballerina would usually having no problem in attempting. She felt such fear upon feeling this firm hand touching her.

"I'm sorry little lady," a voice delicately spoke from above her head. She detected a strange accent, not from around there. "I didn't mean to frighten you. I was sent here to help out…to get your place in order, to make it more sales worthy. My boss sent me here to meet with you. I'm ready to start."

"Who are you, sir?"

"My name is Omar. I am from the Canary Islands, just south of here. I can do anything and everything to make this house look and feel better. Can I take a look around the property, then inside?"

"I guess," Cynthia said naively.

"Great. I'll knock when I'm ready for the inside," he closed his conversation, in a mild and meek, thespian-trained way.

Cynthia walked back inside her mansion, in a state of confusion.

"Do I call someone, or just let it ride?" she asked her now-mutilated mind.

When she entered the house, her cell phone started vibrating violently on the counter and ringing incessantly, with strong emotion.

"Hallo, Cynthia speaking."

"Cynthia, hey, it's me, Willie...no time to explain, but you have to get out of there...*now*...don't trust anybody."

Then, there was a long pause. Next, she heard uncontrollable echoed screams, as though Willie was positioned in a tunnel, or tube of some kind.

"*Don't, don't...don't do that to me*...oh no," he sobbed in the distance, obviously being tortured.

"Oh...Willie...Willie...Are you there? What are they doing to you?"

All of a sudden, there was silence on the other end, followed by a click, then a dial tone.

"Somebody got to Willie. That's why he must not have answered all this time. They have been and most probably are watching my every move. Being Ty's wife has gotten everybody in trouble, or killed, and it's all my fault," she cried hysterically, until she heard the short awaited "knock" on the front door. She slowly got up from the slick marble kitchen floor and took a swig of the robust fresh black coffee that she had just percolated, in order to get a grip on what she had just heard over the telephone, and what seemed to be happening to her now.

Heeding the two warnings from her two friends, she remained quiet and listless, which was really her true character anyway.

Cynthia regained her composure and walked up to the marble entry to answer the door. She had no more struggle left in her. She was worn from defending herself with her every stance and move.

"Excuse me. I'm ready for the inside now, *if you don't mind*," the stranger insisted, with a sly grin on his dark, melancholy face.

She unlatched the door.

Chapter Nineteen

The Suicide

Just as the brusque "worker" barged his way through Cynthia's small doorway, her cell phone went off again, clanging and clanging, monotonously, until this brusque "worker" said, "*Just answer it.*"

Cynthia greeted the caller and heard a familiar voice on the other end. It was Rusty, one of Ty's friends from the Independent Republican Army.

"Cynthia, honey, you must leave your house. Drive far, far away. Some bad men are coming to get you and your belongings," he advised her, trying to remain calm and cool. "Please leave…NOW, don't wait for us to get there. We're on the way."

"Well, I can't yet. You see, I have a gentleman worker here right now. He's looking at all of the damages on the estate, as we speak…"

"*Oh no, you shouldn't have…,*" and the "worker" stole the cell from Cynthia's dainty palm and yelled into the receiver.

"Well, she did, and now it's over. I am Luciano, and this is Italian property now. I have a signed contract in hand, plus everyone involved is ancient history…*ha, ha, ha,*" he laughed into the receiver.

Cynthia grabbed the contract and bolted out the front door, towards the roaring waves of the ocean below, where she finally felt at home. Luciano ran after her, but never even got close to her physically-fit body. She looked down below, then plunged herself onto the rocky waves from the highly-situated cliff, toward her awaited destiny. Serenely, she landed on turbulent water. She did not struggle for air. The Irish boys raced into the driveway to rescue her, not knowing she had already met her freedom down below. No longer would she ever be scorned by anyone. No longer would she ever be betrayed by anyone. No longer would she ever have to hear a lie from anyone. No longer would she ever have to fear any person, or group. She was now at peace, and most importantly, she saved her castle. She was now fully ready to let her head go under the crashing waves. Almost instantaneously, air bubbles on the water's surface could be seen no longer. The Irish clan found nobody at the estate. They were too late. Luciano once had a signed contract in hand, but now his hand was empty, as he stood looking down at the ocean. Herbert was alive, but paralyzed. The feud between the two entities, the Irish and the Italian, was about to become hotter and stronger than ever before. The third mob, Russia, continued being on the side of whoever was winning. Down South, Al Qaeda remained strong. However, ISIS, and now Khorasan and *the others,* were becoming super powerful and moneyed jihad terrorist-extremist groups, making millions each day on black market oil and other illegal sales. Cynthia was dead by suicide. Willie was dead by means of torture. Kimmie was soon to die as well, by a sorry-ass equestrian who nudged Kimmie's horse with the tip of a knife, while she was going over a tall fence.

All properties from the dead were put up for auction, and all confiscated monies were donated to special causes and charities.

Camille looked down from the heavens and thought...
"Ooooohhhhh..
What goes around....comes around...........
Yes, THE GREED, DECEPTION, EGO...
Nothing IS as it really seems.....," Camille
whispered tranquilly to each of the victims,

and all of the serpent-like slayers.......who
wait and wait in purgatory for their numbers
to come up, and their fates to be determined
by the almighty.

"GOOD always triumphs over EVIL," she softly said.
"But DOES IT REALLY?" we all ask.......................

The End

Rather new to the NOVEL circuit, Vanessa Leigh Hoffman has been a writer for over twenty years. She has written articles for several newspapers and written songs for her rock band during this period. This is her second published work, with others already scheduled for publication, including a non-fiction piece about her adopted daughter.

Vanessa was born and raised in Memphis, Tennessee, where she graduated from the University of Memphis with a Bachelor's Degree in Romance Languages. She has been a teacher of Spanish, French, German, English, and Etymology for over fifteen years. She now lives in Saint Petersburg, Florida.